FAIR

**Never deal with** a leprechaun.

Finding a pot of unclaimed gold just doesn't come without a price in the *Monsters, Maces and Magic* RPG world. Stephi discovers this the hard way while tangling with a mean-spirited leprechaun.

With Stephi, now transmorphed into a fairy, the party must do the leprechaun's bidding. Otherwise, Stephi will remain a diminutive fairy with no hope of returning to her former elf self. But leprechauns aren't known for their straight dealing. Neither is Higslaff, a manipulative pawnshop owner who possesses what the leprechaun desires.

Glenn, Kirby, Stephi, Ron and Derek—RPG players trapped in the game world as their characters—set off on a mission to Riven Rock, a city rife with cruelty and corruption. There they must inflict retribution for an attack against the pawnshop owner. Danger and deceit threaten the party at every turn. Can they avoid getting caught up in the brewing war between rival thieves' guilds? Will they survive the journey, and the perils of Riven Rock? As low-rank characters, it'll take all the skill, cunning and luck the party can muster. And that might not be enough.

**Praise for Monsters, Maces and Magic**

"Exciting and hilarious! It feels like a true game with friends." Dueling Ogres Podcast

"I was pulled into the world and could see the rules of the world unfold. This really does feel like a game. A fun game that I am going to have to continue." Casia's Corner

# Books by Terry W. Ervin II

**Monsters, Maces and Magic**
Outpost
Betrayal
Guild
Fairyed

**Crax War Chronicles**
Relic Tech
Relic Hunted
Relic Shield (forthcoming)

**First Civilization's Legacy**
Flank Hawk
Blood Sword
Soul Forge

**Stand-Alone**
Thunder Wells

**Collections**
Genre Shotgun

**Dane Maddock Universe**
Cavern

# FAIRYED

## MONSTERS, MACES AND MAGIC

TERRY W. ERVIN II

**Fairyed- Monsters, Maces and Magic Book Four**



Published by Gryphonwood Press
www.gryphonwoodpress.com

Cover art by Drazenka Kimpel



ISBN-13: 978-1-950920-06-8
ISBN-10: 1-950920-06-2

# Dedication

This novel is dedicated to my mother, Barbara J. Ervin. While I was in the midst of completing *Fairyed*, my brother and I travelled to New Mexico to spread her ashes. During the drive I pondered that I didn't thank her enough for all she did for me, especially as a child growing up. For example, without regular family visits to the local library, odds are I wouldn't be writing this dedication today. Missed opportunities.

# ACKNOWLEDGEMENTS

First, I would like to thank Kathy, my wife, and Genevieve and Mira, my daughters, for their patience and understanding. They allowed me the countless hours to imagine, plot, research, write, revise and edit—all things necessary to complete Fairyed.

Second, I would like to thank my family, friends, co-workers, and the members of Flankers, all of whom encouraged, questioned, and prodded me along to finish Fairyed.

Third, I'd like to thank the folks at Gryphonwood Press, especially Melissa Bowersock for editing Fairyed, and David Wood for his continued support.

Fourth, I'll never be able to say enough about the cover art Drazenka Kimpel created. Her talent and skill captured Marigold transformed into a fairy as vividly as my mind's eye imagined.

Fifth, Brandon Full and his daughter, Thora, named the character Emma in Fairyed. It was a pleasure to work with them while discovering the added dimension the fairy, Emma Glade Flower, brought to the story. Brandon was selected from among the members of Flankers and readers who receive my newsletter.

That leaves you, the reader. You're the primary reason I wrote Monsters, Maces and Magic: Fairyed. Thank you for choosing my fantasy novel from the hundreds of thousands available. I truly hope you enjoy the story. With that in mind, don't hesitate to send an email or post a review to let me know your thoughts. You can learn more about my works at www.ervin-author.com, along with a link to receive my newsletter.

# Chapter 1

**Stephi sat with** her back against the willow tree, observing Glenn and Kirby. The gnome healer and half-goblin thief watched their wooden bobbers intently. Well, the thief more than the healer.

Some wily fish, or other critter native to the Snake Claw River, had been stripping worms from their hooks all morning.

Glenn rubbed his bulbous nose, smiled up at Stephi, his elven friend, and then scanned the area around them. He wasn't too concerned about a monster rising up out of the river. It really wasn't that large of a waterway. No more than a stone's throw across. Well, a stone's throw back when he was a human, back in the real world. Now he was a four-foot, three-inch-tall gnome named Jax, trapped in the *Monsters, Maces and Magic* game world.

The world he and his five friends were trapped in had rules, most of which followed established norms he'd learned to count on while growing up to the point of attending college. So, as the Snake Claw River wasn't exceptionally deep, it seemed like a massive serpent wasn't likely to appear and spew venom on the three, or swallow them whole. How did they know about the river's depth? Pulling up info on a cell phone wasn't an option. The knowledge came from Kirby, who'd assured him and Stephi. The source? His half-goblin friend gathered information about the river from a retired merchant sailor in Three Hills City, the walled city a quarter mile behind them. Where the information was gathered? Through a casual conversation at a small tea house called the Red Brick.

Despite being a half-goblin, with yellow eyes, a muddy-colored complexion and a long pointed nose,

Kirby managed to carouse better than Glenn. Although gnomes were far more likeable, at least according to the game rules—which translated to actual fact in the game world—Glenn just didn't have the knack for pumping random people, or NPCs, for information. The inability was an apparent carryover from who he really was, back in the real world.

Why the city was built about a quarter mile away from the slow-moving river, the retired sailor had no answer. And it didn't make sense to Glenn. Maybe, in the past when the city was founded, nasty creatures *did* reside in the river. Nobody'd want to be close to that.

But the river's current contents didn't concern Glenn. He paid less attention to his bobber than he should, if he wanted to catch fish, and more to the surrounding meadow grassland. Two weeks ago, while fishing at the same spot, a zombie shambling along the river bank attacked them. That was more than reason enough to split his focus.

Petie, Stephi's blue jay familiar, flitted from branch to branch in the willow tree. In theory, the bird was watching for danger. Trusting one's safety to a bird, even one that was uncommonly smart, didn't seem like a sound survival strategy. The world the six others had been sucked into, in the form of their RPG characters, held lethal terrors worse than zombies. Terrors found in the worst nightmares imaginable. Fortunately, those seemed to be far less common than an "average" terror, like the ogre that killed Kim within ten minutes of their arrival in the *Monsters, Maces and Magic* world. She'd died fighting to save everyone else.

The rest of the party, which included Ron, a quarter-elf warrior druid, and Kalgore, a human warrior, survived an adventure into the Dark Heart Swamp and retrieved a magical necklace for the Church of Apollo. In exchange, the high priest cast a Revive the Dead Spell on

Kim.

The spell failed. Or rather Byeol, the warrior monk, failed her System Shock Survival Roll. Now she lay buried in a grave near the willow tree, opposite the river.

Subsequently, the party of five survived a second adventure through the swamp, and some scrapes in Three Hills City. Glenn considered those tiny steps in their long-term goal of escaping the *Monsters, Maces and Magic* world, the one in which a creepy game moderator had sucked them into, or transported them to, or whatever.

It made almost no sense. Nevertheless, they were in the monster-filled RPG world.

Glenn pursed his lips while refraining from shaking his head. He didn't want to distract his two friends from their morning of attempted relaxation.

Ron was a mathematics graduate student, a genius, before becoming Lysine the warrior druid. He believed they were trapped in what he called an "aberrant concurrent world," part of some sort of parallel universe theory.

So far, the only method devised for returning home was to obtain a Wish Spell.

One could say that Wish Spells were about as rare and coveted as a unicorn. Except in the *Monsters, Maces and Magic* world, unicorns almost certainly existed—and would be easier to locate than a wish. A better comparison would be finding a Ford Mustang in the magical, oddly medieval game world.

"Probably crawdads," Kirby said in his half-croaking voice.

"What?" Stephi asked, lifting the brim of the straw hat she wore to conceal her face.

In character generation, Stephi'd maxed her roll for Appearance and, with her elven bonus, she had a 19.5. Gorgeous or ravishingly beautiful were understatements.

Compared to her, supermodels were almost like Cinderella's ugly stepsisters. Concealing her face kept her from drawing unwanted attention from strangers. Her abnormal height and epic chest—a size that would shame any porn star—made blending in even more difficult. Her near-cartoonish figure came about because she allowed a junior high kid to complete her character sheet. She'd laid on the flirty college coed act, egged Kirby on, encouraging responses to gather juicy content for her Sociology 102 paper.

Back then, the fact that she'd rounded up some of the numbers on her character sheet didn't matter. What did it matter if the piece of paper said her elf maiden was two meters tall? It was only a game. And the college assignment was the only reason Stephi and Kim, her sorority sister, and Glenn attended the university's game club meeting. And got involved in the dice and paper RPG that led to their entrapment.

"A crayfish," Kirby said over his shoulder, answering Stephi's question. "You know, like a mini lobster."

Stephi rolled her eyes. "I know what a crayfish is, Gurk. Why didn't you just say that?"

Glenn smiled at his friends' banter. Then frowned. He thought of Kirby by his real name but, like Stephi, whenever Glenn spoke Kirby's name, Gurk, his character's name came out.

That was just one of the many oddities the game world offered. So, Kirby was Gurk, Stephi was Marigold, Ron was Lysine, Derek was Kalgore—and also a jerk most of the time—and he, Glenn, was Jax.

Kirby asked Glenn, "What're you frowning for, dude?"

Rather than bring up his morose thoughts about one of the game world's idiosyncrasies, and risk dragging his two friends' apparent good mood down, he said, "I'm not digging any more worms."

"Awww," Stephi teased. "And Petie was just beginning to like you better than Gurk."

"Whatever," Kirby said and pulled in his line. "Stripped again."

Sitting next to Glenn on the bank, Kirby leaned close and bumped shoulders with the gnome. "Check yours, dude."

Glenn lifted his pole and pulled his line in. The hook was bare.

"What do ya think?" Kirby asked. "Try a little longer, or go back empty handed?"

Going back without any fish meant they'd have to endure Derek's stupid comments. Glenn sighed before shrugging his shoulders. Spending a clear-skied morning relaxing hanging out with Stephi and Kirby was anything but a waste of time. Being the height of an eight year old and traversing the narrow streets of a crowded city? That was stressful. He'd have to deal with it now, or later, so he said, "Sun's starting to get hot. Let's head back."

Stephi leapt to her feet.

Kirby began wrapping his fishing line around his pole. "I think Marigold agrees with you."

"No," Stephi said, pointing west. "Look at that!"

# Chapter 2

**The sky was** perfectly clear. No clouds in sight. Yet, there was a rainbow, vibrant colors almost like neon, arcing across the sky. One end terminated in a coppice of trees not far from the river, about two-hundred yards to the west.

Nobody else around was near the river, except along the small dock area to the east that launched fishing boats and received small river freighters. People didn't do family picnics or go for early morning strolls along the Snake Claw River.

And nobody went near that coppice of trees. They were Duke Huelmer's property, a special species of yew his servants maintained and cut for aromatic firewood. Or so it was said.

Glenn squinted in disbelief. Apparently nobody but Stephi went near the trees. The elf maiden was on her feet, sprinting toward the rainbow, one hand clutching her cloak and the other holding the straw hat on her head. Her rapier bounced along on her hip seemingly in cadence with the undulating waves of her long, dark hair. Glenn long ago gave up pondering the physics of how she ran with watermelon boobs.

Petie flew tight circles above Stephi's head, easily keeping pace.

Both Kirby and Glenn abandoned their fishing poles and grabbed their gear. Gurk only had to snatch up his cutlass resting next to him. Glenn had brought both his cudgel and round shield. A zombie had wandered upon them while fishing once, so traveling unarmed, with what Kirby called Wandering Creature Encounters being an ever-present threat, would be inviting a brutal death. Maybe eaten, or worse.

Stephi was over six and a half feet tall, but she ran with none of the awkwardness of an NBA forward. Her epic chest gave her less trouble than bouncing breasts programmed by chauvinistic video game designers. Kirby scooted along like a shortstop going for an in-the-park home run. Glenn, pumping his arms and stubby legs, lost ground like a dachshund trying to keep up with a greyhound and beagle on the scent.

"Marigold," Kirby shouted. "Slow down!"

Glenn didn't bother wasting his breath. If Stephi didn't listen to Kirby, she wouldn't listen to him. He was further behind and needed every ounce of air.

Stephi half turned, hardly breaking her stride, and signaled her friends forward with her hat. "Come on. Don't you want to see it before it disappears?"

Disappears? Glen thought. Didn't it take rain, or mist, or clouds combined with sunlight to form a rainbow? And this one appeared more tangible than any he'd ever seen. Of course, he was a lot closer to this one.

Stephi slipped into the thick stand of yew trees, and Kirby wasn't far behind. They looked like massive pines but with rounder, fuller canopies. Glenn finally passed between two yews whose trunks were at least twelve feet in diameter. And they weren't by any measure the largest ones.

"Where are you?" Kirby called in his croaky voice.

Stephi replied, "This way, Gurk. Over here."

Glenn angled a little to his left, moving between the massive trees. Only a few scattered plants and shrubs grew beneath the towering yews. They blocked most of the sunlight, leaving everything in a twilightish shadow. It wasn't unnatural, just a stark contrast to the sunshine he'd just left. Fortunately, his gnomish eyes offered superior low-light vision so everything appeared as if in full daylight.

As Glenn made his way toward Kirby and Stephi's

voice, he caught sight of shimmering light ahead. Literally every color of the rainbow danced across the pine needle-filled ground, the bark of the trees, and played upon his eyes. It wasn't blinding, or mesmerizing, just spectacularly awesome. What else could a rainbow actually be?

Glenn found his friends. They stood, staring at the rainbow as it pierced the canopy and narrowed on its way to an open spot on the ground, encompassed by a small meadow area. There, where it struck earth, the colors roiled like a cauldron of iridescence across the lush grass. Bright and flashy, but giving off no sound, no heat. And the woods stood silent. No bugs buzzing, no birds singing, not even Petie.

"Dude," Kirby said to Glenn, glancing to his left as the gnome worked to catch his breath. "You okay? You're sweating pretty good."

"It's not sweat," Glenn said, trying to make light of his perspiration while wiping his sleeve across his forehead. "It's my gnome body crying."

Gnomes were like a cross between a hobbit and a dwarf. He had skin the color of light tea, brown hair, a mustache and sideburns, the latter of which were even damp with sweat. Gnomes were many things, but neither sprinter nor long distance runner was on that list.

"What do you think's causing it?" Stephi asked.

"It might be the Bifrost Bridge, from Asgard," Kirby said. He looked to his right, up at the elf. With her two-inch-heeled boots, Stephi towered over him by a foot and a half. "Odin or Thor might be coming down it."

"Thor?" Stephi asked. "Like in the Marvel movies?"

That wouldn't be good, Glenn thought. Gods on this world wouldn't be like movie actors with a script. They'd be just as likely to violently kick him and his friends aside—or worse—as to smile and wave hello.

"Maybe," Kirby said, lack of confidence in his voice.

Stephi rolled her eyes.

"Okay, what's your explanation?" the half-goblin thief asked.

Stephi stumbled for an answer and settled on, "Magic."

Kirby laughed. "No, duh." He turned towards Glenn. "Jax, what do you think's causing it?"

Glenn furrowed his brow. "I think it's fading."

Kirby squinted up into the canopy. "You're right."

Within seconds the rainbow was gone. On the ground, where it had terminated sat a huge iron kettle, like what hung over a fire pit. Its shape reminded Glenn of a stout flower vase, one he'd trim the sunflowers stick them in.

But there wasn't room for anything inside. Glittering gold coins filled it to near overflowing.

Glenn looked up to see if any sunlight was penetrating the thick covering of yew branches, because gold, while shiny, needed light to sparkle. Except for where the rainbow had been, everything else was twilight, like it should be. Well, Glenn thought, he'd never been in a woods so thick that it was this dim on a sunny day, but this wasn't a woods from his world. And there *was* a break in the canopy…

A shudder ran through the gnome.

At the same time, Kirby said, "Wow."

Stephi leapt forward. Kirby tried to grab her, but his reaction wasn't fast enough.

"Gold," she said and scooped up two handfuls.

Above, Petie warbled and made whistling calls. Glenn understood the familiar because gnomes, according to the *Monsters, Maces and Magic* Player's Guide, got two animal languages. It was due to their woodland heritage. When rolling up his character, Glenn listed one of them as "blue jay" on his character sheet. The bird must've been reflecting his master's emotion because he was singing out, "Joy, joy, joy!"

For a half second, Glenn coveted the gold. Then he shook his head. *Free gold*? Nothing in the game world was free. His hand slipped to the cudgel hanging in the loop on his belt. It had silver wire imbedded in the business end. At the same time, he unslung the round shield strapped across his back.

Kirby must've had the same bad feeling because he said, "Marigold, put it back."

"Why?" she asked.

"Because, me fair maiden," a piercing, cocky voice said, "that all be mine, and mine only."

# CHAPTER 3

**A small man**, shorter than Glenn, stepped out from behind the gold-filled cast-iron kettle. He wore a Crayola green shirt with brown buttons that matched his brown trousers, and a brown bowler hat, which sported a green feather stuck into its brick-red ribbon. His boots were also Crayola green, and came to an upturned point at the toe. His curly red hair held wisps of gray. He had pale skin and freckled cheeks.

The diminutive man carried a club that, for some reason, Glenn thought of as a shillelagh. The weapon couldn't do much damage as its size was proportional to what the man, barely three-feet tall, could wield.

Surprised, Stephi dropped the gold coins and stepped back. "Who are you?"

Rather than answer her question, the man straightened his hat and said, "Exactly who might you be, to be laying hands on me gold?"

Glenn noted the man spoke with an awkward Irish accent. Another of the game world's quirks?

Stephi leaned forward and looked down at the man. "We found it first."

The little man laughed at her, apparently unimpressed with the manner in which she towered over him. Nor did her impressive Appearance Score or feminine assets, each far larger than his head, have any impact. "Who said it'd ever been lost?"

"I think he's a leprechaun," Kirby warned.

Stephi looked back over her shoulder and asked Kirby, "What? Like with that kids' cereal?"

"Maybe a little of that," Kirby said. "But more like those *Leprechaun* movies."

Stephi's eyebrows scrunched together. "What

movies?"

Glenn said, "Nobody's supposed to be in these woods. Let's just go, before the duke's men show up."

"And leave the gold?" Stephi put her hands on her hips. "We need it to get home."

Kirby stepped up next to Stephi and took hold of her left hand. "You don't wanna mess with his kind. It's not worth it."

Glenn wasn't sure why Kirby was willing to forego a huge kettle of gold, but he trusted his friend's instincts and advice. Although Kirby was only a junior high kid in the real world, he knew an awful lot about how the *Monsters, Maces and Magic* game world worked.

"Gurk's right," Glenn said to Stephi. Then he made eye contact with the little man, the leprechaun, if Kirby was right. The man's emerald green eyes looked determined. Bushy eyebrows and prominent crow's feet framing them emphasized that. His teeth, crooked as a rickety picket fence, suggested a hidden malevolence. "Sorry, sir. We just saw the rainbow and—"

Stephi yanked her hand from Kirby's grip before Glenn could finish. "No, we're not leaving. Don't you want to get home?"

"Yer half breed companion," the small man said, disgust dripping from his words, "has the right of it. I *am* a leprechaun, plain and true." He stared up at Stephi. "It's a rarity for yer people, or gnomes for that matter, to be interfering in me people's doings." He pointed his shillelagh up at Stephi and shook it. "Now, you, be off."

"Don't you shake your stick at me, you racist little man. I'm like ten times bigger than you." She leaned forward, menacingly. "I'll take that little stick away from you and—"

"Marigold," Kirby said, trying to grab ahold of her hand again. Then he said to the leprechaun, "Please excuse her. She don't understand."

Stephi yanked her hand away again. Petie released a jeer call and flew down from the branches above, and dive bombed the half-goblin thief. Glenn ran forward and shouted up at Stephi, "Listen to Gurk. Let's go before the duke's men get here and arrest us."

Stephi took a deep breath and gazed back down at the grinning little leprechaun. "I don't wanna hurt you, but we need that gold. I'm sorry but…" She didn't finish the statement. Instead she fired off a quick spell.

The leprechaun blinked once, then sneered. "Oh, that's how ye want to play this, me lady elf?"

Her Slumber Spell had failed. Either the little man was able to resist magic, or he was a creature with too many hit dice to be affected.

The leprechaun rubbed his hands together and Glenn just knew it was going to be bad. The gnome healer charged the leprechaun, intending to bowl him over with his shield.

The little man sidestepped easily.

Kirby flung two darts at the leprechaun. One missed. The second struck, but fell away, leaving no damage.

Stephi's eyes went wide, possibly sensing she'd gone too far. Drawing upon Kim's warrior monk skills, her essence trapped within the soul gem, Stephi attempted a sweeping kick. The leprechaun nimbly leapt over the magic user's booted foot.

The agitated leprechaun completed his spell and pointed at Stephi.

A flash of rainbow colors encased her, then disappeared. Along with it, Stephi was gone. Her blouse, pants and boots collapsed to the needle-covered ground. Her straw hat landed atop the empty garments.

Kirby's face twisted in rage. "Nail the muther with your club!" he yelled, yanking his cutlass from its scabbard.

# CHAPTER 4

**Weeks before, Glenn** witnessed what Ron's spear did to a husk mummy. Nothing. Some creatures were immune to anything but magic, or silver. His cudgel was ringed with silver for just that reason.

The gnome healer charged again and swung his weapon. The little leprechaun dodged again, a sneering grin on his face. Kirby attacked too, and missed. Petie dove and pecked at the little man to no avail. The blue jay may as well have been a moth, being more annoying than anything else.

They'd bitten off more than they could chew. A lot more.

The leprechaun stepped back and uttered another spell. Glenn tried to nail him with the business end of his cudgel before the green and brown clad little man could finish. The little man got initiative, so Glenn failed.

The next thing Glenn knew, he was standing inside of a big cage, shaped like a magical bird cage, with half-inch thick bars that glowed neon green.

The leprechaun's spell trapped Kirby in a cage as well.

"Yer friend is unharmed," the little man said, walking over to his pot of gold. He lifted a coin and examined it.

"Mystical Cage," Kirby said and threw himself at the magical barrier, and fell back, shocked and screaming, like he'd latched onto a car battery's positive and negative posts. "Greater Sylvan Mystical Cage," he groaned.

The leprechaun observed Kirby picking himself up off the ground and shook his head. "Silly goblin half-breed."

Glenn threw his shield at the barrier. It earned the same result as the half-goblin thief.

"It won't affect you the same," Kirby said to Glenn, regaining his composure. Their cages were only five feet apart. "You're a gnome, a woodland creature, like him."

"Yer companion's on the smarter end of things," the leprechaun said to Glenn before tipping his hat to Kirby, "but like I said, yer elf friend is unharmed."

"Then where is she?" Kirby shouted. He tested a finger on one of the glowing green bars.

Glenn heard the sizzling *buzz* as fast as Kirby pulled his finger back. The half-goblin thief shook it and put it in his mouth. Glenn dropped his shield and grabbed one of the bars. It didn't burn. If felt cool and had the consistency of hard rubber. With grim determination he leaned into the bars imprisoning him and slowly pressed his body through.

Once free the gnome hefted his cudgel. "Where is she then?"

"I'm here."

It was Stephi's voice. A little bit faint, and muffled.

"I don't know where," she said. "It's dark and I'm stuck under…some stupid blanket. Or a tent."

Glenn looked around. He didn't see her. Petie, trapped in his own tiny cage on a branch above, chirped and warbled.

Stephi's straw hat, resting on her pile of clothes, moved. A lump like a kitten under a shirt flowed down one of the billowing sleeves. A tiny woman, slender with long wavy hair and pointed ears crawled out. She stood naked, revealing iridescent wings and enormous breasts, in comparison to her miniature size.

The little winged woman spun slowly, looking up and around. Eyes wide, her hands shot up to cover her gaping mouth.

Glenn's jaw dropped too as he stared down. It was

Stephi, no doubt about that, but she looked like Tinker Bell, only a little bigger—if "bigger" could be used to describe her. And she was naked! He tried to look away, knew he should, but couldn't. Curiosity and her stunning Appearance Score…

The leprechaun rocked back and forth on his heels, a smug look on his face. "Well," he said, "now it appears I'm in the vicinity of being ten times bigger than *ye*."

Stephi stared up at him and his crooked-toothed grin.

From within his glowing cage, Kirby said, "You got fairyed!"

The dire shock of the situation kept Glenn from getting aroused. He finally managed to avert his eyes. "And you're naked," he said.

Stephi gasped and covered herself with her arms and hands. She looked around, grabbed her linen blouse's sleeve and clutched it in front of her. Reaching down with her free hand she lifted what had been an ankle bracelet holding the alexandrite gem and cinched it like a belt around her waist.

Glenn took a step toward the leprechaun. "Change her back," he demanded.

"Or?" the leprechaun asked.

"We'll see if the silver in my cudgel will change your mind."

"Don't kill him, dude."

Glenn didn't know if Kirby had that much faith in him, or if it was a psychological ploy. Still, he curled his lip and said, "If he survives the coma, he'll have to learn how to walk without kneecaps. Not busted. I'll dig them out so there's nothing there to heal."

Apparently unimpressed, the leprechaun said, "Look, lad, ye can try and fail, and I'll summon me rainbow and be gone. Or…" He tossed his shillelagh so that it spun once and he caught it by the grip end. "You perform me a service, and I change yer friend back to her original elf self." His gaze darted to Stephi, staring up at the leprechaun and Glenn, her wings fluttering slowly. "Bountifully original proportions and all."

Kirby leaned as close to the glowing bars as he dared. "Brain him. Leprechauns always weasel out of their deals."

The leprechaun spun to face Kirby. "With yer kind, we might. Both bloods that flow in those mortal veins of yours. But not so with gnomes and elves." He glanced down at Stephi. "Or fairies."

Glenn didn't know what to say. The chances of him pounding the crap out of the magical creature before he escaped seemed pretty slim. But if his word couldn't be trusted... Kirby'd played *Monsters, Maces and Magic* dozens of times, or more. He knew the creatures from the Monster Guide, their hit dice, magical abilities, and how they were supposed to act.

"Ye might want to get to making that agreement right quick." The leprechaun flipped his shillelagh again. "Before, as you and your half-breed companion warned, the duke's, or whoever's men arrive."

Glenn bit his lower lip. He looked down at Stephi. "What do you want to do?"

"Like there's a choice." She stomped up to the leprechaun, dragging her shirt by the sleeve behind her. The little man was more than twice her height, but that didn't seem to bother Stephi. She let go of her shirt's sleeve and flapped her wings and flew upward, reminiscent of a butterfly, until she was eye to eye with the little man. She held position there, a little unsteady, like someone peddling their first bicycle with the training wheels just removed.

Glenn was going to say something to Stephi, but just hefted his club and tried to look as menacing as possible. Not really an effective ploy for a gnome healer.

"Speak fast, breakfast cereal boy, and it better be good," Stephi said, leaning close. "Because if it ain't, Jax'll be digging knee caps from your dead corpse."

"Redundant." The leprechaun looked her up and down, and smirked. "And what might be the point of a gnome mutilating a dead body?"

Stephi glanced down. The little man's trousers showed he was enjoying the scene.

"Really?" she said and frowned. In a flash, she flew down, performing a martial arts front kick.

After the solid strike she lost control and crashed to the ground, but mitigated the impact by rolling into it and coming to her feet. At the same time, the leprechaun grunted and staggered back, holding his crotch.

Glenn lifted his cudgel, and stepped forward to follow up on her attack.

Stephi held up a hand, signaling for him to wait.

"Let Jax at him," Kirby urged. "He's been itching for a fight ever since he pounded that husk mummy into a pile of bones and dust."

"We don't have time to wait for your eyes to stop watering," Stephi said. Still a little wobbly in flight, the former elf fluttered upward until she was once again eye to eye with the leprechaun. "What do we have to do before you'll change me back—and it better be good." She pointed up into a tree above. "But first, you're going to release my familiar." She paused and pointed back to her left, her gaze remaining locked with the leprechaun's. "And my friend."

# CHAPTER 5

**"So," Glenn said** to the leprechaun, "all we have to do is get the gold coin stolen from you by a dwarf named Benxcob, who arrived in Three Hills City two days ago from Shatt."

"And bring it back here," Stephi said while sitting on Kirby's shoulder, like a porcelain doll with shiny wings. She was no longer naked.

Shortly after being released, Kirby cut up Stephi's linen blouse to make a long sarape with a strap tied around her waist. She'd decided to keep the soul gem beneath the garment. At first she secured it across her shoulder like a bandoleer, but wearing it as a belt with the gem hanging as a fancy ornament worked better. Making slits in the sarape for the wings with the ends tied together around the neck had been tricky. It took two tries, and the second effort probably wouldn't last. But it was better than a 19.5 Appearance-score fairy standing naked in front of three men as they hammered out an agreement. More than once, Glenn missed having Ron's logical mind and steady emotions on hand.

Maybe it would've been better if Stephi'd stayed undressed, Glenn thought. If she would've done all of the negotiating, he could've just watched. But he knew that was wrong in so many ways. Beyond that, as much as her bare body would've been a distraction for the leprechaun, it would have been doubly so for Glenn and Kirby. She needed their help. She needed Kirby's cunning brain to fashion an agreement where they—Stephi—wouldn't get screwed over.

"And you'll change me back to an elf," Stephi continued. "My original size and everything. No twisting the intent of the agreement or funny business interpreting it. Then, immediately afterwards, we will give you the coin that the dwarf took."

The leprechaun scowled, but nodded. "Pan accursed me luck, an elf arrived first." After muttering that, he stood up straight. "I agree. To obtain the return of me stolen gold coin, I shall undo the enchantment, where you, Miss Marigold, will revert to your original form."

Stephi raised an eyebrow, and the leprechaun cleared his throat before clarifying, "Back to an elf maiden, original size, appearance and everything. No twisting the intent of the agreement or funny business interpreting it. And then I get me coin."

Stephi and Glenn had openly consulted with Kirby while arranging the verbal agreement, but they did all of the direct talking to the leprechaun. It seemed some fae, or sylvan, or nature-based connection between gnomes, elves and, presumably, leprechauns called for a higher level of honesty. Like they were all cousins of some sort.

"How will we know it's the right coin?" Glenn asked. "We don't want to miss an opportunity to get it, or call you back here—you'll know we're here, right?"

"Yes, call for me right here, under these fine and healthy yews." He paused and seemed to stare off into space, listening? Glenn was about to ask exactly how to call, but the leprechaun snapped out of his mini-trance.

"Say Bata Fidil, and me rainbow and me will arrive shortly." The leprechaun's bushy eyebrows drew together and he clenched his teeth before leaning forward and saying, "And no false callings or funny business on your end, or it'll go badly for each and every one of ye."

"Understood," Glenn said. "And the coin?" The gnome gestured to the kettle still sitting behind the leprechaun, its gold coins still glittering. "How do we make sure it's the coin from your kettle? I mean there's a lot of gold coins out there. Some might glow, or the dwarf might've had one crafted to throw off people looking for it."

"That's a pot, Jax the gnome. Not a kettle. And of course, I won't give ye one of mine from it to compare." His eyes looked up to the right, then left, in thought. "Give me a copper coin, if ye have one."

Gurk pulled a coin from his pocket and tossed it to the leprechaun.

The little man deftly snatched it from the air and walked over to his pot. Holding the copper coin in his right hand, he slapped it against the side of the cast iron kettle—or pot—and mumbled a few arcane words.

Then he strode back, inspecting both sides of the coin. He nodded once in satisfaction, then flicked it with his thumb up to Stephi.

Catching it threw her a little off balance, but fluttering her wings kept her from falling. In her hands the copper coin was about the size of a teacup saucer.

"That coin is identical in appearance to all of me gold coins, including the one stolen." The leprechaun rubbed a finger under his nose. "Put it within five inches of me gold coin and the copper one ye have will act as a lodestone."

He balled his fists and put his hands on his hips. "Should be proof enough?"

Glenn thought it was, but looked to Kirby for affirmation. The half-goblin thief nodded.

"I'll be going then." The leprechaun's shillelagh flew from the ground into his hand and he strode toward his pot of gold. "Ye might be thinking on departing swiftly before the duke's men, ye call them, arrive."

While Glenn, Stephi and Kirby stared at each other for a second, wondering what to do, a scything of brilliant colors erupted upwards, forming a rainbow. Without a word or a sound, the rainbow faded, and Bata Fidil, the leprechaun, and his pot of gold were gone.

Glenn ran and picked up his shield lying on the meadow grass. After slinging it across his back, he spread Stephi's cloak out on the ground. Then he tossed her boots, pants, undergarments, what remained of her blouse, straw hat and everything else, except her belt with the scabbarded rapier, onto the cloak.

Stephi stood on the ground, her eyes closed. Glenn knew that meant she was looking through her familiar's eyes.

Kirby picked up her rapier and belted it across his back. "You gather that stuff up like a sack, dude." Then the half-goblin thief gestured to Stephi. "She'll be able to get away, no problem. Me and you are gonna have to make a run for it."

"There's like twenty soldiers coming this way," Stephi said. Her eyes snapped open. "They have spears and crossbows. Two are on horses ahead of them."

Finding the dart he threw at the leprechaun and missed, Kirby asked, "Which direction?"

"From the city," she said impatiently. "They're in two lines now, but I bet they'll spread out or something."

Glenn looked at the stirred up needles and wondered: Were they coming because of the rainbow? Or because someone saw us coming in here? "They'll know we were here," he said.

"They'll know *someone* was here," Kirby said. "If they find this spot. We got everything?"

"I'll distract them, Gurk," Stephi said, fluttering into the air, "so you and Jax can get away."

"How you gonna do that, Marigold?" Kirby peered into the trees, as if expecting the duke's soldiers to be surrounding them any second. "No offense, but you don't look too steady flying."

"I've been bonded with Petie for a couple months. Experiencing things through him. That's helped me a lot already," she assured him.

"What're ya gonna do to distract them?"

"Flash my boobs at them if I have to," Stephi said, growing impatient. "Stop wasting time so I don't have to."

"Where do we meet?" Glenn asked. He shouldered the bundled cloak like a sack. "The willow tree?"

Kirby shook his head. "That's too close. We'll stand out like a couple of cosplayers at a Baptist convention."

Stephi looked at the thief, not comprehending what he'd said.

"How about the dockyard?" Glenn asked. "It's about a quarter mile beyond the willow tree."

"Good idea, Jax," Kirby said. "Different people are always hanging around there." He turned to Stephi. "We're gonna keep low along the river bank. Do what you can to keep them away from there. We only need a few minutes, and then you come find us at the docks."

Stephi nodded, a little wide eyed. Her iridescent wings fluttered a little more quickly. The muscle action in her back pulled at her chest, making it bounce up and down like someone shaking a miniature pair of maracas.

Glenn looked away, pretending he was trying to spot danger. He couldn't shake the vision from his mind. Sure it was arousing, but confusing. With her wings flapping, shouldn't her breasts be bouncing sideways and back, not up and down?

Kirby gripped Glenn's shoulder, snapping him back into the moment. "Dude, you okay?"

"Uhh, yeah," Glenn said.

"We got this," Kirby said. He winked a yellow eye at Glenn. "Come on. If we each roll far enough beneath our Stealth Check, we might even get to grab our fishing poles along the way."

# CHAPTER 6

Glenn, Kirby and Stephi made it back to the Glade House.

The guards on the drawbridge admitting entrance to Three Hills City were a little confused, and disappointed that the towering, buxom elf wasn't with the gnome and half-goblin.

She *was* with them, but in her fairy form, riding along inside a canvas sack that Kirby'd stolen from a laborer around the docks. It smelled a little of fish, which didn't make Stephi happy. But Kirby insisted that fairies were more than a curiosity. They made people nervous. He'd said to Stephi when she balked, "You think dancing on stage without a cloak or bra drew attention? A sparkly winged fairy would turn heads away from that in a second. Fairies got a bad reputation for mischief." His face scrunched up. "Or misfortune. A lot of times somebody ends up hurt." His eyes widened. "Hurt, or dead."

The Glade House, the boarding house where Glenn and his party stayed, was empty, except for Elise. The young maid stood on a stepstool, wiping down the dining room's walls. She turned her head and smiled when she saw Kirby and Glenn.

"No luck fishing," Kirby said and shrugged.

"Too bad."

"Did you hear where Lysine and Kalgore went?"

The maid said, "Sorry, no, Mr. Gurk."

"No problem, Elise," Kirby said, turning to go up the stairs. He took two at a time. Glenn climbed one at a time, his boots clomping the entire way.

When they reached their shared room, Kirby closed the door and slid the bolt to lock it. The room was small, but it had one shuttered, narrow window that offered Petie access to the room, and a place to roost at night. The room held four bunks that folded up against the wall, stacked in pairs like bunk beds. Glenn used a worn mattress on the floor. There were five small trunks that often served as tables, while the bottom pair of folded down beds served as chairs. The room had a magical light set next to the door. The spot where the Light Spell had been cast could be covered by a metallic cup attached to a hinge. The walls were painted a dull yellow and the floor was made of hardwood planks. Since they mainly used the room for sleep, and were out and about during the day, it sufficed.

The Glade House offered an early breakfast, usually of oats and honey, and an evening meal. It wasn't fancy. Usually a decent cut of meat, potatoes or beets, apple cider and bread.

They also had a locked storage bin in the cellar. All in all, clean, safe, and not too expensive. The proprietor, Keri Lovelace, had abilities as an enchantress and was somewhat of a mystery—and made sure things stayed that way. Her two small guard dogs, Rocky and Chili, even liked Kirby. It was rare for canines to befriend anyone with goblin blood coursing through their veins. It was one of the established "norms" set forth in the Player's and Game Master's Guides.

As soon as Stephi crawled out of the sack and onto her bottom bunk, Glenn asked, "You okay, Marigold?"

She fluttered her butterfly-like wings and nodded. Somehow, she'd been able to fold, or collapse them while riding in the sack.

To Glenn she looked like a child's doll, about twenty-five percent bigger than a Barbie doll, sitting on the bed. Once Kirby opened the window and real sunlight reached in, her iridescent wings caught the light and reflected all the colors of the rainbow.

Glenn refrained from mentioning his observation. Rainbows would probably be a sore topic for the foreseeable future. Nevertheless, like rainbows, her shimmering wings were a thing of beauty.

Petie landed on the ledge, and that brought a brief smile to her face. It faded when she looked around at the room. It must've seemed like a cavern to her. Glenn could relate. He still wasn't used to being a gnome, always looking up and having to negotiate a world built for people taller than him.

"If everything's cool," Kirby said, "I'm gonna go look for Lysine and Kalgore. They like hanging out at the livestock auction. Although that might be done by now."

Stephi didn't say anything.

Kirby's eyebrows shot up. "You okay with that, Marigold?"

She nodded and gave him a thumb's up.

He rested a hand on Glenn's shoulder. "I'll be back as quick as I can, Jax." With that, he unbolted the door, stepped out, and was gone.

Glenn stood in the middle of the floor, trying to think of something to say. Before he came up with anything, Stephi's body began to shake, and she broke down in tears.

Glenn's eyes teared up, too. He didn't know what to do, what to say. How could he comfort her? He climbed up on the bunk and sat next to Stephi, his legs dangling over the edge.

Stephi slid over next to Glenn and leaned against him. She wept quietly, hands covering her face.

Although she wasn't saying a word, Glenn thought about Stephi's voice, as a fairy. It wasn't as loud compared to when she was over six feet tall, but it had the same tone. Not higher pitched, like he expected.

Glenn wanted to put his arm around his friend as best he could, but he was afraid he might damage her wings. And an arm around her might make her feel uncomfortable. Stephi was a third of his height—and *he* was short.

What could he say? Everything will be okay? How could he say that? He had no idea, and it'd be a lie. Glenn just shook his head in despair, once again feeling completely lost in the game world. Biting his lip, he did his best to be strong and keep his own tears from flowing.

After a moment he reached into his pocket and pulled out his red and black handkerchief. He unwrapped it, set the few coins it held aside, and offered it to Stephi.

She took it and wiped her teary face.

Even after crying for ten minutes, her eyes didn't appear too red or swollen. Probably her Appearance Score, or some fairy thing. Even with the tears stopped, Glenn knew it was a mask. Behind it, his friend was frightened and hurting, probably more than he'd ever been. Maybe not as frightened as when he'd faced the husk mummy, but that happened so fast, and was resolved fast. Stephi's situation wouldn't be.

"I want to go home so bad, Jax," Stephi said, her voice quivering. "I saw that gold and that was all I could think about—we need it to go home." She took a steadying breath. "I should've listened to you and Gurk.

"He was so little. I thought I could just use my Slumber Spell and..."

She leaned against him and started crying again. Not as out of control as before. Glenn figured she needed to get it all out, especially before Kirby found Derek and brought *him* back.

Glenn gently put his arm around Stephi. "I know what you mean, Marigold. I think about it all the time."

She looked at him. "Really, you do?"

He sighed. "When I'm not trying to figure this world

out. When I'm scared, not knowing how to survive. It's like I hardly ever know what's going on."

"I know what you mean." Once again she took a calming breath. "I guess compared to you, I'm lucky..." She looked down at herself. "Or was...well, still am in a way."

Glenn waited for Stephi to organize her thoughts.

She reached down and fingered the soul gem attached to a silver chain strapped across her chest. The chain looked more like a thin bike chain on her than a delicate necklace chain. "I can talk to Byeol, because she—her soul's—held in my gem." She lifted the enchanted Alexandrite gemstone that dangled from the chain. It was almost half the size of her fist. "And I have Petie. He's not like a person, but he's more than a pet could ever be." She shook her head. "I can't explain it. But those are things you don't have, and I do."

He forced a smile, which became a genuine one. "Well, when I'm hanging out with you and Gurk, I usually feel pretty good. I don't miss home nearly as much."

She leaned in and hugged him.

He laughed. "We sound like a couple of homesick kids, stuck at a summer camp we didn't want to go to."

The embers of mirth in Stephi faded. In a voice that cracked, she said, "Camp Never-ending Nightmare."

**Glenn was still** sitting on the bed next to Stephi, lost in thought, when someone knocked on the door. It made him jump.

"Who is it?" he asked.

"It's Keri." Her worldly-aunt voice was reassuring.

Stephi looked around, eyes wide in panic. "She can't see me," Stephi whispered.

Glenn hadn't thought that far ahead. Then he

remembered what Kirby'd said about fairies, and how people reacted to them. He pointed to the discarded canvas sack on the floor and looked at Stephi with eyebrows raised.

"Keri Lovelace, the owner of the Glade House, where you're staying," the voice said from the other side of the door.

"Just a moment," he said, hopping down off the bed.

"I know what happened, and Marigold's situation."

"Did Gurk talk to you?"

"No, I have my own sources." She paused. "I believe I may be able to help."

Glenn met Stephi's gaze. She gulped and shrugged her tiny shoulders.

Trying to think like Kirby, Glenn asked, "If I might ask, what's your source?" He asked "what" because there could be magic involved. The Glade House's owner was an enchantress, after all.

"I got a message from a friend of mine," Keri said, familiar sassiness in her voice. "She's a wood nymph."

Glenn didn't know what to expect for an answer, but that wasn't it. He'd heard of nymphos, as in nymphomaniacs, but he didn't think that fit. It sounded more nature-like, and he'd heard rumors that Keri had fae blood in her veins. It seemed like half the people were half human and half something else, or maybe a quarter something else, or an eighth. And people always seemed to be hiding something. He scratched his head. Technically, he was hiding something—being a human from another world, trapped in a gnome healer's body.

Glenn again turned to Stephi, with a raised eyebrow.

She stood on the bed, Kirby's makeshift sarape garment hanging from her shoulders, looking like she was ready to flee. Where to, Glenn wasn't sure, until he remembered the open window.

Stephi whispered, "Whatever you think, Jax."

He whispered back, "She's gonna find out, eventually."

"Okay."

Glenn didn't take Stephi's "okay" as a vote of confidence. More in resignation, along the lines of: What else could happen to make things worse?

Glenn moved to the door and reached for the bolt.

Stephi said, "But no dogs."

The gnome nodded and spoke through the door. "Where are Rocky and Chili?"

"On their mats in the parlor, taking their mid-morning nap."

Glenn wondered what use the two little dogs were, other than barking at intruders, and companionship. They did entertain some of the people who stayed at the Glade House. But for Stephi now, they'd be the size of bears.

Glenn opened the door a crack and peered out. Only Keri stood in the narrow hallway, wearing a gray linen blouse, blue skirt that reached to just above the lacing of her heavy black boots, and a white apron. Her hair hung in loose curls down to her shoulder. From experience, Glenn knew when she became angry, her hair somehow straightened.

The boarding house owner had brown eyes that matched her brunette hair. She had full red lips, expressive eyebrows and faint dimples when she smiled. It was normally an infectious smile, as was her laugh.

He opened the door a little wider. "Come on in," he said. As soon as the boarding house owner stepped into the small room he pushed the door closed and bolted it.

Petie, resting on the window sill, chirped a greeting.

Keri looked down at Stephi standing on the bed, frightened and half-ready to fly away. The boarding house owner clasped her hands together and said, "Oh, honey. It's true."

Those words brought on another flood of tears. This time, they weren't accompanied with sobs, just sadness and despair.

After a moment, Keri stepped over to the lower bunk across from Stephi. "May I sit and have you tell me all that happened?"

Stephi took in a deep, unsteady breath and nodded.

Keri pulled down Ron's bed and sat on it. Her booted feet rested flat on the floor. She dropped her clasped hands onto the apron covering her lap. "Whenever you're ready, hon."

Glenn climbed back up onto Stephi's bed and sat next to her as she told the tale, starting from fishing on the river bank and seeing the rainbow, to their trek back to Three Hills City and the Glade House.

Glenn didn't say anything, and Keri didn't ask for clarification while she intently listened, even when a question might be called for. Especially the part about Stephi's vague motivation for taking possession of the gold. Of course, who wouldn't want a pot of gold?

Keri Lovelace had told Glenn, during their first encounter, that everyone should be allowed their secrets. She must truly believe those words.

Although telling the Glade House owner what happened upset Stephi in parts, she worked through them. In doing so, the process instilled a sense of calm by the end. Or maybe it was resignation. Glenn wasn't sure.

After a moment of silence between the three, Glenn said, "Gurk went to find Lysine and Kalgore."

Keri's left eyebrow arched, then she nodded. "I have to ask, Marigold. Why are you wearing that?"

Stephi looked down at her crudely fashioned sarape, cut from her blouse's fabric. "Gurk made it for me, so I had something to wear."

Glenn wondered what else she was supposed to wear. Maybe some infant's clothes, modified by a tailor?

Or a doll's dress?

"You don't know much about fairies?" Keri said. It was less a question and more a statement.

"Gurk does," Stephi responded. "He just didn't have time to tell me anything. We were fighting, and then running from the duke's soldiers and then trying to get back here. And then…"

Keri finished, "And then your half-goblin friend, who's knowledgeable about fairies, went to go find your other two friends."

Glenn suspected that Stephi, being an elf, probably should know something about fairies. Being a "woodland creature" he probably should, too. "Gurk's smart," Glenn said. "He knows a lot more than…he knows a lot about a lot of things."

Keri took a deep breath. "Well, your friend *may* know a lot about fairies, but I certainly don't. Not enough for your concern." Her face took on an intense, serious look. "But I know someone who does, Marigold. You should meet her."

"Who?" Stephi asked.

"Her name is Emma. She's an old…" Keri rolled her eyes in embarrassment. "Better to say, a longtime friend."

"Can she come here?" Glenn asked. "To the Glade House." He wanted to add: Before Kalgore gets here.

Keri's lips pressed together. She shook her head. "No, you'll have to go to her."

"Why?" Glenn asked. "Marigold can't go out. Not when she can be seen. Gurk said people don't like fairies. Hate them and blame them for things that go wrong."

"I'll go," Stephi interjected. She fluttered down onto the floor, next to the discarded, stolen sack. "I can go in this again."

Keri stood, which caused Stephi to shy away a step. "I apologize honey," she said. "I imagine the world's a much bigger place now, and normal things will be unsettling until you get used to them." She straightened her apron. "All the more reason you should meet Emma."

She glanced at Glenn as he hopped down off the bed. "I have a creel basket," she said. "It'll be more comfortable for Marigold."

"A creel basket?" Glenn asked.

"A wicker basket where you stow fish you catch," Keri replied. "It has a lid and shoulder strap. I might've lent it to you, if you and Gurk were better at fishing." She smiled down at Stephi. "Don't worry, it's clean and doesn't smell like fish."

"Okay," Glenn said.

"I'll go get it from the cellar. And I'll tell Elise that you two have gone with me to visit a friend, and that she should share that information with your friends, when she sees them."

Keri paused, and tipped her head. "Be aware, if you haven't already discovered it, Marigold." Her brown eyes widened, to emphasize seriousness. "The touch of iron will be worse than that of a red-hot coal, and steel like a blast of scalding steam."

**Glenn opted to** leave his shield behind, as he often did in town. Having it slung over his back would've made it difficult to also shoulder the strap attached to the creel basket. He had to agree, it was a better solution than a canvas sack. The folded hand towel for cushioning also made a difference.

The gnome healer had trouble keeping up with Keri as she wove around various citizens and workers while making their way down the cobblestone streets. She only stepped around and ahead of slow ones. Those were the ones that travelled a pace more attuned to Glenn's preferred rate. Nevertheless, she never allowed the gnome to fall more than a few strides behind.

The way the Glade House owner observed people and places reminded him of Kirby. She had street smarts. And a lot of friends, or at least acquaintances, as she seemed to exchange a quick nod and smile, or a brief hello, at least a hundred times.

Glenn was pretty sure they were making their way to Duke Huelmer's high-walled keep in the center of Three Hills City. Glenn's keen gnomish nose never got used to the rank odor of the common workers who rarely bathed, or washed their tattered clothes. It was especially noticeable because of the day's rising heat. The hot sun did work to quell the cacophony of sounds, the city's background noise. People put in less effort shouting at each other, or merchants, less intensity hawking their wares. Friendly conversations were brief, while cursing at beasts of burden, and the resulting animal protests, demonstrated a heat-drained energy.

The waves of body odor retreated, as did the frequency of horse and oxen manure piles on the streets. The region around the duke's keep was well maintained, and fewer people travelled the cleaner, quieter streets. Those that were traveling rode mainly in carriages or on horseback to their compressed but impressive estates. Each estate contained unique, tall buildings and elaborate wrought-iron fences. A few porters or delivery men with filled mule-drawn carts travelled toward the keep. The empty carts, or the carts hauling empty crates, were going the opposite direction, past where Keri led Glenn.

Petie easily kept up with them, flying from rooftop to rooftop. Glenn figured Stephi, in the basket, watched their progress through her familiar's eyes.

Finally, when they were within fifty yards of the keep's main wall, Keri took him left, down a short narrow pathway that led between two rows of tall taxis bushes. That path led up to a walled compound. A guard blocked the entry. He wore chainmail and was armed with a halberd resting butt down in one hand and a short sword hanging on his belt. He looked big, and hot, and anything but pleasant. Behind him stood an iron gate with a latticework of three-quarters inch thick steel bars. Beyond it stood a second, similar gate.

The wall was three feet thick and built from limestone blocks. Atop it grew some sort of twisting vines with inch-long thorns. Glenn figured Kirby could probably find a way over, but Glenn knew there was no way he could get over it, at least without a ladder and sustaining plenty of thorn wounds. Ignoring the wall, Glenn doubted Kalgore could take the guard, even if his party member 'rolled' successfully for Initiative every round of combat.

Keri didn't break stride as she approached the guard. Glenn followed, trying to maintain a friendly, unconcerned demeanor.

"I am here to consult with one of the garden's caretakers," Keri said with a friendly lilt in her voice.

The guard smiled, then seemed to catch himself. "Who's your friend, Lovelace?"

She stepped aside. "This is Jax. He is assisting me this afternoon."

The guard eyed Glenn suspiciously. "Have I seen you somewhere before?"

Glenn stepped forward, his boots clomping on the stone path. The taxis bushes were meticulously trimmed. They also formed a sturdy barrier, keeping people on the five-foot wide path. Through the two gates he spotted a host of colorful flowers bordering the path beyond.

"I'm pretty short, sir," the gnome healer said. "So a lot of people overlook me. But gnomes are rare, so when they do notice me, they tend to remember." He shrugged. "I see a lot of humans, but with the crowds, from my vantage, I don't get a good look at faces."

The guard cocked his head. "No…I remember seeing you somewhere…"

Glenn's heart raced. Probably the Blue Bugle, when he was on stage collecting thrown coins while Stephi pole danced. He kept his friendly smile going, counting on the fact that humans tended to have a favorable opinion of gnomes. "Do you ever eat at the Ox Wagon?"

The guard shook his head.

It'd been a long time since Glenn visited the Ox Wagon, so he tried somewhere more recent. "I get tea at the Red Brick. Maybe there?"

The guard shook his head again. "What're you helping Lovelace consult about?"

"Morphation and invasive species." It was the first thing he could think to say. It was completely made up but sounded technical and plausible, he hoped. And sounded right for someone visiting a flower garden.

He gulped. Unless it had nothing to do with the flower garden, and Emma worked inside the duke's keep.

"Okay," the guard said to Keri. He called back over his shoulder. "Brutt, it's Lovelace and a gnome. Open'er up."

A second guard from within the compound used a different skeleton key to open each gate and let them in.

# Chapter 7

**The compound housed** a sizeable flower garden filled with curving paths lined with trellises and large urns filled with flowers. There were rose bushes of all types and small ponds containing flowering lilies and vibrant blue, purple, pink and orange koi fish.

Glenn followed close behind Keri, who seemed to know where she was going. He wanted to tell Stephi what he saw, or open the basket lid so she could see. But Petie was in the compound, flying around and landing on the paths ahead of them. She could at least see through his eyes the climbing morning glories, patches of day lilies, snap dragons, marigolds, irises, tulips, daisies, bachelor buttons, pussy willows and more.

And then there was the legion of bees, a myriad of colorful butterflies dancing on the light breeze, and hummingbirds, at least three different types. All of them flitted from flower to flower in search of fresh nectar.

"Gardeners work during the morning and evening," Keri said, taking a left at a Y intersection. "Afternoons are fairly quiet, unless the duke or other nobles decide to lunch in the garden."

Staying on the stone path that forked multiple times and made numerous turns, from right angle to hairpin, Keri made her way to a quiet corner of the duke's garden. With no one tending the flowers and plants, or visiting, all was quiet, except for some small frogs croaking, insects buzzing and canaries and other song birds singing. The twists and turns, the rosebushes and trellises, and marble statues were arranged to make one feel isolated within the garden. If Glenn were taller, he figured he might be able to see more, get glimpses of the distant boarder wall. What he *was* able to see was the keep's main wall.

As he was staring at it, Keri said, "There is a tunnel that leads from the duke's keep into the garden. Its location is a closely guarded secret."

The way she said it, Glenn wasn't sure if she knew the location of the tunnel's entrance, or not. Probably the way she intended it.

Keri stopped next to a wall of climbing hydrangea framed by several lilac bushes and a pink-flowering dogwood. "Set the basket down, Jax."

He did and looked around. He spotted Petie in the dogwood's upper branches. Glenn supposed someone, Emma, would emerge from the keep's tunnel. But how had Keri contacted her? Did she send a runner with a message ahead? He doubted that, with the guard at the gate. She could've used some sort of messaging spell, if that was possible. Kirby, Ron, or even Derek would probably know.

Not seeing anyone, Glenn lifted the basket lid.

Stephi was sitting, leaning back with her legs crossed, eyes closed.

"Marigold," he whispered. Then he looked up at Keri standing next to him.

"It is perfectly fine for her to come out. This," Keri said, gesturing with a sweep of her hand, "is her element."

Stephi stood and started to climb out, then remembered her wings and flew out, and hovered like a hummingbird. Maybe like one that was a little tipsy.

Glenn averted his eyes, instead of staring. In some ways, with her shimmering wings, beating and flashing in the sunlight, she was that much more stunning. Plus, the way her chest was bouncing, her makeshift sarape might come apart at any moment. He hoped it didn't, even as a creepy part of him sort of—well, hoped it did. And he hated himself for that.

"*Swaa*," a cheerful voice said. It sounded like a practiced feminine soprano.

Glenn looked, and sitting on a lower branch of the dogwood was a fairy. He'd just been looking that direction and hadn't seen her. He was sure she hadn't just flown past him.

The fairy had wings similar to Stephi's, iridescent, but with more pink in them. They were a little fuller. More teardrop shaped, and less butterfly. She had short, blond hair, in sort of a mussed up, fashion model style. She looked a little smaller than Stephi, which made sense since, on average, Stephi had been bigger than most people, except for some massive warrior types, or half-ogres. And the fairy wore a sleeveless, short dress that was made up of flower petals. It didn't look flimsy or about to fall apart. Glenn wasn't close enough to see any stitching. Even so, he didn't think there was any. Maybe some sort of glue?

How could she have avoided being noticed while adorned in a dress consisting of orange, red and yellow flower petals? Her tiny feet were bare, and that made Glenn wonder if she flew south for the winter. Was it warmer to the south? Were winters around Three Hills City bad? He'd never really thought to ask anyone.

"*Swaa*, Emma," Keri said. "These are my friends." She gestured to each as she named them. "Marigold and Jax." She turned to Stephi and Glenn. "Marigold and Jax, this is my friend, Emma."

Emma responded. What she said sounded pleasant, and caused Keri to smile and Stephi to blush while also smiling. The words Emma spoke sounded like Elvish, or Elven. Whatever the language, Jax couldn't understand what was said.

Keri noticed Glenn's blank expression out of the corner of her eye. "Emma, my dear, Jax isn't able to converse in your native tongue."

A brief instant of consternation crossed the small fairy's face. Then she giggled. "Three sunrises filled with apologies, Jax the Gnome. I remarked that Marigold's radiant beauty outshines the loveliest morning glory in the duke's garden. And that she is by long measure the largest fairy I have ever seen, both in height of stem and blossoming display, certain to distract mortal men, should they lay eyes upon her."

Glenn couldn't argue with that assessment. "True words. Thank you for saying them in a way that I can understand."

"Why have you come to spend the height of the sun with me today?" Emma asked. "Certainly not to *consult.*" She raised a feathery eyebrow at Glenn. "Nor to explore *invasive species* within the duke's garden."

"That is true, those are not our purposes," Keri said. "The guards required a reason to admit us on this fine afternoon."

Emma fluttered her wings and laughed. It brought to mind jingling bells mixed with wind chimes.

"The guards are unlikely to know a toad from a toadstool," Emma said, "but they defend the gate like a mother badger does her den."

Glenn wondered if the guards knew the fairy, Emma, was even in the garden. He hadn't seen her until she decided to reveal herself. By the secluded spot Keri had selected, he decided they didn't. He figured most of the nobles that visited the flower garden were unaware as well. That made him feel a little bit special. It wasn't often he felt privileged compared to the rich merchants and nobles in Three Hills City.

Keri returned to the point of their visit. "As you might have guessed, Marigold was not born a fairy. A leprechaun that goes by the name of Bata Fidil transformed her into one just this morning." Keri frowned, then pursed her lips. "From what I know of

Marigold, although an elf, her upbringing has left her unknowing of the fae."

Glenn wasn't sure that Stephi had shared any of her "upbringing" with Keri. But Glenn and his party had been at the Glade House for a couple months. That she and he were relying on Kirby, a half-goblin, for information on fairies, one of the fae races? The logical assumption made sense.

"She is an elf," Keri continued. "Or was, prior to her encounter with Bata Fidil in Polayney's grove."

The fact that Stephi was an elf appeared to both please and sadden Emma.

Stephi continued to beat her wings, effortlessly remaining aloft with only an inch or two in varying height off the ground. She looked down and away. Glenn suspected she was recalling the actions that led to her transformation.

"Like Jax, Marigold is more comfortable around humans than her own kind."

Emma's brow furrowed. "His proper name is Bataí Fidil na Maidine, and he is a wart of a man."

Keri laughed and clasped her hands. "My friend, you say that about all leprechauns, and half the pixies ever born."

"You have a point, Keri," Emma said. "Leprechauns are not long-thinkers and more greedy for gold than squirrels for acorns prior to a harsh winter." For a few seconds, her wings stopped flapping. "Fairies get blamed for half the mischief pixies inflict upon mortals, because the big louts cannot identify one from the other."

Glenn wondered how humans could, assuming those were the "big louts." If they're lucky they get a fraction of a second's glimpse and the pixie—or fairy—is gone. But he didn't express his thought.

Emma leaned forward, resting her hands on her thighs with elbows pointed out. "Bataí Fidil na Maidine?

I would rather spend my morning among the blowflies infesting a wererat's carcass than with him."

"So, more than by name, you know him?" Stephi asked.

"I have had the misfortune to meet him a time or two, many summers past." She sat up straight. "I overheard the duke's daughter and her nursemaid earlier talking of a rainbow descending into the yew grove this morning. I did not know it was Fidil's doing. And I am joyful as a caterpillar devouring a fresh milkweed sprout that I wasn't there to chance meet him again.

"Is that why you're visiting me here in the garden?"

"It is," Keri said. "Marigold knows nothing of fairies and their magic, and their concerns, other than iron."

Emma's mouth dropped open for a second, and her eyebrows shot up. Then she tapped a spot on the dogwood branch next to her. "Please, come sit next to me and tell me about your encounter with the weasel-nosed Bata Fidil. After I apologize to all weasels within earshot for that unpleasant association."

Glenn and everyone else laughed, and Stephi maneuvered herself to stand on the branch, and then sat. She was at least thirty percent bigger than Emma, meaning the small fairy was only a foot or so tall, and built much like a typical Barbie doll.

"You are indeed a tallest of oaks among our kind," Emma said, looking up at Stephi sitting to her right.

"It was the same when I was an elf," Stephi replied with a shrug.

"I must also say, you fly very well with this being your first day as a fairy."

"It's because of Petie, my familiar."

Petie flew down and landed on a branch above them, a few feet away. He chirped happily. Glenn interpreted it as a greeting.

Emma grinned and waved to Petie. "A handsome

blue jay he is," she said to Stephi. "Which means you are a magic user?"

Stephi nodded.

"It also means that when Fidil worked his Transmorph Spell upon you, the enchantment did not strip you of your spell-casting abilities. It may be that you will benefit from what you had and what you have gained."

"Gained?" Stephi asked.

Emma looked down at Glenn, and then for a briefer span, at Keri.

After an uncomfortable pause, Emma said, "Tell me of your encounter with that festering wart of a…leprechaun."

Stephi retold her tale, almost exactly as she had to Keri. This time, she didn't require reminders or input from Glenn. He thought about sitting down on the path, but refrained as he didn't want to interrupt Stephi or accidentally insult Emma. Besides, Keri remained standing.

After Stephi finished, another moment of silence emerged.

Glenn was searching for something to say when the small fairy stood, mostly by effort of her beautiful wings.

Emma offered Stephi a hand to stand as well and announced, "Marigold and Petie will remain with me until after the sun falls below the horizon. I will share with her all she needs to know." She smiled down at Glenn. "She and her familiar shall return before moonrise, when her travels will not easily be viewed by mortal eyes."

Glenn didn't want to abandon his friend, but it was clear both he and Keri were being dismissed. He said, "I'll be sure to leave the window to our room at the Glade House open."

Stephi appeared both nervous and excited. "Thank

you, Jax. I'll see you and Gurk tonight. Don't worry." She clasped her hands. "Keri, I cannot thank you enough."

Keri released a pleasant laugh. "It's my pleasure, hon."

Stephi smiled down at Emma, a knowing smile that Glenn had glimpsed at college, a knowing smile shared between sorority sisters.

Misinterpreting Glenn's absent nodding with raised eyebrows, Stephi said, "Everything's fine, Jax. Petie and I will be okay."

**Glenn left the** garden with some regret hanging in his heart. Even though Stephi said it was okay, he felt like he was abandoning his friend who was vulnerable, both physically and emotionally. Plus, he wanted to linger in the garden, among the flowers. The fragrance and beauty spoke to his heart. He'd never been much of a nature enthusiast. He could recognize a beautiful forest or waterfall, but what he felt at the moment wasn't the same. His game-dictated gnomish nature was to blame.

There was no way he could remain in the garden. He'd be seen, and probably arrested. He wasn't sure how welcome Keri even was to be there for an extended period of time. And if he stayed outside the garden compound, in the rich district, he'd probably be arrested for loitering, or something. Or run over by four magnificent horses pulling a high-wheeled, fancy carriage.

No, even if it was a gnome thing, his human side recognized why spending time there would be alluring. Heck, a duke with power and wealth had created it. Probably to escape from whatever a rich and powerful man would need to escape from.

He looked around and redoubled his efforts to keep up with Keri. After they'd exited the double gates, the Glade House owner commented, "Your step is lighter.

You anticipate a sunrise rather than a sunset for your friend."

"Maybe," he pondered aloud. Then kept the rest of the thought to himself. The *Monsters, Maces and Magic* game world held far more misery, drudgery, desperation and terror than peace and beauty.

While they waited to cross an intersection congested by carts hauling rugs, wagons stacked with cut lumber and bricks, and porters bearing sacks of wool, Glenn looked around. Nobody was close to them, nobody paying attention. He asked the Glade House owner, "What's a wood nymph?"

Keri looked down at him. At first her eyes shot wide. Then her full lips pursed. "A gnome that doesn't know the likes of a wood nymph?"

Glenn gulped. "Sort of like Marigold, I was raised among humans." It was the truth. He didn't add that he'd never actually spoken with a fellow gnome. Ever. And the thought of the first time the opportunity presented itself turned his stomach into a knotted mess.

Keri's head tilted with an eyebrow raised, followed by a look of satisfaction. It was as if a puzzle piece had just fallen into place. She glanced back over her shoulder, the direction of the distant garden compound, possibly fitting another puzzle piece into place.

"Come on," she said, "I'll share a little of what I know of wood nymphs with you."

Instead of trying to make it across the intersection, she led Glenn another direction.

# Chapter 8

**The people at** the Stickley Café apparently knew the Glade House proprietor. Keri walked in, waved to the frazzled waitresses, and the frizzy-haired owner doubling as the secondary cook. She announced, "We'll be using Room Three, the third floor."

The owner replied, "Chelly'll be up when things get under control down here."

The café was finishing up a busy lunch serving wealthier merchants. It seemed there was only one main dish being served. Maybe like Taco Tuesday. Today dish consisted of a grilled fish on a stick, like a fish-kabob, accompanied by a spoonful of corn, several radishes and a round biscuit, all on a wooden plate.

The café contained plain wooden tables and pictures on the wall, mainly of peasants engaged in some aspect of farming. It was warm in the main room. Actually, everyplace was hot on summer days. In addition to modern plumbing, nobody had invented air conditioning. With magic it should be possible. Heck, Glenn recalled his great grandmother calling the refrigerator an ice box. Certainly there was an enchanter that could create ice, and put some sort of fan to blow across it.

The aroma of the fish and fresh rolls caused Glenn's mouth to water. The smell of apple cider made his throat feel dry. Maybe it was the food that drew the wealthier customers. Maybe it was the fantasy world's version of fast food, because everyone was shoveling it in while they spoke. Customers seated themselves and yelled to a passing waitress how many plates for their table. Before departing the customers left a stack of coins on a small tin plate placed upon a wooden stand in the table's center.

The stairway was narrow. The steep steps let off on the second floor before leading to the third. Two big people like Derek, or built like Stephi, would have to squeeze past each other. The stairway lacked a handrail so Glenn climbed using the wall to assist. Along the way he reflected that there were more than a few muscular people like Derek. More on average than in the real world…unless he only hung out at weightlifting gyms. There were also chesty women in Three Hills City but none that measured up to Stephi. Of course, Three Hills City was the only city he'd been in. There was the town, Shorn Spearhead, and a few small villages, or hamlets, or whatever the game world called them. So his observation pool was rather limited.

Then he remembered what happened to Stephi. He sighed.

"We're almost to the top," Keri said, misinterpreting his exasperated breath.

Glenn didn't explain. He just clomped up after her.

When they got to the top there was a door with a lock. Keri had a key.

The hallway was narrow, with narrow floorboards. The floor wasn't completely level. If Glenn dropped a marble it'd roll to a low spot here or there. The hallway led to series of small rooms. Some had doors open with sun-filled windows showing. *Actual* glass windows, although their thickness was inconsistent and their texture was rippled. A few held easels with half-finished paintings. One had a pottery wheel and shelves with finished bowls and urns, already glazed and fired in an oven.

After taking another turn, Keri stopped in front of a doorway and unlocked it using a second key on her ring. Glenn had seen her with the key ring at the Glade House. It held six keys total. Now he knew that, besides the back and front door keys, what two of the others were for. One might be for another room above the café? Otherwise, why would Keri have announced which room she was going to when they entered the establishment?

Keri's small square room was hot and stuffy, and lit with a magical light. It held a narrow desk. A shelf mounted above it was filled with jars holding quills, some smaller ones contained ink. It also held sheaves of paper and a few small wooden carvings. The most interesting was of two small dogs. One was painted brown and white, and the other black and white. They had a striking likeness to Rocky and Chili. Glenn's brain must've been running in low gear, because the likeness was probably the point. They'd certainly been commissioned, maybe from one of the artists that shared the top floor with Keri.

The rest of the walls held shelves filled with some scrolls, but mostly with leather-bound books of various sizes and thicknesses. All but a few appeared old, and none bore titles or identifying information on their spines.

It was obvious the Dewey Decimal system hadn't been introduced to the *Monsters, Maces and Magic* world. Or written into it by the authors of the rule books, or the game moderator that specifically designed the world Glenn was trapped in.

Keri pulled open the two window panes, mounted on hinges along the window frame. Then she lifted the latches that held the two shutters closed and pushed them open so the room could air out. There wouldn't be much of a cross breeze. Fortunately the window faced east, and had already seen the main part of the day's sun.

"You may have my chair," Keri offered, pulling the wooden antique, or at least old but sturdy chair, out from the desk.

Glenn looked at it and said, "I'll be more

comfortable on the floor." When she gave him an uncertain look, he explained, "My feet will dangle."

She gave Glenn a half-grin. "Well, I'd offer you the trunk next to my desk for a foot rest, but it's bolted to the floor."

"Thieves?" Glenn asked, realizing if he used it as a foot rest, he'd have to face the wall and its packed shelves.

"Three Hills City has them, like every blooming city, town or hamlet, and no place or thing can ever be deemed completely safe. I prefer to make it difficult for them." She gestured with her hand to a spot on the uneven floor where Glenn could sit. "Or not worth their effort."

Glenn sat. "This is where you disappear to?"

Keri sat too, and crossed one leg over the other. She then untied one of her boots and began loosening the laces. "Sometimes I go to the garden you saw. I retire here to read, and to study. Sometimes I go other places." She followed her last statement with a squint of her left eye and a nod that caused her curly hair to bounce.

Glenn nodded understanding. She didn't intend to clarify. He squinted up at the shelves' contents. "How long have you been in Three Hills City?"

"Oh, decades." Her answer carried a nonchalant tone.

The answer, again vague, but revealing. Keri Lovelace appeared to be at most in her late thirties, and Glenn didn't think she was a 'hometown' girl, born and raised in Three Hills City.

Keri removed one boot and linen sock and began working on the second boot. "When Chelly or Swela deliver our lunch, we can eat and I will shut the door. Then we'll do our talking." She removed the second boot and sock and set them aside.

She stretched her legs, wiggled her toes with their

red-painted nails, and sighed. "I prefer bare feet to boots." She scrunched up her nose. "But the filthy streets of Three Hills are a far stretch from lush meadows."

Glenn always saw her wearing boots in her boarding house, but didn't say anything.

Keri stood and pulled a book from a lower shelf, one that didn't look often used. She handed it to him.

The book was the size of an abridged, hardcover dictionary. Its leather cover was worn and the pages were thicker and less uniform than those of books he was used to reading. Nothing like university texts. What he held certainly wasn't available as an eBook. Nothing in Keri's room would be. Unless some magic user or enchanter devised a way for words to roll down a scroll. Sort of like the text did at the beginning of *Star Wars* movies.

"Before you begin reading—am I right in assuming as a healer, you've been taught to read the common language? That translated book holds a few maps and drawings, but mostly words."

Glenn nodded affirmation. He could read, at around the seventh-grade level in the game world. That gave him access to most things. Kirby wasn't quite as strong in reading, while Stephi and Ron were far advanced in their ability compared to Glenn. Kalgore, especially as he was a warrior and hadn't taken a skill slot in reading, was illiterate. A fact which vexed the warrior.

Keri peeked her head out into the hallway before turning to stand over Glenn. "You must swear not to divulge that I have a copy of what you hold, or I must return it to the shelf."

Glenn, sitting cross-legged, straightened his back. For half a breath he was unsure he wanted to hold the text, let alone open it. The dire concern passed. Why would Keri wait until this moment to cause him harm? "I swear I won't tell anyone you have it, nor will I share where I learned anything I, ummm, might learn by reading what's in it?"

"That will do," she replied.

"What you hold is a brief history of the dwarves of the Blue Mountains, Jagged Valleys, and Sunken Hills. Well, the last three hundred years' worth, as of its completion fifty-three years ago. It is a translation of the original completed for me twenty-seven years ago." She returned to her wooden chair and leaned back. "As you are a gnome, and a distant cousins of the dwarves, yet raised by humans, it would be good for you to have some knowing of them."

She squinted one eye at Glenn. "And the knowledge may benefit you, as it sounds as if you may be, shall we say, looking for one dwarf in particular."

Glenn nodded understanding.

After Keri returned to her desk, took a sheet of paper from a drawer, and began writing with quill and ink, Glenn rested the book on his lap and opened it.

He turned the pages carefully, yet as quickly as he could, skimming. He found no table of contents, nor any index. It read as if the author had transcribed, word for word, an oral history recited to him—or her. There appeared to be no author listed or identified.

The gnome healer wished Ron was there, with his orienteering and map reading skills, and his booklet that he carried around to jot maps and directions, and pertinent bits of information. But Keri probably wouldn't have approved. Taking such notes without permission likely had consequences far worse than a little copyright infringement.

Keri finished writing and pulled a book from a shelf. With a look of concentration she began leafing through it. Glenn continued with his book, doing the same.

He read and skimmed content for twenty minutes, during which he determined that there were four basic clans, broken down by hair color. Red, blond, brown, and black. There were varying skin colors, from pale white to near coal black, but that seemed irrelevant when compared to the color of a dwarf's hair. They got along well enough, the clans, although they were competitive and frequently envious. They rarely married and had children outside the clan. It seemed, from what he could tell, the hair color of offspring was always determined by the mother. So a black-bearded father would expect his sons and daughters, and those of his daughters' offspring to take the hair color of his wife. Thus, if she was a brown beard, all his children were destined to be brown, and they would be cut off from his clan. And any inheritance to his sons would be counted among the rival, other hair-colored clan.

Such restrictions seemed disturbing. What a screwed up game world. So regimented and constricting. But, deep down, his gnomish instincts felt such regimentation was right and proper. Maybe he needed to find a book on gnomes, or at least ask Kirby or Ron for more of the basics, based on their memory of the Player's Guide, and even the Game Master's Guide.

Glenn was going to ask Keri if she had a similar book about gnomes but he heard one of the waitresses whistling down the hallway. He quickly closed the book and placed it back in its spot on the lower shelf.

Chelly asked, gripping a large wooden tray. "Are you ready to eat?" The middle-aged waitress had a pear-shaped body accompanied by a thin nose and friendly smile. She looked far less frazzled than when he'd seen her hurrying to serve the crowd of customers.

Keri had already cleared her desk. "We are, Chelly, dear."

Glenn stood and backed out of the way as the waitress handed the tray to Keri. On it were two plates, each holding a fish-kabob, a pile of yellow corn, several radishes and two fresh biscuits. There was also a tin pitcher with two tin mugs, and two spoons and two brown cloth napkins. Glenn smelled the spiced apple cider.

"Thank you, dear," Keri said. "Put it on my tab as well as the customary tip. Oh, and if you would, please pull the door closed behind you."

Chelly grinned so wide as to nearly split her thin face. "That is very kind." Her arm showed several pitted scars as she reached for the door. "I'll see not a soul disturbs you."

As soon as the door was closed, Keri handed Glenn his plate and filled his cup with cider from the pitcher.

Glenn thanked the Glade House owner and waited until she was seated and her cup was also filled before he dug in. While he devoured the meal, he pointed up to the carvings of two dogs. "Are those Rocky and Chili?"

Keri gazed up at them. "Indeed they are."

Glenn cleared his throat. "They're fine dogs. Good with customers, even though you said they're for security."

"They make the Glade House a friendlier place. A bit of home away from home."

The gnome thought a moment while chewing a mouthful of corn. "There aren't a lot of dogs in Three Hills City," he observed. "But those that are, and guard places are…well, bigger and meaner. Like you'd expect guard dogs to be." He put his spoon down on his plate. He recalled his first meeting with Keri, in the alley behind her place. She was confronting her cross-alley neighbors. A half-goblin and his half-ogre wife. He didn't think the dogs would've been much help if it would've come to a scrap.

Keri waited patiently as the gnome finished his thought.

"I mean, they're keen to warn you," Glenn said. "But more likely to get hurt than help in a fight."

The Glade House owner paused, her eyes intense, as if she were deciding upon something. "Being relatively new to Three Hills, you may not know that there's a sizeable pack of wererats that lurk in the more ill-reputed sections."

Glenn thought, wererats? Like werewolves, but rats? He didn't ask Keri. He could get clarification from Kirby, or Ron later.

"They were gifts," she said. "Rocky and Chili have what is called Silver Strike. It's a rare ability in canines, and even rarer among humans. Their attacks upon creatures safe from mundane weapons, wood, steel or iron, but vulnerable to silver—as all lycanthropes are—get through. For my Rocky and Chili, it's as if their teeth are coated in silver."

She smiled at Glenn's wide eyes. "Oh, you've got the right of it. My Rocky and Chili are a threat to any wererat in human, or their rat-human form." Her shoulder-length curled hair bounced as she tipped her head side to side in equivocation. "Not exactly dire." She squinted her left eye and focused on Glenn with her right. "However, as big rats sneaking about my establishment? Things tend towards murderous for the filthy creatures."

Glenn nodded understanding. The two spunky and determined canines would tear into rats, no problem.

They went back to eating. After a moment Keri cleared her throat and began sharing information about wood nymphs, and in particular the one named Polayney.

"In addition to the dwarves, another lesson related to history, which will lead to the answer of your earlier question," Keri said, after taking a sip of cider.

"Three Hills City is built on what was once a localized forest of mostly yew trees. Initially an adventuring party cleared the forest of monsters. It was led by a warrior, Zillbann the Black, who'd emerged from the gladiator pits in Shatt. Once the trolls and goblins and even a basilisk had been driven out, back into the Dark Heart Swamp from which they'd spread, or slain, Zilbann established a small wooden fortress for himself and his followers."

Keri took time to eat a biscuit. "You might have guessed, Jax, it was located where the duke's keep is today."

She stared out her study's open window for a moment before continuing. "On the three hills that hold towers today, Zillbann and his people established wooden watch towers. The towers and defenses weren't effective, being they were surrounded by an established forest. So Zillbann's people began clearing trees.

"It was then that a druid, a gnome..." At that, Keri smiled, and took a bite of her fish before continuing. Glenn had finished his grilled fish and was returning to his corn.

"A druid named Glysine of the Shrubbery, who worshiped Pan, led a party of his own adventures. In addition, he is said to have summoned a small host of woodland creatures, mainly satyrs and sprites, with a few centaurs and a friendly hill giant to his side.

"Their objective was to convince Zillbann the Black to cease his clearing the forest. But Zillbann didn't even bother to hear what 'his enemies' had to say. Fierce battle ensued. Buckets of blood from both sides were spilled. Zillbann was felled by the hill giant, but Zillbann's magic user in turn slew the giant with a Fireblast Spell. The result set the yew forest aflame.

"Glysine of the Shrubbery suffered a spear to the back while he was attempting to summon rain to quell the spreading flames. With his death, and with all of his fellow party members slain, the surviving woodland host fled.

"Rains did come, but not before much of the forest had burned, including Zillbann the Black's wooden keep and towers.

"The actual summoner of the yew forest's champions was Polayney, the forest's wood nymph. She had been able to ward a small portion of the trees from the flames, and the magic user, who now led the survivors of Zilbann's side, saw the sense to negotiate."

Keri took a moment to finish her fish and drink some more cider while Glenn sat in thought, trying to imagine the battle. He'd never seen a satyr or centaur. There was supposed to be a hill giant on the far side and north of the Dark Heart Swamp. Maybe it was a distant relative of Glysine's ally.

"Depending whose side you might've been on, it was fortunate, or unfortunate, that the magic user was a lady named Malina the Yellow, for she was devoted to the god Apollo. She was an accomplished spell caster such that she had earned the title of wizard.

"Polayney, the wood nymph, threatened that if her remaining trees were felled, she would blight the land with an enduring curse such that none living upon it would prosper. So a truce was agreed to. Malina promised to leave the surviving yew trees unharmed, and to ward them from harm, as would all those that follow and lived upon the land. Polayney wanted to regrow her forest, but Malina refused. In memory of Zillbann the Black, she would rather see the land blighted than return to forestland."

Glenn sort of wondered why a wood nymph would be okay with goblins in her forest. And why a follower of Apollo would adventure with someone like Zillbann the Black?

He was about to ask but Keri then said, with a measure of scorn, "After all, Malina's side had won the battle."

Keri finished her meal and appeared to be organizing her thoughts, so Glenn worked on finishing his meal and tried to absorb what she'd shared.

Finally, after draining her cup of cider, she refilled both hers and Glenn's from the pitcher, stretched out her legs, gripped her cup and rested it on her right thigh, and continued her tale.

"So it was agreed that south of what is now the south wall of Three Hills City may not be inhabited by people of the city, and kept clear of corpses and structures. A small river port and road was allowed. Trees scattered by nature may grow south of the city. Those may not be destroyed or removed by any of the inhabitants of Three Hills, nor by anyone hired or encouraged to do so. They may be culled by cutting if they reach fifty years of growth. But for each that is cut, Polayney is permitted to expand the size of her yew grove by that same number."

Glenn thought of the willow tree near where he and the rest of the party had buried Kim. Its size meant it was far older than fifty years. Other than the grove, it was the only tree south of the city.

"You see, a wood nymph is immortal, as long as she has her tree and sufficient trees to form a small grove. And her tree is immortal, as long as it has its nymph. She intended to outlast the humans, and slowly regrow the forest."

Keri took several large gulps of her cider. "Malina, however, wasn't fooled. She, using magics and animal husbandry, bred a herd of goats that prefers feeding on young tree shoots and saplings, and are not influenced by a wood nymph's call."

She drained her cup and frowned. "And to this day, the duke maintains that herd of goats, and looses them upon the meadow between the city and the river for one week in the spring, one week in the summer, and one week in the fall to feed.

"As you might imagine, Jax, this has severely hampered Polayney's plan."

Keri pulled back her feet and leaned toward Glenn. "And killing one of the favored goats will earn weeks of torture before your soul is rent and devoured by the demon Wizard Malina summoned and, is to this day, held far beneath the duke's keep."

Glenn knew, in theory, what a demon was. But in this world, they could be worse by many orders of magnitude. He recalled the effect the lich had upon his party, the paralyzing terror inflicted when it, or she, or what once had been a she, simply travelled past their small encampment in the Dark Heart Swamp. A demon was probably ten times worse. That caused him to involuntarily shiver.

Keri frowned, and then a look of concern crossed her face. "Jax, have you encountered a demon?"

"No," he said, his voice quiet and shaky. "But something nearly as bad." He didn't want to explain. "It passed by us in the Dark Heart Swamp."

"Passed you by?"

Glenn nodded slowly, trying to push back the memory. It was still a source of nightmares. He took a deep steadying breath. Not only to settle his voice, but to keep his lunch down. He held up a hand, signaling for the Glade House owner to wait a few seconds.

"Gurk and Lysine said we weren't worth the effort." He stared into her eyes, trying to see if she believed him or not. "Like not bothering to go out of your way to step on an ant."

"It wasn't the dragon," she said.

It wasn't really a question, but he answered it anyway. "No, I've never seen a dragon but, from what I've heard, a dragon would go out of its way to eat gnomes and elves and everyone else in my party."

A moment of silence between them hung in the air.

Keri quirked an eyebrow. “You don’t want to tell me what it was, then?”

Glenn shook his head. “Not today.”

Seemingly satisfied with the answer, Keri said, “Then let me tell you a word or two about a happier subject.” She reached for a sock sitting next to her boots and began sliding it on her right foot.

“Wood nymphs are immortal creatures. That you now know. They are tied to one particular tree upon birth—and don’t ask me what births them.” She grinned. “Not only the size, but the majesty of their grove influences their magical strength. It was unfortunate, or fortunate, that Malina the Wizard was female, depending on your perspective. For wood nymphs, as are river nymphs, beautiful beyond measure.” She half rolled her eyes. “Well, mortal measure. They even surpass in beauty, your friend Marigold.

“Their beauty is such that mortal men can do little to nothing against the nymph’s will, once they have laid eyes upon her. Seeing her unclothed can shock a man’s body, leaving him unwakeable for weeks, or even slay him outright.”

She reached for her other sock. “Gnomes and elves are not afflicted to such an extent, and women are more likely to be jealous than anything else. Most become ill-tempered in the presence of a wood nymph for any length of time.” Keri tipped her head from side to side in equivocation. “Unless they are the sort that desires the company of women more than they do men.”

Glenn rubbed his chin in thought. “What’s their magic like?”

“They have some of the powers of druids, and can speak freely to every natural animal or beast that wanders into their grove.”

That didn’t exactly answer his question but she didn’t seem interested in sharing more. He was pretty sure she knew more. Of course, he hadn't shared about the lich.

Keri reached for a boot and asked, "Would you be a dear and close the window and shutters?"

Glenn looked up, figuring he could reach well enough, but he had a pressing question. "You've been around Three Hills City for a long time. Longer than me and my party."

She looked at him while sliding her right boot on.

After walking over to the windows, he mustered up the courage to ask. Kirby was better at this kind of thing, but she was a friend, or at least as close to a friend as his party had in Three Hills City. "Do you have any ideas on how we might go about finding the dwarf, Benxcob, and get the gold coin back from him?"

Glenn went pale, suddenly thinking he—they—should've been watching the gates. What if the dwarf already left? If he hadn't seen, he must've heard about the rainbow so close to the city. Glenn sure would if he knew the leprechaun had tracked him down to the city.

The gnome healer was almost afraid to say it, but did. "Before he finds out about the rainbow and leaves the city?"

Keri began to laugh, then placed a hand over her mouth, stifling it. "If the dwarf knows about the rainbow," she said, "he won't go anywhere. Not right away, knowing Bata Fidil might be lurking about outside Three Hills."

"Why not?" Glenn asked, truly curious.

"He must be a crafty dwarf," Keri said. "Greedy and crafty, and know something about leprechauns to have stolen, or tricked, Bata Fidil out of one of his precious coins." She slid on her left boot. "He'll know that a leprechaun loses much of his power if he enters a mortal city. What leprechaun would want to confront such a dwarf when so weakened?

"But a crafty dwarf might suspect the sly leprechaun to have recruited someone to enter the city and do the dirty work for him."

"That would be us," Glenn said glumly.

"So, back to your question. Let me think on that a moment." She paused while tying her left boot. While she did, Glenn pulled the window's shutters closed, latched them, and then pushed the two windowpanes closed behind the shutters.

"I heard about your involvement at Higslaff's pawnshop. Your party's presence, and willingness to fight, caught the opposing party of adventurers off guard. And I heard something about Gurk and Josiah the Barber. Gurk tipped off the barber or helped deal with a robbery attempt, or so I heard."

She began tying her other boot, looking down at what her fingers were doing. "You'd know better, I imagine, and I don't need to know your business."

She finished with the boot and stomped it down on the floor. "Rumor has it, they're tied into the local thieves' guild. Gurk might be able to tell you for sure. But, if what I've heard is true, they might owe your party something like a favor."

Glenn nodded to himself. The thieves' guild would know the city, and how to find the dwarf. Plus, there weren't many dwarves in the city. It's just that it was a big city, one that he and his friends didn't know as well as Keri. Certainly not as well as thieves that lived and worked in it.

Then she stood and pointed her index finger down at Glenn. "The guild master is not somebody to get on the wrong side of." She bit her lip. "You just don't. So be sure your friends know that. Especially your mischievous friend, Gurk."

"Thanks," Glenn said. "For what you did for Stephi, and for what you shared." He wondered if the party, or more specifically Stephi and Glenn, owed her a favor.

Glenn put that aside and quickly organized his thoughts. Keri didn't know everything about what had happened at the barber shop and at the pawnshop. Or, if she did, she didn't let on that she did. Secrets, or espionage, or having sources wasn't his thing. In any case, what she'd said was close.

He fixed an earnest gaze on the Glade House owner. "If there's ever anything I can do."

"Oh, don't you worry yourself about that, Jax. If I ever need something from you, I'll be sure to ask."

That answered one of Glenn's questions.

"But right now what *I* need to do is find a decent chamber pot downstairs." She smiled a friendly smile. "I'll lay good coins on the table saying you do, too."

Glenn couldn't argue that, and his face said it.

"Thought as much." She laughed her infectious laugh. "The Stickley Café's apple cider is known for that."

# CHAPTER 9

**Glenn spotted the** one man he wasn't interested in seeing as he and Keri neared the Glade House. It was too late for him to cut down the nearest cross street, or duck behind the group of women carrying sacks filled with their haul of vegetables and dried meats from the market.

Derek stepped off the cobbler's porch and strode toward Glenn. He was a powerfully built warrior, and wearing his breastplate, with his newly acquired longsword strapped in its scabbard along his back. A middle linebacker in armor with a sword.

The big warrior was blond-haired and not particularly attractive. When he smiled, usually at someone's misfortune or after one of his bitingly sarcastic remarks, he showed off that fact that one of his eyeteeth was missing. When Derek rolled up his character named Kalgore the Courageous, he attributed it to a brawl with another warrior, whom he soundly pounded.

Glenn thought—no, knew—Derek was a jerk. But that was mostly in town. Out on an adventure he was an asset to the party. He knew the game's ins and outs. Not as well as Kirby or Ron, but far better than he and Stephi. Derek also never shied from a fight, and willingly took the brunt attacks of some pretty nasty monsters, saving other party members in the process. So Glenn put up with him, especially since they all needed to work together if they were ever going to get back home.

The warrior mopped some damp strands of hair from his forehead. "Where'd you go, gnome?" He looked down, scrutinizing Glenn. "Where's Marigold?"

The fact that he'd stopped in the middle of the

cobblestone street and forced people to walk around him didn't seem to matter. Glenn, however, kept moving. Keri was already out of Glenn's sight. Which wasn't saying much since he couldn't see over anyone's head, let alone shoulders.

"Gurk told me what happened," Derek continued, following alongside Glenn. "Is she in that basket?"

Keri gave Glenn the basket, saying Marigold might need it to get around the city without being seen.

"No, she's not in the basket."

"Then where is she, gnome?" A nasty growl mingled with his words, especially "gnome."

"I can't say exactly, and especially not out here. Where's Gurk and Lysine?"

Derek replied sarcastically, "I can't say exactly." He glanced up at the nearby roofs. "What about her bird? Can you tell me where *he* is?"

Glenn stepped off the street and stopped next to the bench in front of the Glade House. Near it grew some flowers. It reminded Glenn of where he'd left Stephi. A small lump formed in his throat.

"Except for healing, you're next to useless," Derek said, making a fist with his right hand and punching it into his left hand's open palm. "Lysine's in the parlor room, waiting to see if me or Gurk spots you." He peered over heads, down the street. "I'm going to go get Gurk, since you're not saying nothing means we don't have to keep watching for Marigold. Right?"

"Right."

Derek pointed a finger down at Glenn. "Don't you say nothing to Lysine 'till I get back."

"Right," Glenn said again, turning his back on the big warrior before making his way up the porch's wooden steps.

**Glenn sat with** Ron up in their cramped room.

Ron was a quarter-elf warrior druid. His human part gave him his African American features. He was shorter than Derek and lean, but still strong. He wore ringmail, which was leather armor with bronze rings sewn into it. On adventures Ron normally wielded a spear. He also knew how to use a short sword and always carried a scabbarded one on his hip.

Everyone in the party was second rank, or second level, except for Ron, since he had to divide his experience points between two character classes. When rolling up their characters, Ron added druid mainly so that the party had someone who could cast healing spells, besides Glenn. Quite a few times it'd come in handy.

They waited fewer than ten minutes for Derek to stomp in, followed by Gurk. Glenn hadn't said anything about Stephi's whereabouts to Ron. Not because Derek told him not to, but because he wanted to wait and tell Kirby. That, and he was trying to decide how much he should tell, figuring that the duke might not appreciate word getting out that a fairy lived in his garden compound.

They were his friends, and party members, but Keri had confided in him, not only at the garden compound, but in her study above the Stickley Café.

After Kirby closed and bolted the door all four took a seat. Kirby sat next to Glenn on Stephi's cot. Derek and Ron sat on Ron's cot across from them.

"So, dude," Kirby said, "where's Marigold?" He pointed at an item on the floor. "And what's with the picnic basket?"

"She's okay, and it's a creel basket," Glenn said. "You put fish you catch in it."

"Who cares about the stupid basket?" Derek said. "Gurk said she got turned into a fairy."

Glenn expected Derek to make a snide remark about

him and Kirby's pathetic fishing, and not needing a basket. But the fact that he passed up the opportunity and went right to Stephi said the big warrior was worried. Glenn quickly reassessed. Maybe Derek was just curious.

"A leprechaun named Bataí Fidil used a Transmorph Spell on Marigold," Glenn said. "But his proper name is Bataí Fidil na Maidine."

"Dude, you know his name?" Kirby asked. "He only told us to say 'Bata Fidil' to summon him, which makes sense as his name."

"For clarification," Ron said, "Bataí Fidil na Maidine is the leprechaun's *proper* name and not his *true* name?"

Glenn nodded, recalling Emma's exact words.

"True names aren't part of the game's official rules," Kirby said.

Derek interrupted. "How do you know his name and Gurk don't?" He didn't wait for an answer. Instead he glared at Kirby and asked, "Were you even there? Did you really even see Marigold? What she looks like?"

The big warrior turned his gaze back on Glenn. "The thief said some fairytale reject leprechaun turned Marigold into a fairy when she scooped up some of his gold, but just clammed up when Lysine asked why her shirt was shredded." Then his ire returned to Kirby. "Why didn't you stop her?"

Normally Kirby didn't hesitate to verbally spar with Derek. But the last question had to be one the half-goblin continued beating himself up over. As for Stephi's blouse, telling Derek he'd seen her naked would lay a minefield of future embarrassment.

"Kalgore," Ron said, "your line of questioning—"

Ron was an African-American mathematics graduate student in the real world. A genius. Like everyone else, his general appearance blended with that of the character he'd rolled up. Ron's warrior druid was one-quarter elf, so he had slightly pointed ears, unlike Stephi's which were like Star Trek's Mr. Spock. While Derek's hair was a little long and on the wilder side, Ron kept his cut close to the scalp.

The big warrior spoke over Ron and gestured toward Glenn. "The gnome's never played the game before." He pressed his index and middle fingers against his temples, eyes closed with a sneer across his face. "Who the hell doesn't know leprechauns are meaner than shit when it comes to their gold?"

"Enough," Ron said. He didn't yell, but something resonated in his voice. He was the party's leader, and one of the party's members was in trouble. "Discord among us will not improve the situation."

Glenn remained surprised that Derek was so interested in what happened. He was being his boorish self, but in a party-protective sort of way. That was positive, sort of. Or, he was pissed that he missed out on the action. That if he would've been there, he'd've skewered the leprechaun with his sword. Glenn was pretty sure Derek would've gotten turned into a fairy, too. Or worse.

"First," Ron said, "Kalgore and I have only received a brief report. It would benefit all involved, including Marigold, if Kalgore and I possessed detailed knowledge of this morning's encounter."

The party leader rubbed a finger across his chin in contemplation. "It may be that Jax and Gurk have different perspectives on what occurred, much as two witnesses to the same crime frequently do."

"Okay," Kirby said. "I'll tell what I know, and Jax can fill in if I miss something, or tell what he saw different."

Glenn was impressed with Kirby's memory and attention to detail, including the copper coin, which he gave to Ron. Glenn didn't have much to add. He actually learned a few things, like a four-leaf clover was stuck in the bowler's ribbon next to the green feather, and that the leprechaun wore a narrow, gold ring on his right hand's little finger.

"Excellent summation," Ron said.

"So what's Marigold look like?" Derek asked. "Like the picture in the Monster Guide?"

"Sort of like a Barbie," Glenn said. "A little bigger, though." He'd almost said she was a little bigger than other fairies, but caught himself.

"Like a Mariposa Barbie," Kirby said. "Jax is right. She's like four or five inches taller than a Barbie." He bent over and held his hand about sixteen inches off the floor. "Her wings look like a rainbow, like when the sun shines on my grandma's fancy crystal cups in her China cabinet."

Ron asked, "Might I inquire what a Mariposa Barbie is?"

"Sure, dude. It's like a regular Barbie doll but with butterfly wings. But Marigold's are fancier, right Jax?"

"You sure know a lot about Barbie dolls," Derek teased. "You spend a lot of time playing with those Mariposa dolls?"

"My cousin had a DVD and watched it when I had to babysit her," Kirby said, glaring at Derek. "She got it from the stash your mom found hidden under your mattress."

Derek laughed. "Good one, thief. Do they have Bimbo Barbies? Because I bet that's what Marigold looks like."

Glenn told Derek, "Shut up!" the same time Ron said, "Cease."

Kirby stood and pointed a finger in Derek's face. "Call her that again, and you'll be missing more than one tooth."

Derek laughed.

Glenn stood next to Kirby. "Me and you can take

him."

Ron stood, and glared down at Derek. "That was inappropriate humor, and will not be repeated in front of Marigold. If you do, the consequences will be harsh."

Derek held out his hands. "It was just a joke."

"Remember, Kalgore, I'm a thief," Kirby said, sitting down.

"I know," Derek said, nonchalantly. "I'll never see you coming."

"Are we finished?" Ron asked. "It is imperative we proceed with the matter at hand undistracted."

"I'm ready," Glenn said and glanced at Kirby next to him. Everyone sat back down.

The half-goblin thief admitted, "We all got short tempers going with what happened."

"I still ain't clear on where Marigold is," Derek said, "and how Jax knows the leprechaun's name, and the spell he used on her."

"Leprechauns." Ron crossed his arms, then moved his right hand up to his chin. "We should corroborate what we can recall from the Monster Guide and what we remember from encounters while playing *Monsters, Maces and Magic*. Then assess how it corresponds with the firsthand experience of Jax and Gurk."

He held up a hand to forestall Derek's interruption. "Jax indicated Marigold is safe. We shall allow him to share where Marigold is and explain what he has learned momentarily."

Ron lowered his hand and rested it on his thigh. "After that, we shall formulate a plan of action."

"They're immortal creatures, like most fae," Derek said. "Until you run a magical sword through them."

"Yeah," Kirby said. "You need silver or magic to kill them. They ain't affected by iron or steel, like some fae, like fairies."

Derek added, "Green wood, like a club or staff, can

do minimal damage, like one point max."

"They are immune to spells unless the caster is of considerable rank," Ron said. "They are one hundred and ten percent resistant, minus five percent per rank of the spell caster."

"Marigold's slumber spell only made the leprechaun blink," Glenn said.

"She's only second rank," Kirby said. "Besides, leprechauns are immune to Slumber Spells. Charm Spells and poison, too."

"Acid works on them," Derek said.

"Dude." Kirby threw up his hands. "You got a bucket of it handy?"

"There's alchemists in town." While Derek pointed to the hilt angled over his shoulder, and then gestured toward Glenn, he added. "Besides, my sword and the gnome's club, we can't hurt him."

"He was hard to hit," Glenn admitted.

"Due to their high Agility and magical nature, their Armor Class Rating is zero," Ron said.

Kirby chimed in, saying, "And leprechauns are only a three plus three hit-die creature."

"Hit-die?" Glenn asked.

"Means how tough they are. Hit dice is how many eight side dice they get for hit points. Technically you're second rank, and so you're a two hit-dice or hit-die creature. The leprechaun has three d8 plus three hit points."

"But I get a twelve-sided one for hit points," Glenn said.

"The vast majority of creatures are assigned an eight-sided dice," Ron explained. "Player characters are assigned based upon their character class or an average of multiple classes."

Derek scratched his head. "They can Transport Spell using a summoned rainbow, but I don't remember how often."

"It's like every ten rounds," Kirby said, then said to Glenn, "A round counts a combat exchange, but when not in combat, a round equals a minute."

"I believe that is accurate, Gurk," Ron said. "And I believe they have the skills and attack tables of a ninth-rank thief."

"He's a lot tougher than he looks," Glenn said.

"We ain't even talked about his spells." Kirby's brow furrowed. "Transmorph is a really powerful spell, and so's Greater Sylvan Mystic Cage, which he threw." Kirby snapped his fingers. "One I played against used Retard Movement on one of my characters, too." He glanced at Glenn. "Means you're slowed to half speed."

There was a moment of silence, until Ron added, "In addition to randomly assigned high-rank magic user spells, I recall leprechauns are also permitted to cast first and second-rank druid spells, as if they are a fourth-rank druid."

After a moment with nobody speaking, Ron asked. "Any additional input?"

"Yeah," Derek said, "if you got a piece of their gold, it adds twenty-five percent to your Luck Rolls."

"No wonder he beat us," Glenn said, propping his elbows on his thighs and resting his chin in his hands.

"That's why I tried to stop Marigold, dude."

"Yeah, gnome," Derek said. "How do you know that leprechaun's name when Gurk don't? And what about where our Mariposa Barbie party member is?"

Glenn gulped. He'd been listening and so busy learning about leprechauns that he hadn't settled on how he could answer honestly without saying, or giving away, too much.

# CHAPTER 10

**Glenn scratched his** head and told the three party members, "Keri Lovelace took Marigold to somebody who could tell her about being a fairy, since she didn't know anything. Someone who knows more than the three of you combined."

"How do you know that?" Derek interrupted. "We played *Monsters, Maces and Magic* hundreds of times before that sonofabitch GM stuck us here." He cocked his head and raised an eyebrow. "Not counting that shitty night, remind me how many times you played?" His words couldn't have dripped with more sarcasm.

Glenn crossed his arms. "I just know, Kalgore. Trust me on that."

"I have confidence in your assessment," Ron said. He rubbed the tips of his fingers together, left hand's against the right's. "What about knowledge of the leprechaun's name?"

Glenn bit his bottom lip. "You know, I heard Keri Lovelace has fae blood in her?"

All three nodded. They'd heard it, too.

"Well, the same person that's giving Marigold information knew the proper name, after I mentioned the short one he gave us to call him back to the grove."

"When you state *person*," Ron said, "do you equate that with human?"

Glenn uncrossed his arms. He figured Ron suspected something, so he answered with a question. "Are you a person? Is Kirby a person?" He figured that would throw them off, if they considered mixed heritage as the key. It was sort of a lie.

Kirby scrunched his nose in thought. "How did Keri find out what happened to Marigold?"

"She knows a lot of people," Glenn said, trying to be evasive. "She's lived here a long time." He figured it was the wood nymph, Polayney.

"Fae in nature?" Ron asked.

"Why are you interrogating me?" Glenn crossed his arms again. "You want to know, go ask Keri."

"We're asking you, gnome," Derek said, "because you're here and you're a party member."

Ron placed a hand on Derek's shoulder, then said to Glenn, "We are understandably curious, and gathering pertinent information will better enable us to render assistance to Marigold."

"Can't that just wait a while? She'll be back after it gets dark." The gnome healer gestured to the small window that was giving the stuffy room some air. "We just need to leave the window open."

The other three party members watched Glenn in silence, waiting for him to say something more.

Glenn threw his hands up in the air. "I have no clue about fairies and you guys do—"

Derek cut Glenn off. "If you're so worried about knowing, why didn't you ask the *person* who's spilling their guts about it to Marigold?" He held up his hands and made quote marks in the air with his fingers when saying "person."

Glenn ignored him and focused on Ron seated diagonally across from him. "...and how we're going to find the dwarf that stole the leprechaun's gold coin."

Derek sneered but didn't say anything.

Kirby put his arm around Glenn. "Sucks moldy lima beans, dude, when you know something but you can't tell."

Glenn sighed but didn't say anything. Instead he stared down at his boots dangling above the floor.

"Kalgore, Gurk," Ron said, "I shall list game information I recall about fairies. Correct me if I am in error, or supplement the knowledge I express."

Derek grunted and Kirby said, "Got it, dude."

Ron closed his eyes in concentration and began to recite from memory.

"Fairies are immortal, one plus one hit-die creatures.

"They may attack with proportional-sized weapons for one to two points of damage.

"They have sixty percent resistance to magic and are immune to Slumber and Charm Spells.

"They are able to cast a Dazzle Spell, once every turn, or ten rounds. It is an area effect spell, with a range of thirty feet. A successful result will blind victims for one to six rounds. If the victim fails their Saving Throw by more than four, they will additionally be stunned by half the number of rounds they are blinded. During the combat, a creature that has been affected by a Dazzle Spell gains a plus two on subsequent Saving Throws against that spell.

"If the creature makes a Saving Throw versus a fairy's Dazzle Spell, any additional saves versus that fairy's Dazzle Spell during that combat are made at plus four, and plus two versus that fairy at any time, moving forward.

"Fairies may conceal themselves similar to a Camouflage Spell. In nature settings a fairy has a ninety-nine percent chance of being unnoticed by each individual. Ninety percent for each individual actively seeking a fairy.

"In an urban setting, the chances are eighty percent and sixty percent respectively.

"In any of the situations, the individual must be within ten yards and have a direct line of sight to the fairy. It requires one round for a fairy to conceal herself, and once concealed she must remain silent and motionless.

"If a fairy is being observed, any observing individual

will be able see the fairy, despite any Camouflage efforts. Any individual that looks away may attempt to locate the fairy with twice the normal chance of success, if the fairy has not moved more than ten feet from the original location.

"Elder Fairies may animate small objects that are equal to half their weight as Lesser Animate Spell, twice per day.

"A fairy may summon one type of animal or insect, and favorably influence such animals' actions, one time per day. Summoned animals must be within a one mile radius to respond to the summons, and will arrive at their best possible speed."

Ron opened his eyes. "Did I misstate or omit any information?"

Gurk raised his hand, as if he were in school. The half-goblin thief immediately recognized what he was doing, and pulled his hand down before ducking his head, embarrassed.

Ron smiled. "Your response reflected that I employed my 'graduate assistant' voice, Gurk."

Since Glenn had a real interest in what Ron had to say, the monotone voice and steady pace didn't bother him, much. If he would've been a student in one of Ron's college math classes he would've needed plenty of coffee.

Gurk said, "You forgot, fairies walk one-third the speed of humans, and fly at the rate of a trotting horse, with bursts of speed for up to one turn, or ten rounds, once per hour."

"Excellent," the warrior druid said to Kirby. "Anything relevant that I omitted, Kalgore?"

"They're vulnerable to iron and steel."

Ron pursed his lips before licking his teeth, annoyed he'd been unable to recall something so vital.

"You are correct, Kalgore," Ron said, recalling the information he'd read multiple times in the Monster

Guide. His mind's keenness had been degraded by his character's Intelligence Score of fourteen. "Incidental contact causes one point of damage. A steel or iron weapon striking a fairy does an additional three points of damage."

"All fairies are female," Kirby said. "Their male counterpart are pixies."

"Yeah," Derek said. "Except for no wings, pixies are hard to tell apart from fairies." He glanced at Kirby out of the corner of his eye. "Like boys that play with Mariposa Barbies are hard to tell from little girls."

"So they all look like you, dude?"

Derek laughed. "Good one again, thief."

An immediate concern struck Glenn. "Will Marigold have her hit points as a second rank magic user or a one hit-dice fairy?"

Kirby started to answer, but he stopped, letting Ron respond.

"Fairies are a one plus one hit-die creature," Ron corrected, then smiled. "Based upon my memory of the Transmorph Spell's description, Marigold will retain her hit points and her spell casting ability. If she were Transmorphed into a fish, for example, she would not be able to utter the words to complete a spell."

Glenn nodded that he understood.

"Transmorphed into a fish," Kirby said. That'd suck."

"Especially if it was a lamprey," Derek said.

Kirby laughed. "Good one, Kalgore."

Ron frowned in disapproval for a second and looked at the two joking party members, then said, "Through the soul gem, she will also retain Byeol's additional hit points and access to Byeol's warrior monk abilities."

Glenn sighed in relief.

Ron waited a moment to see if anyone had anything else to add. "We shall proceed then to the primary task at hand. Securing the gold coin from the dwarf whom Bataí Fidil na Maidine, identified as Benxcob. Are we in possession of any additional knowledge about the dwarf, other than his purported name?"

Glenn and Kirby glanced at each other, then shook their heads.

"There ain't many dwarfs in the city," Kirby said, then stared at the floor. "It's an awfully big city though."

"One of us should be at the main gate at all times," Derek said. "He could be long gone while we're still wandering around this craphole city, trying to find him."

"He probably won't leave right away," Glenn said.

"And you know this because?" Derek asked.

It felt wrong not to give Keri credit for knowing why Benxcob wouldn't leave. Nevertheless, Glenn said, "If he saw or heard about the rainbow outside, he'd know about Bata Fidil being in the area. Benxcob must know about leprechauns to get a leprechaun's gold, so he'd know about them being weaker in an urban setting."

"Huh," Derek said. "I should've thought of that."

Ron squinted one eye at Glenn. "None of us recalled that information about leprechauns from the Monster Guide. They are unable to summon their rainbow and their resistance to magic is halved, as is their spell-casting ability, when within any settlement larger than a hamlet."

"I heard it somewhere," Glenn said weakly. "Forgot until just now."

No one challenged the gnome about the source of his knowledge.

Glenn continued before anyone pressed how he knew. "Kalgore's right. We'll just be sort of stumbling around looking because it is a big city."

"Sooo you got an idea?" Kirby asked.

"A few things," Glenn said. "Gurk, you're out and around the most. You talk to people, like Patti that works at the Red Brick."

"Do dwarves go for tea?" Kirby asked.

"I do not recall that as a preference listed in the Player's Guide," Ron said.

"Yeah," Kirby said. "The Guide says they prefer beer and ale, sort of like in the *Lord of the Rings* movies."

Not wanting to lose his train of thought, Glenn looked at Derek. "You hang out at the stables a lot. But a dwarf probably doesn't care much for horse riding."

Derek asked, "Yeah, so?"

"Just making a couple points," Glenn said. "Hanging out around the stables is cool, but not going to help us find a dwarf. Lysine talks to the guards around the magistrate's court. If the dwarf gets into trouble, that'll help."

Glenn shrugged. "I pretty much hang out here. I go for walks nearby, but don't really talk to anybody except that lady, Pam, at the market. She thinks because I'm a gnome, I like potatoes. She's friendly and we talk." Glenn smiled to himself and shrugged again. "She doesn't mind because more people buy her potatoes and onions when I hang out next to her cart."

"You *do* like potatoes, dude."

"Funny, Gurk. But she's the only…" Glenn scratched his sideburn, trying to remember what his friends called them. "…the only NPC that I really talk to, and a dwarf with a leprechaun's gold coin isn't going to hang around a farmer's market."

"I get what you're saying, gnome," Derek said, "but you're not going anywhere that helps. We need ideas. A plan."

"Sorry, Kalgore, I'm getting to that." Glenn took a deep breath. "Gurk had that fight with those robbers in the barber shop two weeks ago, and then that big fight started outside the pawnshop while Gurk was trading that goblin shaman's sort of cursed dagger for your magical sword." He faced Ron straight across from him. "And you got those magical rings sewn into your armor for magical protection."

Derek leaned back on the cot. "Rambling again, gnome. Nobody needs a recent history lesson."

"My point is, Josiah the barber and Higslaff the pawnshop owner. They're NPCs that have been around a while and know people, who know people, who could help us. They sort of owe us."

"Maybe the dwarf tried to sell his gold coin to the pawnshop," Derek said, then thought better of it. "Naww, he wouldn't steal it just to sell it to some stupid pawnshop."

"That makes sense," Glenn said, "but it's not what I'm getting at."

"Dude," Kirby said, "I was thinking about that too. Josiah would be better. He probably thinks he owes me more than the pawnshop owner thinks he owes us. The pawnshop dude's more about business and cash. I saw the half-ogre guard on the porch. He was dead, so that means like nine or ten thousand gold to the Church of Apollo for a Revive the Dead Spell."

Kirby grinned, showing his half-pointed teeth. "Bet he had the dwarf guard inside his shop Revived, too. Not many dwarves in town. They might hang out together, from the same clan or something. They got sort of similar names, Bonnar and Benxcob."

"While the names are not completely dissimilar," Ron said, "establishing an association based upon their similarity, at this point, rings dubious."

Kalgore opened his mouth to say something, then began cussing under his breath.

"Bonnar's got a blond beard, if he's been Revived." Glenn, paused, recalling the moment the same spell had been cast upon Kim, and it failed. Or she failed a System Shock Roll.

"So?" Gurk asked, his yellowish eyes focusing on his friend. "You okay?"

Glenn nodded, then went on to explain what he'd learned about dwarves after reading from Keri Lovelace's book.

His three friends listened intently.

When Glenn finished, Ron said, "The Player's Guide states that dwarves organize themselves into clans. It is up to the GM to establish what criteria is used to create such clans."

Derek's face scrunched in thought. "How come you know all that and we don't?"

"This isn't an insult or anything, Kalgore," Glenn said. "I read it in a book someone lent me for a little while."

Derek was touchy about the fact that his character was illiterate. In the real world, Derek was a college student. In the *Monsters, Maces and Magic* world he could neither read, nor write, except at the preschool level. It wasn't like he could have Glenn or Ron sit down and teach him to read and write. As a PC, when Derek gained enough experience points to go up a rank, or level, as a warrior, he'd also get a slot for a skill. He could select Reading and Writing as a skill and, *voilà*, he'd be able to read.

Glenn suspected that was why he and Kirby sucked at fishing. Good thing PCs aren't required to use a skill slot for feeding themselves, or they'd all need to wear a bib at every meal.

Derek looked like he wanted to get mad or be insulted, but just let out a long, hissing breath.

"We're still not any further along finding this dwarf dude," Kirby said.

Ron steepled his fingers a moment. "Gentlemen, I propose this plan."

The other three party members gave the warrior

druid their attention.

"Kalgore, I would like for you to speak with Timz Simman, the silversmith. Determine if he can create a scaled down version of Marigold's rapier, using bronze. Until her situation is resolved, she will require such a weapon. Take Marigold's rapier with you."

Derek nodded. "I can do that. Marigold should have enough gold in her trunk to pay for it."

Glenn put a hand on Gurk's shoulder, keeping him from getting riled.

Ron said, "Jax, I believe Marigold would be least offended if it were you that retrieved the required gold from her trunk."

"All I'll need is a down payment," Derek said. "Nothing fancy. He sort of owes us too, so it shouldn't be more than five or six gold, total."

"That seems like a lot," Kirby said.

"She'll want it to fight with, not some fancy ornament," Derek said. "I'll ask him if he's seen any dwarves, or where they might hang out. I'll make up some BS reason why."

"Gurk, pay a visit to Josiah the Barber. You obtusely indicated he has a network of informants."

"I know what ya want," Kirby said. He looked at Derek out of the corner of his eye. "If bribes are called for, I'll cover it."

"She's got that silver ring with turquoise that's party treasure," Derek said. "She won't be wearing it, so use that."

Kirby didn't say anything to Derek. Probably because what the big warrior said was legitimate.

"Jax," Ron said, "go with Gurk. Gnomes tend to relax individuals and place them in a more favorable mood."

"That'll work," Kirby said. "The barber's probably our best bet on getting a lead on the dwarf." He rubbed his pointed nose. “I’ll check with Patti in the morning. She sees a lot of people pass by. She might recall some dwarf she’s never seen before.”

“Sounds reasonable,” Ron said. “I shall speak with the guards at the Church of Apollo and magistrate’s court.”

Glenn forgot about the church. Being a druid, which was sort of a cleric, and a warrior, Ron seemed to get along with those guards pretty well.

“We have but two hours to accomplish our objectives,” Ron said, “before people close their shops or, in my case, begin their night shift duty.”

“What if Marigold comes back while we’re gone?” Kirby asked.

“We’ll leave a note,” Derek said, his voice showing annoyance. “Lysine can write it.”

Probably to change the topic, Ron said, “It may be after nightfall before we return. I shall be travelling without a party member. As such I shall do my utmost to remain wary of my surroundings and those in close proximity.

“Kalgore, do your utmost to remain aware of potentially nefarious individuals as well.”

Derek scoffed. “Sure.”

# CHAPTER 11

**Kirby and Glenn** hustled to make it to Josiah's barber shop before it closed. Kirby thought the barber lived in an apartment above the shop, but didn't know for sure, and wasn't sure if the barber would go to his apartment after work.

The shop was situated in a poorer part of the city. The streets were missing cobblestones and the horse and oxen manure was more often ground into the stones and dirt than scraped up and hauled away.

Several wooden steps led up to Josiah's barber shop. It had a red, white and blue-striped barber pole next to the door. It was chipped and faded, matching the neighborhood. The shop on the right of the barber shop housed a candle maker. A picture of a candle indicated what it was, along with a wooden sign that read "Candle Maker" in faded white letters.

The door to the shop on the left was boarded closed.

Glenn was impressed. The barber's windows had screens. Not actual screens, but wire mesh that would keep out most of the flies.

The two adventurers hurried up the steps and across the narrow porch. Glenn let Kirby go in first.

The shop had one padded leather barber chair in the center. Along the right were four wooden chairs, each with a seat pillow that looked like an elephant had spent a year sitting on them. A closed door on the left and an open doorway on the right framed a mirror mounted above a counter.

The barber was busy sweeping the wooden-plank floor. He was lanky and on the taller side, but not as tall as Derek. He wore browns, including an apron that held years of stains that washing had failed to remove. He had gray hair, was in the early stages of balding, and offered a friendly smile. He also wore a sheathed dagger on his belt.

"Customer, customer," a creaky voice from near the ceiling called. The source was a gray parrot on a perch.

Josiah leaned his broom against the wall. "Gurk, and this, if I recall, is your friend, Jax."

Glenn had seen the man before, briefly, during the fight outside Higslaff's pawnshop. The barber got stabbed by a poison-covered short sword on the pawnshop's porch. Glenn saw him helped back into the shop by two lady spell casters. The gnome healer had been occupied with recovering from Derek's wounds, ones the gnome had drawn upon himself. After that, the soldiers in the City Guard questioned everyone about what'd happened. Glenn reflected that the pawnshop owner apparently held significant sway, because it had been a *questioning*, and not an interrogation.

The barber had introduced Kirby, Ron and Stephi to the pawnshop owner, who dealt in many things including magical, or enchanted, weapons. Glenn had never spoken more than a friendly greeting to the barber.

"Are you closing up?" Kirby asked.

"Preparing to." The barber picked up a damp hand towel and wiped off the seat of his barber chair. "I can make time, if you gentlemen are here for a cut or shave."

"That'd be cool," Kirby said, "but not today. We're here for something else."

The barber's eyes scrutinized Kirby. Then his gaze fell upon Glenn. "Is the 'something else' a thing best not overheard by passerbys?"

Kirby looked back over his shoulder at the unshuttered windows. "Yeah, dude. That'd be a good idea."

"Okay then," the barber said. He lowered the screens into slots built into the window frame before closing the shutters. He then closed and bolted the front door.

The shop would've been dark, if not for a magical light cast in an open box attached to the ceiling. There was also an unlit oil lamp hanging on a hook.

After looking around at the shelves, mirror and gray parrot, Glenn said, "Those are the only window screens I've seen in town."

Josiah appeared surprised by the comment. "They are my own design, and cost good coin to have built." He gestured to the chairs along the wall. "We can pull those around and take a seat, unless it won't take long."

"We don't want ta take up a lot of your time," Kirby said. He and Jax stood in front of the customer chairs.

Josiah leaned against his barber chair while wiping his hands with the damp towel. "I'm all ears."

"We're looking for a dwarf named Benxcob," Kirby explained. "We need to obtain something he has. We know he's new to the city, but we don't know his clan or anything else.

"We figured you might know people who could help us."

Josiah wiped a hand across his chin. "A dwarf, a name, and recently showed up in Three Hills City. That's all you have?"

Glenn said, "This might not help, but he's probably abnormally lucky."

"Does he know you're looking for him, and what you're interested in obtaining?"

"No," Kirby said, "he doesn't know we're—our party—is looking for him, but he *might* be worried about someone trying to locate him."

"Do you know of any aliases he might use?"

Glenn bit his lower lip. Kirby frowned.

"No clue," Kirby said, "but we know he won't be wanting to leave the city. At least not for a while. There can't be a lot of dwarves in town."

"I've seen only a couple since we've been in the city," Glenn said. He was beginning to realize just how difficult locating the dwarf was going to be.

"There is that," Josiah said thoughtfully. "Does this Benxcob have any known associates?"

Kirby held out his hands and shrugged, before sighing. "I know we ain't got much to go on," he said. "That's why we came to you."

Josiah stared intently at Kirby. "Because of my...*connections*?"

"Mind if we sit down?" Kirby asked.

"Not at all," Josiah said, and climbed into his barber chair.

Kirby opted for the far left chair so his cutlass in its scabbard could hang down. Glenn removed his slung shield and leaned it against a chair before climbing into the one next to Kirby.

"What is the likelihood of this Benxcob agreeably...*relinquishing* what you and your party seeks from him?" The barber examined a spot on his chair's armrest. He licked his thumb and focused on rubbing the spot clean. "Will he see the next sunrise if you meet?"

Glenn hadn't thought on killing him, but it might come to that. A bit of acid crept up his esophagus. If Kirby wasn't able to steal the coin, then Benxcob would have to be given enough gold or whatever to give it up. Not likely to happen. If Benxcob wasn't killed, the dwarf would forever hate them, and would be an enemy, probably out for revenge forever afterwards. That would be bad. The *Monsters, Maces and Magic* world was dangerous enough, without a capable, revenge-seeking dwarf.

What made it even worse was that Benxcob had to be pretty sharp and creative, and probably high level to come out on top with even one coin of a leprechaun's gold. He might be smarter than Ron, a better fighter than

Derek, and more cunning than Kirby. The whole party had barely been able to overpower Mekkart, the Crow Lord. Benxcob might be worse.

"We're not looking to...ummm, stop anyone from seeing sunrises," Kirby said. "Uhh, guessing what's gonna come to him, eventually, he might be better off not seeing sunrises."

Josiah's left eyebrow quirked upward.

"Okay," Kirby said, after scratching his nose, followed by doing the same to the back of his head. "If I tell you this, you can't share it with anyone. Not for any reason."

Kirby waited until Josiah nodded agreement, saying, "Understood. I will not reveal what you're about to divulge."

"Okay," Kirby said, nervousness in his voice. He briefly met Glenn's gaze before continuing. "There was a rainbow outside the city, near the river. You might've seen or heard about it?"

"I did not see it. However, several customers did remark upon it."

"Well, it was there because of a leprechaun. Benxcob swiped one of his gold coins, and the nasty little dude took his anger issues out on one of us. And we gotta get the gold coin back to get things fixed."

Josiah rubbed both hands across the armrests of his chair. "Thank you for sharing. I now better understand your predicament."

Glenn blurted out, "Will you help us?"

"You indicted 'we' suffered the nasty little fae's ire? It doesn't appear either of you are injured or impaired."

"Marigold," Kirby said. He didn't elaborate.

A moment of silence hung in the air while Josiah appeared to deliberate the situation and request.

"We got some gold," Kirby said, "but we ain't rich. Not even close." The half-goblin thief leaned forward in his chair. "I figure you kinda owe me."

Glenn knew, in some sense that Kirby's statement "we ain't rich" wasn't exactly true. The party had earned a sizeable payout in gold for rescuing a wealthy and influential silversmith's future daughter-in-law…well, at the time she was…from a band of goblins that'd kidnapped her. The fact that she was the daughter of an elven baronet played into that payout as well.

The party had taken the gold reward to the Three Hills City Holdings and Exchange and had most of it converted to three diamonds. The Exchange, as it was called by pretty much everyone in Three Hills City, wasn't exactly a bank, or anything like that. They converted gold coins or gold and silver ingots into various gems, or vice versa, for a steep twelve percent fee. They would convert other coinage, such as silver or copper to gold for an exorbitant fee of seven percent. Most citizens, except the wealthy, didn't use them. But Glenn and his party had, which sort of classified them as rich.

They'd also rented one of the Exchange's storage boxes for the hefty price of thirty gold for a year for the smallest box for the diamonds. It was like a modern day's safety deposit box at a bank. Glenn hadn't seen it. Only Kirby had—the Exchange's personnel only allowed one individual into the storage box vault. Actually the squat structure, built with immense, interlocking granite stones, held at least six such vaults. Ron said it was for reasons of security. Anyone attempting a heist would have to succeed in penetrating physical and magical defenses of multiple vaults to achieve a major success.

Glenn recalled observing the ground between the security wall and the fortress-like building ripple. Derek said it was probably an earth elemental. It would stop anyone from tunneling. Plus it could attack anyone above ground attempting to enter or leave without an official escort.

They hadn't placed all their reward in the box. They kept some gold. But overall they were saving to purchase a Wish Spell so that they might escape the game world.

Still people knew that the party had earned a reward. That'd make them targets of thieves. Kirby and Derek letting it be subtly known that the party had secured a storage box at the Exchange made them less of a target for thieves. Kirby going into the Exchange with a small bag of gold and coming out without it made them that much less of a target. Word among thieves got around.

And Josiah was part of the local thieves' guild. Maybe not a major player within it but, being connected enough, he almost certainly knew the party had some gold locked away.

Josiah took a half moment to consider Kirby's assertion. The barber leaned forward in his chair. "I will do what I can," he said. "In lieu of the favor, no compensation on my behalf will be expected. However, others are not so indebted. I will take care of that as needed and we can settle up afterward." He relaxed back in his chair. "Whether this Benxcob is located, or not."

# CHAPTER 12

**Glenn's legs were** beyond tired. He, Ron, Kirby and Derek spent the late afternoon and early evening stopping at shops and taverns that might be of interest to a typical NPC dwarf, as determined by Ron, Derek, and Kirby. No success, unless expended effort counted. If he'd been tracking Fitbit progress, he would've surpassed any reasonable goals. Maybe unreasonable, since his legs required about thirty percent more effort to keep up with Derek, who he'd teamed with.

The sun was well below the horizon. From his spot on the bench in front of the Glade House, Glenn watched the pole men, as he called them, using their hooked poles to lower the slats of the scattered streetlamps. The magical glow didn't work as well as the streetlights outside his dorm room, but they didn't cost anything in electricity. You just had to pay a high-rank magic user an outrageous sum of gold coins to get a reasonably bright light that lasted, well, until someone destroyed or dispelled the enchantment.

Most of the city's night lights ranged between seventy-five and one-hundred watt strength. Lower-rank spell casters charged less, but the magical light they created was proportionally weaker. A streetlamp with a fifteen watt bulb would hardly be worthwhile, to humans. Glenn wasn't sure about Stephi as a fairy but he, Ron and Kirby could see well enough as long as there was a smidgen of light. More illumination, of course, was better since it added color, along with additional depth and detail.

Startling the gnome healer out of his reverie, a blue jay landed next to him atop the bench's backrest. Its warbling chirp announced, "Home. Home."

It was Petie. Stephi must've sent him, knowing Glenn understood her familiar.

The weary gnome hopped off the bench and clambered up the stairs like a distance runner catching his second wind while closing on the finish line.

Petie flew off, presumably to find Ron, Derek and Kirby. They'd staked themselves out at nearby intersections. Blue jays didn't see too well at night. But with the streetlights and the note left in their room for Stephi, the familiar would find and round up the rest of the party in short order.

Keri shot Glenn a brief smile. She was playing chess in the parlor with a merchant that sold exotic feathers. She certainly recognized why the gnome was hustling toward the stairwell. His boots sounded a quick *clap, clap clap*, instead of their normal, slower-paced *clomp, clomp, clomp*.

In the room Stephi sat on the edge of her bed. Her iridescent wings were at rest and her feet dangled far above the floor. "Jax," she said, excitement in her voice.

Glenn didn't know how to respond. What to say. He still expected her voice to be higher pitched to match her miniature body size. It remained her voice, tone and all, just a little quieter. Even though he'd rushed into the room, he decided to play it calm and cool. It was the only way he could pull off hiding his worry. "Hey, Marigold."

His words came out flat and monotone, which didn't match the way he came into the room.

Stephi had ditched the crappy, makeshift sarape. Instead, she wore leaves and bits of bark formed into a dress. It had broad shoulder straps and its length reached mid-thigh. The plant material making up the garment appeared seamlessly glued together. Being green and brown, it was far less colorful than the one the garden's fairy had made from flower petals. The design of Stephi's dress used thin bands of flexible bark to support her breasts, sort of like a built-in brassiere. The leaf material remained supple and flexed like it was still attached to the plant. That was probably part of the magic incorporated when making it, because Glenn just didn't see Stephi or Emma sitting down with a tiny needle and thread, let alone a sewing machine, to make the dress.

"Jax, you're such a dork." She stood on the bed and spread her arms wide. "Don't pretend like you're not happy to see me." She flew up and plastered herself to his chest in a big hug. Well, big for her.

Glenn hugged back. Sort of. He pressed his hands below her back to avoid her wings. He yanked them away, realizing he'd cupped her bottom.

Stephi let go and fluttered back. She put her hands on her hips, but couldn't keep a straight face and laughed as he tried to explain, "I didn't want ta..." He gestured a hug with arms and hands. "…ta crush your wings."

"Me being a fairy, Jax, it's going to take some getting used to. For me, and looks like for everyone." She fluttered back down to the bed and tapped it with a hand, signaling for him to sit next to her. She turned to show him her wings. "Really, they're pretty sturdy but flexible. Like memory plastic or something."

Glenn sat down, leaving a half foot between himself and Stephi, and stared straight ahead. Her breasts still bounced when she flapped her wings, but only a fraction of what they did without her new dress. Glenn tried to think about anything but Stephi in a desperate bid to avoid getting fully aroused. He wondered if this was what it's like for someone who gets off on midget porn. Then he groaned, remembering that, by most standards, he pretty much was a midget himself.

"I've never seen anyone frown quite like that. And blush at the same time," Stephi said. "It's hard to tell with your skin color, Jax, but I can see it." She slid over and put a hand on Jax's thigh. "What's wrong?"

He didn't know what to say and stumbled for words, then gave up.

"It's okay, Jax. Emma's going to talk to the gardeners, who are friends with some of the guards and workers. They're going to help find that dwarf, Benxcob, and we'll get that gold coin back for that jerk leprechaun."

That news, and the fact that Stephi was in better spirits, and far more confident, helped Glenn focus and organize his thoughts. "That's great." He turned to face her. "Gurk called in a favor with that barber. So the local thieves' guild is going to be looking for the dwarf. Lysine talked to some of the guards he knows and Kalgore, some of the folks at the stables and the farrier. So they'll be on the lookout for him, too."

Glenn sighed, some of the excitement draining away, realizing there hadn't been anyone he could get to help. "Keri, downstairs, put the word out, too. Everyone is supposed to be careful about it. Not spread the word too much so that it gets out and the dwarf knows people are looking for him."

Kirby arrived, followed closely by Ron and Derek. They all piled in and closed the door. Derek and Ron sat on Ron's bunk. Kirby sat on the other side of Stephi, on her bed.

Ron and Derek were pretty quiet, their eyes examining Stephi. Seeing her in a diminutive stature with flashy wings was quite a contrast to her normal, elven, six-foot eight with her boots' two-inch heels.

Stephi gave them a second, and then said to Kirby, "Sorry, Gurk, but I got rid of the outfit you made for me." She laughed. "I looked like Homeless Hobo Barbie."

Gurk gestured at her leaf dress. "That looks a million times better."

Derek stared up at the ceiling in frustration. "And you guys gave *me* crap."

"About what?" Stephi asked, her wings beginning to flutter.

Derek's gaze shifted from Kirby and Glenn to Ron. "I said you probably looked like Bimbo Barbie."

Stephi moved her jaw from side to side in thought, then admitted, "That's better than Homeless Hobo." She ran her hands down her dress while panning her gaze across all the men in the room. "No way am I making this into a shorter mini dress showing major cleavage. So don't *even* ask." Her words weren't harsh or angry. They held a teasing playfulness.

Ron cleared his throat. "It would appear that you have acclimated to your situation far better than I would have."

Glenn silently agreed. Probably something to do with the game world aspect. Glenn had gnomish impulses, and things like sleeping cramped up under a bed didn't bother him at all. Maybe Stephi's new fairy nature helped her feel at ease despite being so small.

"Oh, Lysine," Stephi said, "I'm not happy about it. But Emma gave me some tips on being a fairy."

"Emma?" Kirby asked.

"She's a real fairy," Stephi said. "She doesn't, like, advertise she's in the city since most people blame fairies for the tricks and pranks pixies do."

Ron nodded his head knowingly.

Stephi pointed at everyone. Her finger lingering longest on Derek. "Don't any of you say one thing about Emma or there being a fairy—or even hint about any in this dumpy city."

All four men nodded and voiced agreement, including Glenn.

"Emma taught me how to make this dress and a lot of other things."

"Like what?" Glenn asked.

"Close your eyes," she told everyone. "I'm going to

go over by the window. When I say, open your eyes, see if you can see me."

Everyone did as she asked. Glenn felt the slight breeze caused by Stephi's wings as she flew away.

After about ten seconds she said, "Okay, open your eyes."

Glenn did, like the others, and peered at the wall around the window. The only thing Glenn saw was Petie sitting on the sill.

"If she's over there," Derek said, "she's being like a Super Ninja Barbie."

Kirby laughed. "Camouflaged," Kirby corrected. "A natural fairy ability."

"Green Beret Barbie then."

Ron stared intently at the wall. "Gentlemen, train your efforts below the window, near the floor, eighteen inches to the right."

Glenn did and, after twenty seconds of scrutiny, he spotted Stephi's outline. "I see her."

"Where?" Derek said, squinting.

From her concealment, Stephi asked, "Can you see me yet, Gurk?"

Stephi's voice redirected the half-goblin thief's focus a little lower. "Now I can. It's like she's the universe's best chameleon. Like the Predator in those movies."

Stephi said, "I like Super Ninja Barbie better than the Universe's Chameleon Predator." She stood, dropping her fairy enchantment. She'd been sitting cross-legged, motionless as a stone.

Upon seeing Stephi, Derek's eyes widened. "Make that Super Boobs Ninja Barbie."

Stephi rolled her tiny eyes. "I need to practice hiding, but I'm getting better. Just like flying."

"Despite novice skill," Ron said, "if you had not previously directed where I should look, I would have been incapable of identifying your location."

That drew a broad grin from Stephi. Her wings brushed against Glenn's sideburns as she settled back between him and Kirby. That threatened to get him excited in the wrong place. To stop that from happening he bit down on his lip, hoping the pain would cause sufficient distraction.

"Did your sister fairy instruct you in casting a Dazzle Spell?" Derek asked.

"She did. I use my wings for that, too." Stephi's wings became motionless. "Emma also said my ability to hide is better outside the city, unless I can find a group of trees or bushes."

Stephi's face lit up. Glenn looked away so he wouldn't be set off again. He wondered how the other men were managing. Glenn knew for sure he was going to miss the times she wore her formless cloak and concealing hood.

"I can summon pigeons too," she said. "If they're nearby."

"Pigeons?" Derek asked.

"What's wrong with pigeons?" Stephi asked, tilting her head up to glare at Derek. "They'll listen and do what I ask, unless it's, like, suicidal. Like attacking a lion or flying into a burning building."

"Did you get to pick?" Kirby asked. "Sort of like a skill? Or were pigeons assigned to you?"

Stephi turned to Kirby. "Petie gave me the idea."

"Your familiar?" Sarcasm flowed from Derek's voice. "You took the advice of a bird?"

Stephi started to say something but bit it back. After a huff, she said, "We're going to be in this city, and there are pigeons everywhere. The only thing there's more of is rats."

"Rats might be more useful," Kirby said, then leaned away from Stephi, who expressed a look of outrage.

Glenn thought about bringing up wererats in the

city, but thought that moment wasn't the time.

"Rats?" Stephi asked.

"Let me finish." Kirby raised his hands between Stephi and himself. "Spiders, bats, rats and snakes pretty much brand you as Black. Which isn't what fairies are."

Glenn wasn't sure where Kirby was going with that.

Ron cut in, saying, "In an urban environment, pigeons would be one of the most numerous avian species."

"Crows would've been better," Derek said.

Stephi's wings halted mid-flap. "Petie doesn't like crows."

Glenn sensed things might turn into an argument. "Marigold said Emma would get some people looking out for the dwarf."

Everyone turned to Glenn, making him feel defensive. "Well, finding the dwarf's what's important."

"He's right," Kirby said. "We should be out looking for him now."

"While the probability is minute for us to locate him by scouring the streets," Ron said, "determining Benxcob's location while remaining within our rented room is so infinitesimal as not to be worth mentioning."

"What happens if we can't find him?" Stephi asked. "I mean, before he leaves the city?" A wide-eyed look of concern spread across her face. "Then we'll never find him."

Kirby leaned close and started to put an arm around Stephi. Then, having to contend with her wings, and her size, he pulled his arm back.

"I don't want to stay like this," she said. She looked at the party's leader. "If we can't find him, there's something you can—we can do, right?"

"While searching for the dwarf in question," Ron said, "I contemplated what might be attempted, should he manage to evade our efforts."

When he didn't go on, Kirby said, "So, dude, what'd you come up with?"

"The spell the leprechaun, Bataí Fidil na Maidine, cast upon Marigold is susceptible to a counter enchantment." His voice trailed off.

"We could hire someone to cast a Transmorph Spell to fix things back the way they were," Derek said.

Ron turned his head to face Derek. "I had not considered that solution as viable due to the inherent risk being greater than what I would propose."

"Dude," Kirby said. "She'd have to survive a System Shock Roll for the shift to her elf form. And if the spell caster's spell proved unable to override the leprechaun's enchantment, she'd revert right back to fairy form. And have to make another System Shock Roll."

"Those are bad," Stephi said, eyes going wide. "That's what killed Byeol." She looked at everyone, seeking confirmation. "When that priest cast a Revive the Dead Spell on her."

Stephi shook her head and leaned back, clearly frightened. "I don't wanna do that."

Ron rubbed his chin. "Then you will not be in favor of my solution."

"Which is?" Derek asked.

"A Dispell Enchantment Spell. It would have to be powerful as well, to have a reasonable chance of success." He frowned. "And success would entail a System Shock Roll. But only one, should the Dispell Enchantment prove effective in overcoming the leprechaun's enchantment."

Stephi shook her head.

Kirby stomped his soft-soled boot on the floor. "We forgot. Elder leprechauns can cast Retaliatory Contingent Spells." The thief shook his head. "Those suck, and he's probably tough enough to do that."

Glenn asked, "What is a Contingent Retaliatory

Spell?"

Derek's face was scrunched up, like he'd swallowed a mouthful of spoiled milk. "Blowback," he said, "against the spell caster trying to get rid of the Transmorph Spell on Marigold. About as bad as a Skipping Curse."

"What's 'blowback' mean?" Glenn asked, concern heavy in his voice.

"A counter spell directed at the individual attempting to foil the Transmorph Spell," Ron explained. "Greater Lighting Bolts or Greater Curses are commonly selected."

Kirby threw his hands up in the air. "Or a Fireblast Spell, to pay back anybody nearby, including Marigold."

"Can you tell if he did that?" Glenn asked. "If he cast some sort of blowback spell?"

"A Detect Enchantment Spell would address the concern," Ron said. "It may also trigger the Contingent Retaliatory Spell, if it indeed exists."

Stephi pulled her knees up to her chest and wrapped her arms around them. "I don't want to do that." She closed her eyes just as tears began to form. "And I don't wanna be like this, either."

"You already made your System Shock Survival when you got Transmorphed," Derek said. "So stop being a Crybaby Barbie."

"Dude!" Kirby said, jumping to his feet.

"Let me finish, thief." Derek growled. His gaze returned to Stephi. "You don't have to make one, *if* the leprechaun dismisses his own spell."

Kirby balled his hands into fists. "Then what we gotta do is find that stupid dwarf." He sat back down. His yellow eyes focused on Ron, the party's leader. "And get that leprechaun's stupid gold coin."

# CHAPTER 13

**After finally getting** to bed Glenn tossed and turned. Part of it was worrying if they'd find the dwarf, and part of it was he'd decided to sleep in Stephi's bed. Because she urged him to, retreating to his usual mattress and padded quilt under her bed might upset her. She'd curled up on a folded towel inside the creel basket. As best Glenn could tell she hadn't stirred.

Everyone else, from the mutters and rolling over to get comfortable, weren't sleeping well either. Except for Derek.

Glenn finally sat up and decided to go to the washroom. The small amount of light making its way through the open window from the nearby streetlamp was just enough for him to grab his shirt and pants, and sneak out. He was nowhere near as silent as Kirby. Nevertheless, gnomes were woodland beings and that helped—when he wasn't wearing his heavy boots.

By the time Glenn finished, Kirby was standing in the hallway awaiting his turn. The Glade House kept several chamber pots in the tiny common room, along with pitchers of water and wash basins. It was a lot better than some of the other places they'd stayed in. The Ox Wagon Inn came to mind.

Glenn whispered to his friend, "I'm going to the vegetable market before they open and see if Pam might know of someone who could help us."

"Coin-stealing dwarves probably don't shop for potatoes and onions," Kirby whispered back, then grinned. "But you never know."

Glenn nodded once. He knew Kirby was heading to the tea shop to talk to the clerk, or counter person. Derek would say serving wench, even though it wasn't a tavern.

From what everyone said about the game's dwarves, tea didn't sound like their beverage of choice. But Patti saw and talked to a lot of people. It couldn't prove any more fruitless than the party's random search last night.

**Pam, the potato** and onion vendor, was sturdy from her labor. She also bore wrinkles and looseness of skin that age brings. She wore a linen blouse and long skirt that showed evidence of repeated mending. She protected her outfit with a faded yellow apron whose color matched that of her crinkly bonnet. It kept her long, graying hair out of the way.

One of Pam's grandsons helped set up her large cart. It had two sections. One she filled with potatoes, and the other with onions. A grandson helped her each morning, led the donkey away, and returned when the market closed in the late afternoon.

Glenn wandered up after Pam's grandson departed. The sun's rays were just reaching over the roofs in Three Hills City. Some of the potatoes were beginning to show age, having been stored in dark cellars over the winter and through the spring. Most of her large yellow onions appeared and smelled freshly pulled from the ground.

Pam smiled broadly upon spotting Glenn examining her produce and dropping eight large potatoes and an equal number of onions into his canvas sack. "Mighty early for you, Jax. Are you going to stay and visit with me for a short stretch?"

Glenn frowned. "Actually, I can't." He cleared his throat. "Maybe there's something you could do for me?" He verbally stumbled, realizing he should've planned out and practiced what he was going to say. "Actually, it's to help my friend, Marigold."

Pam's eyes went wide before giving Glenn a knowing smile. "Your gorgeous elf friend. The one that hides her face." She winked. "The one that's *only* your friend?"

Glenn sighed. He'd told her at least a hundred times that he and Marigold were friends. He even tried to explain that elves and gnomes weren't attracted to each other in *that* way. Pam never bought it. Maybe because it was only a half truth. He *was* attracted to Stephi. Who wouldn't be? But she wasn't attracted to him, a gnome. Who would be? Another gnome? One he wouldn't be able to relate to?

The gnome healer sighed a second time and looked around. All of the other market vendors were still busy setting up, too busy to listen to a gnome. He decided to press on. "We're looking for a dwarf who's visiting the city. He took something from someone and we want to get it and give it back."

Pam cocked her head and squinted an eye.

Not wanting to get specific, but not wanting to lie, Glenn said, "He took something made of gold."

"Ahhh," Pam said, giving a knowing nod. "Gold and dwarves. More than explains it. What color beard does this dwarf have?"

Glenn shrugged. "All we know is his name, but there aren't very many dwarves in Three Hills City. Not many come here, and he's new. Not one of the regulars you might see."

She chuckled while rearranging her potatoes and onions. "We don't see many dwarves, regular citizens or no, here in the market."

"I pretty much figured that." Glenn scratched his left sideburn. "You said you've been selling here your whole life. Started as a girl, helping your grandmother."

Pam took a deep breath, looking around, possibly recalling the market and her grandmother from at least forty years ago. "That I have." She frowned. "And there's no granddaughter here, learning to take my place."

Glenn knew how that fact ate at Pam's heart. He was sorry he'd brought it up. Two of her five children were already dead. One to an accident while plowing, and the other, serving in the militia and shot dead. An arrow to the throat when the bastards from the Agrippa Empire had come raiding. And Pam had only one granddaughter. She helped her mother with the rug weaving.

"What's this thieving dwarf's name?"

Glenn looked around. In a low conversational tone he said, "Benxcob."

Pam pursed her lips and walked around behind her cart. "I have a nephew who's a guard on the North Wall. There's a small fortified gate there. You know that nobody uses it without the duke's permission. So my nephew doesn't see a lot of folks."

Pam brushed her hands down her apron. The action both cleaned her hands and straightened the garment. "He's up high, though, and tasked to watch both inside the gate and out."

Glenn smiled. "Any little bit will help."

"Well, Jax, you've helped me enough, spending some mornings here by my cart. It's the least I could do." She leaned her forearms on her cart. "His name is Villgar and he has wavy brown hair. But you won't see that because his captain makes the men wear their helmets, summer heat or no.

"You can spot him, sure enough." The potato seller grinned and motioned with her finger along the front of her chin. "A scar right here. Got it from falling while fetching an axe for his father.

"He'll be coming to the North Gard House by way of Kershaw Street. He stands on the wall noon till dusk, so catch him before he has to stand for the captain's inspection, or whatever the soldiers called it.

"Tell him it was his Auntie Pam that sent ya."

Glenn paid her five bronze coins for the onions and potatoes. It was more than they were worth, including a generous tip. He thanked her and hurried back to the Glade House, feeling proud that he'd actually accomplished something.

**Glenn hauled the** sack of food into the Glade House's kitchen, minus one potato. He'd eaten it raw on the way back to the Glade House. Elise was the only person around, so he left the sack of produce with the maid and rushed upstairs.

Stephi wasn't in their room. He'd seen Petie on the roof, so Stephi should be around. No way would she fly around the city in full daylight as a fairy. Maybe she was sitting still, Camouflaged? "Marigold, you here?"

The gnome healer got no answer.

A minute later, Stephi fluttered in through the window. She landed on her bed while Glenn was taking off his boots.

"Jax, you look wiped out."

Instead of telling her about his tossing and turning the whole night, and being still weary from combing the city, he simply said what was obvious. "I am."

"Take a nap."

He shook his head, and glanced out the window. After all this time, Stephi seemed oblivious about how her abnormally high, 19.5 Appearance Score, affected him. "I have to head over to the North Wall in a couple hours." He explained about Pam's nephew.

Stephi clasped her hands, looking hopeful. Then she frowned. "I'm just hanging out on the roof with Petie." When Glenn's eyes widened, she reminded him, "If I sit still nobody can see me."

He grunted acknowledgement. He was tired.

Stephi got to her feet and stood on the bed. She looked down at Glenn sitting on the floor. "Those people behind the Glade House, across the alley. They're nasty."

Glenn nodded. "Keri calls them swamp frogs. I think

it's equivalent to poor white trash."

"If that's true, swamp frogs give poor white trash a bad name."

"I met, or saw two of them that live there. That night we got chased out of the Blue Bugle."

"You mean when you let Rocky and Chili chew up my bra?"

"That wasn't my fault," Glenn protested. "You have two bras now."

"I know, Jax. I was just teasing you." She looked around and then down at herself. "Weird as it might sound for me to say, I hope I'll fit into them again someday. Soon."

Glenn's mind was running slow. It led to a moment of silence. He decided to put the subject back on the neighbors. "Did you see the half-goblin, Roary, or his half-ogre wife, Buellean?"

"Maybe I saw him. There's at least three half-goblins there. One of them dumped their chamber pot out the back door."

Glenn shook his head and stifled a yawn. "That night I met Keri, she was yelling at them because they'd tossed one out and it got on the back of her building."

"Last night was the first I came close to sleeping. I really closed my eyes and sort of dozed off, like being half asleep. Closest to sleep since we got sucked into this world."

Glenn remember that elves didn't sleep. They sort of daydreamed for a few hours at night, but weren't really asleep. He couldn't hold back the next yawn.

"Get some sleep, Jax," Stephi urged. "I'll wake you up in plenty of time."

Glenn scratched his head and stared down at the floor beneath Stephi's bed. "Since the window's open I'll sleep in my usual spot."

**A small hand** pressed on Glenn's face while a female voice called him from sleep. It was Stephi. "Get up, sleepyhead," she whispered. "Lysine and Kalgore fell asleep a half hour ago, so keep quiet."

While not totally refreshed, a sense of purpose urged the gnome to wakefulness. "Okay, thanks."

Within five minutes he'd dressed, gathered his shield and cudgel, and made his way down the steps and out the door. He bit into a raw cucumber Keri had tossed him.

Glenn didn't like to venture out alone when the streets were busy, especially when he didn't know exactly where he was going. Actually, even when he was with a party member, he didn't like it. Usually it felt like being a seven-year-old trying to make his way through a crowded shopping mall on Christmas Eve. He couldn't see very well, and everyone was intent on their own specific goal. That he was armed with a cudgel with a shield strapped across his back did afford him some deference. *If* people noticed him.

He reached Kershaw Street an hour before Villgar was to go on duty. The street was fairly wide and lined with large workshops. The largest ones built wagons, carriages and carts. Glenn climbed and sat atop a barrel sitting along the front of a cooper's shop.

He didn't have to wait long. Within five minutes he spotted a man with wavy brown hair, probably in his early thirties with a deep scar angled across his chin. He wore chainmail armor with a crossbow slung across his back and a scabbarded short sword on his hip. He carried his helmet under his arm and strode with a purpose.

Before the wall guard reached him, Glenn waved to get the man's attention.

Upon seeing the gnome a small smile crossed the man's face. Once again Glenn was thankful people tended to have positive reactions to gnomes. Kirby said it was due to a plus ten percent modifier to Reaction Rolls when he encountered NPCs. It was one of the few benefits to being a gnome.

"You're Villgar, right?" Glenn asked after hopping down and making his way to the guard.

The man slowed his pace. "I am."

"I'd like to talk to you a moment, if you don't mind."

Villgar scowled and kept walking.

Glenn hustled to keep pace. "Your Auntie Pam told me I should talk to you."

The scowl retreated and was replaced by a quirked left eyebrow. "About what?"

There was little shade at the current hour but Glenn spotted a narrow bit of it next to a two-story warehouse. He gestured toward the wooden wall. "Can we talk there? I promise I'll be fast so you won't be late."

"Oh, my gnome friend, I assure you, you won't keep me from roll call." The wall guard followed Glenn into the shade. "Are you the gnome fella that hangs around and helps my aunt sell potatoes?"

"And onions," Glenn replied and offered his hand to shake. "I'm Jax."

"That's right," Villgar said. "My aunt mentioned your name, but the fact that you were a gnome is what stuck with me."

Villgar stood with his back against the wall, placing himself completely in the shade. "Okay, what can I do for you?"

"I know this is a long shot," Glenn prefaced. "I'm looking for a dwarf named Benxcob. He's new to town, and I don't have a description. Just a name."

"Does this have anything to do with my aunt?"

"Nothing at all to do with her," Glenn said. He watched as a wagon pulled by a team of oxen and filled with lumber creaked by. "I don't know a lot of people.

Your Aunt Pam said you didn't see a lot of people out this way, but a dwarf might stick in your memory."

"You're right. I mainly watch the North Gate. Nobody uses it, unless they have the duke's permission."

"So, in the last week or so, you haven't come across a strange dwarf? Here or maybe on your way to work?"

"No, sorry. I can't say that I have."

Glenn frowned in disappointment. "Could you keep an eye out?"

Villgar started to nod, then lifted his right hand and snapped his fingers. "I did hear about a dwarf a couple days back. Him and some big guy were winning big at the Copper Crown."

When the wall guard saw Glenn's eyebrows shoot up, he clarified. "It's a gambling tavern, south of the New Square Tower. Not a place I'd go in to but my friend, Noll, he goes there."

"What'd he say?"

"Some big warrior and a dwarf were accused of cheating at the dice table. There was a fight and the big guy ruffed up the bouncers pretty good. Noll said they left on their own, taking their winnings. The owner told them they weren't welcome back."

"Your friend Noll didn't mention any names?"

"No." Villgar shifted his helmet to his right hand and started down the street, toward the gate.

"Maybe I could talk to Noll?"

Villgar sucked in air through his teeth. "Probably not for a couple days. He's part of the mounted patrol. They go out for three days. Sometimes up to a week."

The guardsman sucked in a breath. "I gotta go, but I'll ask around."

Glenn bit his lower lip. "It'd be a drawback if he knew I was looking for him."

The wall guard's left eyebrow quirked up again.

Glenn said, "It has to do with gold that he shouldn't

have."

"Owes you coin?"

"Not me, but I'm helping a friend out trying to get it back." Glenn shrugged. "You know dwarves and gold."

"I got ya. I'll be careful asking around."

Glenn thanked Villgar and hurried back to the Glade House, pleased with how things went. He was frustrated that he didn't have a better lead. But it was a lead he could share with the party.

# CHAPTER 14

**"Dude, Mos Eisley** has nothing on the Copper Crown," Kirby told Glenn and Stephi. The two were sitting on her bed when he'd entered the room just ahead of Ron and Derek.

"I believe we have discovered a hive containing more scum and villainy," Ron added, a goofy grin crossing his face.

With nothing better to do that evening, Ron, Derek and Kirby went to the Copper Crown in search of information. Glenn and Stephi got to hang out at the Glade House, and Glenn decided to stay in the room. People were starting to ask about Marigold and he didn't want to lie. The cover story was that she'd left on a caravan to meet an elven friend in Shorn Spearhead.

Derek groaned and shut the door behind him. "No nerd-festing."

"Dude," Kirby said, plopping down on Stephi's bunk. That placed Stephi between him and Glenn. "You don't like *Star Wars*?"

"*Star Wars* is okay," Derek said. "Kylo Ren's a pathetic villain." He slapped Ron on the back before plopping down on his bunk across from Kirby. "You do realize Lysine is a complete *Star Trek* geek."

Ron took a seat next to Derek and stretched his legs out. "That is an accurate statement," he said. "I find structural aspects of the *Star Trek Universe* far more interesting in comparison to the *Star Wars Universe*."

Glenn watched every episode of the *Next Generation* when it'd been available on *Netflix*, and scattered episodes from all the other *Star Trek* series, and all the old movies that featured the *Next Generation* crew. *Star Wars*, he'd seen all the movies to date, either on *Blu-ray* or at the theater, but wasn't well versed in their contents or "lore."

Stephi spoke up, asking Ron, "You don't find Princess Leia or Rey interesting?"

An hour-long discussion ensued. For a short time Glenn forgot that he was a gnome trapped on an aberrant concurrent world. It appeared the same for everyone else. When the discussion stalled while discussing why Spock was a better sidekick—Ron referred to sidekicks as "right-hand men"—than Chewbacca. Everyone fell silent, looking from each other, to the room around them.

Ron broke the silence. He explained how Spock's death saving the crew paralleled Kim dying while saving the party. Everyone realized Spock got a second lease on life. Kim didn't.

It was depressing.

After an awkward thirty seconds of silence, Derek released an extra-loud sigh. Fumbling, he pulled a small bundle from a sack. He reached across the span between the beds and proffered something wrapped in a white cloth to Stephi.

"It ain't exactly Rey's lightsaber."

Stephi took the gift and quickly unwrapped it to find a rapier and scabbard scaled down to her size.

"It's bronze," Derek said, "except the Silversmith, Timz Simman, insisted on coating the blade with some sort of hardened silver."

Stephi flew over and hugged Derek's arm. She stretched up and planted a kiss on his cheek. "Thank you, Kalgore."

Derek grinned wide, his missing tooth making him look a little goofy. He flicked his left hand, pointing at Ron with his thumb. "It was his idea. I just did the leg work. I also commissioned him to make a dagger with silver in the blade. Might come in handy dealing with leprechauns or something."

Sometimes Derek surprised Glenn. Most of the time he was a major jerk. But, after his Bimbo Barbie crack, he'd been pretty decent.

Stephi shot over to Ron. She hugged and kissed him as well. Her wings' shimmering couldn't hold a candle to her broad smile.

"Marigold," Ron said, "I suggest that tomorrow, at the earliest opportunity, you commence practice with it. Wielding a rapier in flight may prove challenging."

Then she frowned and her wings slowed in their flapping. "What good will it be? It's so small." Her shoulders sagged. "I'm so small."

"Come on, Marigold," Kirby said. "It'll do one to two points of damage per hit. Everything adds up in a fight."

"Gurk is correct," Ron said. "Additionally, do not discount the fact that you retain the ability to cast Mystic Missile and Slumber Spells, in addition to your fairy-based magical abilities."

Derek made mock rapier thrusts and cuts with his big hand. "Musketeer Mariposa Barbie."

"I got it," Stephi said, failing to suppress a smile.

Kirby patted Glenn on the shoulder. "Me and Jax'll make you a practice dummy."

Derek glared at Kirby. "It better not look like me."

Ron was the first to laugh, followed by Kirby, then Stephi. Glenn was the last to catch Derek's self-deprecating joke.

When everyone stopped laughing Ron broke the returning awkward silence. "We were unable to ascertain if the dwarf at the Copper Crown was Benxcob."

"If anyone knew," Kirby said, "they weren't sharing. It's not exactly a sharing, *Kum Ba Yah* sort of place."

"The big guy, though," Derek said, "is named Rex. A lot of people know him. A warrior-type who henched for a party of adventurers for a few years."

"Henched?" Stephi asked.

"Was their henchman," Kirby said. "Like Blizz is for us, except instead of handling the animals, he was more like Jurome. Fought alongside the party."

Glenn hadn't thought of the man-at-arms in a while. He'd died helping the party defeat some mercenaries trying to kill White Birch, the daughter of an elven baronet they'd rescued.

It reminded Glenn, once again, how dangerous the *Monsters, Maces and Magic* world was, and that taking the gold coin away from Benxcob would probably end in violence.

"The hour is late," Ron said. "It would behoove us to secure as much sleep as possible. None of us knows what the morrow might bring."

"In other words," Kirby said, "Dad Lysine's saying, 'Go to bed because we all got to get up early, work all day, and ain't nobody getting a nap.'"

# Chapter 15

**Kirby burst into** the room while Glenn was holding the end of a stick with a mildewed tarp wrapped around it. He was maneuvering it back and forth and side to side while Stephi practiced coordinating rapier-thrust attacks with her flying ability. She wasn't very good at it, in Glenn's opinion, but showing improvement. Having someone like Derek or Ron there to give advice would've been handy. They knew sword handling techniques. Stephi's connection to Kim through the Soul Gem wasn't useful. She only had warrior monk skills, and none of those involved rapiers.

Stephi kept wearing the silver chain holding the alexandrite gemstone, the soul gem housing Kim's soul, as a belt. Ron had carefully wrapped strands of green silk around the chain so that it didn't chafe her leaf dress or make any noise. He offered to get the remaining bit of silk he'd secured fashioned into socks or leggings. Stephi declined the offer. Like all fairies, she preferred to remain barefoot.

"Dudes," Kirby said, unbridled excitement in his voice, "Josiah told me where that dwarf is staying." He took a second to close the door. "You know what's even better?" The half-goblin thief didn't wait for Stephi or Glenn to respond. "He's been invited to a second floor poker game at the Blue Bugle! Tonight!"

Stephi, fluttering several feet above the floor, slid her rapier into its scabbard.

"Oh, Gurk."

That was all she could manage but Petie chimed in from his spot on the window sill, chirping and warbling. Glenn interpreted it as "Wanted, wanted, wanted."

Gurk said, "Send Petie to go get Lysine and Kalgore

so we can organize a plan."

**It was dusk** when Glenn and Kirby reached the Blue Bugle. The party had spent the day scouting routes from the gambling and entertainment tavern to the Laughing Goat Inn. It was about a half mile, and not a straight shot back. That meant alternate alleys to set their ambush and hope no members of the City Guard were patrolling nearby. And that Benxcob went straight back to where he was supposed to be staying.

Josiah the Barber had given Kirby and Glenn stamped copper tokens that would allow them entrance without question. He also had a contact named Josie—if that was her real name—who'd point out Benxcob when he came into the Bugle for his poker game. It was assumed that Josie could locate a half-goblin and a gnome among the crowd. The bill for the barber's efforts came to fourteen gold, nine silver and two copper coins. Glenn wasn't sure if that was excessive or a bargain, but everyone pulled from their stash and paid the location fee, as well as for passes for Ron and Derek to get into the Bugle. Whether that much coin was excessive or not, it was worth it, if they got the leprechaun's gold coin.

Derek and Ron were to arrive fifteen minutes after Glenn and Kirby. Once Benxcob arrived and was identified, Glenn and Kirby were to depart and hang out at the Crow's Gullet. There they'd wait for Petie to let them know when the dwarf left the Bugle.

Stephi was to keep track of the dwarf, relaying instructions to Glenn and Kirby through Petie so that the pair could be ready to lure Benxcob into one of the ambush alleys. Ron and Derek were to follow at a distance, far enough behind that they wouldn't be noticed. It all hinged on Stephi. That made her anxious. She had to fly above the roofs and Camouflage herself while keeping track of the dwarf, communicate with

Petie, and make sure Ron and Derek knew where the ambush would be.

The Blue Bugle was a wooden building with sturdy framing and actual windows. The front was single story and wide, but it extended back to become a three-story structure. Painted on the wall facing the street was a large blue bugle. With so much of the population being illiterate, the painted depiction made sense to Glenn

There was a small admittance line to get into the Bugle. Glenn had his cudgel in its loop and his shield across his back. Kirby carried his cutlass in its scabbard and bandoleer of darts. Everyone in the Blue Bugle was armed. Some had small swords, or short swords or maces. There were a few with long swords in scabbards on their hips or strapped across their back, the way Kalgore preferred. But everyone had at least a hunting knife or a dagger.

Weapons could only be drawn and used in self-defense, under penalty of imprisonment—or death. And if a patron wouldn't allow himself to be disarmed by the blue-clad security teams, the same punishment could be expected. Allowing weapons, but also having harsh penalties to even draw them except in defense, seemed odd to Glenn. What about the *Monsters, Maces and Magic* world wasn't odd? Maybe if he gained more experience points and went up a rank or two, he'd better understand…not!

Kirby and Glenn reached the pair of doormen armed with short swords and offered their copper tokens. Normally it cost three silver coins for admittance. In return, their right hand was painted with a green dye and the door was opened for them.

Having been in the establishment once before, the pair cut through the meandering crowd and found a high table with two stools along a wall. Its placement wasn't optimum for viewing the stage, being at a good angle off to the left-hand side. But it did offer a glimpse of the upper two levels from across the room, sort of like one of those hotels where one could look up at the mezzanine and the second floor. Up there the larger-stakes gambling took place.

Kirby put his soft-soled boot on one of the tall stool's spindles, enabling Glenn to climb up. Once Kirby was seated, they looked around. Two hulking bouncers that could double for Arnold Schwarzenegger in his prime guarded the spiral stairwell leading up to the gambling area. That was where Benxcob was supposed to be invited.

The bottom floor had several rows of benches arrayed up near the stage, which was near the back of the first level. Located beyond the stage was the kitchen, storage, offices, and whatever else the Blue Bugle needed for the place to run.

Behind the benches stood nine round tables tightly arranged with seats for between four and eight customers. Those tables were larger and lower compared to where Glenn and Kirby sat. That made them more appropriate for dining. Most of the high tables like Glenn and Kirby's sat along the north wall. Along the south end of the large, low-ceilinged room, was a gambling area. There were tables with a few people playing cards around them, what looked like a blackjack table, and one where people were shooting dice. The dealers and those running or monitoring the tables wore blue, similar to the doormen. Several of the men were pretty large, and wore short swords or sabers on their hips.

Despite the magical medieval setting, the place had an Old West gambling hall melded with a modern theater club vibe. There was an open floor area where customers mingled. Nobody danced.

The place continued filling up with merchant men

and women in linen and silk outfits. Some were pretty conservative while others sported odd patterns, with reds, blues, oranges and greens. Convenience and ease of wearing weapons seemed more important than deadliness. No halberds or spears or spike-headed flails. A few men and two women wore larger swords strapped across their backs. Glenn smiled, knowing that despite the oddity, they'd manage to sit comfortably, just like he did with his shield. Game world rules.

There weren't any other gnomes, mostly humans with a few half-elves mixed in. There was a dwarf working behind the bar along with a couple human bartenders. Glenn recognized the dwarf being there the other time they'd been in the Bugle.

"Most everyone's human," Kirby whispered to Glenn. "Merchants, based on their clothes and weapons. Here to have a good time, showing off a little wealth, and avoiding the common riff-raff."

Glenn nodded agreement to the obvious. He appreciated Kirby making sure Glenn was aware, and helping him to learn. Yes, three silver coins for admittance, a little less for attending servants, would keep the poorer folks out.

Glenn leaned close to Kirby. "Crowded, but not as crowded as last time."

A spindly thin waitress with braided black hair that dangled past her waist came up to their table. "What'll you two be having?"

"An ale for me, and a mead for my gnome friend," Kirby said, pointing his thumb at Glenn. "Not the rot-gut stuff, but not your best neither. We got some coin tonight, but we ain't rich."

The waitress eyed the green marks on the gnome and half-goblin's hands and said, "I'll take care of you two, no problem." She gestured toward the stage. "The Albino Leper Man is going to be doing some singing soon." She leaned close. "He ain't diseased, mind you. Just his stage name."

"Stay sharp," Kirby whispered, leaning close, "and hope at least one of us makes our Observation Roll."

Glenn gulped.

Kirby must've caught his friend's concern. "Don't worry, dude. Spotting a dwarf among humans—and if we don't get stinking drunk—we'll get massive bonuses to our roll. Plus, I'm a thief, so I'll get an extra plus two."

Glenn wondered where the 'roll' exactly took place. Some great game master in the sky? With this weird world it was within the realm of possibility.

While they waited and watched for any dwarf, and for their contact, Josie, the bard on stage warmed up. He sat on a low stool with a large harp resting between his legs. The sound as he plucked strings carried pretty well.

The Albino Leper Man was definitely pale, but his eyes weren't red. And his short-trimmed hair wasn't white. It was faded blond. The gnome decided the stage name, or a weird NPC name, was one some GM had made up. He frowned. Maybe the creepy GM that had trapped them in the game.

The Albino Leper Man wore a black linen shirt and breeches, and a sleeveless vest sporting a vivid yellow and black checker pattern.

By the time their spindly waitress delivered the drinks and Kirby paid—they didn't want to have a tab since they might need to leave at any moment—the bard was prepared to sing his first tale of the night. Except for the murmur and occasional laughing and backslapping from the gambling taking place on the opposite side of the large main floor, everyone was quiet and surprisingly attentive.

After an impressive musical flourish from his harp, the bard announced in a clear tenor voice, one with a hint of a nasal tone, "The Fall of the Winterlands."

Nods, whispers and grunts of approval came from all around Kirby and Glenn.

As the bard sang his tale, his eyes closed and his fingers plucked strings with confident grace.

*When the God-Emperor came down like a wolf on the fold*

*And his cohorts were gleaming in purple and gold*

*And the sheen of their spears was like the stars on the sea*

*When the Kratzfians marched and laid siege to Akbe.*

*Like the leaves of the forest when summer is green*

*That host with their banners at sunset was seen.*

*Like the leaves of the forest when autumn has blown*

*Half the host on the morrow lay withered and strown.*

*Belagusta had aided with a fiery blast*

*And the Wizard of Winter felled more as he passed.*

*Montremain had slain generals with the Chaos Blade's charm*

*And Meltarm had battled all who dared Justice harm.*

*But there stood defenders, eyes open, mouths wide,*

*Through the ranks marched the God-Emperor, determined in stride.*

*Belagusta challenged first, and was decimated onto smoke*

*Then Archimedes, Mage of Ice Mountain, was the next to be broke.*

*The mortals all stood, spirit broken and pale,*

*'Till Benemere the White rode forth, in gleaming white mail.*

*The ranks were all silent as he battled alone.*

*He perished unheralded, with trumpets unblown.*

*The Kratzfians moved forward to press their advantage,*
*The defenders stood ready, courage as could manage.*
*The cresting attack took them over the walls*
*The fighting raged on, in doorways and in halls.*

*Telecarn, Cancer, Chi, and Sir Joshua too*
*Fought on like windstorms, and thousands they slew.*
*Aimen and Emperor battled near side by side.*
*Akbe was in crumble with nowhere to hide.*

*The pocks of resistance were being destroyed,*
*The fate of the Winterlands none could avoid.*
*Like Grahmlaug before, died defending his land,*
*Like the Hold of the Sea Princes, who'd failed to stand.*

*Covered in blood, crimson to the feet,*
*The Emperor of the South with sword raised, jeered defeat.*
*Ravaged his way to the embattled town square*
*Issued the God-Emperor to meet his end there.*

*Once again it halted, the bloody conquest*
*All eyes turn toward it, the despotic contest.*
*The defenders knew their last hope, their last gasp,*
*As a sun weary wanderer, one daring an asp.*

*Like fell darkness he came, came out of the night*
*Like cold blackness he struck, struck with all of his might.*
*Against such force, no mortal could stand*
*Even one so mighty, with the Chaos Sword in hand.*

*The Aimen knew this, and claiming his right*
*With Hammer of Justice, wagered into the fight.*

*The two battled on, relentless. The God-Emperor laughed.*

*Then laid them low with his strength and his craft.*

*The men of the Winterlands battled on, relentless, to the last.*

*The God-Emperor laid them low with his strength and his craft.*

It was quite a tale, sounding both dire and epic. But Glenn was totally lost when it came to the names and places. One thing he was sure of: He didn't want to meet the God-Emperor. The gnome healer was pretty sure the lich that had passed by his party in the Dark Hart Swamp, and left them all a cowering mess just by her near presence, was equal to a mage. And the mage in the bard's tale got snuffed with apparent ease. Like everyone else.

He made a mental note to ask Kirby or Ron about the bard's tale when he got the chance. To Glenn, the tale meant that the *Monsters, Maces and Magic* world they were stuck in had some sort of extensive history. A violent one, like so much else in the game world. It also meant any adventures to the Winterlands wouldn't be anywhere near the top of his list.

The crowd began tossing coins onto the stage, a sort of payment of which the Bugle kept twenty percent. Glenn learned that from a previous backstage experience while fleeing hostile patrons. Kirby hurled a few coins, too. They looked like iron pieces to Glenn. Unlike when he was on stage, the patrons weren't targeting the bard, or trying to get him to run from one side of the stage to the other.

The bard planned better, too. A young girl with a push broom did the coin-gathering job. And nobody hurled coins at her for amusement.

While the Albino Leper Man began another tale, this one telling of a nearsighted captain of a cargo-laden sailing ship, a cute woman with freckles and sparkling green eyes wandered up to the table and addressed Kirby.

Glenn guessed the young woman was their contact. She was a little on the chubby side, dressed in a brown linen blouse and wool knit pants that reached mid-calf. She wore sandals and her feet were dusty, like she'd done a lot of walking that day. She pushed aside a curly auburn lock and said, "One never can tell exactly who the Bugle staff will let in these days, let alone how many."

She picked up Glenn's tin mug of mead and finished it. After licking her lips, she slid the mug back on the tall table, shrugged with a smile, and wove her way back into the growing sea of patrons, most of which were moving toward the additional benches the blue-clad Bugle staff were placing. Apparently more customers than expected wanted to listen to the bard.

Glenn ignored that and focused his attention toward the entrance. A half moment later a dwarf swaggered in. He had a long, bushy beard, coal-black in color. Like all dwarves, he looked sturdy, like he could swing the hell out of the war hammer hanging from his leather belt. One end of the weapon was blunt and the other spiked. Crack a skull or pierce it, neither result would be pleasant.

The dwarf, Benxcob, had on leather armor. But instead of rings sewn into it like Ron's armor, this one had steel disks riveted to it, patterned like the stars on the U.S. flag.

Following behind the dwarf strode a big, clean-shaven man with straight hair, a little on the greasy side. It framed his face dominated by a hawk-like nose. Beneath his chainmail vest, he had broad shoulders. The man scanned the crowd as if looking for someone to bludgeon with his mace or stab with his dagger, both weapons secured to his belt.

Kirby tapped Glenn on the shoulder, drawing his attention away from the dwarf and man.

Glenn turned to see what Kirby wanted.

"Don't stare at them, dude," the half-goblin thief whispered, leaning close. "That'll give us away."

"Oh, sorry," Glenn muttered. He tipped his empty mug toward himself and stared into it.

"And don't do anything that'll make you stand out. We're a gnome and half-goblin among hundreds of humans, so it's already bad enough."

Kirby was right. There were a few elves and half-elves in the hall. He'd seen one half-goblin woman, but that was it.

Kirby leaned close and whispered again. "Josie's clueing Lysine and Kalgore in."

Glenn's eyes shot wide. He hadn't seen his two party members enter the Bugle. He'd been too enthralled with the bard's musical tale. Because of that he probably got minuses on his Observation Roll.

The gnome focused his attention on the stage even though he wasn't listening to the bard's voice and harp. Looking for Ron and Derek, or even Josie, would probably be a bad idea, too. He sucked at being a thief, and trying to spy on people.

Kirby hopped off his tall stool. "Come on, dude. Time to go."

They made their way out, which might've surprised the doormen—customers leaving so soon—had it not been for Kirby holding his stomach and groaning a bit. Glenn thought about putting his arm around his friend, like he was supporting him, but he was a gnome. His kind weren't supposed to be friendly toward goblins, or half-goblins. So being with Kirby was odd enough already. It reminded Glenn of how stereotypically narrow-minded the world's NPCs were. Of course in mythology, and even children's fairy tales and movies, goblins were always evil and nasty. And gnomes tended to be happy, friendly good guys. They never palled around with goblins. The game's creators apparently based the game's cultural norms on such literature.

He shrugged to himself and kept pace with Kirby as they made their way to their assigned destination: The Crow's Gullet.

**Kirby attracted significantly** more stares than Glenn at the Crow's Gullet. It was an outdoor tavern sort of restaurant. It had a large roofed-over porch where customers could sit outside and enjoy the fresh air, what there was of that, and the sites, mainly carts, carriages and citizens making their way to and from various establishments.

The Crow's Gullet was known to be frequented by mercenaries, henchmen and adventurers. That helped the two blend in. Even more important was the fact that it was slightly less than midway between the Blue Bugle and the Laughing Goat Inn, where Benxcob was supposed to be spending his sleeping hours.

The Gullet was known for its meats. Both Kirby and Glenn opted for the oil-broiled catfish, which had been dipped in lard, spiced with salt, black pepper and thyme and broiled in a large oven. The fish was served skewered on a stick.

Beyond being a place to blend in, the Gullet's roof offered Petie a place to perch and await word from Stephi. The familiar was to warn Glenn, sitting in the establishment's open porch, that the dwarf had left the Bugle. The other benefit was that the Gullet sold a necessary prop for their ambush. Clay jugs filled with cheap whiskey.

The evening passed slowly and Glenn's nerves

became more and more on edge. The pair nursed their meal and their mugs of weak cider. While the alcohol content was low, the bladder filling was high. Their choice of drink also earned some snickers from those seated nearby. Fortunately it never went further than that.

Around eleven at night a couple of drunks began arguing in the middle of the cobblestone street.

Glenn watched with interest. Both men were armed. One carried an axe and the other was armed with a small sword, good for little more than thrusting. Both men wore gambeson, or thick padded jackets for armor. To Glenn they appeared to be warrior types. Maybe men-at-arms, hired by merchants to protect wagons travelling dangerous roads from city to city.

Both men leaned close, locking stares. An exchange of creative cuss words commenced, mixed with comments about one's mother sleeping with flea-ridden goats and the other's father favoring maggot-infested pig corpses.

Both Kirby and Glenn remained silent while many dining on the Gullet's porch leaned against the wooden rail to observe. There was sufficient light for humans to pick out details. The Gullet's customers began shouting encouragements. "You gonna take that from him?" "Who lets a man insult his mother like that?" "Only a yellow coward would take that insult lying down!"

When the louder man went for his axe, the thinner one drew his sword.

Kirby elbowed Glenn. "City Guard."

The other patrons also spotted the four guardsmen coming around the nearby corner. Glenn wondered if they'd been summoned or if it was an unfortunate coincidence that the patrol route's timing brought them to this street during the drunken argument.

As usual they wore chainmail vests along with blue

and red-striped sashes reaching from left shoulder to right waist. Each had donned a Norman helmet with a thin nose guard extending down the front and two-inch wide metal plates that hung down on either side, protecting each guard's temples and jaw while leaving hearing unimpaired. They were armed with spears and short swords and, as always, looked like they meant business.

Everyone on the porch went silent. A few customers grinned, a few sneered in disgust, but most watched on, eager and expectant.

The leader of the guardsmen, a corporal by the two black stripes on his sash, blew a shrill whistle and ordered the still-arguing men in the street, "Disarm."

Both inebriated warriors turned to face the four enforcers of the law standing twelve feet away.

The axe-wielder cocked his head. The swordsman turned his stance unsteadily.

"We're just talking here in the street," Axe Man loudly explained.

Swordsman gestured with his sword over his head. "There's plenty of room for you all to march around." He lowered his sword. "We don't mind."

It wasn't clear if the men, in their state, understood the gravity of the situation. Maybe they were strangers to the city. Glenn had been told that no one messed with the City Guard.

The corporal again ordered, "Disarm. Weapons on the street."

The two drunks lowered their weapons, but didn't drop them.

Swordsman asked, "Why, kind sir?"

At some unobserved signal the four guardsman advanced to attack, two against each defender. The drunks, sensing the danger, stepped back and raised their weapons instead of dropping them. To Glenn, it was unclear if dropping them at that point would've made a difference.

The swordsman managed to knock one spear thrust aside with his narrow blade but the second guardsman succeeded in his attack, drawing blood from the thin drunk's left shoulder. At the same time Axe Man, suddenly enraged, charged to clash with the corporal and accompanying guardsman.

While Swordsman's fight appeared somewhat choreographed, with him dodging and thrusting, twice with minor success, Axe Man's turned into a close melee with his axe and fist against short swords. The corporal took a glancing axe-blow to the helmet, but shook it off within seconds. Shortly after that Axe Man collapsed under a hail of sword blows, most of which came after he was down on the ground.

Swordsman, unable to defend against two attackers, fell with one spear tip piercing his kidney and the other spear impaling him through the gut.

Everyone on the porch winced and frowned but said nothing. While some sentiment might lie with the two fallen men-at-arms, maybe even a little guilt for egging them on, nobody dared speak out.

The corporal's intense glare at those watching from the porch motivated the Gullet's customers to return to their tables. Glenn and Kirby watched out of the corner of their eyes as the two dead drunks were dragged away by the guardsmen.

"That might be good for us," Kirby whispered. "They might not be back by the time the dwarf comes by."

"Or," Glenn lamented, "it might mean they call in extra men because there was trouble."

"I don't think so," Kirby said, shaking his head and returning to his wooden mug half-filled with cider. "At worst, a replacement patrol, if the first one has to report or do paperwork."

Kirby's opinion didn't convince Glenn. He hid it by lifting his own mug to his lips.

An hour later, around midnight, while Glenn and Kirby were discussing the bard's song, Petie sounded off. "Warning. Warning."

The bird's jeering whistle stopped the Gullet's table chatter for no more than a half moment. After shrugs and short laughs, and speculation if a cat or a rat had startled the bird, everything went back to normal.

Kirby was up, corked-jug of whisky under his arm. Glenn left two silver, six copper and four bronze coins on the table and waved goodbye to their quiet and unassuming waiter.

Once on the street, Petie landed on a crossbeam beneath a porch. His song and single bob, Glenn interpreted as, "One."

That meant the dwarf was on the primary route back. Glenn shared this with Kirby and they meandered toward the pre-selected alley.

"Okay," Kirby whispered, after taking a swig of the cheap whisky, swishing it around in his mouth and spitting it out, before spilling some on his leather armor. "We need to hang around, but not be noticed." He scratched behind his ear. "Don't look like we're loitering."

"Shouldn't we hide out in the alley then?" Glenn asked, unsure how to not appear like he was loitering, when that was pretty much what he was doing. That, and getting butterflies in his stomach.

Kirby showed him how to walk slowly, stopping to look at something, notice a bat flitting overhead or adjust a buckle on his tunic, not make eye contact, yet be aware of who was around them and what they were doing.

The streets were sort of quiet after midnight. Most people moved directly toward where they wanted to be with little deviation. There *were* predators out there.

Glenn hoped that Josiah, through his supposed connection with the thieves in town, had directed those folks who prowled the dark streets to leave Glenn and his party alone, at least for this night.

The sky above was mostly clear with the unfamiliar stars sparkling. The moon was on the rise, now visible above the buildings, unless the gnome wandered too close to one of them. Then he couldn't see it.

Petie landed close again, signaling, "One," then, "Near."

Glenn relayed the message to Kirby, who then grinned in anticipation. Glenn wondered how Kirby could do that? How could he feel excited about what was going to happen? Kirby was a junior high kid. He'd been living a rough life as a social outcast, but…

Glenn tried not to stare at an obvious prostitute, identified by her tight short dress, high boots and corset that thrust her breasts upward. What really gave it away was that the parts of her breasts that weren't *supposed* to be showing edged above the low-cut white blouse.

Startling himself, Glenn remembered he wasn't supposed to stare, or draw attention.

The half-goblin thief signaled the worried gnome healer with a tip of his head. Silently the pair left their spot in front of a hat maker's shop.

They meandered across the street to the narrow alley that ran between a furrier and a cobbler's shop. Both establishments had second story apartments above and storage sheds behind them. The alleyway was muddy with a few stray weeds sprouting along the edges. The best thing was the placement of streetlamps. They left the alley's opening in shadowy darkness. A perfect place for a cutthroat or mugger to get the drop on someone.

Glenn followed Kirby into the darkness. There were a few carrion beetles buzzing around a dead cat. It looked like a carriage ran it over earlier in the day and someone tossed it into the alley. The moon was reaching just the right height, so that its light touched the first few feet of the apartment above the furrier's shop. That setup reflected a scant bit of light down into the alley, giving both Glenn's gnomish eyes, and Kirby's half-goblin ones enough to see like they were in a bedroom with a nightlight.

Kirby crouched down and looked around the corner of the cobbler's shop, just above the level of its porch. It made Glenn wonder. Almost every business had a porch, and the vast majority of those were on the narrow side. Kirby saying, "There they are," snapped the gnome healer back to worrying about the task at hand.

"There's three dudes ahead of them," Kirby said, his voice cracking in excitement. "Looks like two merchants and a hired man-at-arms escorting them. Our dwarf is about twenty feet behind, with that big dude we saw with him earlier." Excitement filled the thief's whispers. "Rex, I think his name is."

Glenn remembered seeing the warrior follow Benxcob into the Blue Bugle. Remembered Rex's hawk nose, big mace and long dagger, and armor. Derek, or maybe Ron, said he'd been a henchman for adventurers.

The gnome healer bit his lip and squeezed the business end of his cudgel. He felt the inlayed lines of silver, cold and smooth, against his fingers. His cudgel's head wasn't perfectly smooth anymore, having been in more than a few fights, many of them for his very life. So, of course, Glenn thought to himself, Benxcob wouldn't wander the streets alone at night.

Thinking on that gave him a really bad feeling.

Kirby uncorked his jug, took a swig and spit it out, a little of the spray hitting his boots. He wanted to smell the part. "Show time."

The thief must've seen something in Glenn's eye. "Just pretend. Let your gnome personality show a bit.

Lysine and Kalgore are right behind the dudes."

Glenn nodded. He sure hoped so.

Kirby staggered out, leaning against the corner post supporting the cobbler's porch. He curled a finger in the loop attached to the jug's neck and rested it on his forearm and bicep while lifting it to his lips.

Glenn came up, reached over and snatched the jug away, spilling some of the whiskey. "No more!" He turned his body so that the jug was out of Kirby's reach.

"Aww, mannn," Kirby slurred. Then he pretended to just take notice. "Dwarf dude," he said, pointing unsteadily at the black-bearded dwarf tromping down the middle of the cobblestone street. "T-Tell my frrriend to give me back my boozzze."

Benxcob slowed his stride and glanced over at Kirby. The big man, Rex, said, "Ignore the little ox turd."

The dwarf looked pretty angry. Glenn smiled meekly while observing the dwarf's clenched teeth and drawn eyebrows.

Benxcob continued walking, and growled up at Rex, "When did you become a goblin lover?"

"Aww, mann," Kirby said again. "Youu won't tell my frriend 'cause yourr mommm loves my pops?" Kirby leaned forward. "He's a goblin, ya know."

"Come on, Benx," Rex urged, looking around. Apparently he spotted someone down the street, behind them. "He ain't worth it."

The dwarf started forward again, shouting over his shoulder, "Your pops preferred goats to your mother, half-breed."

Kirby pretended to start getting sick, then stood up straight and pointed. "That'sss it, dwwarf," he said like some revelation had just struck him. "The scraawwwny goat your pops bedded to bringgg you b-birthed into the world has a betterrr beard than you."

The instant the dwarf turned on his heel and began

stomping toward Kirby, the half-goblin thief clutched his stomach and pretended like he was going to heave. He staggered back into the dark alley.

Rex followed behind the dwarf. "Benx, this ain't going to make things no better."

Glenn steadied himself to play his part. He set the clay jug on the ground. "Mister," he said, holding out his hands in a placating gesture. "He didn't mean it. He's drunk." The gnome healer stepped back, giving Benxcob wide berth.

Glenn wanted to flash a glimpse down the street, reassure himself that Ron and Derek were close. He didn't. Instead, he looked up at the trailing human. "Sir, not you too?"

The man looked neither frustrated nor angry, nor concerned. The glint in his eyes and half smile suggested amusement.

Keeping out of arm's reach, Glenn trailed the human, Rex, into the dark alley.

# CHAPTER 16

**When the dwarf** was thirty feet into the alley, about ten from Kirby, the half-goblin thief stood up straight. He didn't waste time or words. "Benxcob, you took a leprechaun's gold coin. We're here to retrieve it." There was no slurring of words, and his croaking half-goblin voice held confident authority.

The dwarf pulled the war hammer from his belt. "I don't have what you're looking for, you squirted pile of pig shit." He laughed deeply. "Even if I did, a smart leprechaun would've sent more than the likes of you."

"Hand it over." Kirby drew his cutlass and pulled a dart from his bandoleer. "It ain't worth dying for, dude."

Glenn unslung his round shield and pulled his club. He'd been in only one fight since advancing to a second-rank healer. His was the only class he knew of that got a d12 roll for hit points. With twenty-seven hit points, he could hang in a fight a lot longer than before. But, even at second-rank, his "to hit" chart still sucked, meaning he couldn't hit opponents worth a crap.

Glenn didn't lift his shield to the ready position and held his cudgel so that it drooped toward the ground. "I don't want to hurt you," he told the big human warrior.

Rex turned his head as if just noticing Glenn. "Don't worry," he said. "If it comes to fighting, you won't."

The words didn't sound like bluster to Glenn. He gulped and gripped his cudgel a little tighter. Outmatched or not, he wouldn't let the man get to his friend. The dwarf and his hammer would be plenty enough for Kirby to handle.

"Dying?" Again, Benxcob laughed. "You should've thought on that before offering me insult."

"Relinquish the gold coin."

Glenn recognized the voice. He would've heard Ron coming into the alley, but for his racing heartbeat filling his ears.

Ron strode past Glenn, seeming to ignore Rex. Derek entered the alley and stopped two strides from Rex, opposite Glenn.

Benxcob turned and maneuvered to place his back to a shed's wooden planks. It only required a few steps since the alley was less than ten feet wide.

"I find it improbable that you remain unaware of the rainbow terminating in the stand of yew trees between Three Hills City and the Snake Claw River two days past." Ron stopped and rested the butt of his spear on the ground. "That should serve to inform you that Bataí Fidil na Maidine has tracked you here, to Three Hills City."

While Ron spoke, Rex reached into a hip pocket and produced a metallic case shaped like a pocket watch. As Ron finished, Rex flicked his thumb and the metal device snapped open. Light, equivalent to a forty-watt bulb, emanated from it.

Rex dropped the enchanted case to the ground at his feet. He sighed while reaching for his mace and dagger.

"Hey, look up here everyone!" It was Stephi, fluttering down from the moonlight. She stopped five feet above Kirby's head.

Knowing what was coming, Glenn raised his shield.

Even from behind his shield, a flash of scintillating light shone through his closed eyelids.

"Damn all fairies," Rex cursed, raising his dagger hand to block the spell's effect a fraction of a second too late.

Much as he hated to do it—both his true self and his gnomish instincts—Glenn charged the human warrior. The plan drilled into him by Kirby and Derek: If the dwarf refuses, we strike first. Stephi will Dazzle Spell him, and anyone with him. When they're blinded, attack.

Somehow Derek missed Rex with his +1 +2 vs. ogres magical longsword. Glenn however, got in a good strike at the warrior's back, going for the leg where he didn't have chain armor. It was a solid hit, at least five points of damage, maybe six. The blow didn't faze his target.

Sneering, Derek grunted and faked a charge. He pivoted at the last second, bringing his sword down, this time connecting with the opposing warrior's forearm. He drew blood, but such a hack should've cut to the bone. Glenn whiffed his second attack as the man shuffled out of the way.

Rex had apparently recovered from Stephi's spell because his crushing mace swing was on target. Derek barely managed to interpose his shield. Rex's dagger thrust, however, struck home, biting into Derek's shoulder.

Glenn charged in again, realizing they were in a fight for their lives, a fight they were likely to lose. This guy took solid hits and kept coming. Rex was more than a first or second rank warrior.

The fight between Glenn and Derek, and Rex was quiet, except for shuffling of feet across the muddy ground, grunts, and weapons striking shields, flesh, or armor. On the other hand, the fight with Kirby, Ron, and Stephi against the dwarf had all that, plus Petie diving in, jeer calling, and fluttering away, while the dwarf shouted foul curses. Kirby taunted with phrases like: "Your mom's so ugly she lost a beauty contest to a medusa."

For their part Stephi and Ron went at the dwarf in determined silence. Maybe they were worried about the City Guard hearing the commotion almost as much as Glenn was.

Benxcob kept his back close to the wall, not allowing anyone to get behind him. Ron slashed and jabbed with his spear while Kirby threw darts and made fast cuts with his cutlass.

Stephi dove in but got clocked with a hammer blow before her small rapier could find Benxcob's blood. The solid hit sent her tumbling to the ground. Since she wasn't screaming in pain, the hammer's steel hadn't touched her skin.

Rex was pretty nimble on his feet as he exchanged blows with Derek. Despite breast plate, helmet and shield, Derek suffered crushing blows from Rex's mace. Glenn drove in again, and scored a glancing blow with his cudgel. Rather than back away, he chased after Rex as the hawk-nosed warrior dodged Derek's sword thrust.

Out of the corner of his eye Glenn spotted a pink flash. Stephi had loosed a Mystic Missile Spell. Petie continued sounding off but Kirby was silent.

Glenn couldn't worry about that. He drove his shield between Rex's legs, trying to trip him up, to no avail.

*Clank.* Rex's mace caught Derek with a glancing blow across the helmet. The toughest fighter in Glenn's party staggered back and collapsed against one of the shop's walls.

Another pink flash announced Stephi releasing her second, and last, Mystic Missile Spell. Kirby was down, but Ron was still up. However, it was now Benxcob who advanced. The dwarf chuckled with confidence.

Glenn had to hope his two friends could finish the job. He'd do what he could to keep Rex off them…for as long as he could.

Rex turned on Glenn and kicked out, sending the gnome sprawling backwards. Glenn kept his balance but, instead of following up on his attack, the warrior stepped back and gestured with his mace toward the other fight. "I'm done with this fight, little guy. Go help your friends."

Glenn risked turning his head. Ron was against the wall, his right arm hanging limp, and trying to fight with his sword left-handed. The gnome glanced back up at the hawk-nosed warrior, afraid he'd finish off Derek if given the chance. But his friends were losing. How much would his cudgel change that?

Then Stephi's spell went off. Glenn wasn't prepared. He could only see spots, a kaleidoscope of flashing colors and nothing else.

For a second he cringed behind his shield. Then he thought of something better. Remembering where Derek lay in relation to where he stood, Glenn blindly shuffled that direction. When his boots found the big warrior's prone body, he knelt and hastily muttered the words for a Minor Heal Draw Spell, taking all of Derek's wounds upon himself.

Benxcob growled, "Where are you at, you dark bastard." The dwarf had fallen victim to Stephi's spell. "Try that again, you fairy bitch."

Within seconds, Glenn's head ached. A fractured forearm, broken ribs and a stab wound to his shoulder appeared. He would've gasped at the sudden influx of pain but, with broken ribs, it might've proven too much for him to remain conscious. And he needed to.

Glenn's sight was returning when Derek stirred. The big warrior sat up.

"Rex is done fighting us," Glenn said to Derek. "Go help Lysine and Marigold."

Ron had taken advantage of the second Dazzle Spell's effect and healed himself using his Minor Cure Spells. He'd stood ready, spear in hand to go another round with the dwarf. Stephi hovered near the ground, between Kirby and the dwarf. She held her small rapier at a guard position.

Even before Glenn released the spell energy to begin healing himself, Derek was on his feet, sword and shield in hand. He spent a half second assessing Rex's intentions before charging to aid Ron and Stephi.

Benxcob recognized the true threat and turned to

face Derek. "Rex, you—"

The dwarf didn't have time to finish his statement as he and the freshly healed warrior clashed. As always, Derek went all out and exchanged blows, giving as good as he got. Ron joined him, as did Stephi and Petie, mainly harassing and distracting the dwarf.

Within moments the dwarf suffered a whack from Ron's spear shaft to the back of his head. Finally, hit points depleted, Benxcob collapsed beard first into the damp dirt. Except for huffing from Ron and Derek as they caught their breath, the alley fell silent.

Glenn got to his feet. He watched Rex warily.

The warrior had sheathed his dagger. He nodded to Glenn and slipped his mace's shaft through the loop on his belt.

"So, you're a healer," Rex said. He picked up his light case and snapped it closed.

Glenn wasn't the only one in the shadowy moonlit alley watching to see what the hawk-nosed warrior would do next. Ron, Stephi and Derek hadn't put their weapons away.

Rex tipped his head toward the party members standing over the downed dwarf, signaling for Glenn to accompany him.

"He lost his special coin in a poker game tonight," Rex said, walking up to Benxcob's prone body. "A rigged one." He stared down.

"Jax," Ron said. "Heal Gurk."

Glenn had already been moving that direction. He'd seen his friend's chest rise and fall, but that didn't mean he might not slip into death at any moment.

Ron turned to Rex. "Not to insult your honesty, but we intend to search Benxcob's person for the gold coin we seek."

Rex shrugged, then held out his hand. "Your spear."

Glenn knelt next to Kirby while warily watching the

group surrounding the downed dwarf.

With an eyebrow arched in curiosity, Ron leaned his spear's shaft toward the warrior.

Glenn gulped, thinking that was pretty stupid. Stephi's wide eyes and quick-fluttering wings said she agreed. Derek, on the other hand, watched with interest.

Rex took the spear, deftly spun the weapon so that its tip pointed down, toward the dwarf. Without hesitation, or apparent concern, he drove the spear's tip into Benxcob's back.

Stephi's hands went to her mouth as she gasped. She fluttered higher into the night air.

"That was harsh," Derek commented, "for someone you travelled with."

Rex crouched down and retrieved the dwarf's hammer. "We planned to leave the city tomorrow. After his big haul at the Bugle." He twisted the shaft before yanking the spearhead from the body. He casually wiped the blood off on the dwarf's pant leg. "With a leprechaun on the hunt." He took a half second to glare up at Stephi. "I thought on how that might've turned out for me."

"And you get the hammer because?" Derek asked.

Glenn hurriedly mumbled the words to his spell and rested a hand on Kirby's unconscious forehead. He hadn't exceeded his total hit points he was able to cure—one for one transferred to his body, and two to one for curing injuries he directly received. But, from the look of Kirby's wounds, he wouldn't be able to fully heal himself. Not after bringing Derek up to full strength. Glenn knew it was better to have Kirby up and ready than to have himself at full hit points.

"Because none of you can stop me," he said, looking around, daring any one of them to argue the point. "And he owes me good coin. Plenty of it."

Derek bristled but knew the score.

Glenn thought about the tactic his party used against

the Crow Lord. But, with Stephi being so small and all of them showing some injuries and, at the moment, none of them were on the same page…

"We could Crow Lord him," Derek said, his voice low and threatening.

Well, Glenn thought. Derek's thinking along the same lines. That made Glenn reconsider the plan's merit.

Ron shook his head. "The hammer is not our objective."

Rex quirked an eyebrow. "You had a run in with that cocky bastard, Mekkart? Fancies himself the Crow Lord?"

"What of it?" Derek asked, sheathing his long sword.

"We defeated him in one confrontation," Ron said. "And cooperated with him on another."

"Huh," Rex said, then gestured to the body of the dead dwarf. "He's got no gems or coins left to speak of. But he's got an enchanted tooth in the back that allowed him to eat anything that wasn't rocks, metal or…crystal." Rex shrugged. "Or that's what he said. Can't say I saw him eat dirt or tree bark or anything."

"I'm on it," Kirby said, getting to his feet, mostly recovered from his wounds. He pulled a pair of small pliers from a boxed tool kit. Glenn remembered them as his thieves' tools.

"I'll search him for anything else." Kirby made eye contact with Glenn. "Wanna help?"

Glenn nodded and helped Kirby roll the dead dwarf over. Flipping over a corpse and checking it for valuables was something Glenn would've never done in his real life. But the gnome adventurer had little problem with it. He figured the goblin part of Kirby had even fewer qualms.

"Best hurry," Rex said, turning to depart. "Saw the guards chasing a lady thief that crippled a carriage's horse and tried to rob the riders. Soon enough some snitchy citizen'll point them this way."

"If Benxcob no longer has possession of Bataí Fidil na Maidine's gold coin," Ron said as the warrior walked past, "might you share who currently has possession?"

"Some smooth-talking guy. Wears a hat with funny glass eye-pieces."

Ron asked, "Might he have been named Higslaff, owner of a pawnshop?"

# CHAPTER 17

"That Josie took her sweet time telling us the dwarf didn't have the leprechaun's coin," Kirby complained in a harsh whisper. While they'd been hiding the dwarf's corpse in the alley so it wouldn't be immediately found, the cute female thief working for Josiah found the party and warned them. About twenty minutes too late.

Ron and Derek were in the hall outside the party's Glade House room. One waited while the other used the chamber pot in what could be called, in the broadest sense, the bathroom. Stephi was on the Glade House's roof, Camouflage Spell up and watching for any possible trouble coming their way, unlikely as that might be. Ron believed an additional ninety minutes of vigilance would suffice.

Glenn, sitting in their rented room with Kirby, frowned before replying. "She had the City Guard patrol chasing her." He didn't have to explain how bad things would've gone if the guards showed up in the middle of the alley fight. His friend was frustrated and annoyed, and just venting.

Glenn's shoulder ached where some of Kirby's transferred wounds hadn't been fully healed. Instead of sleeping on Stephi's bunk, he decided to sleep in his normal spot under the bunk. Nowhere near comfortable as his dorm room's bed, or his one at home. Not even close.

**Derek was at** Josiah's barber shop. He was there to find out what he could about last night's events, and get the magical tooth implanted.

After Kirby pulled Benxcob's enchanted smoky-white crystal molar, it returned to an incisor shape.

Derek volunteered to chance the magical implant without having it identified, especially since the party really didn't have much spare gold. Plus, Derek already had a missing tooth and, compared to everyone in the party, he ate the most.

Ron suggested that Josiah might assist emplacing the tooth, and also might possess a method to match it to the enamel of Derek's teeth.

Glenn, Kirby, and Ron sat on the porch to Higslaff's pawnshop. Stephi reclined inside the creel basked carried by Kirby. Petie kept watch from atop a roof across the street. They intended to be the first "customers" in the shop as it opened, and eliminate any chance someone might purchase the leprechaun's gold coin—if the pawnshop owner intended to sell it.

Glenn had suggested they go to the barber shop a couple hours before sunrise and try to get Josiah out of bed, and find out where Higslaff lived. Both Kirby and Ron nixed that idea. So now they waited. It was almost as bad as sitting in the Blue Bugle, waiting for Benxcob to arrive and Josie to point him out.

Stephi warned everyone before leaving that the pawnshop owner was a selfish jerk and wouldn't give them the coin. He'd want something outrageous for it.

What choice did they have, except to find out? Deep down, Glenn thought it'd be sort of funny if Kirby had to pull out Derek's new tooth, if they needed it for a trade.

The three got plenty of stares from merchants and workers moving down the street. Kirby munched on an apple and Ron kept busy scribing something into one of his small, leather-bound journals. Normally he jotted maps, directions, significant historical or current people, and bits of odd information that might be useful in the future. Glenn sometimes listened to him recite pages to Derek, since the warrior couldn't read.

That was almost as boring as reading the listed facts.

But Glenn took the time to review new notes every few days. Better to be informed and safe than ignorant and sorry.

Bonnar, a stout dwarf warrior, was the first pawnshop employee to approach. His job was internal security, and he sat upon a short stool all day. He had piercing blue eyes and a thick brown beard that did little to mask a perpetual frown. The war hammer he carried sort of looked like Benxcob's.

Glenn didn't know much about weapons. Closer inspection as the dwarf climbed the porch steps showed the etching on the shaft and leather grip were different from Benxcob's. Bonnar's chainmail armor appeared in pristine condition despite having endured a Fireblast Spell, a spell which slew its wearer.

Ron was already standing, with Glenn and Kirby scrambling to get to their feet.

"Bonnar, sir," Ron said.

The dwarf slowed. Something he appeared unaccustomed to doing, but the party had helped kill an assassination party attacking the pawnshop.

"Yah," the dwarf warrior said.

"If perchance, Higslaff is already within his shop, would you mention our desire to meet with him at his earliest convenience?"

Bonnar eyed the gnome, half-goblin and quarter-elf and nodded once. "Yah." Then he turned, produced a key from a pocket and opened the door. Before closing it, he carried out a chair and placed it next to the door.

Glenn knew two things. First, the door had a slot for a wooden bar to secure the door from the inside. Second, the chair was for the outside guard, Thogg, a broad-shouldered half-ogre brute.

Even before the three sat back down, Kirby said, "There's the porch guard."

Thogg approached using lumbering strides that

somehow suggested latent nimbleness. He carried his large battle axe resting across his shoulder. The half-ogre's angular face was anything but handsome and his thick leather armor was a size or two too small, making his muscles appear even larger. His long strides made up for the less than determined pace. His seven-and-a-half foot height encouraged others to step aside.

"Good morning, dude," Kirby said, quirking a half smile.

Thogg didn't use the two steps to climb atop the porch. His size made them unnecessary. He leaned his axe against the wall next to the sturdy wooden chair and plopped down. "I hate mornings." He stretched out his legs and shot Kirby a tusky-toothed grin.

Kirby said, "All I got to say about that, dude, is I hope the day ain't too hot."

The half-ogre guard died during the attack on the pawnshop, too. A sneak magical attack took him out. The owner had to have paid thousands and thousands of gold coins to get both him and the dwarf guard Revived.

Ron leaned out from under the porch, checked the sky, and then squinted at the intimidating guard. "I suspect today's top temperature will be nearly identical to yesterday's peak temperature. However, I would not be surprised if there is a stronger presence of cumulus cloud formations by late afternoon."

Thogg scratched his blunt nose. "Druid, huh?" In addition to security, he was sort of a screener, allowing only those who had legitimate business into the pawnshop.

Ron tipped his head in acknowledgment. "So I have been trained."

"Druids are good," Thogg said. Another grin creased his angular face, which didn't seem possible, or at least not common.

A long moment of silence followed.

To fill the conversational void, Kirby asked, "How long you been working for Higslaff?"

The half-ogre looked Kirby up and down. "The boss won't hire you."

Kirby laughed. To Glenn it sounded uncomfortable.

"Good thing I'm not looking for a job," Kirby said. He placed his hands on his hips and rotated his shoulders, as if trying to remove a crick from his back. "No doubt, he's a good dude to work for."

"How long until the shop opens?" Glenn asked.

"When Coleen Sammae opens door, shop opens."

Glenn refrained from rolling his eyes. Giving the big guard a reason to kick him off the porch, or worse, didn't seem like a good idea.

"We arrived quite some time ago," Ron said. "We witnessed Bonnar arrive and place your chair. At that time I requested that he let your boss know we hoped to meet with him upon his shop opening."

"You selling, pawning or buying?" He raised an eyebrow and cocked his head. "Or you looking for a job?"

Ron shook his head. "We are here to inquire about an item we believe your boss is in possession of. None of us are seeking employment."

Glenn wondered if Coleen Sammae arrived for work early, or if there was a back door, or if Higslaff slept in his office or some other room in the building.

Before he had time to consider, the shop's front door opened. Coleen Sammae leaned out. She was an enchantress, a little past middle-aged with her graying hair wrapped in a bun. She wore a long cotton dress, gray with turquoise buttons. She also wore turquoise earrings and a large turquoise pendant on a woven silver chain. The last time they'd seen her she'd worn a white silk blouse and black leather trousers stuffed into calf-high boots, along with gold and rubies.

She handed Thogg a wooden mug and a wedge of pale orange cheese, and said to him, "We're open."

Glenn smelled the scent of lemon tea in the cup. The cheese was a mild sort, if he accurately interpreted the odor.

The enchantress observed the party. "Higslaff will see you."

Kirby picked up the basket containing Stephi before following Ron and Glenn into the shop.

Glenn's nose detected a hint of something burnt, an aftereffect of the Fireblast attack two weeks past. The shelves appeared identical to those previously in the shop. They were probably the same ones, but much of the merchandise on those shelves was different. Behind the back counter, however, the fancy-inscribed trident still hung on the wall.

On the stool in the corner, where Bonnar normally sat, a boy with hair the color of damp straw sat, erect and alert. It was Vernie, the shop owner's nephew. Normally he cleaned and ran errands. At the moment he clutched a sheathed dagger and his brown eyes appeared eager to pull it. Eager to show he knew how to use it.

Good for him, Glenn thought, until he runs up against someone higher than first rank.

Coleen Sammae led them to the oak display counter along the back of the shop. She lifted a hinged portion near the middle. Then she gripped a section of the shelf that was mounted on the front of a concealed door, and pushed it open.

"You know the way to the stairs to the boss's office," she said to Ron. "I'll follow you up." As the party members passed her, she turned and said to Vernie, "Watch sharp. I shall return in a moment. Two at most."

Ron led Glenn and Kirby through the storage room to the stairs that took them up to Higslaff's office. Glenn observed that the storage room's shelves were nearly empty. It made sense since the fire attack destroyed many of the items displayed in the main room. The attack was an opening move in a thieves' guild conflict. Kirby called it a low-grade guild war.

Higslaff's office was on the second floor. It held a sturdy, utilitarian desk which didn't resemble anything like the polished oak counters and shelves in the display area on the floor below.

Higslaff sat behind his desk. He was a man approaching the far end of middle age. He wore Victorian-type leathers, and a bowler hat, complete with a set of goggles with magical jeweler's double eye loupe mounted on them. Glenn had seen steampunk cosplay outfits before, and Higslaff's wardrobe wasn't too far off. The shop owner was closer to stocky than thin, and about as tall as Ron. Not only did he appear confident and able to handle himself, he had no qualms about taking a sword into a fight. At the moment, he only wore a dagger on his hip.

The loupe on the goggles enabled the shop owner to detect enchantments, as well as accurately estimate the quality and value of gemstones.

Behind the desk stood a narrow window too small for even the most anorexic of goblin thieves to squeeze through. Shelves with scrolls, books, unused quills and small urns containing ink filled the wall around the single window. As with all of the pawnshop's rooms, magical light provided illumination.

To the left of the owner's desk, as he faced the stairs, along the adjacent wall stood a long work table. Next to that table, on a padded stool, sat Bonnar. His war hammer rested on the table, within easy reach.

Bonnar was present for a bit of steel and muscle, and intimidation. That was pretty obvious to Glenn.

Three stools sat arranged in front of the desk. Ron took the center stool, while Kirby climbed on to the left.

Ron placed a foot on one of the right-hand stool's crossbars, enabling Glenn to climb onto it.

Kirby set the creel basket on the corner of the desk, to which Higslaff said nothing. Instead he gave the three men a casual smile. "It is my understanding that you wanted to meet with me."

Ron leaned forward an inch or two. "That is correct. It is our understanding that you came into possession of a certain gold coin during a poker engagement last night at the Blue Bugle."

Higslaff leaned back in his chair. "In the course of my success at the table, I did come into possession of a gold coin with latent enchantments that have yet to be determined."

Ron reached into a pocket, which caused Bonnar to tense. Glenn wasn't happy about being closest to the dwarven security guard. He was glad he'd healed himself up and Ron had used one of his Minor Cure Spells on Kirby.

"Might it resemble this coin?" Ron placed the copper coin provided by Bata Fidil on the desk.

Higslaff leaned forward and picked up the coin. He examined it. "Looks identical, except for the type of metal." Placed the coin back on the desk and slid it across the desk so that it stopped in front of Ron. "How'd you learn I had this coin?"

Ron picked up the coin and placed it back into his pocket. "An associate of the former owner indicated you won it while engaged in a poker game."

"What did the obnoxious dwarf have to say?"

"He indicated he no longer had possession of the coin we sought."

Higslaff quirked a thick eyebrow. "Were those his last words?"

"I do not believe so," Ron said. "Why do you ask?"

Kirby cut in, saying, "Cuss words. After I informed

him his mom was so ugly she lost a beauty contest to a medusa."

Ron glared at Kirby. The thief rolled his eyes. "Dude, it's not like he doesn't know."

"Might you relinquish the gold coin to us?" Ron asked.

Glenn hadn't ever played *Monsters, Maces and Magic*, but he knew the answer to that. Under similar circumstances, a pawnshop owner would laugh in the face of anyone who asked that. Glenn even told Ron that, but the druid warrior said that it wouldn't hurt to ask first.

"I am hard pressed to understand why I should," Higslaff said. "I won it at great risk of losing much of value."

"Dude," Kirby said, scoffing. "You won it by cheating."

The pawnshop owner cocked his head back in disbelief. "Why would you say that?"

Kirby pointed to Higslaff. "You got your sources." Then he pointed to himself. "I got mine."

Glenn held a straight face, wondering if Kirby's bluff would work on the accomplished poker player. Or maybe he wasn't so accomplished without things weighted in his direction.

After a few long seconds Higslaff tipped his head in equivocation. "Let's just say that the coin's previous owner was cheating simply by virtue of carrying the subtly enchanted item. He lost that advantage when he threw it in the pot after I raised." Higslaff raised his eyebrows and lifted his hands palms up, effecting a look of exasperated innocence. "What could be done but to turn the tables on him, so to speak, to balance things out?"

"Could be done?" Glenn asked. Like Kirby, the gnome healer didn't feel very diplomatic. "How about letting us know so we didn't almost get killed." Glenn made an educated guess. "Josiah convinced you to invite Benxcob into the poker game, and you knew why."

"It was Josiah's operation, not mine," Higslaff said, a hint of annoyance rising in his voice. "If there were problems with contingencies, take it up with him."

Ron interjected in a steady, quiet voice, "It is imperative we that we gain possession of that coin."

"Why is it imperative?" Higslaff asked.

Kirby stood, throwing his hand up in the air. "Dude, we saved your sorry ass hardly two weeks ago."

Bonnar reached for his weapon. A small shake of the pawnshop owner's head called the dwarf off.

"That you did, but it wasn't exactly, shall we say, an altruistic measure." He nodded toward Glenn. "Jax here, and the warrior, Kalgore? They became involved because they believed the rest of their party was in danger."

Higslaff noticed the basket on his desk jiggle just a bit.

"But we didn't have to help you fight in the street!" Kirby barely kept his voice restrained. "We did anyway!"

Ron put a hand on the half-goblin thief's shoulder, keeping him seated on the stool.

The pawnshop owner clasped his hands together. "That is why I am meeting with you, here and now, without an appointment."

Kirby rolled his eyes. "Save your shop and your ass, and that gets a meeting without calling ahead for an appointment?"

Higslaff looked at Kirby, a little confused. "Again, I ask, why do you want the coin?"

Stephi, apparently tired of laying curled up in the basket, remaining quiet, lifted the lid and stood. "Because," she said, "the leprechaun who did this to me wants his coin back before he'll turn me back."

Maybe Josiah had told Higslaff, because Stephi

popping up, like some sort of fairy-in-the-basket magic trick, didn't throw him off, much. That didn't mean her 19.5 Appearance Score and scaled-down epic chest didn't have an impact.

Her appearance, however, very much surprised Bonnar, as evidenced by his unfinished question, "Wha…?"

All Glenn could think was: That won't benefit the dwarf guard during his next employee evaluation.

"What do ya want for the coin?" Kirby asked, clearly frustrated. "You already know we ain't got a lot of coin to buy it."

"I don't suppose you have the dwarf's hammer?" Hisglaff asked.

"That, we do not possess," Ron said.

"We got his enchanted tooth," Kirby said, working to keep his temper. He might be pissed off more at Rex than at Higslaff. "Ya want that?"

Sensing there might be trouble, Bonnar was on his feet, hammer in hand.

Glenn shifted in his stool and unslung his shield. He figured pulling his cudgel would escalate things toward a fight. But pulling a shield might do enough to let the warrior dwarf know Glenn and his party meant business. Even so, he didn't have the size or intimidating sneer Derek did. It was unlikely any gnomes in the game world ever possessed the likes of that.

Higslaff gestured a hand for Bonnar to stay where he was. Then he leaned back in his chair, adjusted his hat, and proffered a sincere smile. "Let's all take a brief moment to relax."

"Agreed," Ron said. Surprisingly, to urge compliance, the warrior druid was forced to stare down Stephi and her fluttering wings longer than he did Kirby.

When everyone managed to slow their breathing, and maybe their heart rate, Higslaff said, "I have a proposal."

He leaned forward, resting his forearms against the edge of his desk. "One where I'll extract a measure of revenge, and you, my friends, will gain a measure of payback in the process." He rubbed his hands together like what he was about to say excited him. "And you will earn possession of the leprechaun's enchanted coin."

Anything but mollified, Kirby remarked, "Ain't none of us your friend."

Even if true, Glenn didn't have to make a Diplomacy Roll to realize Kirby's words did more to alienate than to endear.

Ron added, "Your machinations have steered us from the amiable path to true friendship, toward a more adversarial business relationship."

"Understood," Higslaff said, unconcerned. After that, he revealed his proposal.

Negotiations began.

# CHAPTER 18

**With the enchanted** tooth filling the gap, Derek looked less like a thug. Even so, somehow it didn't measurably improve his Appearance Score.

Glenn wondered if makeup, or lack of makeup, would affect one of the game's basic stats. Or if taking steroids might affect a Strength Score.

He figured to ask later. At the moment they were waiting for Kirby to pay Patti for their biscuits and honey, and tea. The Red Brick was mainly a carryout business for merchants and laborers, and the main morning rush was over. Normally, they would've just remained and discussed the issue around one of the two standing tables for customers. But a fairy might unnerve Patti. It would definitely attract unwanted attention from any customers or passersby that might lay eyes on Stephi.

They could've gone back to the Glade House to discuss the pawnshop owner's proposal, except that Stephi increasingly felt antsy, or agitated. She needed nature. Plants and sunshine rather than an urban setting, surrounded by stone, bricks, dead wood, and the constant threat of iron. Ron stated it was a deep need related to her inherent fairy, or fae, nature.

Who was to argue? So the party wolfed down their biscuits and tea before heading out to Glenn and Kirby's fishing spot near the willow tree. Near Kim's grave.

**Once outside the** wall Glenn asked Ron, Derek and Kirby, "What's the logic behind ranks? I get that gaining experience would make someone a better swordsman or spell caster. But more hit points?"

Derek snorted a laugh. "What brought this on,

gnome?"

"I really nailed that Rex guy. He just sloughed it off, like I hit him with a Nurf bat." Glenn threw his hands up in exasperation. "I bet that guy could take a swipe from a grizzly bear and laugh. Heck, he could lay on a Florida beach for hours without sunblock and not even get sunburned."

"Dude," Kirby said, "ranks and hit points are the only way the game can allow humans, like Derek with a sword, to eventually stand toe to toe with ogres, and maybe dragons."

Derek interjected, "Hey, who says I can't take out an ogre."

Keeping pace, Kirby squinted up at the big warrior. "You're second rank. Ogres are four hit-die monsters." He held up a hand to stall Derek's objection. "You got a good Strength Score, so you get bonuses to hit and to damage. That definitely helps. Still…"

Derek reached back over his shoulder and placed a hand on his sword's grip. "What about my sword?"

"And you got a magical sword," Kirby admitted. "But it's only plus two against ogres. You and an ogre probably deal out equal damage, and with your breast plate armor, you have a better armor class. But the ogre's gonna have more hit points, and has a better 'to hit' chart."

Derek grumbled, but didn't disagree.

"To answer the other portion of your query," Ron said to Glenn, "I believe, under the Florida sun scenario, such a warrior would suffer the effects of sunburn, despite having a large reservoir of hit points."

They were off the road and crossing the meadow grass. Stephi was no longer in her basket. Instead she rode on Derek's shoulder. There were still scattered people on the road, and might see her. Maybe mistake her for a giant butterfly, maybe not. Sitting on a shoulder until they were nearer the river would be less conspicuous than flying around. Her Camouflage ability helped disguise her, especially from anyone at a distance.

Stephi kept stretching her arms out, soaking up the sun. She was definitely tired of riding around in a basket.

"But not the bear?" Glenn shuffled faster to keep up. "I mean I get bears, ogres and dragons having more hit points, because they're bigger and they're monsters. And husk mummies because they're magical undead..."

"That's the point of the game, dude," Kirby said. "*Monsters, Maces and Magic* would get boring if all you could do is fight goblins or lizard men. Wouldn't matter how good you are attacking and defending with a sword if you came up against a dragon. One bite and you're dead, dude. Don't even think about surviving its breath-weapon damage. Be like a scarecrow against a flame thrower."

"When I get enough ranks and hit points," Derek interjected, swinging his fist as if he were wielding a sword, "I'll go toe to toe with a dragon." He shrugged, showing a lopsided smile. "At least for a few rounds."

"Takes a party effort to kill a dragon," Kirby said.

"Gnomes gotta watch out, though." Derek smirked at Glenn. "Dragons always swallow them whole, first."

Stephi smacked Derek on the top of his head. "You're making that up."

"Working at being Domestic Abuser Barbie?"

Stephi stuck out her tongue.

"You are correct, Marigold," Ron said, attempting to redirect the conversation. "Kalgore's assertion with respect to a dragon's preference for gnomes is a fabrication. It is not found in the game rules."

"I watched my brother play videogames," Stephi said. "Those games weren't anything like this world. More army soldiery stuff with tanks and explosions. But he leveled-up *a lot* faster than we are. I mean, he completed missions and collected loot and guns and bombs—."

Kirby cut in, "You mean grenades?"

"Grenades, whatever." She rolled her eyes. "After a big fight or two, he'd have enough experience to level up." She threw her hands up in the air, just like Glenn had. "I should be fifth or sixth level by now, not second."

"Video Voyeur Barbie?"

Kirby snickered at Derek's comment.

Stephi pointed at Kirby. "Don't encourage him."

"Rank, not level," Ron corrected, scanning the area around them.

The road had turned west, before angling south to the small port. They kept walking south, across the meadow grass, toward the river.

Stephi's wings fluttered. "Rank, level, whatever."

Glenn looked away from Stephi, down his at boots as he trudged through the thick grass that reached up to his knees. Her beauty, especially in the sunlight, distracted him. He said, "I get killing a monster giving experience points toward going up a rank. But gold coins looted off the bodies or from their lairs?"

"You also get experience for getting magic items too," Derek said. "Not a lot, which always sucked about this game." He looked around in the sky and across the terrain with his lip curled. "Sucks about this world."

Glenn couldn't argue. But more than gaining few experience points for finding magic was far from the only thing about the world that sucked.

"*Monsters, Maces and Magic* was designed to focus on role playing rather than rank advancement," Ron explained. "While the experience point totals listed to advance a rank appear comparable to similar tabletop role playing games, experience gained for slaying creatures is less. Each gold piece secured is worth merely half of an experience point compared to similar tabletop games. An enchanted item's contribution to experience points earned is one twenty-fifth the item's gold coin value, as listed in the Game Moderator's Guide."

Derek thumbed over his shoulder—the one Stephi wasn't sitting on—toward the hilt of his sword. "And you get none for buying or trading for a magic weapon."

"Any enchanted item," Ron corrected.

"They help you on adventures," Kirby said. "Help you survive. That's their real value."

Petie flew down, landing in the meadow grass. He came up with a small grasshopper in his beak.

"So the game focuses on role playing," Glenn said, scorn in his voice. "Which we're *literally* doing."

"And encourages long-term campaigns," Ron said.

"Which we're *literally* on." Glenn kicked at an especially thick tuft of grass, nearly tumbling in the process.

Kirby grabbed Glenn's arm and steadied his friend.

Instead of laughing at Glenn's near tumble, Derek smacked a fist into the palm of his other hand. "When we get back," he said, "my fists'll be doing some *long-term campaigning* on that shithole GM's face."

**They sat in** a circle under the willow tree's shade, ten yards from the river. Derek leaned his back against the tree. Ron sat to the big warrior's left and Kirby on his right. Glenn sat between Ron and Kirby, with Marigold squeezed in between Glenn and Kirby. With her natural-leaf green garb, except for her shimmering wings, Stephi nearly blended in with the grass.

Glenn had to keep himself from sneaking glimpses of her. He noticed Derek didn't bother. For some reason the big warrior wasn't affected in the same way Glenn was.

Despite Petie in the willow tree above watching for approaching danger, Glenn did his best to remain vigilant. Less than a month ago a zombie with some sort of blue-glowing Tracking Gem imbedded in its forehead stumbled across Jax, Stephi and Glenn while they were fishing.

That, and the gnome didn't want to be surprised by the leprechaun. The others didn't seem concerned. They all remained confident Bataí Fidil na Maidine wasn't in the area, and wouldn't return until he was called.

"So, we're like, going to do this, right?" Stephi asked, concern in her voice.

The pawnshop owner wanted them to travel to Riven Rock and complete a retaliatory attack on a business owned by a member of the guild currently working to expand into Three Hills City. The guild to which Higslaff, and Josiah—and Josie—were members, headed by some powerful guy that went by the name Black Venom, obviously opposed that expansion effort.

If the party did his bidding, the pawnshop owner would give them the leprechaun's gold coin as payment.

Trying to take the coin from Higslaff didn't seem feasible. And whoever he eventually sold or traded it to, if he didn't keep it himself, would probably be a good measure more difficult to take it from.

Kirby said, "Of course we are, Marigold."

"You say that like it'll be a piece of cake job," Derek said. "It's not gonna be, you know."

"I know," Kirby said with a scowl. "We all know. But his idea of us going in the town as part of a small trade caravan makes sense. Safer than us travelling alone. And wagons are a good way to get into a city without questions." He scowled again. "Well, not as many questions."

Derek's lip curled. "And we're doing him another favor by guarding the wagons and helping him turn a profit."

"He's giving us scrolls for Stephi, to cast some tough

spells," Glenn said. "They'll even be written fairy-size."

Glenn shot a quick glance at Stephi. He usually avoided bringing her small size up—like she didn't notice her tininess pretty much all the time. He noticed his short stature at least a hundred times a day.

Glenn's mention didn't pull her attention away from Derek. He was against the adventure, or at least leaning that way. The big warrior was going to be outvoted, even if Ron was against it. No way would Kirby vote against getting Stephi back to her normal self. Glenn would risk about anything for her, and for Kirby, too.

"Working on the assumption that we accept this adventure," Ron said, "we will require sufficient details with respect to the city of Riven Rock, and the business therein, and probable security the business employs."

"You can bet they'll be expecting payback," Derek warned. "Remember, their attack on the pawnshop didn't end so well for them."

"That's because of you and Jax jumping in right away," Stephi said. "You cut off that magic user's arm and fought that cleric and other warrior, remember?"

"Yeah," Kirby said, "but we'll be smarter than them."

Glenn picked a few strands of grass and twisted them together. "Higslaff didn't give us much information about the target for his payback."

Ron explained, "He will refrain from providing details until we accept the adventure."

"Right, dude," Kirby said, his hands becoming animated as he spoke. "Otherwise we might tell the target, because he's being a jerk by not giving us the coin."

"That's just wrong," Stephi said. She tried to cross her arms over her chest, then pounded her fists on the ground instead. "He should've given that stupid leprechaun's coin to us."

Derek fingered his new tooth. Josiah had painted it

to match his others, and used some sort of spell to make the paint durable and not rub off. "Remember, this world's got zero charity."

"Well," Kirby said. "There's gonna be three, maybe four wagons, and he'll have some men guarding them, along with us. We'll have him commit to a minimum number of men-at-arms." The half-goblin thief scratched behind his ear. "But those'll be *his* dudes…"

Derek was about to say something when Kirby snapped his fingers first and said, "Since Higslaff said he'd fund the venture, we'll get folks of our own." Kirby grinned like a beggar who'd just found a twenty dollar bill in his coat pocket. "And Mr. Pawnshop Dude can pay for it."

"Like who?" Stephi asked.

"Blizz," Kirby said.

Blizz was an old half-goblin animal handler that had travelled with the party twice into the Dark Heart Swamp. Him and his donkey.

Before Stephi could complain about Blizz being a creep that stared at her every chance he got, Kirby added, "Plus, we could get our own man-at-arms to go with us. One old animal handler and one lousy man-at-arms? No way he'll turn us down for that."

The half-goblin thief gestured to the two warriors in the group. "Kalgore and Lysine, you guys gotta know someone who can do that, or know how to find someone.

"Blizz can help with driving the horses pulling a wagon. That'll free us up more."

"Right." Derek grinned menacingly. He nodded once at Kirby. "Even better, it'll come out of his pockets, not ours."

"An item to consider," Ron said. He waited until everyone looked his way. "Taking on this adventure, even if we succeed, may draw us into this war between rival thieves' guilds."

Derek asked Kirby, "You know what's going on with that, thief?"

"Is it gonna be really a war?" Stephi asked.

"It's more like rival street gangs fighting over turf," Kirby explained to Stephi. "Except they're using daggers and swords and spells, instead of guns."

Kirby plucked a long piece of grass and stuck the end in the corner of his mouth. "From what I've heard, a few killings on both sides. My guess is the Riven Rock Guild has been planning this for a long time." He pulled the piece of grass from his mouth, examined the tip, and bit back onto it again. "Years, and it's just getting started."

"I say we vote about going on this adventure," Derek said, laying heavy on the sarcasm. "We already know we're going."

"Any additional discussion?" Ron asked.

Everyone shook their heads.

Ron nodded once. "Those in favor of attacking the property of the rival guild on Higslaff's behalf in order to secure Bataí Fidil na Maidine's coin, raise your hand."

All five hands went up, Glenn and Stephi's more enthusiastically than the others.

"The party shall proceed with the mission," Ron said.

"You realize," Derek said, his intense gaze focusing on Stephi and Glenn, "if we don't get killed, and get caught instead, better hope it's the city's guards that did the catching.

"That way we'll probably just get thrown in some dungeon prison for twenty years." His gaze dropped for a few seconds while he stared intently at the grass in front of him. "If we survive in there that long."

Derek refocused his gaze on Stephi. "They'll probably just lock you up in an iron bird cage, and make you perform for the warden, or whoever, like some

Caged Canary Barbie."

A menacing grin crossed his face. "Lysine and Gurk'll back me up on this." He leaned forward, locking eye contact with Glenn. "If it's thieves that catch us…they'll do some nasty things before we die. Things that'll make those old *Saw* movies look like kindergarten playtime." The grin fled Derek's face and his voice reverberated dire seriousness. "With none of us walking away."

# CHAPTER 19

**Blizz, the aging**, bandy-legged half-goblin looked crestfallen when the four wagons pulled out and Stephi was nowhere to be seen. He wore baggy pants and sandals and a tattered wool shirt covered by what Glenn would call a canvas poncho with a hood.

Glenn scratched his sideburns, suddenly realizing the half-goblin animal handler was dressed pretty much exactly the same way when he joined them on their first adventure into the Dark Heart Swamp. And during the second, too. Each time, his clothing took a beating, like everyone else in the party. But the old half-goblin seemed to find identical garb—always worn and never new.

Come to think of it, pretty much every NPC seemed to have one outfit, or at least a single theme. Keri Lovelace, owner of the Glade House, sported some variation, depending on what she planned on doing for the day. But Pam, the potato and onion vendor, always wore a linen blouse and long skirt that showed evidence of repeated mending. Over her outfit she always wore a long, faded yellow apron whose color matched that of her crinkly bonnet. Sometimes she had a scarf instead of the bonnet.

Glenn frowned. Even he pretty much wore the same leather jerkin and boots, day after day. Sure, Derek had upgraded his chainmail armor to include breast plate and, before she got fairyed, Stephi switched out colors for her hooded cloaks and blouses, the latter tending to get destroyed during adventures. But still, there remained a consistent pattern. Even at the moment, her leaf-based fairy outfit looked exactly the same from day to day.

Just another of the RPG world's quirks.

The gnome healer snapped his thoughts back to the present. Back to Blizz the henchman, or hireling.

Blizz sat slouched forward on the wagon bench. He looked like someone who'd just discovered he'd read the numbers on his lottery ticket wrong, and he hadn't won a mound of cash. He held the reins to the pair of sturdy horses. The horse team was tasked to pull a wagon filled with clay pots of honey. Those rested atop a load of eight-foot long, one by twelve inch boards. Ron said the wood was red oak.

The old animal handler's donkey, Bristle, trailed behind the wagon, tied to it with a length of rope. No way would Blizz leave the small beast of burden behind in the care of someone else.

The wagon Ron drove was half filled with wooden crates containing candles packed in straw. Those too sat atop red oak lumber. The remaining space held food and gear for the party and the drivers of the other two wagons, and the five men-at-arms, plus their captain. The captain was really a guard captain of a small squad of mercenaries. He was probably a second-rank warrior. No higher than third, and not a City Guard Captain. That job held notably more prestige.

In addition to the regular five party members and Blizz, Derek had recruited a man-at-arms as well. His name was Mardin. He had dark skin like Ron, wide-set eyes and a laugh that was more goofy than warrior-like. He wore chainmail for armor and had a helmet, like the other men-at-arms and the guard captain. While they all had longswords and bows, Mardin, who looked to be pushing forty, had a saber and crossbow. They all, along with Derek, rode horses. Mardin's mount was a long-eared mule, gray with patches of black and named Spots. The lack of a creative name pretty much matched Mardin's personality.

Although nobody in the *Monsters, Maces and Magic* world understood the name of Derek's mount, Glenn and Kirby thought it was funny. Because Derek said this mount had about as much spunk as his grandma's underpowered and worn-out Ford Taurus, he named the horse Four Banger.

The other two wagons were loaded down with red oak lumber. The lead wagon also carried a dozen sacks of wool, while the second wagon in the procession hauled sacks filled with onions, in addition to the lumber.

All Higslaff's men, or hires, had been told that a fae would be joining them on the trip. Other than an initial questioning look and a sarcastic comment or two, they didn't seem to care. Nobody in the party told Blizz anything, as far as Glenn knew. It was probably the same with Mardin.

The wagons pulled away from Three Hills City's main gate. Ron's wagon was the third in line and Blizz's last. Within minutes the half-goblin driver spied Petie circling above the wagons. The animal handler looked around before scratching his head, and sighing. Glenn wasn't sure what to say. Stephi was hidden, resting in the creel basket that Keri gifted to Kirby.

To Glenn it seemed like a pretty small caravan of covered wagons to be heading into the Border Lands. It was said to be a lawless region that acted as a buffer between the Morrin Confederacy and the Agrippa Empire, centuries-old enemies. Three Hills City, located within Vandike, one of the lesser kingdoms comprising Morrin Confederacy, was about seventy miles north of the Riven Rock. Once they crossed the Snake Claw River they'd be in the Border Lands for about fifty miles. Then an additional twenty miles, or roughly a good day's travel, past some unmarked border to reach Riven Rock. Twenty to thirty miles a day, depending on the weather and if the roads remained good. The roads were hard-packed dirt created by decades of compaction by wagon wheels. There were supposed to be bridges maintained over streams, with no major rivers beyond the Snake Claw.

Crossing the wide Snake Claw River a quarter mile beyond the minor port required a flatbed barge. It hauled one wagon and team of horses across at a time. A team of eight oxen pulled the barge across, guided by thick ropes strung across the river. It took the handlers and several men to keep the horses under control during the crossing.

Supposedly, over the centuries, a bridge hadn't been constructed as a security measure. The river served as a barrier to slow any potential invasion from the Agrippa Empire. A bridge would prove an enticing target to capture and hold as part of any invasion.

The ferry service provided job security for the barge laborers and a profit for the owner. Glenn wondered how the contract for the crossing station was obtained, because there was only one, with no apparent competition. Heredity? Favor from the duke? Bribes? Bidding? Or just being the meanest and most ruthless? Probably a combination of five methods. In any case, coins were exchanged, this time supplied by the pawnshop owner and paid through Nickson, the guard captain.

While riding the creaky wooden barge across the river Glenn sat on the wagon's bench. Ron, Kirby and Blizz focused on keeping the team of horses calm. Glenn spent the time stressing out over not having selected Swimming as a skill. The river's current fought against the securing ropes, making the ride across anything but smooth. It was almost as bad as the time he'd spent in a canoe. At least then he had a paddle and *some* control.

Glenn watched as the far shore drew near. He didn't envy Stephi having to keep out of sight. Still, she had

Petie's eyes to see through. And she'd be out of the city's urban surroundings. That'd certainly make her feel better.

**Somehow Glenn managed** to forget how uncomfortable sitting on a wagon's bench seat could be. Despite a folded blanket, the rocking and bumps inflicted by the road through a vehicle lacking any sort of springs, or any serious attempt at shock absorbers, made his backside sore and his arms weary from steadying himself. Having longer legs, where his booted feet could reach more than air without stretching? That would've helped a lot. The good thing was, if he retained his spell strength, he could use it on himself just *before* sunrise. It'd fix up any minor bruises and soreness.

The gnome healer sighed. The forthcoming opportunity to heal would prove little comfort as he struggled to sleep, bruised and sore, during the night. He'd wait until just before sunrise because, just after it, his spell strength replenished. The RPG world held so many unexpected dangers. No way he'd waste a spell for minor comfort when it could cost a party member their life.

Glenn continued to think it odd. Not only the game world's appointed time for spells to become available for memorization. Even more, wouldn't it make more sense for White to be at noon, or something? Gray at sunset, and Black at midnight? Instead the game's rule books established Gray and White reset at sunrise. Black at sunset.

The gnome shrugged to himself. The game's rules were unbreakable, like his world's laws of physics, such as gravity. And that meant dealing with the effects of the ride while trying to get a good night's sleep. More proof that the *Monsters, Maces and Magic* world wasn't created with creature comforts in mind.

The day's travel proved slow and plodding. Glenn guessed about three, maybe four miles per hour. Someone walking briskly—well, a human like Derek—would've kept up. Still, those wagons were heavy and the horses struggled up the occasional long incline that climbed maybe five feet every hundred yards travelled. And the drivers had to keep the wagons from picking up too much speed during similarly angled declines.

The land was dry with patchy grass and thorny stands of shrubs making up ninety percent of the foliage. Mardin managed to nail a large rabbit with his crossbow. Two of Nickson's men-at-arms shot and killed a small boar with their bows while scouting ahead.

The flat terrain and sparse vegetation made the likelihood of a large band of brigands, or bandits, or whatever they were called, sneaking up on the small caravan or laying an effective ambush less likely. The men Higslaff hired appeared to be competent. Add to that the party, with Derek, Kirby, and Ron, plus Petie's elevated eyes, and Glenn felt relatively safe. Who knew? Maybe there was some sort of giant worms like in the *Dune* books or the *Tremors* movies. Little good his cudgel would be, and a gnome would be a bite-sized snack. Healing up inside a big worm's stomach would be a losing proposition. Besides the digestive juices, Glenn figured he'd suffocate. Or, as Ron would say: Perish due to asphyxiation.

Glenn couldn't figure out why he was in such a morose mood. Maybe it was because all he could do was sit and get jostled about while pondering how bad things were for him, and how much worse they might get.

Just prior to stopping for the night, Blizz spotted Stephi. The old half-goblin became the happiest person in the whole caravan. Maybe the happiest being within a hundred miles. Her fairy stature and wings didn't appear to surprise or concern the old animal handler. He just grinned and did his best to catch glimpses of her whenever he could. When she came near the other riders or drivers, they frowned and looked away. Like acknowledging her would bring bad luck down upon them. Glenn bet not one really looked closely, or her beauty would've overcome at least a few of the men's disdain.

**After the day's** travel, while Ron, Derek and Blizz tended to the horses, Kirby and Stephi left the circled caravan to fetch a little additional meat for dinner. The plan was for her to Dazzle Spell another few rabbits and for Kirby to finish them. That left Glenn to gather what he could for the fire while Mardin stood watch. Gathering dried sticks from the thorny bushes always proved a mini-adventure. Fortunately, Ron warned the gnome healer about the thumb-sized fire ants he needed to watch out for.

The plan was for Stephi to clue Blizz and Mardin in about her presence before cooking the meal. Blizz had pretty much figured that out. As the trip progressed, the captain, his men-at-arms and the other two drivers would determine Stephi was friendly to the group. Ron said the captain knew that fairies weren't the same as pixies, and had been told to expect a fairy accompanying the caravan.

Glenn didn't know why they just didn't introduce Stephi directly, but Ron believed it'd be taken more in stride if the men sort of got used to Stephi, and experienced nothing bad happening. Kirby preferred the other men staying sort of scared and uneasy. They'd be less likely to conjure up any bad ideas against her. Whatever the case, the result made things easier on Stephi, who was more than a little self-conscious.

Blizz remained more than excited to see Stephi, even a pint-sized version. After pulling a cooked rabbit leg from the fire, he grinned. "My old eyes kept telling me it was you," he said to her when she flitted down a few feet from him. "You're the prettiest thing my old eyes ever laid eyes on. All smalled down, you're even prettier." He shook his head. "Starting out, I fell to thinking something bad happened to ya, and your adventuring friends was just too sad to say."

Stephi's smile gleamed at the bandy-legged half-goblin's words. "I'm really glad you hired on with us again. Bristle is my favorite donkey in the world."

Glenn was sure Blizz would've preferred the last complement directed at him, but he showed his pointy-tooth smile and continued eating. His eyes frequently rove over to where she'd flown back to settle between Glenn and Kirby.

Mardin was more at a loss for words. Stephi's abnormal beauty pretty much stunned him. The fact that she was a fairy simply piled on. Sitting next to Derek, the man-at-arms ate his entire meal without saying a word, or even letting out one of his goofy chuckles.

The other men-at-arms, wagon drivers, and the guard captain caught sight of Stephi's fluttering wings. Glenn heard them mumble some about trickster fairies and bad luck, but the captain wasn't having any of it. He berated them for not knowing the difference between a pixie and a fairy. He ordered them to talk on something else while they ate their share of roasted hog.

In truth, Glenn didn't know the difference either, except pixies were male. Of course, he was ignorant of a lot of things in the RPG world. But he was learning.

Ron stood watch for the camp, along with Petie, during the meal. Yonn was the only man-at-arms hired by Higslaff that looked over a couple times at Stephi after the captain's orders. Yonn was a blunt-nosed man that looked like he'd run into a few too many walls as a child. Maybe continuing the habit well into adulthood.

Each time Yonn glanced Stephi's direction, he

frowned.

**Only once did** the party's caravan encounter one moving toward Three Hills City. It was larger, having eight wagons, with twice as many men-at-arms types. Rules of the Road Etiquette dictated that the smaller caravan pull off and allow the larger one to press on. Blizz explained that to Glenn. He also said, "If there's the same number of wagons that both got, those with their shadows pointing closest to the direction they're going get road rights. If'n the sky gots too many clouds or it's night, the leader of the two caravans with the biggest horse, or steed." Blizz uttered the last word with sarcasm in his voice, then took the opportunity to spit onto the dry ground. "The bigger one's group gets road rights."

Glenn squinted ahead as Blizz followed Ron's wagon pulling off the rutted trail.

Blizz continued, saying, "Except for sunlight, those other differences mightn't be right off evident."

Glenn nodded agreement.

"There's always the chance for fightin' if ya want," Blizz said. "But out in the wilds, most civilized folk don't go for that."

Derek and Nickson sat on their mounts along the opposite side of the road while the larger caravan passed. The bigger caravan's leader joined the two and engaged in a brief conversation.

Petie remained out and about while Stephi retreated to cover within the wagon. The passing wagons carried crudely formed ingots of iron and copper. Heavy loads that the teams of four oxen labored to pull.

After the party's caravan pulled back onto the road, Derek rode alongside Ron's wagon, speaking with Kirby and the warrior druid.

Then Derek slowed his horse until it plodded alongside Glenn's wagon. "Jax," he said, "and Hide-A

Lot Barbie, about noon we'll reach a small stream, close to dried up."

"Her name's Marigold," Glenn said.

"Listen up, gnome. There's a bridge at the stream. Camped out near it is a group of brigands. Ten or twelve of them. Probably won't mess with us, but we should be ready."

"Okay," Glenn said, wondering how the other caravan knew they were brigands. And why Derek figured they wouldn't bother their caravan.

Blizz stared at Glenn with one eye squinted, his gaze dropping to Glenn's hand gripping the head of his cudgel. "Don't be worried none, Jax." He leaned back and spoke over his shoulder. "Marigold, if'n you're concerned, you might want to sit up here, next to me a short spell." He patted the bench seat. "While I shares with Jax why the group of thieves ahead ain't worth frettin' over."

The animal handler seemed to look for reasons to have Marigold near him. Who wouldn't? Unless you had some prejudice against fairies. Which a lot of folks apparently did.

Rather than sit, Marigold decided to flutter next to Glenn. She might not be comfortable around Blizz. More likely, Glenn figured, in addition to wooden dowels, a fair number of iron nails and brackets held the wagon together.

"Why shouldn't we be worried about a fight?" Stephi asked. "Kalgore seems worked up about it."

Blizz said, "Aww, Kalgore's more itching to stick his sword in someone's belly than showing concern."

"When isn't he?" Stephi said, her iridescent wings shimmering in the sunlight. The horse team quickly became accustomed to her flitting presence. Maybe because she represented something in nature that normally didn't bother other creatures. The horses became accustomed far faster than Nickson and his men had. More accurately, they were still working on it.

Blizz chuckled to himself. "That's true. But if the number of road thieves counted is accurate, they'd wanna have more than twice our number, unless'n they got themselves a fancy spell caster."

Glenn knew the animal handler wanted to share more, so the gnome obliged by asking, "Why?"

"They might win and take our stuff, wagons and horses, but they'd get hurt pretty good, so it ain't worth it." His eyes angled up in thought. "See, most alley cats can kill a rat in a fight. But if the rat's big enough, or mean enough, the cat'll look somewhere else. A cat that gets bit up, it'll be weaker, even after it eats the rat. It'll have to hunt on even smaller rats then. That's, until it heals up." He flicked the reins, urging the horses to pick up a little speed so that they didn't fall behind. "If the wound is somethin' that don't end up being crippling. Or a full-on healthy alley cat don't find the weak one and kill off the competition."

The small band of mounted brigands camped on the far side of the stream, a hundred yards beyond the stone bridge, didn't prove to be a threat. As predicted, Petie and one of Nickson's scouting men spotted the brigands' scout, so there was no surprise.

All they did was watch while the party's caravan watered their horses, refilled canteens, and bucket-filled the water barrels.

What did prove a threat an hour later, and came as a surprise, was the Wandering Creatures Encounter.

A manticore.

# CHAPTER 20

**The Monster Guide** describes manticores as monsters whose bodies resembled a lion's, but twice as big. They have a human face rather than feline, with wide mouths holding double rows of razor-sharp teeth. Bat-like wings allow them to fly. In the air they're anything but graceful, being Maneuverability Class F.

By the laws of physics, they shouldn't be able to lift off the ground. Even a kindergartener could figure that out. But that notion of flight followed the physics of the real world, not the *Monsters, Maces and Magic* one. While birds like Petie could out-maneuver a manticore in the air, that didn't translate to any benefit for land-bound people, or horses. Especially since the maned, male manticores bore tails ending in a ball packed with four-inch spikes. Those spikes served as barbed projectiles. Once launched and striking a target, the spikes acted like a bee's stinger, pumping virulent venom into the victim.

It was about noon when one of the men-at-arms near the caravan's front cried out, "Manticore!"

Glenn was sitting next to Blizz when the alarm went up. Kirby was in the wagon, balled beneath a tattered blanket, sleeping. Derek trailed the caravan on Four Banger while Stephi rode in Ron's wagon, just ahead Glenn's.

Blizz pulled on the reins, stopping the horse team. He pulled the brake lever before standing on the bench. One hand shaded his eyes as they scanned the sky. Glenn didn't stand, but stopped looking left and right and began checking the sky.

Kirby stuck his head out of the wagon, accosted by a serious bout of bedhead. His anxious voice croaked,

"Someone shout manticore?"

"Yep," Blizz replied.

"Those are eight hit-dice monsters." Kirby threw his bandoleer of darts over his shoulder. "Their tails shoot venom spikes."

Two of the mounted men-at-arms rode past Glenn's wagon, their horses galloping across the hard-packed trail. Glenn recognized one as Yonn. The other was a youth barely able to grow a beard named Fitzrack.

The horse team in front of Glenn commenced stomping, their ears up and noses flaring.

The half-goblin animal handler pointed ahead, almost straight up. "This ain't no good." He hopped down off the bench seat before staring back up at Glenn. "Me and Bristle's gonna hide under this here wagon. You might think hard on joining us."

Captain Nickson shouted orders. "Dismount. Tie your horses. Grab your bows."

Stephi flew out from her wagon. She moved off to the right before ascending. Petie kept close, like an aerial wingman. Ron stood two strides off the road, spear in hand.

Derek rode up, past Glenn's wagon. He struggled to control his mount. Ron snatched and held the reins of the panicking horse, allowing the armored warrior to dismount.

On instinct Glenn ducked under his round shield as the huge creature shot past overhead. The horse team neighed and reared before dragging the wagon forward. Blizz snatched a wooden pole resting on brackets off the side of the wagon and slid it in between the rear wheel's spokes. The result was to "rough lock" them.

None of the other drivers thought to do that.

Dismounted, Mardin held the reins of Spots while gripping the bridle strap of one of Ron's horse team. Standing between a terrified mule and horse looked dangerous, but not equal to facing a manticore. The gnome healer's opinion reaffirmed upon hearing the manticore's screeching roar. It sounded like an enraged lion, one tangling with an amped-up speaker squelching ear-rending feedback.

Glenn attempted to climb off the wagon but tumbled to the ground. The team bucked and pulled the wagon, despites the brakes and pole locking the rear wheels. The trifecta of sight, smell, and the manticore's roar drove the equines frenzied with panic. Everything fell into chaos. Exactly what the black-maned, tawny furred beast intended.

Blizz stayed under the wagon. He scooted along, keeping pace with the wagon's sporadic jolts forward. The only animal seemingly under control was Bristle. Blizz held the donkey by a thin rope and calming words, when he could manage them. The sturdy donkey stumbled and shook but followed right behind the wagon.

Glenn internally groaned. Nearby grass patches, scattered tangles of thickets and small trees with spindly leaves offered little cover. Beneath the wagon with Blizz was really the only place to hide. The way the wagon jolted and skidded forward made that a risky option. He spun around, looking left and right, and gulped.

A gnome healer fighting a manticore? How many hits could it take from his cudgel? And it flew! Glenn had a sling with a few stones, but he didn't know how to use it. In game terms, he wasn't trained, or Proficient. Which meant he'd be lucky to hit the broad side of a barn. What chance did he have of hitting a flying monster—an eight hit-dice monster? And how much damage would his little stone actually do—would it even make a difference? Besides the nasty teeth and claws, what about the spikes?

Glenn tensed and gripped his cudgel. An eagerness to confront the bat-winged beast surged within him. The healer's timidity stemmed from his rational mind, who he really was. An average human facing a mythical beast with nothing more than a club. He'd have a better chance against a normal grizzly bear. The boldness was the game-world's gnome influence.

Resolve mounted.

Stephi was up there chasing after the monster. Glenn wouldn't abandon her.

The manticore wasn't terribly fast in flight. Even though it appeared to be gaining on Yonn and Fitzrack fleeing on their mounts, the big beast began to pull up—until the younger man-at-arms lost his balance and tumbled from his racing mount.

Yonn, on his mount, didn't slow. He didn't realize Fitzrack wasn't following until the riderless mount drew abreast a hundred yards later. By that time the manticore had dropped upon the stunned man and tore out his throat.

Stephi, being no fast flier herself, arrived several seconds too late to save Fitzrack. She fluttered ten yards above the manticore and shouted, "Hey, look up here, you mangy cat man!"

When the manticore raised its bloody maw Stephi released her Dazzle Spell.

The monster stared up at Stephi and snarled, "Fairy bitch." The scintillating light burst had failed to blind the monster.

Stephi fluttered in place, confused by her spell's impotence. Or the fact that the horrific beast shouted and called her a bitch.

Gurk shouted, "Marigold, his tail!"

Stephi didn't back away. She didn't comprehend the danger.

The manticore raised his tail and released a spike. It flew at her as if propelled by a $CO_2$ cartridge. Petie dove down, slammed into Stephi and knocked her aside. The spike missed her and knocked loose a few of the blue jay's tail feathers. Before the blue and white feathers floated to the ground, Stephi came to her senses. She wove and dodged in the air, doing her best to evade two more tail spikes launched at her.

Derek and Captain Nickson, along with the four men-at-arms still with the wagons, including Mardin, had drawn their bows. In Mardin's case, he'd cocked his crossbow. They stood in a line on the road, just past the panicking horses.

Ron shoved the reins to Spots and Four Banger into Glenn's hand. No way his four-foot, three-inch frame could control one panicking mount, let alone two.

Blizz darted out from beneath the wagon, took the mule's reins and tied them to one of the wagon's spars. Glenn struggled with Four Banger as the horse dragged him around.

Blizz took the reins from Glenn. "I got this one too, if'n you're wanting to fight."

Glenn nodded and scooped up his cudgel from the ground.

For some reason the horse settled a little when the half-goblin took control.

Their wagon continued skidding forward. Someone had stuck a pole between the spokes of Ron's wagon, slowing its progress, and the drivers of the other two wagons continued shouting and cursing, trying to keep their mounts from bolting. In return, the horse teams continued to snort, neigh and buck, and lurch their wagons forward. The mounts of Captain Nickson and his men had fled the road the instant their riders dismounted. They were already hundreds of yards away and showed no interest in slowing.

"Thanks," Glenn said to Blizz and trotted back around the wagon. He made it in time to see the volley of arrows and single crossbow bolt sail toward the manticore. The beast had been running along the road, chasing Stephi. At that moment it chose to leap, taking flight.

"Marigold, go left!" Gurk shouted. She responded just in time to avoid the scattered rain of arrows. It'd been a hundred shot. Someone must've rolled a twenty because one arrow bit into the manticore's shoulder.

The beast tore the shaft free with his teeth, spit it out, and continued to pick up flight speed.

Glenn bit his lip. The arrow proved to be little more than an annoyance, as had Stephi's Dazzle Spell. Using the sling hanging from his belt would be worse than useless so he hefted his shield and readied his cudgel.

"Stand in front of Lysine," Gurk urged. The thief stood just behind the line of men-at-arms. Derek was on the left with his bow. Ron stood on the opposite end, in the bristly grass, ready to hurl his spear.

Glenn scurried around in front of Ron and glanced up at the warrior druid. The quarter-elf's eyes and concentration remained focused straight ahead.

Over the horse-neighing din, Gurk shouted to Glenn, "Use your shield to protect Lysine from spikes."

Glenn nodded, sweat on his brow, both from the day's heat and nerves. The gnome turned to see the manticore flying toward the line, keeping little more than ten feet above the road. Stephi and Petie trailed high and off to the left. A pink, tennis ball-sized burst of energy shot from the fairy into the manticore's flank.

Stephi's Mystic Missile Spell did nothing to slow the beast.

The guard captain shouted, "Release!" Somehow arrows missed. Ron and Mardin took their turn when the beast closed to twenty yards.

Ron's spear sailed high. The crossbow bolt missed low. But Derek had waited, too. His arrow caught the monster in the left forepaw.

Glenn watched the monster's tail. The gnome shifted left to keep himself between Ron, recovering from his spear throw, and that tail. The manticore dove down and snapped at one of the men-at-arms, knocking the bow aside and clamping its jaws down on the man's shoulder.

The hired soldier screamed. At the same instant the manticore whipped its tail around and sent a pair of spikes Glenn's direction. One found purchase in a second man-at-arm's stomach. The other, Glenn managed to intercept with his shield. Even so, Ron had dodged to the side, hitting the ground and rolling. Smart move, Glenn thought, figuring the warrior druid would've evaded the intercepted spike.

The airborne manticore held the screaming mercenary in its jaws and dragged him across the ground. Kirby leapt and slashed with his cutlass, nicking one of the manticore's trailing legs. Maybe the hit encouraged the beast to release the man-at-arms. Maybe it was the man's flailing fit. Or maybe the attacking monster just wanted to gain altitude. In any case, the screaming man tumbled across the hard-packed road. At the same time, the spike-stricken man crumpled to his knees.

Ron helped the stricken man yank the four-inch spike from his stomach, but it was too late. Too much venom had already been injected.

The wide-eyed man fell back, writhing in pain.

"With me," Guard Captain Nickson shouted, his sword held high. Only Derek, Ron and Mardin followed. The remaining man-at-arms backpedaled a dozen feet before turning to run the down the road, chasing after Yonn.

It seemed Yonn had finally turned around, but wasn't exactly galloping full speed back toward the battle.

The spike-poisoned mercenary lying on the ground

began convulsing and frothing at the mouth. Glenn couldn't do anything for poisons—especially to combat a toxin as virulent as the manticore's.

The bitten man-at-arms lay still as well, foaming blood seeping from his mouth. Either the bite's ferocity or the beast's toxic saliva could've done him in. Whatever the case, it didn't matter.

Glenn gripped his cudgel tightly and turned to follow Kirby, Ron, Derek and Nickson.

Ahead of the gnome healer, Ron shouted up at Stephi. "Retrieve the scroll!"

She nodded and dove toward the covered wagon. The wheeled conveyance continued lurching forward while Blizz sheltered beneath it. From within the wagon, the fairy shouted, "What spell should I use?"

"Lightning!" On foot, Derek pounded past. "That'll blast the hell out of it!"

The manticore rose up and then dropped down atop the horse team at the head of the caravan. The lead wagon turned sharply before tipping. The horses screamed, or that's how it sounded to Glenn. Even so, the manticore's bellicose roar somehow drowned them out.

The other wagons' teams went left while Ron's went right, off the road. Blizz gave up hiding and climbed onto the bench in an attempt to regain control. Bristle trotted alongside. Spots and Four Banger neighed, following while fighting their tied-off reins in a bid for freedom. Ron's wagon, with no driver, was out of control, as was the second wagon. The driver had bailed and sprinted back down the road, then veered off it when he spotted the poisoned man-at-arms suffering his final death throes.

The manticore had taken down the lead wagon's team. One horse lay with a broken back. The other had its head bitten off. The bat-winged monster spun in a tight circle to finish the driver whose legs were pinned beneath the tipped wagon. He should've fled, too.

Ron shouted, "Leave him be, you foul beast!"

Derek continued his charge, shield ready and sword held high. A snarling battle cry emanated from his lips.

Kirby and Nickson trailed behind, followed by Mardin. All were too far, would be too late to save the hapless driver. The man screamed while his arms shielded his face and throat. To no avail.

The massive jaws snapped down, through one arm and clamped onto the terrified driver's face.

Stephi fluttered up into the air, angling for a height far above the manticore. She held a small scroll in her hands, and finished unrolling it.

The manticore spun and climbed atop the fallen wagon to face his oncoming foes. It spread its wings and released another screeching roar. It was met by Derek's sword, followed by a bolt of lightning flashing down from Stephi's scroll-cast spell.

A thunderclap sounded, drowning out both the roar and Derek's battle cry.

Wooden shards and splinters erupted outward, many flailing against Derek's armor. The warrior had closed while the others had slowed to give Stephi's spell room.

Knocked from its perch, the feline monster rolled a dozen yards before unsteadily regaining its feet.

The Minor Lightning Spell had blasted the manticore with great effect. One wing hung wrecked. A raw burn, three feet long, stretched across the monster's back. Blackened flesh outlined the smoldering wound.

Derek charged around the shattered wagon, sword raised and shield facing front. Stephi's spell had left the big warrior unscathed.

Glenn remembered Kirby saying the lightning spell did six d6 of damage. The mission's plan was to use the spell to blast a door open. He also remembered Derek had a magical fulgurite that protected its wearer from lighting strikes.

The manticore ignored Derek. Instead, the wounded beast leapt back onto the wrecked wagon and then skyward. Its extended claws came within two feet of reaching Stephi.

Before the manticore landed, Derek caught it in the shoulder with his magical long sword.

The beast came down hard, front left leg collapsing upon impact. Ron came in, opposite side from Derek. The warrior druid hacked deeply with his short sword. Nickson followed with a sword slash, but failed to penetrate the monster's furry hide.

Glenn spotted one of Kirby's darts sinking into the monster's throat.

Even after all of that, the manticore was still up. It spun to face Ron, and caught the warrior druid with a nasty paw swipe. The warrior druid staggered back, wounded but undeterred.

At the same time two tail spikes shot toward Derek. One deflected off his steel helmet and the other stuck in his shield. Pea-green fluid flowed down the shield, the spike pumping as if it'd penetrated flesh.

Glenn raced forward, past Ron, and swung his cudgel. A paw from the big beast knocked the gnome's attack aside, foiling his attack. But that gave Kirby and the guard captain their opening. Sword and cutlass both found flesh in the monster's side and flank, staggering the beast.

Derek ducked in low, beneath the spiked tail, and slashed at its base, severing the prehensile limb. Blood gushed from the wound, as it did from the side and flank wounds. With a rictus look of pain and surprise, the eyes of the twisted human face rolled up, and the beast collapsed.

Glenn, wanting to be sure, slammed his cudgel into the monster's side. The gnome healer heard at least one rib crack. Equally cautious, Kirby shot forward and drove the tip of his cutlass into their unmoving foe's throat and twisted the blade.

The half-goblin thief withdrew his weapon's blade and grinned. "He's deader than a possum that tried to cross a road."

The guard captain turned and snarled at Kirby. He gestured angrily with his sword. "So is a driver and three of my men."

For a split second Kirby stared at Nickson, dumfounded by the guard captain's remark aimed at him. Then the half-goblin thief sneered. "Since you're so good at counting, Guard Captain Nickson," Kirby said, leaning closer, his face turning ugly, "how many of your men ran?" He gestured with his bloody cutlass. "Everybody else was too busy fightin' to count."

Derek stood behind Kirby, bloody long sword held ready.

Nickson leaned forward, unflinching, with his own sword in hand.

Ron, wounded and a little unsteady on his feet, wedged himself between Kirby and Nickson. "Our efforts will be better spent burying our dead," he said, "and retrieving our mounts."

Stephi fluttered down. "And you getting healed, Lysine."

"I shall attend to that task myself, Marigold. Momentarily."

"Don't be silly," she replied, rolling her eyes. With a flick of her tiny hand she gestured to the gnome healer. "Jax, put your club away and get over here. Can't you see Lysine's hurt?"

Silly? Glenn thought. Adrenaline from the life and death struggle still pumped through his arteries.

The gnome took a deep breath, shrugged, and trotted over.

**The task of burying** the dead men-at-arms—Fitzrack, Pyetin, and Erlon, and the driver—fell to Kalgore and Yonn. Fortunately, the caravan had only two shovels, or Glenn might've had to pitch in. As it was, he stood guard. Ron, Captain Nickson, the surviving driver and the other man-at-arms moved the contents from the wagon Stephi's lightning bolt wrecked to the three surviving wagons.

While the gnome healer was sturdy and strong enough to haul sacks of onions and wool, he wouldn't do it as quickly as someone with longer arms and legs. And efficiently maneuvering the long red oak boards? Better he put his eyes and ears to work.

Blizz was busy tending to the stressed horse teams while Stephi and Mardin had gone out to round up the mounts that had fled the battle. Kirby busied himself collecting parts of the manticore he thought could be sold or traded to an alchemist, or maybe a magic user that had need of such exotic items. He'd commandeered a wooden crate and already filled it with the spiked tail Derek had severed, along with two wine bottles filled with blood. He added claws and teeth to the box. The teeth required precision and patience as they were coated with venom. Last, he used a knife to shave the black mane and stuffed it into a sack.

Glenn wasn't sure how his friend could do it. The face was that of a human. Larger and far more grotesque, but still. Maybe Kirby was destined to be a taxidermist, should they ever make it back home.

The gnome made his way across the dirt road to check the terrain that direction. Whoever came down the road, seeing the broken wagon, horse carcasses, and whatever Kirby left of the manticore, was sure to know there'd been a battle. The four vultures circling above had to be a sign of death to anyone or anything nearby. People, other scavengers, predators, and monsters.

At that thought, Glenn trotted up to Ron, who was pausing in his labor to ladle a drink from one of the water barrels. "Lysine, shouldn't we get moving?" The gnome gestured skyward. "That has to be drawing unwanted attention."

"Your concern mirrors my thoughts, Jax." He proffered the metal ladle to Glenn, offering him a drink.

Glenn shook his head. "How long until they get the horses rounded up?"

"Marigold, even more notably in her current physique, has an affinity with animals, especially herbivorous." He drank deeply, emptying the ladle. "Both wild and domesticated."

There was no arguing that, but it didn't exactly answer Glenn's question, or address his concern. He looked around, half expecting to spot an ogre, or another manticore nearing the disorganized caravan.

Ron rested a firm hand on Glenn's shoulder. "I acknowledge your wariness, and desire to vacate this area and to proceed toward our destination." He returned the ladle to its hook and tamped the barrel's lid back into place. "Maintain vigilance. I shall endeavor to expedite what remains to be accomplished."

Glenn said, "Okay," and returned to his assigned task.

Neither the brief conversation, nor his vigilance, alleviated the notion that something bad—or something else bad—was on the way.

# CHAPTER 21

**Glenn sat on** the wagon bench next to Blizz. The old half-goblin was driving the horse team of the trailing wagon. It, like the two others ahead of them, was more heavily laden, and moving slower. Guard Captain Nickson and Derek were riding their mounts ahead of the poor excuse for a caravan. Mardin, on his mule, trailed the wagons, watching the road behind.

Ron drove lead wagon, and Kirby sat next to the middle wagon's driver. The zero-rank hireling remained jittery, even though the manticore's carcass was an hour behind. A competent adventurer's nearby presence was supposed to bolster the driver's confidence. Glenn didn't think it was likely to work.

Glenn was trying to decide if Yonn, and the other surviving man-at-arms under Captain Nickson named Slarg, had maneuvered their mounts between the second and third wagons because they were still nervous. Or to maybe catch a glimpse of Stephi inside the covered wagon.

He also wondered if men-at-arms in the RPG world served as Red Shirts. If they did, Yonn and Slarg seemed aware of their peril. Mardin, not so much. The gnome recalled Derek saying, "Men-at-arms added targets and soaked up damage."

Whatever the case, the gnome knew the mounted men-at-arms' position frustrated Blizz's similar viewing efforts.

Truth be told, Glenn didn't mind seeing Stephi. Even pint-sized, it was an understatement to say she remained easy on the eyes. What the half-goblin driver and the men-at-arms probably hadn't figured on was that Stephi slept in her natural leaf and bark attire. They weren't going to catch any flashes of her naked body.

Glenn was pretty sure he wasn't projecting what might be his desire on the two men. At least that's what he kept telling himself. To switch thoughts, and alleviate the feeling that they should expect another Wandering Creatures Encounter, he asked Blizz, "Besides that lich that passed us in the Dark Heart Swamp, was that manticore the nastiest creature you ever came across?"

Blizz took a moment, pursing his lips, reflecting on the memory that still gave Glenn nightmares.

Finally the half-goblin shook his head. "Naw, Jax. Can't say it is." The animal handler flashed a pointy-toothed grin at the gnome. "Not that a manticore ain't nothing that won't make the average fella dampen his trousers, mind you."

It was Glenn's turn to flash a grin. "That makes us both above average."

After a quirked eyebrow and a half-second hesitation, Blizz released a hissing snicker. "True, Mr. Jax. True. But you was out there with your club and I was sheltering under the wagon."

"True," Glenn agreed. "But you helped me with Spots and Four Banger. We each have our skills and talents."

Blizz licked his teeth and nodded agreement. "That's why I don't hire out to fight."

The gnome and half-goblin rode in silence for a few minutes, until the animal handler spit onto the side of the road. "Trolls, now they're plenty fierce, but the worst I saw was a big ol' mountain giant." Blizz tipped his head up. "Stood tall as two ogres."

Glenn's eyes widened. "While working as a hireling?"

"Yep, that's back when hired outta Riven Rock."

"What happened?"

"That adventuring party took him down. The fire

wizard that'd hired me finished the mountain giant off with what he called a Flame Lance Spell." Blizz squinted his eyes. "Well, it took three of them spells, plus the cleric's mace and the warrior's bastard sword."

Blizz scratched his chin and spit over the side again. "That mountain giant was pretty mighty. Stomped on the fighter, killing him good. And did number of the cleric's magical armor. Pret-near broke every bone in that cleric's body."

"But they won," Glenn said.

"Yeah," Blizz said. "You and Lysine can't hold a candle to how that cleric could heal up broken bodies, including himself's. Didn't do no good, though."

The gnome healer's eyes widened. "What happened? A second giant—or a troll?"

"Naw. An Apollo cleric took him on a day later.

"And a paladin ran his sword clean through the fire wizard who'd hired me." He frowned. "Well, it was more bloody than clean, but you gets my point."

"What'd you do?" Glenn asked.

"Well, I cut loose the dead fighter Bristle'd been toting." He shrugged. "Happened about fifty miles to the west of here. The paladin and Apollo cleric didn't bury the fighter, or the wizard or cleric."

"They hired you?"

"Sure did. My previous employer'd been talking on getting the fighter revived, but I don't think his heart was in it. Leaning more toward some sort of Reincarnation Spell,'cause it'd cost less coin."

That reminded Glenn of his party discussing options after the ogre'd killed Kim.

Their wagon was falling behind, so Blizz flicked the reins to urge the plodding horse team on.

"Bristle carried the dead cleric and warrior's armor and weapons," Blizz said. "All the way to Three Hills City. Stayed hiring out of there after that. Lot nicer place than Riven Rock."

Something about Blizz's tale seemed odd to Glenn. "You didn't mention any names, Blizz."

"Nope," Blizz replied. "Never do."

"Why not?" Glenn asked, thinking that being able to offer references would help the animal handler get hired, especially since he was a half-goblin.

Blizz squinted one eye, appraising the gnome healer. "Your friend, Mr. Gurk, says you're a good fella. Brave and loyal and all, but sorta hinted you're a little naive on some things." Blizz quickly added. "Nothing wrong with that—kind of a gnome trait, ya know."

Glenn clenched his teeth. It was true. He didn't know a lot about *Monsters, Maces and Magic* and the RPG world it'd formed. But he was learning.

"See," Blizz continued, "adventuring parties got secrets. Spells they can use, magics they got in their weapons, dungeons they ain't finished off and might come back to someday."

Glenn said, "Ahhh," and nodded his head slowly. That meant any of his party's secrets were safe with Blizz. "Is that pretty standard among henchmen and hirelings?"

"Nope, it ain't. Least ways not so much in Three Hills City." He gave a half grin. "You all were smart in hiring me."

"But it's that way in Riven Rock?"

"For folks like me that's smart," Blizz replied. "Folks there in Riven Rock ain't so, uumm, nice, as they are in Three Hills City."

Glenn thought back to the time he, Kirby and Stephi got jumped by a gang of street thugs in Three Hills City. And the fact that Ron insisted everyone always travel in pairs…

"You mind sharing some of your knowledge with this gnome?" Glenn asked. At first he offered a toothy smile. Then his eyes became serious. "So I don't get mugged, or knifed in the back?"

"That's rightly smart of you, Mr. Jax."

The bandy-legged animal handler both informed and entertained Glenn through colorful recollections of persons and places, interspersed with highlights of various things he'd witnessed. Most of those involved violence.

The pair, half-goblin animal handler and gnome healer, kept at it a couple hours, until Derek shouted, "Got a lone man on foot, approaching from ahead, on the right."

# CHAPTER 22

**Stephi, with Petie** as her wingman, flew out toward the approaching man. Derek, Guard Captain Nickson and Mardin formed a line and trotted their horses toward the man, across the dry, scrub grass and rock-strewn landscape.

The small caravan kept plodding along. Even so, Glenn stood on the bench seat and scanned the countryside. A lone traveler might be a distraction.

Blizz watched the gnome carefully, ready to steady him if needed. "See anything, Mr. Jax?"

"No," Glenn said. "Just thought bandits or something might try to sneak up on us from the other direction."

Blizz laughed uneasily, like something was troubling him, too. "I like the way yous're thinking."

Despite the plodding hooves and creaking wagon, Glenn heard Stephi nearly one hundred yards away. "Ewww," she said. "He smells."

The man had stopped and gazed up at the fairy holding station twenty yards above.

Stephi dipped a little lower, and then began moving away. "It's a goblin, with one of those glowing blue crystals stuck in his forehead."

Glenn thought back. A zombie lizardman with a glowing blue crystal in its head approached him, Stephi and Kirby while they were fishing along the shore of the Snake Claw River. That one had smelled like a pile of day-old pig intestines from a slaughter house tossed out to rot under a hot sun.

The instant the memory fell together for Glenn, Stephi shouted, "It's a zombie!"

As she fluttered up and away, the goblin-zombie

moved to follow, still looking up.

Petie called out a warning, sensing his mistress's distress.

The faint blue glow flared.

Derek kicked Four Banger, urging his mount into a gallop as he drew his sword. Nickson and Mardin followed.

"Keep backing away, Marigold," the big warrior shouted.

"Why?" Marigold asked. Before Derek could answer, she let loose with her Dazzle Spell.

The horses reared. Both Derek and Mardin fell from their saddles. They landed hard on the ground. Captain Nickson regained control of his mount, but the animal balked moving forward. Blinded like the other two horses, all three neighed in fright and confusion.

Mardin curled up in a ball on the ground until his mount moved away from him. Then he stood unsteadily, also temporarily blinded.

Derek had rolled away from his horse, cursing. He got to his feet and began stomping toward the goblin zombie. "Just stop," he shouted.

"But you told me to back up," Stephi replied.

"That was when I was on my horse!" Derek trotted forward, sword held two-handed, cocked back. "Just keep its attention—and don't flash us again."

"I wouldn't mind a proper flash, none," Blizz said with a snicker. Then the half-goblin animal handler met Glenn's angry gaze. He frowned. "Didn't mean for that to slip out."

Deep down, Glenn woundn't've minded for a quick flash to happen. The base thought tightened his throat. He didn't respond. Instead the gnome healer turned back toward Stephi just in time to see Derek cleave the goblin zombie's head from its body.

The zombie didn't realize it was dead. Well, that the

necromantic magic hadn't quite been sundered by the warrior's blade. It required a second hacking attack from the big warrior to fully end the confrontation.

**After Derek smashed** the still-flaring crystal with a thirty-pound rock, and set fire to the goblin zombie's body, the party's caravan continued down the road.

Glenn knew the overloaded wagons couldn't move fast. The weight was already a strain on the wagons' wheels. Odds were they'd use up each wagon's spare on the rutted, rocky, weak excuse for a road. Luckily they'd stripped the four wheels from the lightning-blasted wagon, plus its spare.

Listening to the bumps and creaking wheels, the gnome healer thought back, recalling what Kirby told him and Stephi about Tracking Gems. Evil clerics or magic users attune an enchanted crystal to what they're looking for. The spell caster in question stuck his Tracking Gem in the forehead of a goblin zombie and sent the undead creature out to find…whatever.

That type of enchanted crystal offered some basic guidance. If the blue crystal gets close to whatever it's set to seek, like within a half mile, depending on the strength of the creating spell caster, it'll direct the carrier—like a zombie—right toward the sought object.

Glenn wondered if the object could be a person. What he kept coming back to was that the higher-rank the spell caster, the more powerful the tracking. Sometimes the Tracking Gem's creator could tell if the creature bearing the gem was close, if the spell caster happened to be holding a shard of the Tracking Gem and concentrating on it. Sort of like GPS, but not as accurate. Maybe even see the target through the blue crystal.

Stephi was kept out of sight within the covered wagon Blizz drove. Glenn rode on the bench next to him.

Kirby stuck with Ron, who drove the lead wagon. Derek rode Four Banger alongside. Glenn was pretty sure they were discussing the last Wandering Creature Encounter. And he was pretty sure it wasn't a random Wandering Creature Encounter. Not one with some random dice roll directing its occurrence. Rather one directed by some intelligent force. One with a purpose.

# CHAPTER 23

**The party pressed** on until early evening. They pulled off the road to camp within sight of another group of wagons. Their destination was apparently to the north. Ron, Blizz, Derek and the other driver managed to get one of the lead wagon's wheels changed. Cracked and wobbly as it was, Glenn guessed it didn't have more than another hundred turns left. It was probably a low estimate, but it wouldn't hold up against too many more rocks or twisting ruts. Captain Nickson said they should reach Riven Rock before noon despite their slow rate of travel. No way the replaced wheel would've lasted that long. Actually, Glenn wondered about two other wheels, one of them on the wagon he rode.

Glenn sighed. Even if wheel failure was one of his worries, the wagon wheels weren't one of his responsibilities.

Ron believed a campfire would be a good idea, so Glenn was assigned to gather whatever bits of wood he could find. Some of the scattered thorny bushes seemed to be the most likely source.

Kirby accompanied him, as did Stephi. She flitted above, watching for danger. Kirby stalked along, making his way around rocks and stands of scrub grass. His gaze flicked left and right and even up into the darkening sky.

The hot air wicked up sweat from Glenn's skin. His gnome nose smelled bone-dry dirt. Sort of a baked sandstone and acrid bark scent. Better than road dust and weary horse.

Something was bothering Kirby, leaving the half-goblin thief agitated. Glenn cleared his throat about it when Kirby signaled with Blizz's hand axe for Stephi to drop closer.

"Captain Nickson, Yonn and Slarg are jumpy as hell," the half-goblin thief whispered. "Our guy, Mardin, is worried as hell, too."

"I'm a little on the freaked out side, too," Stephi said. "That ugly manticore and creepy zombie goblin? Who wouldn't be?" When neither Glenn nor Kirby agreed, she asked, "Jax, aren't you freaked out—just a little?"

Glenn tossed down the canvas tarp next to a dead thorn bush and began unfolding it. "I'm more worried than freaked out, Marigold." He expected Kirby to chime in. The thief didn't.

Instead, Kirby said, "This might be the first time in a month I've agreed with Kalgore." Kirby examined the bush. Eyes squinting, the thief strategized how he might reach the good wood without getting scratched up by the thorns. "Burning a few of the red oak boards to lighten the load makes sense to me."

Glenn stepped back from the tarp. "But not to Lysine and Guard Captain Nickson."

"Yup," Kirby said. "Because they ain't the one who has to deal with these thorns."

Stephi glanced around. "Are you sure it isn't because the wood is worth a lot of money?"

"The coin the wood's worth is reason enough for Lysine," Kirby said. He hunched low and pressed a dead branch up with his forearm, counting on his leather armor for protection. "But not for that guard captain."

The half-goblin thief scrunched up his pointed nose and then got to work with the hand axe. Once he had the first couple of branches chopped off, the thorn-scratching job got easier.

While Glenn dragged the branches onto the tarp, Kirby said, "Me and Lysine were talking. Kalgore, too."

Kirby glanced around warily, then watched Glenn place his heavy boot on the main stem of the first branch before carefully grabbing and snapping off the smaller ones.

Impatience written across her face, Stephi asked, "About?"

"That zombie today with the Tracking Gem."

Glenn stopped working and crossed his arms. "I don't think it was a Wandering Creature Encounter either."

Kirby's yellow eyes widened. "Really? 'Cause that's what we decided, too. About the lizard man zombie with a Tracking Gem, too."

Glenn thought back to their encounter with the undead lizard man while fishing along the bank of the Snake Claw River. Something important had been decided, and he'd been excluded.

Stephi crossed her arms, mimicking Glenn. Except her action pushed up her breasts, causing more cleavage to show. Kirby's eyes widened at the sight. Then he frowned and got back to work.

The gnome's growing anger helped him suppress a smile. A top-heavy fairy fluttering in place with arms crossed and a scowl. An ironic image, in a cute sort of way.

"Why are you surprised?" Stephi asked. "Jax is smart." Her hands went to her hips. "Me, too." She huffed. "Stop chopping, Gurk, and look at me when I'm talking.

The half-goblin thief complied.

"Why didn't you include me and Jax in the big discussion?" She didn't wait for an answer. "Because we don't know anything about the stupid game we're all stuck in?"

She flitted down and stopped, nose to nose with the half-goblin thief. "We might not have known much when we first got here, but we've been learning." She pointed an accusing finger at Kirby. "Tell me. How are we supposed to learn more if we're always left out?"

Glenn nodded in agreement. He felt much the same way.

"Ummm," Kirby started. "Because you were on the other wagon. And Kalgore rode up and started talking about it?"

"So?" Stephi said, not buying it.

"Come on," Kirby said. He gestured open palmed with his left hand. His right still held Blizz's hand axe. "Kalgore and Lysine are tight friends. Like we three are." His voice faded on the last sentence, showing uncertainty.

Glenn scowled in thought. Kirby's statement made sense. Derek put up with Glenn, probably because they were party members from the real world stuck in the same predicament. Not like he'd come asking Glenn for input or advice. Derek was friendlier with Stephi. Mainly because she was easy on the eyes. Or so Glenn figured.

Stephi winged herself a few feet away from her nose to nose position.

Before Glenn verbalized his agreement, Kirby's left hand clenched into a fist and his right dropped the hand axe onto the dry, hard-packed ground. It balled into a fist, mirroring the left held down at his side. "Whatever, dudes. I came over here to tell you first chance I got." His intense gaze moved away from Glenn and Stephi and focused back on the camp. "When none of the *freaking out* men-at-arms could overhear." He spun around and faced the other way.

Glenn often had to remind himself that Kirby was actually a junior high kid, and prone to teen-driven emotions. And his half-goblin game heritage constantly pressed a darker emotional tinge—at least if it was anything like Glenn's insistent gnome tendencies attempting to steer his actions.

"Whatever," Stephi said, her hands again on her hips as she flapped a few more feet above the ground. She spoke to Kirby's back. "Did you tell Kalgore and Lysine that we should be involved in the discussion about the creepy zombie goblin—that was after *me*?" She rushed an answer, not giving Kirby a chance. "That would be a 'No.' Right?"

Kirby turned back to face Stephi. His eyebrows drew down and a sneer filled his face. Things were going to get bad if Glenn didn't intervene. He stepped between the two. "I'm interested in what you have to say, Gurk." He shot a glance over his shoulder, up at Stephi. "We both are."

The gnome turned back to the angry half-goblin. "We're just a little miffed at being left out." He held out his hands, palms up. "Think about it. You would be, too."

"That's why I'm here, telling you now." His clenched, partially-pointed teeth never separated while forming those words.

The anger was way beyond what Kirby had ever shown, Glenn thought. At least toward himself or Stephi.

Glenn took in a breath. "So, what did you guys determine is out there looking for us?"

Kirby's demeanor changed. He looked around, eyes wide, then involuntarily tucked his head down a couple of inches when he whispered, "That lich we saw in the Dark Heart Swamp." He gulped. "And it's not looking for us." He pointed up at Stephi. "It's looking for the Soul Gem."

Very little wood got cut and gathered in the five minutes it took for Kirby to explain what he, Derek and Ron had pieced together.

**Stephi and Glenn** lay tucked under the same blanket, each on top of a sack of wool in the covered wagon. They'd shared the first watch, along with Mardin. Now, unlike Blizz who snored away beneath the wagon, neither could sleep. Both lay worried and cold, Glenn within inches of shivering.

The gnome healer's mind kept recalling the horrible encounter with the lich, Malthia the Cursed, riding her black steed. A fiery-eyed Gehenna steed. The moment in the swamp when he'd frozen in place, so terrified he couldn't run, or duck and hide. It was the lich's Aura of Fear and Dread that'd affected him. Low-rank adventurers didn't even get a Saving Throw against it.

Stephi startled him when she whispered, "You think Lysine's right, Jax?"

He rolled over to face her. His low-light vision showed her head peeking out from beneath the gray wool blanket. Her green eyes held wide.

Lysine determined the lich had recruited the swamp's goblin tribe to help attack the Outpost where the party'd slain the husk mummy. They'd gone there to get the amulet that made the wearer invisible to undead. Apparently the husk mummy used the amulet to kill the previous occupant: a vampire. During the search, before the underground complex flooded, Stephi found the Soul Gem under the staked vampire's skull.

Apparently the husk mummy wasn't unaware of the magical gem lying hidden, easily within her grasp. Apparently Malthia the Cursed was aware of its existence. And was aware of the fact that some adventurers had whisked it away. And the lich was searching for it—for them—for Stephi, who now wore the Soul Gem. The magical item that housed the soul of their fallen party member, Kim.

The moment after Kirby'd explained it all, Glenn wracked his brain to come up with another theory. Who else might be sending the zombies with Tracking Gems? They required a high-rank wizard to create. At least twelfth rank.

The only other people who knew the party had the Soul Gem was the High Priest of Apollo and his assistant. The church offered a Revive the Dead Spell cast upon Kim in exchange for the amulet that made the wearer invisible to undead. When Kim failed her System Shock Roll, her soul went into the vacant Soul Gem. Until that moment, no one in the party knew the alexandrite gemstone was enchanted, let alone its magical properties.

The Church of Apollo wouldn't create undead. Nor would it need a Tracking Gem to locate Glenn's party. They'd been living at the Glade House in Three Hills City since the day Kim's soul entered the gem. And they were a *White* church. They wouldn't create undead. Nor would they share such information, especially with someone Black, someone with connections to a lich. And if they had shared info about the party, then seeking the Soul Gem through zombies wouldn't be necessary.

With both eyebrows raised, Stephi propped herself up on an elbow. She repeated her whispered question. "You think Lysine's right, Jax?"

Glenn was less than a foot from Stephi's 19.5 Appearance-score face, which threatened to distract him, so he forced his gaze down toward the line where the two sacks packed with wool pressed together.

The gnome responded with a question. "That it's the lich that created the lizard man and goblin zombies?"

Out of the corner of his eye Glenn saw her small head nodding.

"That's what Kirby said Lysine determined." The fairy magic user's voice shifted from frightened toward conspiratorial. "And that it's a good thing that creepy zombie saw us heading toward Riven Rock."

"Right," Glenn said. "Means the lich'll be less likely to search for us in Three Hills City." Even saying "lich" sent small chills up his spine. No way was he going to say the lich's name out loud. Maybe taboo or superstitious or whatever, but saying it wasn't a good idea.

Stephi nodded again. "What are you frowning for? That's what Gurk said." She sat up and clasped her hands together. Her iridescent wings spread wide. "And when I get changed back to being an elf, the lich thing will still be looking for a fairy in Riven Rock." At the statement's end her voice rose above a whisper, filled with excitement.

That put even more pressure on the party to succeed, so they could get the leprechaun's coin from the pawnshop owner.

With the speed of an arrow, Stephi shot over and embraced Glenn with a hug. It was like an infant's hug, but stronger—and sexier. Glenn hugged back, lower to avoid her wings. That brought his hands down to her bottom. He yanked them away, embarrassed.

Stephi didn't even seem to notice. She puckered her lips and gave the gnome a quick peck on the cheek before shooting back onto her sack, pulling up the blanket.

"I feel so much better, Jax. Don't you?"

Glenn looked down at the blanket and pulled it up. "Yeah," he said. "I do, Marigold." He forced mirth into his hushed voice. "Now maybe we both can get some real sleep."

Minutes passed and he heard the quick but steady breathing coming from the beautiful woman next to him. The gnome healer couldn't sleep, replaying the encounter with the goblin zombie. Derek shouted Stephi's name, Marigold, before he hacked it to bits with his sword.

Did Tracking Gems not only allow the creator to see what's around them, but hear, too? Glenn vaguely remembered some crystal balls in *Dungeons and Dragons* being able to do both—he thought. That was a long time ago, when he played. And now, although he was in a game, part of the game, the question caused spurts of acid to well up from his stomach.

He'd have to ask Kirby, or Ron. He'd wait to ask until a moment when Stephi was too far away to hear.

# Chapter 24

**Glenn awoke from** his fitful sleep to Ron's grinning face. The warrior druid had opened the covered wagon's canvas flap, letting in faint light.

The still drowsy gnome rubbed his face. The sun hadn't risen yet, but it would soon. Outside, Blizz was talking to his donkey, and someone was gathering up the horses to hitch them up. An advantage of middle watch was a few minutes extra sleep.

"I have excellent news to report." Ron's hushed voice held restrained excitement. He leaned black and glanced left and right before leaning forward again. "After a seemingly interminable time, I experienced the dream!"

Glenn didn't get what Ron was saying. The first thing that came to mind when "dream" was mentioned, was his last nightmare. The one he'd sweated through before mid watch.

"*The* dream?" Stephi asked. "Really?"

"Indeed," Ron said, nodding his head in assurance. "In it, I was availed the opportunity to peruse my character sheet."

Then Glenn remembered his dream, when he advanced to become a second-rank healer.

"I earned sufficient experience points to advance both in warrior *and* druid."

Glenn didn't think often enough about experience points, and how important they were, especially for Ron. He was multi-classed, so he had to split those earned equally.

"I had been calculating..." He scrunched his face and bit his lower lip before continuing. "The battle with the manticore pushed my totals past the minimum experience points required."

Stephi stood, then fluttered forward. Glenn realized that fairies didn't seem to do much walking. Heck, it took him forever to get anywhere walking and her legs were shorter than his.

"What's that mean, Lysine?" Stephi asked. "Do you get more spells?"

"An additional first-rank druid spell," he said. "And eight additional hit points." His renewed grin nearly split his face. "I rolled remarkably above average, with a nine on my ten-sided dice and a five on my eight-sided dice, plus my Constitution Bonus. In comparison, an average pair of rolls would have netted a mere six points."

Glenn recalled back to his experience. He got a twelve-sided dice for hit points, and had a better Constitution than Ron. It wasn't exactly a physical roll, but Glenn distinctly remembered in the dream, seeing the black dice with white numbers roll across a wooden table. Weird was an understatement.

"What skill did you take?" Stephi asked.

His voice fell into lecture mode, reminiscent of his days as a math grad teaching assistant. "A character earns one skill per rank, or level, of advancement, Marigold. Being multi-class and advancing a rank in each of my selected classes, I earned two Skill Slots."

Glenn sat up straight, interested in what the warrior druid had selected.

"I opted for Tracking and for Religious Studies." Ron squinted one eye and nodded once in assurance. "I pondered long and hard for this event. Both skills have proven useful in past games. Thus, they are likely to be of benefit in our current predicament."

Glenn initially took Gem and Precious Stone Appraisal when rolling up his character and Basic Construction when he advanced. He knew Stephi had initially taken Dance. He was curious about her second Skill Slot.

"What skill did you select Stephi, when you moved up a level?"

"Rank," Ron corrected.

"Oh, I never told you. I took Running." She flapped her wings and looked down at her short legs. "Not a lot of good it's doing me now." Still fluttering in the air she kicked her arms and legs in gear, running in place. "I bet I could've gotten a full-ride scholarship for track before that creepy leprechaun."

Ron rubbed his chin. "With your good sixteen Coordination Score, and your exceptionally tall and lithe elven stature? There is little doubt."

Glenn considered asking if she'd run the hurdles, but declined.

Stephi commented, cupping her leaf and bark-covered chest, "Good thing this idiotic world doesn't care if you have ginormous boobs. One of the few things they don't do is slow me down."

Ron began saying, "I believe the archetypal video game females influenced—"

Derek cut him off. "Hey, Lysine," he said, walking toward the tent. "Tell the gnome and Sleeping Beauty Barbie to get moving and help break camp."

Ron suppressed a smile. "The more expediently we prepare, the sooner we shall arrive at Riven Rock."

"How long will it take?" Stephi asked. "We'll get there today, right?"

"By noon, barring any unforeseen events. Actually, the craggy hills of the city are within sight."

Glenn gulped and folded up the blanket. The world continually threw unforeseen events at them.

Stephi flew up to Glenn, hauling one of his clunky boots. She dropped it next to him. "Come on, Jax." She laughed. "Kalgore called *me* Sleeping Beauty, not you."

# Chapter 25

**It didn't bother** Glenn that the weather and terrain changed by simply crossing a river. That GM that sent them here probably drew the map. With a city named Three Hills City? Because it contained three hills…quite the imagination.

Things remained hot and dry. The road improved slightly, widening from a two-rutted trail. There was even evidence of gravel having been spread across some sections in years past.

They spotted a goat herder and his two sons. Not surprisingly the vests covering their tattered linen shirts were made from goat skin. The father walked with a staff. The two sons carried spears. Their three dogs looked like oversized border collies, but with wiry brown fur. They, like the herders, looked anything but friendly.

Glenn estimated the goat herd contained well over a hundred. He was pretty sure it wasn't a flock. He didn't think flock was the right word because the men were goat herders. Just one more thing in the game world he wasn't sure of. He wouldn't have known it in the real world either. But he could've Googled it. In the *Monsters, Maces and Magic* world, the closest thing he had to Google was asking Ron.

In any case, the goats were certain to do a number on the scraggy grass and plants trying to survive the harsh conditions. Maybe there was a rainy season? Gravel had been placed where the road looked to have washed out sometime in the past.

Also, off the main road, usually with a beaten trail leading to them, stood scattered clusters of shacks. Glenn would've called them cottages, but they looked too makeshift and rundown to qualify as anything else but a shack. Some had livestock, goats, chickens, or pigs, penned or staked out around them. People moved around, most doing something industrious, such as tanning animal hides, sharpening spears or axes, maintaining the pens or rickety fences, or a myriad of other tasks.

All appeared poorly dressed with floppy-brimmed hats. There appeared to be very few women, and the children appeared to be boys. Glenn guessed that the women kept inside, and the girls all kept their hair short. Lice and fleas were common enough among the poor, so short hair made sense.

As the small caravan approached within half a mile of Riven Rock, the road leading to the city widened enough to accommodate traffic both directions. There, however, wasn't anyone heading toward their caravan. Stephi, from within the wagon, said there was a road leaving the city going east. It had some traffic, but mostly carts and people on foot. Glenn knew she was getting her information from Petie flying overhead.

Riven Rock itself appeared to consist of two steep, craggy hills. Each stood at least four hundred feet in height. It might be that they were once one large hill, split apart by some major cataclysm centuries ago. There didn't appear to be much dirt or plant life on the steep hillsides. Rather, holes pockmarked their limestone faces, most holes having ledges beneath. Glenn's strained eyes spotted stairs and walkways. Some were carved into the hillsides and others were built of wood or metal. Occasional ladders haphazardly connected them. Glenn thought a blindfolded giant hurling rusted fire escapes torn from 1940s era buildings at the hillside would've offered a more rational layout.

Along the base of the craggy hills sprawled a menagerie of structures. Squat towers, paired towers, squatter buildings, with a few being multi-story topped with steeply pitched roofs. Most were of brick or wooden construction. From it all, streams of sooty smoke rose into the air. Coal, Glenn's gnomish nose told him. That, and dried animal droppings.

Further from the hills stood winding lines of shacks similar to those they'd passed. All Glenn could think to call it was a "shanty town." Fewer wispy streams of smoke rose from it. But more scents of human waste, sweat, and despair hung in the hot air.

"Quite a sight," Blizz said, leaning close to the gnome healer. "Like I was tellin' you before. A lot meaner of a place than Three Hills is." He pointed. "In them tunneled hills, that's where plenty of them with gold coins and gems live. Nearer the hills, that's where your artesian workers are found. And those with coin dig down, not build upwards, like they do in Three Hills."

Blizz looked to the horses, urging them to speed back up with a flick of the reins. Once that was done, the animal handler looked back at Glenn. "Those with little for their cook pot surround them richer folk, further out. Beneath the hills, lining and burrowing into the crevasse, some calls it The Fissure, is where the *real* business gets done."

"Who's in charge?" Glenn asked.

"The Council of Three."

The half-goblin animal handler snapped the reins to keep the horse team plodding forward. "We'll be taking the Circling Road." He nodded and pointed with his gaze to the left. "That'll take us around East Way in."

Glenn wasn't sure if he wanted to know more about the Council of Three or about The Fissure. He figured two hills that might've once been one gave the city its name, Riven Rock. He guessed the split continued down into the earth, The Fissure. So he asked, "Who are they? The Council of Three?"

Blizz rubbed a finger under his pointed nose and

shrugged. "Don't know. Never saw even one of them, myself. But don't no one crosses them."

"No one?" Glenn had a pretty good idea, but decided to ask. "Something happens to someone who does?"

"No one with half a brain," Blizz corrected. "Saw two fellas accused runnin' for their lives. Runnin' like a pair of coyotes with their tail hairs afire. Maybe they got away." The animal handler leaned over the side of the wagon and spit. "Saw plenty others get arrested. Either way, never saw any of 'em again."

The old half-goblin scratched the side of his nose. "Forced down into the lead and silver mines. Under the boot of them dirty dwarves." He spat over the side of the wagon again. "Never saw them again. Sure as the sun never fell on their face again."

After a moment of silence, Stephi, who'd been listening, said, "Other side of the hills. There's green. Trees and crops, and people with hoes working."

Trying to throw off the oppressive mood setting in as they neared the city, Glenn said, "Don't tell Kalgore there's hoes out there, working."

Blizz shot the gnome a confused glance.

Stephi huffed. "Whatever. That's all men think about." She paused. "If you want to get with *those* hoes, better bring that muscle-brain warrior with you. There's guards with shields and spears walking around the outside of the short wall surrounding it all. Clearly protecting the hoers from horny gnomes."

"I know gnomes is woodland types and all." Blizz scratched behind his ear. "That don't explain what clearin' weeds has to do with bein', ummm, horny?" He met the gnome healer's amused gaze. "Working a hoe's hard work."

"That it is," Glenn said to the animal handler. Then he said over his shoulder, "Or so I've heard."

"Oh, shut up, Jax," Stephi said. "You're sounding

just like Gurk."

Stephi moved closer to the front of the wagon. "Blizz, what's going on there? All the guards? Are they like slaves or something?"

The thought of slaves wiped the grin from Glenn's face.

"Oh, the guards ain't keeping the hoers in. For poor folks, they got a good job working. What they're cultivatin' is what feeds the folks with coin. Orchards and root crops like potatoes, carrots and onions. I think it's called a conglom-rate of earth and water wizards that bring up water needed." The old half-goblin grinned and shot a quick wink at Glenn. "Everyone else? They eat gulch worm jerky and fungus gruel."

Keeping just within the covered wagon's shadow, Stephi said, "Ewww. No way."

Blizz was pulling Stephi's leg. Glenn thought Blizz was trying to pull his leg, too.

Then the gnome healer wondered. Usually, the best humor held elements of truth. After a moment, he more than suspected that gulch worms and fungus gruel *were* real things. And real people *did*, at least occasionally, eat them. At least in this world.

# CHAPTER 26

**Taking the East** Road into Riven Rock was more depressing than Glenn anticipated. The shacks and smell of squalor travelled over the clay brick barrier lining each side. It'd take more than the ten feet beyond the road and five-foot high wall to safeguard his gnomish olfactory system. It'd take two hundred yards and a hundred-foot-high brick wall. He did his best to ignore the stench.

"Ewww," Stephi said. "Is there like an overflowing sewer or something?"

"The eastward breeze isn't helping any more," Glenn said. "At least you don't have a sensitive shnozz like me."

"Think I'll keep hiding back here and focus on what Petie smells."

Blizz frowned, and snapped the reins on the horse team. "C'mon, boys. Not much ferther."

Glenn started to say, "Birds don't have a good sense of smell," and then tapped himself on the side of the head, emphasizing the *duh* moment.

Blizz let out a sigh, then scrunched up his nose. "I kinda forgot the fancy fragrance." He leaned close to Glenn. "You get used to it."

Glenn huffed, trying to breathe with his mouth. "I hope so."

"You know where we're going, Mr. Jax?"

The party had been silent about their ultimate target, a glass blower's shop. But their first objective was Krogman's Wagon Shop. Not only was it a place to park and repair their wagons, the owner was the party's contact. Supposed to be the one person living in Riven Rock the party could trust—at least according to Higslaff the Pawnshop Owner.

Glenn answered, “Krogman’s Wagon Shop.”

“Krogman’s…Wagon Shop?” The half-goblin’s eyes drifted up in thought. “There was a spry young fella that went by the name of Krogman. Sorta like me back when I was young.” The half-goblin seemed to smile at some long-past memory. “Krogman…he was a wheelwright, but that was a lot a winters ago.”

Blizz’s thoughts snapped back to the present. “If’n he bought out the shop from Hagelberger, I know where it sits.”

Ron was counting on Guard Captain Nickson to lead the way. Derek rode up front, next to him. Slarg and Yonn rode alongside the small caravan, slipping in between the teams and wagons when necessary, but keeping folks away. Mardin brought up the rear.

The roads were wider than in Three Hills City, once they got past the shanty town and the brick wall. Glenn figured it was because the town wasn’t restricted by a wall. That said, it wasn’t as well planned, with streets angling and veering in and out.

The buildings were mostly made from clay bricks and wood. Some canvas coverings and a few rusted metal supports. The squat towers were built with limestone. Unlike Three Hills City, almost no shop or apartment had a front porch. And the people, while there were plenty like in Three Hills City, they appeared more downtrodden. Dustier and more depressed. Almost no one smiled and all spent more time looking at the ground in front of them, instead of up and around them. Somehow, they avoided getting run over or bumping into fellow travelers.

Progress was slow. The horse teams pulling the extra-heavy loads wearied with the stopping and starting. They snorted and stomped and strained. Concern built on Blizz’s face.

Finally they made it to the wagon shop.

It was a large, barn-like structure. The base, up to about five feet, consisted of limestone slats pieced together bound by mortar. Vertical wooden planks made up the upper part of the two-story building. They'd been painted brown, but the paint was pockmarked, like it'd endured a sandblaster's passing attention. White block letters on the brown planks above the door, a little faded, read: *Krogman's Wagon Shop.* Underneath, in smaller lettering, it read: *Sales and Repair. Wheels fixed.* Beneath the words was a simple white painting of a wagon, along with a broken wagon wheel next to a fixed one.

Sounds of work—shouts, hammering and scraping—emanated from within the wide doorway. One of the two sliding doors was blocked open.

The three wagons pulled off the street and parked in front of the shop. Ron's middle wagon blocked the doorway.

Derek strode up to Glenn's wagon. "Old man," he said to Blizz, "you and the other driver, see to the horses. Slarg and Mardin are going to fetch water for the teams. Gurk's going to talk with the owner of this place." After gesturing toward the barn-like shop, he glanced up at the sky. The sun was well past its apex and fast on its way down. "Lysine, Nickson and Yonn are going to look at getting buyers for what we brought." Without looking at the wagon he continued, his voice a little lower, "We'll need you out of the wagon, Hide Away Barbie. Get to the roof, without drawing attention."

After saying that, Derek grinned wide. "Me and you, gnome, get to stand guard, and make sure no one gets curious about what cargo we're carrying."

Out of the corner of his eye Glenn saw Kirby make his way into the wagon shop. Ron was already resting on Four Banger's saddle, ready to blend back into the street's traffic.

Blizz stood and shook life back into his legs. "Sure

thing, Mr. Kalgore." He climbed down and got to work.

Glenn climbed down on his side and came around the wagon. He'd stood night watch and other types of watch. But he wasn't normally the first choice for doing so in a city.

The gnome healer strode as fast as his short legs would carry him without breaking into a trot. He stopped and stood next to Derek.

The big warrior glanced down at Glenn. "We got the easy job. Just look mean and pay attention. I'll go over by the lead wagon, you stick here."

"Got it," Glenn said.

Derek started to walk away, then turned back and frowned. "I said look mean, not look like you're watching a parade or something."

Glenn stared up at Derek, a quizzical look on his face.

"Even short as you are, with your club and shield, a mean look'll discourage folks from slowing or getting curious." He paused, staring up and down the street. "Don't want to have your club out. Town guards might not like that."

Glenn tried to mimic Derek's look.

"You look like you're constipated." Derek rolled his eyes. "Draw your eyebrows down and maybe clench your teeth some."

Glenn tried. Derek looked around and away before shaking his head.

"Strap on your shield, gnome, and let your arm hang down your side. It's got a lot of combat scars on it. Shows you've been in a lot of scraps."

The gnome healer did as instructed.

"Now, if someone slows and looks your way, make eye contact. Maybe twitch your eye some—like Clint Eastwood does when he's getting angry."

Glenn looked up at Derek and gave the eye twitch a

shot.

"Don't wink, gnome, like you're looking to date me." He rested a hand on his armored hip. "Give the look like someone just deflated Marigold's boobs—no wait. Nobody's gonna fret over messing with a depressed gnome."

"Look, Lysine, I'm a healer, not a warrior."

"Yeah," Derek said, "And you know what else? Your mom's a skanky whore."

"What?" Glenn said, his hands balling into fists.

"That's it!" Derek said. He patted Glenn on the shoulder. "Keep that look."

**It took about** forty-five minutes for the two men-at-arms to haul enough buckets of water to satisfy the horse teams, and for Blizz and the other driver to check the horses and feed them some oats. Glenn got bored watching people, sneering or doing whatever, whenever someone glanced his way. Every now and then he went and checked the other side of the wagon. No way would he ever make a good security guard.

Derek frequently glanced over at Glenn from his post, and occasionally offered an approving head nod. Other times, a disappointed head shake.

Glenn wondered what could be taking Kirby so long when Derek wandered over to stand next to the gnome healer. The big warrior gestured with a hand back to his right. "Yonn and Mardin are going to watch over there." Derek rocked on his heels, still managing to look angry to passerbys. "You did okay, for a gnome healer."

Glenn wasn't sure if that was a real complement, and waited for the other shoe to drop. It didn't. After a few minutes of eating dust, he pointed over his shoulder at the wagon and asked, "You want me to get my canteen?"

"Good idea, gnome."

After the two shared a drink, Glenn said, "That

tooth, does it change the flavor of things?"

"Not really. Did try eating grass. It tasted like grass." The warrior shrugged. "But I didn't throw it back up like a dog."

"I was thinking." Glenn rubbed his sideburn. "About your tooth."

"Yeah, gnome. What about it? You want it to try eating grass or something?"

"No. I was thinking about White Ash's father, an elven baronet. And then there's Duke Huelmer, in Three Hills City."

"There's plenty of nobles. You think they might want my tooth?"

Glenn nodded. He held up a hand to forestall Derek's certain protest. "In our world, didn't kings and dukes and queens have tasters, so they didn't get poisoned?"

Derek squinted in thought. "Maybe I recall something from some Shakespeare play mentioning that."

"That tooth, if it allows you to eat anything, it'd allow you to eat poison too, right?"

Derek's mouth opened with a retort, but then he stopped and squinted in thought again. "I think you might have something there, gnome."

The two went back to watching carts pulled by oxen, and porters with crates and sacks passing by.

"When we're done with this mission," Derek said, "tell Lysine about your idea." He reached down and slapped Glenn on the back. "You're starting to figure things out on this world, Jax."

The slap caused Glenn to stumble forward a step. Derek probably did it on purpose…but Derek had called him Jax, instead of Gnome. In a weird way, that sort of balanced things out.

# CHAPTER 27

**Krogman was a** wiry man with a thick mustache and thinning hair on top. He wore a heavy linin brown shirt with narrow red striping below the collar. It reminded Glenn of something a square dancer might don.

From the shop owner's constant grin erupting beneath his mustache and the way he exchanged jibes with his workers, Glenn pegged the man as a practical joker. If this game world, and especially the stinky, oppressive town, had anyone who played practical jokes. Or ones that weren't in some way sadistic or cruel.

The inside looked just like a barn, with a loft or second floor area, and the floor was made of thick boards, worn smooth from years of service. Two sweaty men wearing nothing more than trousers and boots were replacing split boards lining the bottom of a freight wagon. Another two or three men were on the shop's upper floor, hammering and sawing. A third man, sweating more than anyone else, wearing a thick shirt and leather apron, labored at a small forge, hammering out nails and brackets.

While Glenn and Derek stood guard, Krogman had inspected the wagons, mainly the wheels, whistling and shaking his head. Kirby followed him, not saying a word. After Ron and Guard Captain Nickson got back, bringing along a potential buyer, the repair shop owner made himself scarce—until Ron, Derek, and Blizz, along with Nickson, Slarg, Yonn and their driver took the wagons to the buyer's warehouse. That left Glenn, Kirby and Mardin to guard their pile of gear sitting inside, just to the right of the main door.

Stephi had retreated into her basket. It rested next to the pile. Petie took station in the rafters of the wagon repair shop.

After making sure all the workers were on task, Krogman signaled for Kirby to follow him into the shop's office.

"Dude," Kirby said to Mardin, "watch our gear." Then he flicked his head, motioning for Glenn to accompany him.

Like any competent and reliable man-at-arms, Mardin took position between the doorway and the pile of satchels and packs.

Glenn hustled to keep up with the half-goblin thief. "What's he want?" Glenn whispered to Kirby. The gnome was pretty sure Krogman couldn't hear over the shop's din.

The office was cramped with little more than a shelf with stacks of papers held down by ornamental wheel hubs and a desk beneath it. The desk was mostly clean except for a pair of pliers, a ballpeen hammer and small lock box that Krogman appeared to be in the middle of repairing.

The shop owner uncovered a sconce that held a small torch, revealing a Light Spell cast upon it. It wasn't very strong, maybe equal to a twenty-five watt bulb. He pulled the wooden door closed.

"I'd offer this to one of you." The shop owner pointed to the office's sturdy red oak chair before his easy smile faded. "But I don't think this'll take long—or it better not."

"What is it, dude?" Kirby asked.

"Nickson," Krogman said, his voice monotone. "I remember him from about nine or ten years back. He worked as muscle for Villar's guild here in Riven Rock."

"The thieves' guild in Riven Rock?" Glenn whispered.

"Yeah, dude," Kirby said in a tone suggesting Glenn should zip it.

The gnome healer bit his lip and stepped back in front of the door. "Sorry."

Higslaff was connected to the thieves' guild in Three Hills City, a member of importance, Glenn realized. His pawnshop was attacked in the opening stages of a guild war. The Blue Bugle was second, and some low level guild operatives were killed.

And Higslaff sent them to Krogman, his contact in Riven Rock. Glenn wasn't sure why he hadn't grasped Higslaff's importance. He had the pieces, just never put them together, until that moment.

Krogman reminded Glenn of an auto mechanic. He didn't look like a thief. But Josiah the barber wasn't a thief either. Or at least he didn't live the life of one. Glenn stopped biting his lip. He really had no clue what Josiah did at night, on during his off hours. Non Player Characters apparently had more complex lives than he thought. Even if they wore the same clothes most of the time, and kept to the same routines.

Or at least some NPCs.

Even though there continued to be hammering and sawing and muffled banter on the other side of the door, Krogman kept his voice low. "Nickson may not know what your party's up to, but he knows Higslaff sent you. He was pretty chummy with a lot of the..." The shop owner's mouth pulled to one side and his eyebrows arched. "He might be loyal to Higslaff. But he might be *more* loyal to Villar and his gang."

"And if it's the latter," Kirby said, face scrunched up, "we're screwed."

"If screwed means dead, then yeah."

Kirby's intense gaze met Glenn's. The half-goblin thief's off hand gripped the top of his scabbarded cutlass. "Damn. We've got to figure it out."

"And fast," Krogman said.

"Me and you should follow him, Jax. Find out if the

guard captain intends to screw us."

Glenn nodded. It was an unfamiliar city, but Kirby was an experienced player, and a good thief. And a good friend. He might need Glenn's cudgel as backup. Or his healing.

Kirby returned his gaze to Krogman. The man leaned back against his desk, arms folded. "Give me and Jax directions to where they took the wagons. We'll follow him from there."

"What about us getting the rooms?" Glenn said. In an even lower voice, just above a whisper, he added, "And Marigold? We could use Petie."

Krogman said, "I can send Voisard to the Sulfur Ash Inn to get your rooms. I don't know anything about a Marigold and Petie."

"Mardin can stay with our stuff. We can leave, saying we're getting rooms, just going earlier. There ain't a lot of blue jays here in Riven Rock, right Krogman?"

"No," the shop owner said, "can't say that there is." He'd seen the blue jay fly in and land in the rafters. So had all his men, except the blacksmith.

"If Nickson's up to something, and sees Petie, that'll tip him off." Kirby turned to Krogman. "Petie's the bird."

Krogman nodded. "A familiar?"

Kirby nodded affirmation to Krogman, then turned to Glenn with a wide-eyed sense of urgency. "Jax, go get Marigold and bring her in here. Krogman can explain things to her, and she can explain herself to him." Absentmindedly running his left hand across his bandoleer of darts, he added, "We gotta get moving, 'cause I got a feeling we don't got time to waste."

# CHAPTER 28

**Glenn followed Kirby** through the unfamiliar streets. Dust lined the gnome's nostrils, dampening some of the odor of stale sweat and animal waste. Whoever ran Riven Rock wasn't as attentive to the latter as the duke was in Three Hills City. Of course, the absence of moisture in the air helped mitigate the effect. It was a lot better than the squalor of the shantytown surrounding the more established part of the city.

Fortunately they only had to keep to major roads to find the raw materials broker's warehouse, and only made one wrong turn along the way.

Glenn did his best to look like he belonged, instead of a tourist. He observed signs and shop fronts, trying to burn them into his memory, all the while doing his best to avoid eye contact with anyone. That included hired guards and street sellers peddling their wares. Eye contact, Kirby said, would make him memorable, instead of just part of the crowd. And they didn't want to be memorable. Being a gnome and a half-goblin among mainly humans was bad enough.

They reached a trio of brick warehouses just as Blizz, Ron and the other driver were pulling the heavily-laden wagons into the warehouse on the far right. Outside, a middle-aged man with thick arms and a beer gut counted out gold and silver, before dropping it into a large pouch and handing it to Nickson. Derek and Yonn watched.

"Come on," Kirby urged. "We'll duck around the corner and see what happens."

Glenn trotted to keep up with the half-goblin thief until they came alongside a two-wheeled cart pulled by a mule. They kept pace with it, keeping the creaky contraption between them and Derek, Nickson and Yonn as they passed by.

"Here," Nickson said. Glenn heard the sound of coins clink. "Take this back to Krogman's, and I'll meet you at the Sulfur Ash Inn."

"Where you going?" Derek asked. His voice sounded gruff and slightly suspicious.

"There's a place I can post that we're interested in hiring a few guards for the return trip. If I do it tonight, word'll get around and we'll have a better chance of getting some that are competent."

That's all Glenn's gnome ears could make out before they were out of earshot. A few seconds later he followed Kirby, ducking around the corner.

While Kirby did his best to casually peer around the warehouse's corner, Glenn stood next to him. "Did you hear what the guard captain said?"

"Total BS," Kirby hissed. "Back off, he's coming this way."

The pair turned and strode away, the half-goblin more calmly than the gnome. Ahead a pair of laborers lifted empty wooden crates from a stack onto a flatbed wagon. The sturdy horse team snorted as the thief and healer stepped in front of them. They remained there until the guard captain crossed the intersection.

"Come on," Kirby whispered. "Stay way behind me, but don't lose sight. If we get separated, I'll meet you back at Krogman's." Without waiting for acknowledgement Kirby scurried back toward the intersection and stepped around the corner. As soon as the half-goblin thief was out of sight, Glenn hurried to follow.

# CHAPTER 29

**Twice Glenn lost** sight of Kirby as the half-goblin thief wove through the streets, occasionally ducking down an alley or using a group of pedestrians or a slow-moving wagon for cover. The thief made it look so easy, like he had an intended destination and wasn't tailing someone.

Glenn, on the other hand, knew he looked like a semi-lost gnome—which he was. He had a pretty good idea the direction to the wagon repair shop. Back over his right shoulder. And the odor becoming more pungent said they were nearing the outer shantytown. The sun was getting low, but that didn't bother Glenn, at least not visually. His gnomish eyes offered low-light vision, superior to humans. Kirby's half-goblin eyes were even better at night, for which Glenn was thankful.

What he wasn't appreciative of was that pedestrian and merchant traffic was falling off. Sure, there was some traffic from street peddlers and their carts going home. But few of those were heading the shantytown's direction. Glenn just counted on the fact that, if he kept moving fast enough, it was less likely that locals with nefarious intentions would have time to react and jump him.

The buildings were getting shorter—no two or three-storied types. The wood and brick construction steadily increased in shoddiness and disrepair. And the streets became narrower, more twisting, and filled with debris and rotting refuse.

A lanky man wearing scuffed and mended leather armor stepped out of the shadow of a leaning hovel on the verge of collapsing. The figure bore layers of scars across his face and his lips split in a nasty grin, showing a set of teeth that held more complex angles than the shack he'd emerged from. The most notable thing about the man was the barbed hook sprouting from his right arm, where his hand should've been. It was sort of like those Glenn saw in old pirate movies as a kid. But those weren't usually rusted. If the guy scratched himself hard enough to draw blood, a case of tetanus was sure to afflict him.

But the thug proved he wasn't suffering from lockjaw when he said, "Hey, little gnome, whatcha—"

Glenn didn't give the man time to finish his question. Instead he veered toward the man while pulling his cudgel. Delay meant he'd lose track of Kirby, and it'd give the thug's band time to surround him. Experience from a previous fight in Three Hills City said the guy'd have backup.

Without a word Glenn swung his cudgel, even as the hook-wielding thug drew his rusted weapon back, prepping for his own swing. Everyone in the game world thought of gnomes as inoffensive and easy-going. This determined gnome's quick action gave him Surprise Initiative.

A sickening *crunch* said Glenn's attack did something nasty to the man's knee. Glenn guessed he'd rolled a 20, and maybe got a Critical Strike, because the scarred man collapsed onto the street.

He was down but not done, and started to shout. Glenn's boot drove past the defending forearm and knocked in a few teeth. The man rolled to the side, causing Glenn's follow-on smash with his cudgel to miss and rebound off the street's hard-packed dirt. Undeterred, Glenn pursued the man, not allowing him a second's respite. Another swing impacted the man's lower back—maybe his tail bone. It wasn't nearly as solid as the first hit, but dropped the man. A final boot to the ribs ended the fight, with Glenn victorious.

Immediately he looked up and swiveled his head left

and right while unslinging his shield. Nobody was charging him. But the emerging locals shouted and hurled debris at him. Broken boards, cracked pottery and rocks. Glenn ducked behind his shield and shot off to the left, down a narrow walkway as fast as this short legs would carry him. Other than escape, his only thought was that he couldn't let the guard captain spot him.

# CHAPTER 30

**Glenn rethought running** headlong down the debris-cluttered path. Within ten feet he'd startled a trio of rats, each more than a foot long—discounting their tails. He stopped and listened. There was no going back down the path to the scene of his fight. He had no clue where the current path led. Locals certainly did, and none followed after him.

He decided to cut right, squeezing between two weather-worn shacks. Their brick foundations were eroding. A hand rubbing against the planks making up the walls would come away with dozens of splinters. But there was enough room for his gnome frame to squeeze through, if he held his shield ahead of him, sideways. If a group eventually did give chase—the shouting hadn't died down—they wouldn't expect their quarry to make an immediate turn. Plus, it would keep him moving the direction he'd last seen his party member. Losing track of Kirby almost frightened him more than facing an angry mob. Almost. Otherwise he would've backtracked onto the street.

It became obvious where residents dumped their chamber pots. Glenn did his best not to scrape against the walls, so that only his boots would require a thorough cleaning. He breathed through his mouth, shallow breaths and thought of pleasant things—like fishing on the Snake Claw River with Kirby. And gorgeous Stephi, lounging under the nearby willow tree.

He came to a sludgy puddle of human waste and whatever else. Moisture in the dry city was odd, and a couple of large rats were taking advantage of it. One of the big rodents stood on its hind legs, observing the gnome's approach. At some unseen signal they all scampered away.

Glenn did his best to straddle the muck. Then he passed between another five rickety buildings to his left and four to his right. He came to a T. Both paths were wider than the one he'd just taken. Holding his breath, he went right, heading back toward the street he'd just ducked off of.

A gaggle of ten or eleven people were on the street, watching as two men dragged the hook-handed thug from the middle of the street. Glenn kept to the side of the road, a few feet from each shanty hut and forced himself to walk away from the crowd. Kirby once told him it was better to walk like you belonged. Running was more likely to draw attention. With the darkening shadows of the sun nearly set, he kept moving, not looking back.

A pair of strong-armed laborers with short-cropped hair and bad teeth walked past Glenn. They ignored the gnome, being more interested in finding out what they'd missed.

After ten or fifteen seconds, the gnome healer remembered he was tracking Kirby, and began scanning ahead. He didn't see his friend. A moment of panic started. A gurgle of stomach acid bubbled up, but he swallowed it down and kept moving, doing his best to pretend like he belonged...belonged in the slums of an unfamiliar and oppressive city...in a world based on *Monsters, Maces and Magic*, a role playing game.

At the moment that was his life and, if he wanted to keep it, he needed to find his friend.

# CHAPTER 31

**Glenn kept moving** at a steady pace down the winding street, searching ahead, and watching at forks and cross streets.

"Pssst!"

Glenn looked right, his hand falling to his cudgel resting in its belt loop.

It was Kirby. The half-goblin thief signaled Glenn to come over to him, off the street between two buildings. One appeared of superior construction for the area. While that wasn't saying much, maybe it was important.

Kirby put a finger to his lips, urging silence.

Glenn felt an urge to hug his friend, but refrained. Instead he leaned close as the thief whispered into his ear. "Listen." Then the half-goblin pressed an ear against the dry wood.

The gnome followed suit, pressing his ear, and listened.

"So, you's here to pay your debt?" It was a strange, creaky voice that Glenn didn't recognize. I was sort of croaky, like Kirby's.

"Nobody's got that much gold." Glenn recognized that voice. Guard Captain Nickson's.

"Then whatcha doin' here?"

"I got something better than gold."

"What's that? Magic?" Whoever was speaking laughed.

"Information," Nickson said, clearly annoyed.

Glenn clenched his teeth. Information? The only thing he knew was that Higslaff sent him and his party to Riven Rock. He didn't know exactly why, but he might be able to guess. To do a little payback for damage to the pawnshop owner's property and the attempt on the pawnshop owner's life. Slimy bastard, Glenn thought. He fought to keep his breath quiet and steady.

The half-goblin thief seemed to have better control. The only sign of anger expressed itself in his yellow eyes.

"What information you got that's worth more than gold?" the sturdy shack's owner asked.

"Information that's too important for your ears, my old friend."

"Ha! Long as you got a price on your head, we ain't friends. Thinking on killing you and bringing Vineada your head."

"You can try." Nickson's voice was little more than a growl. The clink and scrape of metal said the guard captain had gotten to his feet.

"Your fancy armor and sword don't impress me."

"Set up a meeting, Nibber. I want to talk to Veneada."

"Why don't you go yourself?"

It was Nickson's turn to laugh. "I'm no fool. Odds are she'd have me killed first and wonder why I was there second."

"True," the croaky voice said. "What's in it for me?"

"You owe me, Nibber." The creaking of wood said Nickson had sat back down. "My sword stopped Lobo from doing you in."

"Bahh, that was more than ten years ago."

"Ten years of life you wouldn't have lived."

After a moment of silence Nibber hissed. "This'll cancel that life-debt, Nickson. But not here. At the Warthog Well House."

"When?" Nickson asked.

"Least an hour, maybe three," Nibber said. "Might depend on Veneada's mood."

"Has she changed any?" Nickson asked.

"She's started going gray." Nibber laughed, and there wasn't a hint of mirth. "Made her meaner."

"Okay," Nickson said. "I'll be at the well house in an hour."

Kirby signaled for Glenn to follow. The pair crept around to the back of the sturdy shack. They leaned their ears close and listened.

"No ways I'm gonna be seen with the likes of you, Nickson. Least ways not until the price is off your head."

"What do you suggest?"

"I go set up your meeting. You wait five minutes, and then make your way to the well house."

"Got anything to eat?"

"Ha!" Nibber said. "Help yourself. Might be your last meal."

The sturdy shack's door creaked open and closed.

Kirby drew Glenn away from wall, behind the one next door. Inside it, someone could be heard snoring with another occupant humming some sort of rhythmic tune.

The half-goblin leaned close and whispered into Glenn's ear. "We take him when he comes out." Then, in a few sentences, he outlined the plan.

"You good with that?" Kirby asked before leaning away to see Glenn's expression.

Glenn bit his lip but nodded yes. He'd been in one fight already tonight, but that one didn't end with death. The one they were initiating would—with Nickson's, or theirs.

# CHAPTER 32

**Glenn waited, kneeling** down in the shadow of the sturdy shack. The moon wasn't up, but there was still dusk's light, and a clear sky began showing its array of twinkling stars. Kirby was waiting on the other side of the shack.

Guard Captain Nickson was a noisy eater, chewing something crunchy and smacking his lips. Was it the guard captain's last meal? Glenn wondered what he would want for his last meal. Certainly something better than what Nibber left behind for Nickson.

The five minutes waiting seemed like fifty. In the real world, Glenn would've never contemplated, then followed through with a killing—well, maybe, if his family were in danger. But he'd use a pistol or shotgun. Not a cudgel. His Neutral Gray alignment seemed to ease the decision. The fact that he was an adventurer, and had done some killing already, of both humans and monsters, made it feel like a reasonable course of action. How would all of this violence affect him when he got back to the real world?

Glenn shook it off. He had to survive to get back to the real world. If he didn't follow through with the plan? Didn't fight? Everyone—Stephi, Kirby, Ron, and even Derek, would be dead, and none of them would get home. It'd even end Kim's slim chance.

Guard Captain Nickson began grumbling to himself. What he said wasn't clear.

Time was up. Glenn wanted to unsling his shield and have his cudgel ready. But that wasn't part of the plan. The goal was to throw the guard captain mentally off balance, give Kirby a shot at a Stealth Attack.

Glenn hustled out onto the street and moved about

five yards away from the sturdy shack's door. That placed him almost a whole shack away. Nobody was on the street. It was almost like cockroaches, but in the opposite way. At night, in the dark, they came out and were everywhere. Flick on the lights, and they scattered for cover. In the shantytown, in the day folks were out and about. Darkness, and the residents scattered for the cover of their hovels.

The door creaked open and Nickson stepped out. Glenn began walking forward before the guard captain pulled the door closed. When the guard captain caught sight of someone his hand went to his sword's grip.

"Hey," Glenn said, "what're you doing here?"

"Jax?" the guard captain asked, squinting in the darkness.

Something alerted Nickson of impending danger. Maybe it was experience, or a sixth sense. Maybe Glenn didn't play his part well enough, or Kirby's movement wasn't silent enough. Failed his Stealth Approach Roll?

The guard captain spun and backed away, into the middle of the street, foiling Kirby's approach.

The jig was up, since Kirby was around the corner, cutlass in hand.

"Ho," Nickson said, drawing his sword from its scabbard. A malicious grin creased his weather-worn face. "You two aim to kill me? A lowly half-goblin thief and pathetic gnome healer?"

Glenn didn't know what to say. He prepared his shield and cudgel. They'd do his talking.

"We're going to deliver your head to Veneada," Kirby said, a sneer in his voice, louder than Glenn thought necessary. "Since there's a price on it."

"What? How do you—"

Nickson didn't bother to finish, having to duck a dart Kirby threw left-handed.

If Kirby failed to take Nickson down with a Stealth

Attack, the backup plan was to attack him from both sides, and keep him off balance.

The guard captain, however, wasn't playing along. Even as Kirby closed, Nickson charged the half-goblin. The pair clashed and separated before Glenn reached them.

Nickson had a shallow thigh wound. Kirby'd come off worse, with a gash along the side of his head, just above the ear. Glenn charged in, swung his cudgel and missed. The gnome pressed his attack, but the guard captain got a kick past the healer's wooden shield and sent his shorter foe stumbling back.

Kirby came in again, his cutlass biting into chain mail instead of flesh. Nickson countered with a sword thrust that nearly skewered Kirby. The nimble thief danced aside, avoiding the killing blow by a fraction of a second.

Glenn realized they were playing into the guard captain's hand. He had superior armor and weapon skills, and they weren't using their two-on-one advantage. This part of Riven Rock wasn't like Three Hills City, with city guardsmen on regular patrol. No one was going to interfere.

Instead of charging in, the gnome shuffled forward, shield interposed, and cudgel cocked back, ready.

"Thinking of running, are ya?" Kirby taunted. "I see it in your eyes."

"Cut like that," Nickson countered. "You'll bleed out soon enough. Then it'll be just me and the gnome."

"Nahh, dude. I'm just getting—" Midsentence, Kirby rushed in.

Glenn closed in the same instant and simply whaled away. Grunts and curses said Kirby was going at the guard captain with all he had. Glenn got in two good hits against the guard captain's back before his friend dropped to the hard ground. Nickson yanked his sword's tip from the mortally wounded half-goblin's gut and spun to face the persistent gnome.

Nickson hadn't come away unscathed. His cheek had been slit open so that molars showed through the wound. Glenn didn't know what rank the guard captain was, but he'd taken at least three cutlass hits from Kirby and two cudgel strikes from Glenn. That had to be fifteen hit points dealt to him. If he was second rank, he had to have only a few hit points left. If he was third rank, a lot more. Glenn had a lot of hit points himself, and could heal up to twice his total hit points inflicted by his foe. He could win this.

But Kirby lay on the ground, unmoving. Maybe he was already dead—if he wasn't, he only had a few rounds before he was. Time was against Glenn. Nickson knew that.

The casual defensive stance said as much.

Glenn made a decision. It was going to be all or nothing. Both he and Kirby would survive, or neither would. Mumbling spell words under his breath, he raised his shield and charged at, then past the guard captain. He stopped above his friend, knelt down and completed his Minor Heal Draw Spell, taking on all of Kirby's wounds.

The appearance of the head, shoulder and gut wounds were painful, but the gnome healer had suffered worse. And he had enough hit points to remain conscious, to keep his shield between the attacking guard captain and himself, and his friend.

Still on his knees, Glenn attempted an attack, and failed. The guard captain batted the gnome healer's shield aside, and hacked down with his long sword.

Glenn took it in the shoulder. He nearly passed out before muttering the words to trigger his Minor Heal Draw upon himself. Before he collapsed, he saw Kirby, healed and refreshed, roll away and spring to his feet, cutlass in hand.

"Round Two, dude."

**The immense pain** nearly caused the gnome healer to pass out, but he managed to keep his eyes open and a firm grip on his cudgel as the healing magic mended the wounds he'd taken upon himself.

Uninterested in taking on a fresh and revived assailant, the guard captain turned and ran. The move initially caught Kirby by surprise. It might've been a prudent tactic for the guard captain to put distance between himself and the recovering gnome healer in order to deal with one foe at a time. But he didn't turn to fight. Instead he was brought down from behind by the nimble thief.

The man died with a dart plunged through his left eye and into his panicked brain.

The gnome healer gathered his shield and trotted up to the thief who stood over their dead foe.

"What do we do now?" Glenn asked his friend in a hushed voice. "We can't just leave the body here."

"Sure we can, dude. Who's gonna care?" Kirby looked around, and then squatted down and began searching the dead man's pockets. "Too dark for any humans to get a good look at us anyway."

Glenn figured his friend was probably right. Dusk in the shantytown quickly transitioned to shadowy darkness. Then he recalled something and squatted down next to his friend. "Nibber will be back." Glenn pointed to the body. "He *knew* that Nickson knew something important, and thought it was enough to get out from under whatever he'd done."

"Yeah," Kirby said. "Sounded like he was risking his neck."

Glenn peered at the body, then around it. "Nickson's soul is still attached to it, right?"

"For three days," Kirby confirmed.

“Maybe this Vaneada person can find a cleric or witch or someone that can talk to his ghost.”

The half-goblin’s yellow eyes widened. “Right, dude. And this backstabbing asshole’ll snitch on us in a second.”

Glenn didn’t bother to say that was already the guard captain’s plan.

“A tethered soul makes it easier, but all they really need is the body.” The thief looked around again. “I don’t know any good place to dump a body in this dried-out city.”

“You look for those things?” Glenn asked.

“Sure. Know six good ones in Three Hills City.”

The gnome leaned back from his friend.

“I’m a thief, dude.” Putting the coins he’d taken into his own pocket, the half-goblin hissed in frustration. “Anyplace will be better than leaving it here.”

Glenn wondered if bodies were just left to rot. Maybe someone would push them to the side or toss them over a fence. Not like a decaying corpse would add much to the shantytown’s horrendous odor. That brought an idea to mind.

The gnome healer slipped his cudgel into its belt loop. “I know a place.”

# CHAPTER 33

**Glenn asked, "How** do you know they have a wheelbarrow?"

"I saw the dude roll it in while I trailed him," Kirby said, pointing down at Nickson's corpse. "There's probably even a wheel track, if you wanna check."

Kirby refrained from throwing his hands up in the air. "Not only is this dead dude too big for either of us to carry far, it'd draw too much attention, even in *this* neighborhood."

"And a dead guy in a wheelbarrow wouldn't?"

"Stop stalling. Longer we're here, more chance for things to go bad—er—worse bad."

The nervous gnome peered around. Already doors and shutters were cracking open for the locals to see onto the street. Although they were already talking in hushed voices, Glenn leaned close to Kirby. "He whispered, "How do I act like a dwarf?"

The thief had already told Glenn that they'd be more likely to open up the door to a dwarf than a half-goblin, especially the one who killed a guy in front of their shac—umm, home. And that being a dwarf was better than a gnome, since there were supposed to be a lot of dwarves in the city. Although Glenn hadn't seen one.

"You ever see *Lord of the Rings*, dude?"

"Dwarves talk like that."

"I don't know. Dwarves don't talk to folks like me." Kirby pointed at his face. "They either cuss, spit or just wanna fight."

Glenn bit his lip and nodded. "I'll do my best."

"You do that, and I'll get traitor dude ready for a ride—oh, and get a tarp or blanket or something. If you can."

Glenn relaxed his shoulders, practiced a few phrases under his breath, and walked up to the nearby shack and knocked on the door.

No one answered, or said anything, but he'd seen the door slide closed just as he approached. So he knocked again then said, in as deep-throated Scottish accent as he could muster, "I and my fine friend are in the market for a wheelbarrow, lad, and I know you've got one handy."

No response, so he knocked again. "Next time I'll be knocking with my…thumping club, and your door doesn't look fine enough to endure that."

Speaking in the deep, eccentric accent pinched at Glenn's gnomish throat.

He tried to think what Gimli from the movies would say. "Being late meeting my ale-drinking mates always puts me in a sour mood, lad, and you don't wanta be dealing with an angry dwarf, do ya?"

From the other side of the door came a voice. "Ya can't have my wheelbarrow. Got to have it for my job." It would've sounded forceful, except that it cracked the last few words.

"No fretting, lad." Glenn took a breath and cleared his pinched throat. "I'll pay you good coin for its use."

"You'll bring it back?"

The voice was definitely a man's. And there was movement inside, indicating more than one person beyond the door.

Glenn glanced over his shoulder to see Kirby gesturing for Glenn to speed things up.

"What'll you pay?"

"Depends on the quality of your wheelbarrow. And I expect you to throw in a tarp, or blanket, too."

"You're going to use it to take the warrior you killed to…Vaneada?" The last word, the name, came out as little more than a whisper.

"You have the gist of it." Glenn put his hands on his

hips, figuring someone might be peering at him through he cracks. It was dark, but certainly his outline could be seen. "Now roll your wares out so I can have a look, or I'll have to come in. And that might get bruising and bloody."

The door opened and a tall fellow with big hands and sunken eyes looked out and down at Glenn. From behind, someone lit a lantern.

The tall fellow's eyes widened. "A dwarf with no beard? What happened to it?"

Glenn had sideburns and muttonchops, but no beard. He said the first thing that came to mind, only half maintaining his accent. "Lost it in a wager, and I'll bust the jaw of anyone that reminds me of its loss again."

The tall fellow jumped back, leaving the door to swing open. He dropped a rusted hand axe on the floor.

Inside, with the man, stood a rail-thin woman holding the lantern. The interior had a few hooks with garments on them, and a table constructed from planks and scraps of wood. Their bed was little more than a jumble of rags and blankets. The place smelled of horse and goat manure, and Glenn guessed it came from the wheelbarrow tipped up against the back wall, and the flat shovel leaning against it.

Even if the pair looked harmless and intimidated, no way was he going into the shack. "Roll it on out and let's have a look."

The man complied and stepped back, remaining in the doorway. It would work. Glenn had no clue how much a wheelbarrow went for. Nevertheless, he reached into his pocket and pulled out the handkerchief that he wrapped his coins in.

While Glenn did that, the wheelbarrow owner said, "Nibber usually does the killing that needs done around here."

Reasserting his accent, Glenn replied, "Nibber is off

to let Vaneada know about the dead man."

The wheelbarrow owner ducked his head at the mention of Veneada, whoever she was.

"Three silver for your wheelbarrow."

The man's eyes widened. From inside the house, the woman's scratchy voice said, "We were hoping for four silvers."

From the man's expression Glenn knew he'd offered too much, and that the woman was the barterer of the two. "The generous coin is to buy your silence about me and Pippin—mind you, lad, not from Nibber." Glenn put a scowl on his face. "But from nosy neighbors."

The man nodded, as did the lady.

"I believe I purchased the wheelbarrow, your silence, and a blanket?"

The man turned his head to the woman and gave her a sharp look. She hurried and brought out a tattered wool blanket.

Glenn placed the three coins in the man's shaky hand.

The man asked, "Do you want help loading the body?"

"No, thank you lad," Glenn said, moving around to take the wheelbarrow to Kirby. He looked back and failed to hold back a half smile. "Pippin and I got it."

As he pushed the wheelbarrow away, and before the man shut the door, Glenn heard the woman say in a hushed voice, "Mighty friendly, for a murderin' dwarf."

The man whispered back, probably due to adrenaline pumping in his veins, "Pippin's the mean one that done the killing."

The woman let out an exasperated gasp. Behind the door, Glenn caught the woman's muffled reply. "Ask a mother how a babe named Pippin grew up to be a nasty knifer."

**"That was perfect**, dude."

Kirby and Glenn were already back on the street, pushing their empty wheelbarrow. Empty except for the guard captain's armor, wrapped in the blanket. Kirby had the dead man's scabbarded sword strapped across his back.

Glenn had helped lower Guard Captain Nickson's corpse into the sludgy excrement puddle he'd run across between the dilapidated shacks.

Like before disposing of the body, their stroll garnered nary an ounce of interest. The few individuals that were out and about held no interest in anybody else's business.

"Why'd we lay him down face up?" Glenn asked as Kirby tossed the dead man's boots between a burned out shack and the neighboring one that had just barely survived the heated encounter.

Kirby quirked an eyebrow. "You really want to know?"

Glenn figured he probably didn't, but replied, "How am I supposed to learn how things work in this world?"

Kirby nodded. "Well, it probably works the same way in our world." He'd used the flat of Nickson's sword to push his legs, arms and torso down as far as they would go—about ten inches—so the disgusting excrement sludge covered most of his body. But Kirby had been careful to keep the face clean.

Glenn had a hard time forgetting the pallid face, slashed cheek exposing teeth. Luckily his low-light vision didn't offer vivid color.

The half-goblin thief kept pace with the gnome pushing their wheelbarrow. He said to his shorter friend, "I'm hoping the big rats we scared off'll come back and eat his face."

Glenn grimaced. Thinking on that, he turned away.

"Pretty gross, I know." The half-goblin licked his

semi-pointed teeth. "Even if the body's found right away, nobody should recognize him."

"Remember," Kirby said, making eye contact with his friend. "The dude was an NPC. A traitor worse than Benedict Arnold."

Benedict Arnold, Glenn thought. Kirby was a junior high kid, and probably just learned about the Revolutionary War traitor in an American History class.

Glenn was pretty sure he'd lost another piece of himself, his *real* self. But he'd gained something—something he wasn't sure he wanted. A small knowledge of how to survive in the game world.

He glanced over at his friend, Kirby, whose eyes darted from place to place, seeking potential danger. Kirby'd proven once again his advanced knowledge of survival measures through playing *Monsters, Maces and Magic*.

And had probably lost a lot more pieces of himself than Glenn.

# CHAPTER 34

**Glenn struggled more** than usual to keep up with Ron.

After returning to Krogman's and then to the Sulfur Ash Inn, Kirby and Glenn got a meal of cornbread and ale, and then went upstairs to the party's rented room to tell their tale. Three cots. That didn't mean Glenn would spend the whole night sleeping on the floor. Everyone would spend a share of the night in the hard wooden chair, keeping watch. The men-at-arms slept in another room, one with a fourth cot for Guard Captain Nickson. That one had a cloth napkin tied closed around a cut of corn bread, waiting in vain for the guard captain to make his way to the inn, eat it and then join his fellows in sleep.

Blizz and the other driver, Simmer, slept at the stable. Glenn learned that it was a common thing, with hammocks strung above the horse stalls. There seemed to be a sort of community among the drivers and handlers staying there. It was likely that Blizz would've stayed near Bristle even if he'd been offered a spot in the inn's common room.

The only person happy with Nickson's betrayal and the subsequent outcome was Derek. He gave Kirby, sitting across from him, a thumbs up. He slapped Glenn on the back in approval so hard that a sizeable bruise wasn't too far out of the question.

Glenn struggled to sleep. What little he managed proved fitful.

**Drowsy-eyed, Glenn** followed Ron to the Work Lines near the Copper Bucket, an important well house in the built-up part of the city. If they, themselves, couldn't find a driver and a couple men-at-arms, Ron intended to contract the services of a hawker to secure potential recruits for the jobs.

Yonn and Slarg were both distressed at their captain's failure to return. They'd left with Ron and Glenn, but hurried on ahead, annoyed at Glenn's slower pace. The gnome was pretty sure they not only respected Nickson, but didn't want to be ordered around by Derek. Their actions and attentiveness said they respected Ron. Instinctively they knew Derek would somehow bully them. As such, they avoided being with Derek whenever possible.

Derek and Kirby left to scout the area around the glassblower's shop. Mardin and Blizz, and the other driver, Simmer, were to split time hanging out at the wagon repair shop and caring for the horses at the nearby stable.

Each wagon was to be rotated in for inspection and repair, especially their wheels. Stephi's job was to hang out at the repair shop. Camouflaged under the eaves, along with Petie, Ron assigned her to watch for potential trouble.

While Glenn and Kirby had apparently taken care of the situation, a good thieves' guild, if curious or motivated, or both, wouldn't have too much trouble discovering what happened to Nickson. Especially with magic at their disposal. That included who might've been involved in the guard captain's death.

Rather than being forced to trail behind, Ron maintained a pace that allowed Glenn to walk beside him. Morning traffic packed the streets with everyone intent on a purpose or errand.

Ron occasionally referred to one of his small leather-bound books, following instructions garnered from Nickson while on the trip to Riven Rock. Those were amended with few notations after Glenn suggested the party leader consult Blizz.

Glenn depended on the towers in Three Hills City to keep from getting lost. At that moment in Riven Rock, he was hopelessly lost. His nose could find the shantytown slums, unless the wind changed. On the other hand, Ron's sketched maps and Orientation Skill delivered them to the Work Lines.

The Work Lines contained anything but a line. It was a loud open area with barkers and hawkers calling for skilled and unskilled day laborers of all sorts, from brick layers to porters. Men, and a few women, milled about, with gaggles and waves moving toward one barker here, or a hawker there, coming away dejected or filing out with an employer.

Glenn tried to make sense of it. Ron's Intelligence and experience better suited him to the task. Plus, his stature, compared to a gnome's, offered a better physical perspective. Because of that, Glenn watched Ron's back. Kirby would've been far better, but the gnome healer could identify a pickpocket or individuals with more nefarious intentions well enough.

Time and again Kirby reminded Glenn the one spotted easily is the decoy. It's the one or two that aren't easy to spot, those that move in while the decoy raises distraction are the threat. Bumps, distracting sounds, or odd antics meant something was going down.

"You see Yonn or Slarg?" Glenn asked.

Distracted, Ron said, "I have not." He sighed. "Utilizing Blizz's purported network among animal handlers appears to be a more suitable option." A quirk of a smile crossed the warrior druid's face. "Men-at-arms, on the other hand…"

Glenn stuck close as Ron wove through the gaggle of NPC humanity toward a cluster of men. There were about fifteen of them. Each maintained a no-nonsense glare, standing tall with chests puffed out. A few had pieces of armor but all carried some sort of a weapon.

Maces and spears dominated the mix. One had a crossbow slung across his back.

Ron marched up to the group of men. They appeared closer to thugs than trustworthy mercenaries or guards.

The warrior druid placed his hands on his hips and eyed the cluster of armed men, each doing his best to impress with rigid stances and hard looks.

"Raise your left hand if you are a competent horse rider."

Seven of the men raised a hand. Two of them raised their right hand.

Glenn got the "left" part of the question. A guard that knew left from right had some education, or military training. Still, with a fifty-fifty chance, that didn't weed them all out. But why didn't all of them raise their hand about being competent on a horse? That took them out of the chance for a job.

Ron pointed to four who'd raised their left hand and said, "Attend." Without looking back he led the four to the outskirts of the Work Line area. Glenn trailed behind, trying to figure out why the party leader selected those four. The one with the crossbow made sense. Being able to shoot a monster from a distance was a plus. Of the other three, one had a flanged mace, one a short sword and the last, a spear. The crossbowman wore a thick leather jerkin with broad metal studs riveted to it. The spearman and the swordsman each wore a chainmail shirt. The man with a mace looked stronger than the others by a good measure, but only wore a buckskin vest over a thick linen shirt.

"I am hiring men to guard a small caravan as it ventures north. It is not my intention to return to Riven Rock. The span of service will be one week."

The four men nodded in acknowledgment.

The warrior druid held out his hand. "Hand over

your crossbow for examination." The warrior druid inspected its condition and workings, then handed it back. He did the same with each candidate's primary weapon.

Glenn walked around behind during the process and then returned to Ron's right-hand side. The four men ignored the gnome.

Ron handed the swordsman back his short sword. "This weapon will not endure combat. You are dismissed."

The swordsman's shoulders slumped. Without a word he trudged back into the Work Lines.

"I am Lysine," Ron said, "and this is one of my associates, Jax." He gestured to the gnome. "What is the name each of you opt to go by?"

The crossbowman said, "Trumble,"

The mace-wielder replied, "Kronk."

The spearman said, "Harold."

"Payment shall be a serviceable sword, for you, Trumble. A mail shirt for you, Kronk, and for you, Harold, a round shield and helmet."

The men's eyes widened.

"While the proposed payment for such a short term of service may sound extremely generous," Ron said, his voice low and serious, "we encountered a manticore making our way to Riven Rock. Ill-equipped men-at-arms will be of no value in such a fight."

Glenn recalled the manticore and eyed Trumble, Kronk and Harold. They looked even less equipped and formidable than the men-at-arms the manticore killed. He refrained from gulping and nodded agreement to Ron's assertion.

"Is that acceptable?"

The three men nodded and voiced agreement.

"Excellent." Ron reached into his pocket and withdrew several index card-sized slips of paper. Taking out his pencil, he jotted down the names of the men. "Take these to the Sulfur Ash Inn and proffer them to the proprietor for admittance."

Questioning looks crossed the three hirelings' faces.

"Give them to the guy running the inn," Glenn clarified.

Unconcerned about the failed communication, Ron continued. "Arrangements for meals and an overnight parcel on the common room's floor have been made. Retrieve your gear for travel and report to the inn prior to the noon meal."

After the hired men departed, Ron turned to Glenn. "Before you inquire, the individual bearing the short sword carried it as a mere ornament. The pommel was suspect and I believe the entire hilt assembly shall come apart upon rigorous combat."

Ron looked around, getting his bearings. "Krogman recommended a weapons and arms dealer. You shall accompany myself or Kalgore there and assist in selecting gear for our most recent hirelings."

"Okay," Glenn said, hoping he'd accompany Ron.

"Gurk impressed upon me the necessity, when opportunities present themselves, of including you and Marigold in activities as they relate to adventuring."

"Thanks," Glenn said, then expressed what was on his mind. "I didn't see Yonn and Slarg. Did you?" It wasn't really a question.

"After questioning the hawkers and barkers with respect to Guard Captain Nickson, they were to join us." The warrior druid released a huff of frustration. "That they failed to do so is an occurrence of somber concern."

**Traversing the city** with Derek frustrated Glenn.

The gnome healer hustled to keep up with the big warrior. That meant people crossed between Glenn and his party member, throwing him off stride. Occasionally they fell in line between the two, if the gnome allowed the distance to grow too great. And he had to watch if Derek stopped abruptly. Otherwise, the gnome's face would run into the sack Derek carried over his shoulder.

The large sack contained Guard Captain Nickson's armor, helmet and sword, and didn't slow the big warrior down in the least. The scabbarded-sword's hilt stuck out of the canvas sack. It rocked and bobbed, and provided the gnome a beacon to follow. Glenn mentally compared it to a shiny fishing lure, enticing a frustrated fish to chase after it.

Glenn would rather have accompanied Ron and Kirby. They'd gone to scout the glassblower's shop. Ron believed keeping the gnome and half-goblin separate while on the public streets was prudent, citing the incident that resulted in the guard captain's demise. People had witnessed it. The cover of a dwarf, beardless due to an ill-conceived bet, might prove an interesting tidbit of a tale to tell over breakfast, lunch or an evening's bitter ale. Hopefully more so than a gnome going around with a half-goblin.

Derek veered right, off the street, and stopped next to a stone building with a large arching door propped open. They'd crossed and circled around most of Riven Rock to the distant side of the southern hill. The gnome's nose said they were near the continuation of a slum area that made up the outskirts of the big city. Somewhere beyond that were the planted trees and crops Stephi described.

The building's first floor had narrow rectangular windows on either side of the steel-reinforced door. The steel-framed windows held steel bars set into them. The upper two floors had similar windows. From Glenn's angle it was hard to tell if those windows had thicker or thinner bars.

"Long haul, gnome, and you didn't even complain

once."

Glenn smiled up at his party member. That was almost a complement.

Krogman suggested Frank's Arsenal when the party said they wanted to sell off the guard captain's gear. It was nowhere near the wagon repair shop or the Sulfur Ash Inn.

Carts, wagons and porters continued past on the street, contributing grumblings, conversation, shouts and animal noises to the constant din.

"We're gonna trade this good armor and sword for some functional crap armor and weapons for our new henchmen," Derek said. "I can do that well enough, but if there's an exchange of coin involved, you make sure the counting is done right."

Glenn knew better than to give the big warrior a hard time about his low Intelligence Score and basic illiteracy. In real life Derek was a college student, and that situation is one that grated upon him.

"Sure thing," the gnome said. "You know more about armor and weapons than I'll ever know."

"Damn straight on that."

The proprietor of Frank's Arsenal was named Arnold. His grandfather, Frank, opened the weapons shop several decades ago. Arnold wasn't intimidated by Derek's size, strength or meanness. The short, wiry fellow probably dealt with warriors all the time. The owner carried a scimitar on his hip, but the real deterrent to trouble was the brutish half-ogre wearing a battle-scarred breastplate, and who looked like he knew how to wield his war hammer. The guard never said anything. He watched patrons carefully from his position near the entrance, occasionally picking some sort of nut from a clay bowl resting on a tall, three-legged table. The guard smacked his lips while he ate.

Derek might not have a high Intel Score, but he

knew how to barter. They came away with a decent mail shirt, a short sword that had seen some wear but remained serviceable, a helmet that had had more than a few dents hammered out of it. But the leather inside was new. They also obtained a round shield the same size as Glenn's, made of steel instead of wood. They even came away with six gold, two silver and four copper coins.

With the refilled sack over his shoulder, Derek looked up and down the street. "Since I did such a good job trading, gnome, me and you can get a good lunch."

Glenn glanced up at the big warrior. "Is that a good idea?"

"Sure," Derek said, adjusting the load over his shoulder. "Lysine and Gurk'll take most of the afternoon scoping out the place and the area around it. And I'm hungry as hell."

The gnome healer figured the second reason was more important to Derek, but he was hungry and thirsty, too. Derek was right. Kirby said it'd take at least two days to check out the glassblower's shop for patterns of activity and weaknesses.

"Sure, but no place with nuts on the menu," Glenn said.

"Pissed you off too," Derek replied. "Any other place I'd've smashed the tusked asshole in the face for being so damn annoying."

Glenn wasn't so sure Derek could take the half-ogre guard. At least not as easily as implied. Suggesting that wouldn't go well. Glenn withheld a sigh. Hanging out with Derek sort of sucked.

The big warrior's stomach growled. "Come on, gnome. I saw a place that looked like it's got grilled goat ribs."

# CHAPTER 35

**The party sat** under a stunted pair of acacia trees, intent on completing their discussion before nightfall. Being outside the city helped make certain they wouldn't be overheard. They might stand out to a passersby on the road several hundred yards away. If anyone questioned the party upon their return, they'd enjoyed a picnic. Three loaves of bread and a half-pint of honey in a clay jar provided the food. A shared waterskin, along with the shade, helped fend off the dry heat.

Glenn wasn't really hungry but, since Derek didn't share their spending good coin on a meal, Glenn didn't either. He felt a little guilty about it. He planned on mentioning it sometime down the road.

Stephi sat on her travel basket placed between Glenn and Kirby. Derek, sitting between Glenn and Ron, leaned his back against one of the acacia's trunks.

Ron dipped his torn piece of bread in the honey and passed the jar to Derek. After chewing for a moment, savoring the taste, the warrior druid swallowed and cleared his throat. "Sterjin's Glass Receptacle Fabrications offers a formidable challenge to our objective."

That wasn't news to Glenn. No way Higslaff would've sent the party on a cake adventure. Besides that, Ron and Kirby's somber mood since returning from their scouting mission couldn't mean anything else.

"Dude," Kirby said, "just call it Sterjin's Glass or Sterjin's like everyone else in the city. Or just 'the glassblower's shop.'"

Ron glanced to his right. "Precision matters, Gurk. Of those comprising our party, only you and I had knowledge of the establishment's proper name."

Uncowed, Kirby said, "And now Kalgore, Marigold and Jax know how everyone but *you* calls it." The half-goblin grinned and made eye contact with Derek. "Keep the honey moving around."

Derek pressed a large piece of bread into the honey jar, then shoved it into his mouth. Packing the bite into a cheek, he complained, "This tooth makes everything taste a little bland, like it's been dipped in water." He scowled and shoved the jar into Glenn's hands.

Glenn held the jar for Stephi while Ron began again. "Sterjin's Glass Receptacle Fabrications offers a formidable challenge to our objective."

The warrior druid ignored the half-goblin thief's rolling eyes. "Utilizing a Detect Enchantment Spell, I was able to observe magical warding on the entrance, specifically the door frame and the door itself. The window frames are similarly warded."

"That's bad," Derek commented before shoving a plain piece of bread into his mouth.

Kirby leaned over and took the jar from Glenn's grasp. "It gets better," the half-goblin thief said before dipping bread and cramming the morsel into his mouth. "Meaning worse." The wad of bread muffled his words.

"Indeed." Ron took the proffered clay jar. "Upon entering, the Detect Enchantment Spell ceased." He looked from Derek to Stephi. "The spell's duration had not yet elapsed."

"So, it cancels detection spells," Derek said. "Is that all?"

"Gurk and I were not able to determine parameters of the warding."

The big warrior's face twisted in anger, like someone just insulted his mother. "Could stop anything Scroll Casting Barbie tried casting through it."

Glenn looked to Stephi to see if Derek's comment bothered her. She gave him her 'whatever' look, but didn't say anything.

Apparently unfazed by the warding concern, Kirby sat up straight. "Dude, tell them the cool part next."

Ron raised an eyebrow as he glanced at the half-goblin thief.

"The glass guardians," Kirby said. "They're life-size, totally nude chicks…uhh." The half-goblin's muddy skin showed signs of flushing as he looked away from Stephi. "I meant to say unclothed warrior women made of glass—with wicked crystal daggers."

Stephi rolled her eyes in exasperation. "Why doesn't that surprise me?"

"My heirloom item vibrated when I came into close proximity, which indicates they are in some fashion, enchanted."

Glenn asked, "Like the silversmith's golem in Three Hills City?"

"Silver golem's gotta be a lot better than glass," Derek said. "Even if there's two of them."

"The enchantment process to create a glass golem fortifies them," Ron said. "Makes them far more durable than might be expected of mere glass."

"Like bullet-proof glass?" Stephi asked.

"Yeah, sort of," Derek said, excitement draining from his voice as a thought surfaced. "Remember that adventure when we tried to loot that collapsed Athena temple?" His gaze shifted from Kirby to Ron. "The glass knight guardian really kicked our ass."

"Indeed," Ron said. "At that point in the campaign our characters were all fifth rank."

"But we were pretty much out of spells when we fought it," Kirby said.

Derek leaned forward. "We had more spells then, than we have now. Even when we're fresh." He reached over and took the honey jar from Ron. "And you said there's two of them."

Kirby looked down and frowned. "It gets worse." His yellow eyes met Ron's hazel ones. "Tell'em."

Ron took a deep breath. "Please refrain from commenting or asking questions until I complete my observation so that I will be less inclined to omit any important details.

"Gurk will then clarify or rectify any omissions, and possibly supplement with his observations."

While everyone acknowledged with a nod or an affirmative word, Ron lifted the waterskin to his mouth and drank. He wiped his lips and passed it off to Kirby.

"As Gurk noted, there are two elegantly crafted glass statues that incorporate formidable-appearing crystal daggers into their design. As they have been identified as enchanted, or magical, creatures, a logical assumption is that they are golems.

"The interior of Sterjin's Glass Receptacle Fabrications is similar to that of Higslaff's pawnshop. The exterior consists mainly of granite and limestone construction."

Ron pulled a small leather-bound book from his satchel, opened it to a page near the middle, and passed it to Derek.

"Visitors to the establishment first step into a large display room. The entry door is made from red oak and is reinforced with steel bands, and opens into the display room. I estimate it to be thirty feet deep and forty feet wide. The flooring is stone as are the walls. The shelving is built into the walls, and reaches up to the eight-foot ceiling. Both shelves and ceiling are constructed from red oak. Four limestone pillars support the ceiling, and presumably the structure's second story.

"The only windows in the establishment are narrow, being approximately eight inches wide and four feet tall. Two are set to either side of the main entry door and are filled with stained glass. Intense Light Spells equal to one-hundred-watt bulbs, render the windows decorative.

"A four-foot-tall granite counter runs lengthwise across the room, separating the display area from the work area. On the left is a door that presumably leads to a storage area, and access to the second story of the building. Gurk and I observed it opened briefly, revealing spare tongs, metal blow-pipes and other equipment necessary for creating high-quality glass jars, vases, and bowls.

"The right-hand portion of the work area has two granite tables set several feet apart, in front of the door leading to the furnace. To the right and left of the furnace are two pairs of three ovens stacked atop each other up to the ceiling.

"There is a constant, intense flame within the furnace, yet there is no evidence of any fuel source to maintain the flame or heat. One might imagine coal with a constant bellows or some sort of magically pumped liquid fuel."

Ron held up a finger to forestall Derek's question, and then continued.

"It seems there are two glass-blowing artisans on duty at a time, each pair working eight hour shifts, and the shop runs twenty-four hours a day. In addition to the artisans, there is an assistant behind the counter and there is a guard. The guard we observed was human. He wore breastplate, had a round shield, and was armed with a mace and a short sword. A steel helmet rested on a hook next to where he sat on the customer side of the counter, along the left-hand wall.

"Finally, there is what might be termed the shop foreman. He also serves as salesman. Both Gurk and I suspect the individual we observed is an enchanter, armed with a small sword and wearing a gold ring of impressive quality, which leads me to suspect the ring may have magical properties.

"While there are many glass items for sale on the shelves, the artisans read specifications written upon slate chalkboards, which the assistant occasionally erases and updates from a ledger. It is plausible that most of their work is contracted in advance.

"The two glass guardians, formed to the shape of six-foot-tall, voluptuous females stand to either side of the main entrance. They are tinted blue, crystal clear, and have sculpted sapphire eyes.

"The business does allow one to observe the process for several minutes, before the salesman inquires if the individual intends to contract the services of Sterjin's Glass Receptacle Fabrications, or purchase off the shelf. Inquiring about services and prices, it is logical to surmise that only the wealthiest of clients, or those in desperate need, might afford Sterjin's Glass Receptacle Fabrications' offerings."

Kirby cut in, "I could negotiate him down."

Ron frowned. "The stated fee for their crafted items, I believe, is purposefully inflated to discourage those without sufficient need and or resources to depart without further inquiry."

Kirby again interrupted Ron, offering him the jar of honey. "We saved ya some, dude. It's almost empty."

The warrior druid thanked Kirby, then said, "While I finish my portion of bread, provide the remaining pertinent details of our scouting endeavor."

"Right." Kirby grinned and scratched his nose. "So, after arrogant salesman dude talked to Lysine, then sort of gave us the brushoff, we went back outside.

"There's a two-story brick building to the right that's a bakery."

Ron cleared his throat. "Interpret left as to the east, with Sterjin's Glass Receptacle Fabrications' entry door facing south on the east to west running street."

"Yeah, right, east. Bakery's on the corner." Kirby

glanced to his left, at Ron. "Talking to a few people, when we got the bread, the upstairs floor is apartment rooms for the glass-blowing guys. On the left is a building just like the bakery, but with no business sign telling the type of business. It's deep as two buildings, so it sort of makes the two-foot wide alley a T, with the narrow parts going north and south. It ain't rundown or boarded up or anything. Me and Lysine think it's like the business offices and supply storage for the glass place. The big storage building's *west* wall," Kirby said, emphasizing the compass direction, "has a door that's super big with a short ramp up to it, and wagon ruts, too. The front door is sort of normal, but looks pretty sturdy, with a latch for a padlock. Probably for at night."

Kirby scrunched up his face. "Some dude with a sword sort of watches the business office and the glass shop from the street."

Kirby shook his head. "He's either the worst thief in the world, or wants people to know he's there for a reason." The half-goblin thief nodded his head while thinking to himself. "Bet they got, like, someone watching twenty-four seven.

"Bad thing is that there's only like about a foot between the buildings along the sides and a little over two running between buildings behind. In this town there's sharing walls or a couple feet. Plus, I saw iron rails partly dug into the ground. They got two-inch nail spikes sticking up. Nobody's gonna want to try squeezing between Sterjin's and the bakery or storage place."

Kirby reached over and picked up the empty jar sitting next to Ron. He said, "Tell'em about the pottery shop and the pipes and what we figured they're for, Lysine, and the shoemaker dude."

Grinning, the half-goblin began scraping his finger along the inside of the jar, licked the bits of honey and bread crumbs off his finger, and began the process again.

Ron cleared his throat. "The elderly cobbler. His single-story shop, also of brick construction, is on the corner, behind or north of the bakery, and east of the pottery shop. The cobbler presents himself as an ill-disposed individual who mistreats his apprentice."

Ron didn't elaborate, other than offering a look of disgust.

Kirby said, "Beats on him pretty good, by what we saw and the bruises."

That upset Glenn, causing a scowl.

Stephi said, "He shouldn't be allowed to do that. Why didn't you do something, Gurk?"

Gurk flinched, ducking his head. "I wanted to, but Lysine said we were on a scouting mission." He made eye contact with the party leader. "If the opportunity presented itself, we can take action."

Stephi's wings fluttered in irritation and asked Ron, "Why'd you stop Gurk?"

Derek cut in. "We're here because of you, Miss Do-Gooder Barbie. If Lysine or Gurk got marked as troublemakers, everybody'd be watching them if they ever went back around there." He leaned forward. "You wanna try doing the mission with only me, you, the gnome and your bird?"

The big warrior sat back. "I ain't dying to help some apprentice that gets thumped when he does something stupid." He pointed sharply at Stephi. "But say the word, Stupid Miss Do-Gooder, and I'll kick the cobbler's ass for ya, and you can stay a fairy forever."

Glenn jumped to his feet, fists balled. "You take that back."

Derek remained seated. "What? We're here because she did something stupid and she's wanting to do something else stupid."

"Men!" Ron said sharply, then continued in a

moderate tone. "Gentlemen, after engaging in a brief discussion, Gurk and I determined it wise to refrain from intervening, by and large, for several of the objective reasons Kalgore suggested."

"Yeah," Kirby said, yellow eyes glaring at the big warrior, "we get it, but you didn't have to be a—"

Ron leaned forward and snapped, "Gurk," cutting the half-goblin thief off. Then he motioned to Glenn. "Jax, please return to a seated position."

Glenn sat down in a huff, glaring at Derek and Ron. "If you already decided we're not going to do anything about it, why'd you even mention it?"

"So that everyone in the party would be aware," Ron said. "And refrain from intervening, even though our natural inclination is to do so."

Except for Derek, Glenn thought, but didn't express it verbally. The gnome healer could hardly stomach the big warrior's crossed arms and smug expression. Instead he reached out and took Stephi's tiny hand in his and squeezed gently.

Pent up anger in his voice, Kirby said, "Just tell them about the heat pipes and the elemental fire spirit."

# CHAPTER 36

**Glenn hustled to** keep up with Kirby. He understood his friend's urgency. Being seen together by the wrong person wasn't top on their list. Nor was wandering around Riven Rock in the dark, even though they were prepared for trouble. Glenn carried Stephi in the creel basket. Petie moved from rooftop to rooftop ahead of them.

Her fairy abilities, coupled with her magic user spells, and even some of the abilities she could channel from Kim, offered a potential nasty surprise. If she'd've been around for the fight against Guard Captain Nickson, it would've ended with a lot less of Kirby's blood being spilled.

That thought made the gnome healer wonder if the blood left in the street in front of Nibber's shack could end up being a clue to implicate his half-goblin friend. It'd be mixed with hard-packed dry dirt and rock. That had to lessen the chances.

Derek and Ron remained at the inn, interviewing a potential driver Blizz suggested. A woman named Lilac. The old animal handler said he'd worked alongside her before. She was good with animals, steady when fighting breaks out and, like him, wasn't the sort to talk about previous employers.

Plus, as party leader, Ron realized the current peril of pairing Kirby with Derek for the interview. He'd gotten pissed about Derek calling Stephi stupid. More than Glenn. A little time apart and working on the mission would soothe hard feelings. Glenn could hardly wait for Derek to do something that he could rub the big warrior's nose in.

"We're not going to make it back to the inn before

dark," Glenn said as they approached the intersection that led to the bakery from the east.

"Nope, dude." Kirby stopped to allow a rustic carriage with a driver atop and four figures inside, partially hidden by breeze-rippled curtains, to pass. The team of four horses trotted sharply. Sitting on the back of the carriage, buckled into a narrow seat with pegs for footrests, was a guard with helmet, breastplate, cocked crossbow, and short sword.

"C'mon, dude." Kirby signaled for his friend to move quickly across the road. "Guess they're like you and don't wanna be out after dark neither."

As always, Glenn's short legs required him to hustle to keep up.

"Don't look too long," Kirby said after they crossed the street ahead of a gaggle of porters with large wooden crates on their shoulders. "Dude in leather armor with the short sword, leaning against the front of the glass blowing shop. He's the local guard for sure."

The half-goblin and gnome backtracked a few steps and moved along the street, north, past the side of the cobbler's shop and turned left to walk past it and past the pottery shop. The pottery shop's exterior was lined with deep blue tiles, hardened and shiny.

Good advertisement, Glenn thought. People would remember the building.

"Marigold," Kirby said in a whisper, knowing her keen fairy ears would hear. "Have Petie find a spot to watch the guard, but mostly the glass shop. See who leaves and how they lock up."

Glenn recalled that they were supposed to work three eight-hour shifts, so closing down didn't seem likely. But locking when they didn't want customers made sense.

He also recalled that Ron had detected another magical creature with his heirloom necklace. By entering the bakery, cobbler's shop and the pottery shop, counting on the necklace's detection range, the magical creature was located in the northeast corner of the glass shop, bottom floor, right where the furnace was.

With no apparent use of coal, wood or any sort of liquid fuel to fire the glassblower's furnace, initial thoughts were that the owner of Sterjin's utilized some sort of permanent magical fire to create their expensive glass wares. The magical creature brought the notion of an elemental fire spirit. Ron witnessed intense flames from within, so he, Kirby and Derek were convinced.

Glenn had no clue exactly what an elemental flame spirit was. That said, any fiery creature that melted glass was one he didn't want to cross.

The pipes extending from the glass blower's shop, which were described as about fifteen inches in diameter to the baker's shop and twenty-four inches to the pottery shop, almost certainly provided heat for both operations. The bakery didn't show any use of coal, whereas the pottery shop did. But Ron estimated that the kiln's coal or wood capacity was insufficient to reach adequate temperatures. Plus, a hired man to pump a bellows through a pipe from the back wall to the kiln made him suspect where supplemental heat came from. Sterjin's Glass Receptacle Fabrications.

The pipe from the glassblowers to the baker, while being smaller, aligned with the elevated base of the main oven, much like a pizza oven. The larger pipe to the pottery shop ran along the ground, and was framed along the sides with brick and a rusting iron grill across the top.

Kirby had been more interested in the pipes than Ron when they discussed the building arrangements. Ron was more concerned with the magical warding on the shop's entrance. He discussed creating a small battering ram, like what law enforcement used to break doors down when raiding a drug house. But fretted if magic might protect, or even react, against such a physical assault.

"Marigold," Kirby whispered. "I'm gonna write a note for Petie to take back to Krogman's shop." He shot Glenn a wicked grin. "Us three are gonna do some breaking and entering, and see if we can sneak in the back way."

# CHAPTER 37

**With Stephi camouflaged** atop the building across from Sterjin's Glass, Kirby led Glenn west, toward one of the hills.

"We need some supplies," Kirby explained.

"You been in those hills?" Glenn asked. "In the tunnels?"

While Glenn had felt trepidation going into the unknown underground, especially as darkness fell, his gnomish heritage sort of looked forward to it. Gnomes didn't dig in mines and live underground in the same way dwarves did, but they often lived in the hollows of massive trees, or small communities dug into hillsides.

"Me and Lysine explored a little. The big crack in the ground ain't bottomless, but it's pretty deep. They lower mining dudes down in a bucket, with big ropes and pulleys. The horses tied to the ropes make the Budweiser Clydesdales look like ninety-eight pound pushovers."

That Glenn hadn't gotten to see it sort of disappointed him. He got to spend time with Derek instead.

Kirby slapped Glenn on the back. "They got an easy system for directions, dude, but ya can still get lost. Me and Lysine got mixed up twice, and it screwed up his sketches in his map book."

As the pair of adventurers got closer to one of the main entrances, the road leading up to a hole big enough for a school bus, more and more people seemed to be streaming in. Not legions, but twenty or so men, mostly laboring types in groups of three to five, tromped in. The scene reminded Glenn of Friday nights on campus. Upperclassmen streaming uptown, toward the bars.

"We ain't gotta go in far, Jax, but if we get separated,

remember squares on the ceiling means you're going deeper inside and round—like the sun—means you're going toward an exit."

Glenn eyed his friend with an arched left eyebrow. "Signs?"

"You'll see, dude." He patted the gnome on the shoulder, then handed him a thick piece of chalk. It looked like powder blue sidewalk chalk his kindergarten niece drew with.

"I'll explain," Kirby said. "Trust me."

Right, Glenn thought. A gnome following a half-goblin into an underground complex filled with revelers and who knows what all else. And the half-goblin is really a junior-high-aged kid. What could go wrong?

Then he remembered. Kirby might be only twelve or thirteen in the real world, but in the *Monsters, Maces and Magic* world, the kid had far more experience. *And* he was a skilled thief. Glenn rested his hand on his cudgel and felt the weight of his round shield strapped across his back. He was a healer, with a lot of hit points, and a gnome. Most people liked gnomes.

**Turned out, gnome** or not, most people ignored Glenn, and Kirby. A time or two, a band of drably dressed laborers wearing sandals or heavy boots brushed past them, intent on some destination, one that likely involved drinking and entertainment.

Glenn wondered if there were places like the Blue Bugle beneath the small mountains. He doubted it. The corridors carved through the big hill—big as those he recalled driving through in Kentucky and Tennessee—were low and wide. Eight feet wide and no more than seven feet tall. Stephi, the old, non-fairy Stephi, would've had to be careful.

The stone corridors were pretty straight, lit by

magic. The Light Spells were on the weaker side, being either fifteen or twenty-five watts in strength. Plenty strong enough for his gnome eyes. And for Kirby's half-goblin, despite the globes tending to fade out for several feet instead of their coverage overlapping. That provided an odd feeling as they walked ever deeper into the hillside.

Glenn discovered what Kirby meant by the round and square signs. Every fifty or so feet, a circle and square were painted on the ceiling, stacked parallel with the hallway. As best Glenn could tell, the white square was placed, showing the direction deeper. The white circle indicted the direction to go to find a way out. The corridors were fairly straight, but the intersections, both T and four-way, were rarely ninety-degree affairs. Occasionally ladders or stone stairways, carved into the walls, went up or down. They were wide as well, about four feet, so two people could squeeze by each other.

They took one down, after taking a left, down a thirty-degree forked corridor. The level below's circles remained white but the squares were tan.

And there were plenty of shops, at least from what Glenn could tell. None had hinged, swinging doors, but he saw many had some sort of door hidden in a set-in a slot a foot or so in the arched doorways. Others had gates that could be dropped, much like stores in malls did, when they closed.

Unlike in Three Hills City, there were no official city guardsmen to be seen. But in the tunnels some hulking, muscled men in armor with maces or axes stood by some of the shopfronts. Always in pairs. They weren't Riven Rock city guards. Glenn pegged them more along the lines of Rent-a-Thugs. Their disdainful visages mingled with eyes eager to detect some reason to attack one of the riffraff streaming past. That encouraged Glenn, the short gnome, to avoid eye contact. To give them wide berth.

Glenn's nostrils took in odors of sweat and bad breath. His bulbous nose also detected scents of flowery perfumes and exotic herbs, alcoholic beverages, smoke and some oily cooked meats. Smells lingered because the progress of unwashed bodies seemed to be the only thing moving the air.

One double-wide doorway emitted purple light. Inside lounged scantily-clad women. One of the three had a chest even more epic than Stephi's. But her Appearance Score was nowhere near Stephi's, and the woman's alluring smile didn't reach her eyes.

Kirby grabbed Glenn by the arm, dragging him forward. "Dude, don't get distracted. We're almost there."

"Where?" Glenn asked, spotting some sort of roulette wheel spinning in a deep alcove. A cluster of men crowded in front of it, grumbling or laughing rancorously. One even cheered.

"Here," Kirby said and pulled him into a smoke-filled room. It was a bar, of sorts. No tables filled the space, only a U-shaped granite bar running along the three walls, with iron stools bolted to the floor. Dwarves mainly filled the seats, with a few humans. Three barmaids tended to the customers, bringing steins of ale or beer from a room—or series of rooms—beyond. One of the women had to be a female dwarf. Glenn instinctively recognized this, by the wispiness of her brown beard. She stepped up on some sort of platform to serve the laborers, trading friendly jibes and insults. The muscles framing her stout upper body and chest, hidden beneath a sweat-stained linen blouse, were impressive.

Glenn noted all the stocky dwarves, like the waitress, had brown beards. They all smelled of coal smoke, sweat and burnt iron. Unlike the men in the bar, who carried the scents of wood, animal waste and sulfur.

"Stay right here," Kirby said and elbowed his way

between two men, flashing two silver coins. "Two bottles of liquor, to go."

Eyeing the silver, a human waitress with braided black hair and a scar over her left eye asked, "What kind, shorty?"

"Jack Daniels."

The barmaid squinted across the bar at the half-goblin. "Jack who?"

"Uhhh, what ya got?" Kirby asked, suddenly at a loss for words.

The two workmen sitting at the bar the young thief had squeezed between glared down at Kirby.

Glenn stepped up behind his friend. "He means whisky, if you have any, ma'am."

The black-haired woman looked past Kirby. When her eyes fell on Glenn, she smirked, then rolled her eyes and smiled. "Two more copper, or what you'll get, my little gnome, will leave you puking before morning."

Glenn didn't care for the "little" remark, but it came without the harshness of an intended insult. "Two coppers, plus a third, if you can get it to us quick." He smiled and winked, coming up with the only thing the barmaid and patrons in such a questionable bar might accept. "We got dates waiting on us."

**"Thanks, dude." Kirby** led his friend out into the night air, leaving the tunnel behind. Most of the foot traffic going in had abated. "We needed something in a bottle, and they don't have beer or ale in bottles. And asking for wine in that place didn't seem like a smart move." He shrugged. "All I could think of was what my dad kept in the cabinet above the stove."

"No problem," Glenn said, looking around, making sure nobody was paying attention as they made their way back toward the pottery maker's shop. He pulled the thick piece of chalk out of his pocket. "What'd you give this to me for?"

"Really?" Kirby slowed almost to a stop. "Sorry, I thought you knew. Mark the walls in case you get lost. I knew where I was going, but if we got separated, it'd help you from going the same way, again and again." The half-goblin thief shrugged. "Works better in a cave than with people around." He took the chalk and demonstrated against a wooden building as they walked. "A quick flick can show the way you came from without drawing much attention."

Kirby handed the chalk back. "I got more, dude. That's what makes us a good team. We cover for each other."

That complement felt good. So often Glenn felt like he was more a burden than an asset—other than healing.

"So, what's the plan with the whiskey?"

"I'll explain as soon as we get Marigold to fly down so she can hear it, too."

**Glenn stood between** buildings a half-block away. He watched the guard clad in leather armor smack at his neck, then curse and wave his hands back and forth, before slapping at his face.

Stephi had noted a guard watching the road from atop Sterjin's Glass. That caused a change in Kirby's plan. Stephi used her Slumber Spell on the roof guard, then hauled the whisky bottle up to the roof. Once there she poured some down the sleeping man's throat—without waking him—and spilled some on his clothes. Getting drunk and falling asleep on duty wouldn't go well for the guard. In any case, he wouldn't be likely to mention the event for fear of what might happen. That was Kirby's theory.

Since Stephi had only one Slumber Spell memorized,

and they only had one bottle of whiskey, Kirby told Stephi to use her fairy ability to summon as many pigeons as possible. Then have them unleash as much bird poop as possible all over the dude standing guard.

How Stephi could "communicate" with the pigeons and suggest a course of action, Glenn wasn't sure. But it was magic. And it was working. At least thirty of the birds arrived, flying tight circles overhead and landing on nearby roofs.

The guard stopped his foot patrol and looked up at the commotion. From the way the guard rubbed at an eye, while spitting, said at least two pigeon poo bombs struck home. Gobs of white continued raining down. Many missed, but enough landed in the man's hair and all over his leather armor to make it look like he was on the losing end of a paintball fight.

While Stephi's pigeon distraction was going on, it was up to Kirby to pick the lock to gain entry. One of the scattered light poles, with a weak Light Spell, barely reached to the pottery shop's front door. That left Kirby visible and exposed. Nevertheless, the risk didn't seem to bother the half-goblin thief.

Being a second-rank thief, having an eighteen Coordination Score, and his half-goblin Racial Bonus for that particular thieving skill, Kirby estimated he had a fifty-fifty chance of picking the padlock.

After a minute, Petie bobbed his head twice, indicating success.

Glenn slipped his cudgel back into its belt loop. Relieved he didn't have to confront the guard, the gnome made his way from shadow to shadow toward the pottery shop.

He didn't see Stephi standing in the small gap between the cobbler and pottery shop, Camouflaged against the wall. Risky, Glenn thought, with the iron spikes pointing upward.

"Be fast," she whispered. "My pigeons are empty."

Glenn half jumped, and looked down her general direction, then gazed up and down the quiet street. He knew she was supposed to be there.

Stephi added, "Gurk thinks this is some sort of a game."

"Technically, it is," Glenn said and kept moving at a steady pace, knowing her little fairy face would be scrunched up and a light shade of pink.

The gnome made it to the door, pushed it open and slipped inside.

"Pretty quiet, dude," Kirby whispered into his ear. Even with his low-light vision, everything was dark and shadowy. Then he added. "The pottery dude's baking some of his stuff, so it's too hot. Let's try the baker's."

"Maybe we should call it a night and try again tomorrow," Glenn whispered.

"No way. We try this tomorrow night and them guards'll know something's up." He rested a hand on the gnome's shoulder. "Same deal as before, but Stephi'll have to distract the guard."

Less than ten minutes later, Kirby and Glenn were inside the baker's shop, with Stephi returning to her watch position, this time between the bakery and the glass shop.

"How do you think she managed to get him around the corner?" Glenn whispered as they made their way behind the counter, heading toward the oven.

"Maybe she flashed her boobs," Kirby replied with a mischievous grin. He picked up a large pair of oven mitts. "Give me your everlast candle."

After checking behind the big set of ovens, Kirby said, "See this lever?"

Glenn nodded. The steel bar was attached to the pipe, set to pivot and elevate something blocking the air flow when pressed down. "I bet that lets the heat in."

Kirby nodded. He pulled the oven's big iron door open. "When I get inside, pull the lever so I can see where the pipe goes."

"It goes into the glass shop's furnace."

"I know, dude. But I want to see if the thing's lined with clay or if it's steel. If so, Marigold won't be able to make it through them. Iron, or anything with iron in it, burns her now that she's a fairy. Remember?"

"Steel lining or no, I'm not sure she'll fit through this pipe."

"I know." The half-goblin rolled his yellow eyes. They probably built this pipe the same way as the bigger one that leads into the pottery oven."

Kirby looked into the oven before donning the oven mitts and crawling in. Then he fumbled to open Glenn's everlast candle.

"Lever it, dude."

Glenn did as asked, pressing down on the lever.

"Oh, that's hot," Kirby said. "Heat's prickling my face."

Then he added, "Oh, well, that sucks."

A sizzling pop accompanied a split-second of light, like a camera's flash, and emerged from the oven's open door. The same instant a muffled cry echoed from within the oven, followed by a dull, *thump* on metal. Next came the smell of smoldering fabric, and burnt flesh.

# Chapter 38

**Glenn released the** vent's lever and raced around to the oven's front. Kirby's legs dangled out, unmoving. Without hesitation, the gnome grabbed hold of his friend's ankles and hauled back. He then shifted the unmoving body's weight sideways so he could lower Kirby to the hardwood floor.

Trails of smoke wafted up from the blackened oven mitt. Sticking through the charred end were two blackened fingers. Not wasting time to see if his friend was dead or alive, Glenn immediately began a Minor Healing Draw spell, and took the damage upon himself.

The gnome healer's heart fluttered and skipped several beats. He fell back against the oven, clutching his chest, despite the pain in his right hand.

Kirby's hands twitched and his left leg kicked out. After groaning for a second, he sat up and wiped the drool from his right cheek.

The half-goblin thief's eyes shot wide. "Jax!" He scrambled over and knelt next to his friend. He leaned over and gripped the gnome's shoulders as his croaky voice cracked, saying, "Don't die, Jax. Come on—ya gotta pull through."

Glenn released a pent-up breath. His heart fell into rhythm, and he began to breathe.

"Man, you scared me, dude."

Still a little disoriented and weak, Glenn forced a half-grin. "Like you didn't scare me?"

"Let me get your candle, close up the oven and get us out of here."

"What happened?" Glenn asked. He propped himself up, getting to one knee.

After retrieving the candle and closing up the oven,

Kirby helped the gnome to his feet. "Tell ya, later."

**Ron admonished Kirby.** "Your actions were both impetuous and inadvisable. You were fortunate to have survived the Minor Lightning Spell contingently placed to eliminate individuals curious enough to explore mysteries related to…" Ron paused, then ended, saying, "The glassblower's furnace."

The party was crowded into their room in the Sulfur Ash Inn, huddled around Glenn's everlast candle.

"Yeah, thief," Derek said. "Lucky you made your Saving Throw."

Ron nodded affirmation of Derek's statement. "And fortunate that Jax's Minor Healing Draw Spell re-established your heart's stable electrochemical system."

Glenn knew that he'd taken on Kirby's heart damage. Luckily, healing fixed what the Minor Lightning Spell disrupted. Maybe that required a Saving Throw as well?

"I know, I know." Kirby sounded anything but repentant. "But now we know what to expect if we wanna go in through the pottery shop's pipe." He shot a nasty grin at Derek. "To screw with the furnace."

That was the new plan. Rather than a frontal entrance effort and dealing with the entry door's magical protections, attempt something not quite as direct, but equally destructive.

"I still got the fulgurite," Derek said, placing his hand over his chest where the magical item hung beneath his mail shirt. "So any lightning won't bother me."

"The intense heat generated by the fire elemental spirit is the next obstacle." Ron rubbed a forefinger across his chin. "During my undergraduate studies, my dormitory roommate was an art major. He spent many hours engaged in artistic endeavors, which included elementary glassblowing and pottery manufacture. Relevant to our current situation is what I recall from assisting him in his studies.

"Achieving a temperature of one thousand one hundred degrees Celsius is necessary to work glass."

"Celsius, dude?" Kirby threw up his hands. "Who uses that?"

Ron frowned. "In my former state, making the mental conversion from Celsius to Fahrenheit would prove trivial. As I am now, it requires pencil and paper to properly implement the formulaic conversion."

Glenn bit his lip. Ron's Intelligence Score, as Lysine, was a fourteen. In real life, as the graduate student studying mathematics, he was a genius. Probably equivalent to an eighteen. More than just about anything else, the loss of mental abilities disturbed Ron.

Stephi fluttered up from her place in the circle and rested a hand on Ron's shoulder. "Do the calculation yourself, Gurk. You used metric measurements to trick me into having ginormous boobs."

"They ain't exactly ginormous now," Derek said. "Mini-Metric Marigold Barbie."

Stephi huffed. Her wings fluttered, carrying her higher into the air. "They're ginormous to me, Kalgore the Courageous."

Her wings' rapid beating caused her breasts to bounce like agitated maracas beneath her leaf and twig garments. Either she was trying to emphasize her point, or didn't notice it happening. Either way, it wasn't good.

Kirby flinched after realizing he'd put his foot in it then, and now. "No problem, Lysine." He averted his gaze from Stephi and spoke louder than necessary, refocusing attention on himself. "A thousand, one hundred degrees."

"Our present forms, they force each of us to endure deficiencies," Ron said, "or that which hampers us."

Glenn agreed with the warrior druid. Being short was none too fun. Stephi was suffering that doubly…plus her huge breasts. They always drew unwanted attention. Derek was illiterate, and Kirby suffered with being an unattractive half-goblin in a highly prejudicial and bigoted world.

"A more colloquial near equivalent would be standing in a blazing bonfire," Ron said. "On the other hand, to fire clay requires a temperature of nine hundred fifty degrees, Celsius."

"Which is why there was coal in the pottery place," Kirby said, "but not in the baker's. You don't need a thousand degrees, Celsius or regular Fahrenheit to bake bread."

Derek cleared his throat. "Don't druids have a first rank spell that protects you from heat?"

Ron closed his eyes in thought. "That is correct, but not likely useful for our purposes. Minor Heat Resistance protects an individual from temperatures up to four-hundred fifty degrees Fahrenheit." The warrior druid glanced and the thief and raised an eyebrow, then smirked. "The Player's Guide utilizes the Imperial or U.S. Standard system of measurement.

"To endure the glassblower's furnace harnessing what we believe to be a fire elemental spirit, would require a Major Heat Resistance Spell."

"That's like a fourth or fifth-rank spell," Kirby said.

"What about getting a scroll?" Marigold asked.

Wrinkles appeared on Ron's forehead. "That is a possibility."

"There's potions that'll do the trick protecting ya," Derek said. "We've got manticore parts to trade."

Kirby slapped Derek on the back. "Yeah, dude. This city's gotta have an alchemist somewhere."

A knock on the door, followed by a gruff yet feminine voice silenced everyone. "Lysine, it's Lilac."

Lysine removed the chair blocking the door and opened it, allowing a stocky woman to step in. If anyone might be accused of being built like a barrel, it was this driver. But, unlike drivers the gnome had seen, this woman wore a chainmail shirt and carried a war hammer slipped through a loop on her broad belt. Her unruly, straight brown hair barely reached her shoulders and framed an unremarkable face, except for its nose. It was bent at an angle, obviously broken and not properly set to heal.

The woman quickly took in the group, except for Stephi. She'd backed against the far wall and worked her Camouflage magic while everyone else had gotten to their feet. Lilac looked up to meet Ron's gaze after the warrior druid closed the door.

"Lysine, sir, there's a couple of men from the local thieving guild downstairs questioning your hired mercenaries."

The warrior druid's hand quickly went to the grip of his short sword. "Explain."

"They're mostly questioning your man, Mardin. They want to know if the party is in the inn. Mardin indicated that he believes the party leader and gnome are, but isn't sure where everyone else is."

Derek started to say something but Ron held up a hand to forestall questions.

"Did these men go to the innkeeper first, or straight to our hirelings?"

"Straight to the hirelings. Mardin, Trumble, Kronk and Harold. I was not sitting with them, and they probably don't know you've hired me."

Glenn bit his lip. The local thieves' guild had done most of their homework.

"The name Yonn was mentioned. Mardin's reaction gave away he knew who that was. Said he hadn't seen him and some other mercenary, or their captain since this morning."

"Remain here," Ron said to her. He clenched his teeth for a second. "Jax, you and I will go downstairs and exit, concealing that we are aware of the questioning in progress. We shall proceed to the Dusty Brick Inn and secure rooms.

"Kalgore, you shall wait in this room while Marigold determines if the men in question remain, or if they followed us. If they follow Jax and myself, you three are to surprise the questioners, and secure what information you are able. Otherwise, remain here until they depart. Then make your way to the Dusty Brick."

Ron turned back and addressed Lilac. "When appropriate, inform Mardin, Trumble, Kronk and Harold to remain here for the remainder of the night. At noon, all of you are to pack up and seek instructions at Krogman's Wagon Repair Shop."

"I believe the guild men also questioned the other drivers," Lilac said. "Blizz ain't one to talk. To encourage Mardin, they indicated roughing Blizz up pretty good."

"We are aware of his professional conduct," Ron said, brewing anger showing in his hazel eyes. He turned back to the rest of the party. "Jax and I will attend to Blizz first, and then make our way to the Dusty Brick Inn. Adjust your plan of action accordingly."

# Chapter 39

Ron departed the Sulfur Ash Inn with Glenn trailing behind. The warrior druid made a quick nod of acknowledgement to Mardin, who was at a table with two men in leather armor. Each was seated on the bench to either side of the man-at-arms.

Glenn didn't allow his gaze to linger. Best to let the thieves from the rival guild—rival to the guild in Three Hills City—think that they'd been overlooked as inn patrons. The warrior druid carried his spear, so Glenn knew it might come to a fight.

Once outside Ron halted, looked both ways, and then began a line of conversation with Glenn that focused on estimated time for the wagons to be ready, anticipated cargo, the possible need for additional horses. Not satisfied, he continued, assigning Glenn to secure travel provisions for the party, drivers, and hired men-at-arms. Derek would secure oats for the horses due to the harsh terrain. He discussed travelling further south, to Fountain Springs.

Glenn nodded and occasionally asked a question, such as a preference between beef or goat jerky, or potatoes or carrots, radishes or onions. The gnome healer thought he was playing his part fairly well.

Periodically the pair of adventurers slowed to allow other nighttime travelers to bypass or cross ahead of them. This part of the city was better built-up than where Glenn and Kirby fought Nickson. Wider streets and more posts with Light Spells meant fewer shadows. Still, the gnome was happy to have a warrior walking beside him.

Glenn didn't dare turn around to see if they were being followed. If Ron did, Glenn didn't catch him doing it.

Then they made a turn, heading back toward where their horses were stabled. Where Blizz and Simmer watched and cared for them.

Ron's anger had ebbed, but Glenn's concern for the bandy-legged, old animal handler hadn't. He sort of guessed why Ron chose a roundabout route. To give Kirby and Derek, and Marigold, the opportunity to get the jump on the two guild thieves.

They finally made it to the stables which, of course, were locked up.

Ron stood at the side door, knocked once. "Blizz," he whispered. "This is Lysine. Jax has accompanied me."

A moment later Simmer lifted the latch and let the pair of adventurers in. A look of relief spread across the wide-eyed driver's face. "Mr. Lysine, Blizz is over here." He signaled for them to follow.

"Return the bar to its place," Ron said over his shoulder to Glenn, then followed Simmer past a dozen stabled horses to where Blizz lay, sprawled out on a spread of straw. A rag pillow supported head. Dried blood caked around his nose and swollen lips indicated the severity of the beating he'd endured.

"He's alive," Simmer said, "but I can't get him to wake up. They said if I left the stables before sunrise, they'd kill me, and finish Blizz, too." The driver looked up at several other drivers lying in hammocks. The dim lantern light revealed several nods in affirmation of Simmer's statement.

Glenn moved to begin his spell, but Ron placed a hand on the gnome healer's shoulder. "Allow me to utilize a Minor Cure Spell. You have expended much of your healing ability already this day, and I have yet to utilize any spells this day."

Glenn wasn't eager to feel the pain the half-goblin animal handler suffered. Nevertheless, he wanted to heal the loyal hireling.

Ron placed a hand on his chest, where the wooden symbol of Gaia hung, and uttered the words. He then touched the old half-goblin. Within a minute, most of the swelling that afflicted Blizz's face disappeared. The dried blood remained. After a second spell the injuries from which the blood had welled were gone.

The old animal handler stirred to consciousness and a wide smile split his face.

"Mr. Lysine and Mr. Jax, I knew you'd show up. And I thank you."

"It is us," Ron said, "that should be thanking you."

Simmer'd watched the healing. He stepped back and looked away, at the stable floor.

The warrior druid got to his feet, and examined Simmer. The man had a black eye.

"I told them where you were staying," the driver said, his voice barely above a whisper. "They were going to beat me like they done Blizz."

"Rest assured," Ron said to the remorseful driver, "the matter is being addressed by Kalgore and Gurk."

"Oooh," Blizz said, "payback's a coming around." A wicked, pointed-tooth grin filled his face. "If there's two better porters of payback in this black city to deliver it, no mother's whore of a demon'd want to meet them."

**Glenn and Ron** sat at a table in the corner of the tavern attached to the Dusty Brick Inn. Ron was on his second ale while Glenn nursed the mead in his clay mug. While it wasn't sweet, the gnome could taste the honey.

It was closing in on midnight, and Ron had rented a large room for the party. Petie'd landed on a post outside about a half hour earlier. The familiar bobbed and warbled, indicating everything was okay, before flying off.

The tavern scene was familiar to Glenn. A wooden-plank floor with round tables and wooden chairs. It leaned toward a bar from the American Old West, but with an Irish pub influence. Visiting *Monsters, Maces and Magic* taverns was sort of like visiting a string of hotels. All the rooms looked mostly the same.

The person or persons who thought up this *Monsters, Maces and Magic* game world, in many ways, lacked imagination. Or motivation to use imagination.

"Do you ever get scared, here, Lysine?" Glenn asked. He didn't exactly plan to ask that question, but the words somehow slipped out. The gnome healer shrugged to himself and pressed on. "I get scared a lot, but seems like you never are."

The warrior druid took a long drink and set his tall mug down on the worn table. "I believe each of us experiences fear, my friend." He suppressed a smile. "Even Kalgore the Courageous."

"Really?"

"Absolutely. Despite what your feel inside, you have accounted for yourself well. Fought with the heart of the stoutest of warriors."

Glenn looked up at his party's leader, and shook his head. He took a long drink.

"It was you, Jax, who defeated the husk mummy, despite the terror in confronting such a vile creature. Without your valor, all of us would have perished."

"Once, and I got lucky."

"Have you forgotten the swamp harpy confrontation?"

"No." Glenn shook his head again. "But when it comes to a fight, I hardly make a difference."

"Your character class is a healer. The combat tables are least favorable, equal to that of magic users." He tapped an index finger on the table. "A party consisting entirely of warriors would not fare nearly as well compared to one balanced with an assortment of character classes."

Glenn laughed. "Five warriors like Kalgore against us? They'd hack us to pieces."

A rare smirk of humor crossed Ron's face. "What if Marigold released a Slumber Spell? Even if the warriors did prevail, how long would it take them to recover from their inevitable wounds? What might happen if they met with a Wandering Creatures Encounter while so wounded?"

Still unconvinced, Glenn asked, "How do you deal with being scared?"

Ron signaled for the olive-skinned waitress to deliver another drink for himself and Glenn. "During my undergraduate studies, I researched and wrote a report discussing B-17 bomber crews of the 8th Army Air Force battling against the Third Reich during World War II. The crews fought in horrendous weather conditions, against determined foes. They endured both waves of Nazi fighters and eighty-eight millimeter anti-aircraft guns sending up tremendous flak barrages.

"A high percentage of bombers and crews were lost during missions over Germany and occupied France. Yet most crewmen continued to fly against the enemy. The targets selected, the weather, what the enemy would throw against them…was out of their control. Mission after mission, how could that not be frightening? What the crews could control was how well they did their job and how well they looked after each other. How could that not be bravery?"

Glenn slowly spun his mug on the table while pondering Ron's words. "So, as party leader, you sort of see yourself as the pilot? And each adventure is a mission with dangers, some known and others not?"

"I believe you have missed my point, Jax." Ron glanced up at the wooden beams above, supporting the second floor. "Each person has the potential within him-

or herself to overcome paralyzing fear. To do what is right, and just and prevail."

When Glenn didn't respond, Ron continued. "An observation I once heard on a Youtube video is relevant to this conversation. It described life as tragedy tainted by malevolence. While one might argue that as an accurate description of the true world—our world—evidence, at least anecdotal evidence, indicates such is the state of things in this aberrant concurrent world we now inhabit."

The warrior druid leaned toward the gnome, his gaze intense. "Despite such egregious conditions, I have undertaken to ensure all in our party achieves the opportunity to return home."

He leaned back. "I believe we, as a party, can surmount this world's malevolence."

Glenn always wondered what made Ron tick. He knew logic and determination were at the core, driving him.

"Lysine, I think you're at least as brave as any B-17 crewmember."

"Your complement is appreciated, Jax, but overstated."

The discussion with Ron was less logical and precise. It was more wandering than he was used to hearing from the party's leader. He was probably as unprepared for the discussion as Glenn. Maybe even less used to sharing feelings and insights. Ron's closest friend was Derek. Glenn couldn't imagine engaging in a deep, revealing conversation with that jerk.

The gnome pushed his drink aside. "How many bomber crewmen ever stood against a manticore, with only a spear and sword?"

"That statement implies I stood alone against such a creature. Clearly, I did not."

"Now it's you who's missing the point."

# CHAPTER 40

**"Gnome, if you** see that sorry bastard, Yonn, let me know." That was the third time the big warrior told Glenn that.

Ron assigned Glenn to accompany Derek to the alchemist to see if there was anything available to protect someone from intense heat, like that found in the furnace at Sterjin's Glass. In the meantime Ron and Kirby were arranging for supplies for the wagons, and doing a little last minute recon of Sterjin's.

Rather than being a sunny and dry morning, with building heat, it was a partly cloudy morning with building heat, and dust in the streets. Glenn thought about wearing a handkerchief across his face, but figured that might draw attention to him, maybe even as someone planning to rob some place.

The streets were busy and Glenn wasn't likely to recognize anyone while trying to keep pace with Derek's long strides. Ahead of them a pair of donkeys pulled a cart stacked with cages holding chickens and roosters. Combined with the din of the busy streets, Glenn decided to risk a conversation.

"So those two guys you and Gurk jumped, they just believed you?"

Derek shifted the sack he carried over his shoulder. "They were looking for information and weren't too bright."

Glenn scratched his sideburn, feeling it damp with sweat. "You said they were higher rank than you?"

Derek turned his head left and right, then glanced over his shoulder. The big warrior was probably looking for Yonn, or Slarg, more than to make sure he and Glenn weren't being followed.

"Higher rank, but like I said, dumber." Derek picked up the pace to get around the poultry cart. "Plus, even your half-goblin pal can be pretty intimidating." Derek stood up straight. "Not as much as me."

After they got ahead of the cart, Derek slowed down. "I saw that one of them had a dagger with a dark paste rubbed on it. Twisted it out of his hand before either of them could do anything. I licked the blade and just glared at them while doing it. Made'em think we were tougher than them.

"Remembered what you said about the tooth neutralizing poison." The big warrior slapped Glenn across the back, not as hard as usual. "That was smart thinking."

"They just wanted to ask questions about the guard captain. One of them had a magic bead that glowed green when someone tells the truth and red when someone lies. The knife guy asked if we knew what happened to Nickson. I shrugged and said he left, saying he was going to see about hiring more mercenaries, since we lost a couple fighting a manticore.

"Bead glowed green." Derek grinned. "See, magical gems and beads like that don't follow words only. They pick up whether the statement is true or false. So as far as the bead was concerned, I told the truth—which I did. But they missed the shrug. They were watching to see what the bead showed. And I actually did tell the truth, overall—assuming you and the thief told the whole truth."

Derek gave a crooked grin, signaling he was joking. "Then the bead guy asks your buddy thief what he knows about Nickson's disappearance. So Gurk tells him that he'd heard the dude had a gambling problem. Green glow again, and I said to the dumb thief holding the bead, 'You want to know what I know?' The bead guy says said, 'Yes.' So I tell him people that ain't good at gambling disappear all the time. Green again, and the bead's magic was used up."

Glenn wasn't sure he followed it all, or that Derek had the explanation right, but didn't question him.

Derek glanced around then smiled down at Glenn. "Those two were too dumb to ask good questions and stop us from making statements that'd use up the magic." Derek tapped a finger to his temple. "A GM pulled that trick on us once."

Glenn was going to ask if they'd asked dumb questions too, when learning the lesson. But thought better of it. He knew what the big warrior meant. Wrecking Derek's good mood wasn't worth it.

Something caught Derek's eye. "There it is, up ahead." He picked up the pace, going around a creaking wagon piled full of coal. "Oh, and your buddy Gurk said these guys might be tight with the local guild, so just follow my lead."

Wonderful, Glenn thought. Could've told me that, say, any time before thirty seconds until arrival?

**The exterior of** Brombar's Mixtures and Elixirs impressed Glenn. A three-story granite building with several pipes extending far above the structure's slate roof. He'd seen them from a distance a couple of times, and now knew what they belonged to. A good landmark to gauge where he was within the city—besides the stench. The glass windows framed in steel, with thick steel bars in front of them made sure nothing but light got in. The entry door set into an alcove looked pretty stout. When Derek pushed it open, he mumbled to himself, "Ironwood."

The interior, on the other hand, was anything but impressive. Well lit, with magical light supplementing the natural sunlight. But the air was hot and stuffy, and filled with stuff that made Glenn's gnomish nose feel like little ants were running around in his nostrils. Other than that, a red oak table, whose top was scratched and marred by divots and stains, sat in the center of the front area. Behind it sat a man in a padded chair reading a leather-bound tome. The only thing adorning the wall behind him was another door. From its looks, probably ironwood. There was metal slot cut into it. Closed.

Derek moved to take one of the two three-legged stools across from the man. Once seated he popped the filled sack down on the floor next to him. Glenn thought about climbing onto the other stool, but decided against it. Instead he slid it aside and stood next to the seated warrior.

The man looked up from his reading, placed a thin copper bookmark in the pages before closing the book and setting it on the corner of the table.

The guy was a salesman, if Glenn ever saw one. A waxed, handlebar mustache, slicked back hair and a broad, insincere smile. His silk shirt was white with silver buttons and his breeches were dark blue. He wore high boots with silver buckles. As far as Glenn could tell, he wasn't armed.

In a bored-sounding voice, he asked, "May I be of assistance?"

Derek looked around, as if realizing for the first time how empty the ten by twenty-foot room was. "You don't look much like any alchemists I've ever met." He pointed. "Shouldn't you be grinding up unicorn horns or heating some glass vials over a candle?"

Ron insisted that Derek do the main talking, but that Glenn should be ready to step in and help the deal along. It made sense since, at least game-wise, Derek had bartered a lot more than Glenn, and knew what kinds of potions and other things alchemists in the game could make. Those would help with any "dice rolls" related to negotiations.

And they both knew that the establishment was tied in with the local thieves' guild. Probably like Higslaff's pawnshop was in Three Hills City.

Glenn kept a pleasant expression on his face, instead of showing annoyance at Derek's intentional omission of that guild connection, until the very last minute.

The salesman rolled his eyes—certain to get Derek fired up—and said, "While I am well versed in chemicals and exotic components, and wield a *really mean* mortar and pestle, my specialty is in sales and service."

Despite the condescending tone, Derek appeared to take it in stride. That wasn't like him.

"Oh. Okay," he said agreeably. "We got some stuff while adventuring you might be interested in." He reached into the sack he'd been carrying and began placing the items on the table. "This all came from a manticore."

First he placed a sack stuffed with black hair from the manticore's mane, then a smaller sack holding eight claws on the table. From the bottom of his sack he pulled out a wooden crate. Placing it on the table and resting a hand over it, he said, "In there's the tail with spikes and some teeth. You'll want to be careful, because they probably got some dried poison on them."

The salesman let out a long sighing breath. "The correct term would be venom."

Derek knew the difference between poison and venom. Glenn was sure of that.

"Yeah, right. Venom. And we got two corked bottles of blood that my friend has in his sack." The warrior signaled for Glenn to put them on the table.

"We drank the wine and washed them out with water before putting the blood in—just after I killed it with my sword." Derek pointed over his shoulder with his thumb at his magical long sword's hilt.

The salesman stood and examined the claws and

black mane hair dismissively.

Glenn realized the man hadn't given a name, and Derek omitted sharing his or Glenn's. Seemed odd.

After examining the contents of the small wooden crate, the salesman uncorked one of the bottles. He waved a few fingers over the top to draw out the resulting odor of sour, rotting flesh. He scrunched up his nose and replaced the cork.

Pushing the bottle back to the center of the table, he said, "Manticores are uncommon creatures, and a challenge to slay." He gestured at the table's contents. "You harvested some parts that are useful in creating a number of potions and elixirs." Then he sighed. "However, the method of harvest and preservation can be described as crude, at best."

Derek scratched his head "Well, it was a desert, and we lost a couple henchmen killing the monster."

Maintaining an uncaring tone, the salesman said, "A word of advice?"

"Yeah?"

"Should you ever be afforded the opportunity to harvest a manticore again, consider the tongue and heart."

Derek nodded sharply, then said to Glenn standing next to him, "Remember that."

"I will." Glenn kept his voice upbeat with a happy gnome smile on his face. "Thank you for the advice, sir."

The salesman sat back down in his seat. "Despite the quality and condition, I can take what you've brought today off your hands, depending on your asking price."

"Oh," Derek said. "We're not looking for coin. We want to trade."

Derek stood up from his stool, becoming animated, gesturing with his hands. "See, we were fighting some goblins in the Dark Heart Swamp, and found their treasure hoard."

Derek looked at the apparently unimpressed man across from him. "Goblins are crafty and mean. Especially a shaman.

"See, their tribe used some old mine as a lair. They built a hole in a wall near the bottom, with treasure an arm's length away." Derek frowned. "One of our guys stuck his hand in to grab some of it. Rubies and stuff. A flame appeared. Burnt his arm to the bone in hardly a second."

Glenn noted the mixture of truth and fiction in Derek's tale.

The salesman steepled his fingers. "So you seek something to protect you against fire?"

"Yeah," Derek said. "Exactly. Me and him want to go back, but neither of us wants to stick our arm in there—without protection."

"Hmmmm," the salesman said, tapping an index finger against his lips. "Mightn't a Major Resist Heat Spell suffice for the task?"

Derek cocked his head, like that was a dumb question. "Neither me nor him," he said, pointing to Glenn, "cast spells like that. So scrolls won't work either."

"You only need protection for one arm?"

"Right," Derek said. "It'll be mine." He lifted his right arm. "All the way up to the shoulder. Maybe a little extra for my other arm, if something at the bottom needs two hands to pull out."

"You are proposing a straight trade? Your harvested manticore parts for something alchemical that will protect your arm, or arms, from an intense flame."

"An intense *magical* flame that'll char to the bone in seconds." Derek held up a hand, indicating he had more to say. "Oh, and it'll have to last a little while because I'll be feeling around for gems and pulling them out."

"That is understandable," the salesman said. "I

believe we have something in stock to suit your need."

The salesman swiftly departed the room through the ironwood door behind him. Was the slit there just for show? Or was someone behind, listening.

Glenn started to ask a question, but a sharp look from Derek made him pause. Still, he'd started to speak, so he finished with a different question. "Do you want to get goat ribs for lunch?"

Derek was about to explode until his mind processed the question. Catching himself, the big warrior played along, snarling, "You know I hate eating goat, gnome. Gives me the shits."

Glenn's eyes widened. He wanted to laugh, but held it back. "That's what caused it all through the desert?"

Derek gave Glenn an unfriendly glare, saying there'd be payback, then returned to his pretend, easy-going personality. He adjusted his position on the stool. "You can eat goat ribs. I'll get turnip and onion stew."

The turnip and onion stew sounded tasty to Glenn's gnomish taste buds, but he didn't comment, and silence between the two adventurers reigned for the next few minutes.

Muffled noises from the busy street made it difficult for Glenn to be sure. It sounded like there was someone else besides him and Derek in the room, breathing. Glenn didn't say anything to Derek because, if he was right, it'd be stupid to mention it. Or so he figured.

A moment later the mustached salesman returned, holding a stoppered glass vial twice the size of Derek's thumb. An assistant followed him out, a youth of about ten years of age, with dark skin and alert eyes. His heavy linen attire was roughly stitched together and he pushed a small wooden cart.

The salesman moved directly to the table and returned to his soft chair. The assistant remained near the now closed door.

The salesman reached across the table and placed the vial in front of Derek. "This Lotion of Exceptional Fire Protection will ward your arm from intense magical heat, created by fire or even the likes of a branding iron, for no less than thirty minutes—once applied."

Derek leaned down, squinted one eye and examined the vial's milky blue contents. "Doesn't look like much in there." The warrior held up his muscular arm once again. "My arms ain't scrawny."

"Rest assured, there is a sufficient amount. It requires only a thin layer, and the protective lotion's blue color helps to ensure complete coverage. That is obviously important, before you would insert your sword-arm where a magical fire is certain to be triggered."

"How do you spread it on?"

"Apply it directly to the skin. No clothing or…" He examined Derek's battered and repaired breastplate and mail sleeves. "Armor, being made of metal, an inorganic material, the protective lotion would not adhere—or stick well. Most clothing's porosity is problematic. Complete saturation is necessary, as even pinprick-sized gaps in coverage would provide a channel for the assaulting heat to penetrate.

"Application is best accomplished with an accompanying individual's assistance." The salesman's gaze shifted to Glenn for a fraction of a second. "Pour a small amount on the arm and spread it with a finger. Pour a little more and spread again. In tight spots, between fingers, for example, the assistant should apply a small amount to his finger and spread it across such areas."

The mustached man waited a moment to see if Derek comprehended. Then he continued. "The protective lotion has a high viscosity, meaning that it won't roll or drip off your arm onto the floor. Yet, it will spread to a very thin covering, which is all that is required. A thick application will not protect your limb, or limbs, any more than would a thin application.

"The assistant should use the same finger at all times while spreading until all areas to be exposed to the concerning heat are covered. This will ensure maximum coverage for your appendage—or should I say, your hand and arm."

Derek snorted, holding back a laugh. Glenn refrained from rolling his eyes.

"What if the gnome misses a spot?" Derek asked. "Like where my fingernails meet the end of my finger."

"The result would be painful, and allow damage due to the intense heat to occur. It would not be as severe, as with full exposure, but it could inhibit your ability to successfully feel and grasp small items."

Derek nodded understanding. "Will my grip be slippery, like I got hog's grease on me? What about the hair on my arms? Will it get burnt off?"

"Your grip will be minimally impaired, as if your hand is damp with water." The man smoothed his handlebar mustache with his fingers, in thought. "It is likely the hair follicles will be coated in the process, and thus, protected."

The big warrior glanced down at the quiet yet attentive gnome. "What if my assistant gets some splashed in his eye? Will it blind him?"

The salesman looked over at Glenn, even more dismissive than he'd been of the manticore items. The gnome continued to stand to the right of his seated partner.

"Your assistant would see the world tainted blue, through that eye, for the duration of the lotion's protective effect. But he would otherwise remain unimpaired."

"So, like his eye would be safe from the heat of a red-hot poker? But if he closed his eye, it'd burn his eyelid?"

"Except for the pressing force of the poker directly against the eye, yes," the salesman said. "I believe you have a clear understanding."

Glenn cleared his throat, then asked, "If it takes me three minutes to apply the Lotion of Exceptional Fire Protection, the area I applied it first would elapse in being protected three minutes sooner than the last place? Like his fingers first, than say, his bicep, done last?"

"That is correct," the salesman said, nodding once. "Exposure to oxygen in the air is what limits the duration."

"So, if I had a bucket of this lotion stuff," Derek said, "a red dragon could breathe fire on me and I'd be okay?"

"Indeed, but those flames would melt your sword. And if you inhaled at the wrong moment, the heat drawn in would sear your lungs."

"Because I couldn't put any on my sword, and even if I wiped some of the lotion up my nostrils, the dragon could just bite my dumb, unarmored ass."

"That would be an expected result."

Derek asked, "If the gnome got it in his eye and he cried tears, would it wash the lotion stuff out?"

"It would not. The lotion will adhere to the eyeball itself."

The big warrior offered Glenn a goofy grin, much like Mardin's. "Just joking about the crying."

After a few seconds of silence, presented with no additional questions, the salesman clasped his hands together. "So, my warrior friend, we have a deal?"

Friend, Glenn thought. The slimy sales guy was getting the better end of the deal. Or was dead certain he was.

"Not yet," Derek said, his normal, unpleasant disposition emerging. "I want to test it."

The salesman leaned back a fraction of a second,

noting the change in Derek's voice and bearing. "I can provide a mundane flame—"

Derek cut the salesman off, not moving his eyes from the man. "Gnome, get out your candle."

Glenn hopped to retrieving his everlast candle from deep within his satchel, and placed it on the table.

Derek glared directly at the salesman whose gaze flickered over to his right, then forward again, while the big warrior asked, "It can be opened and closed right, without losing effectiveness—due to oxygen in the air?"

The salesman instantly regained his composure. Glenn guessed Derek either failed, or the salesman succeeded, against some sort of intimidation roll. He sometimes forgot how the game world worked.

"Indeed," the salesman said. "And the glass vial will resist normal strikes, and the stopper requires effort to pull out, as you will see." He gestured to the vial. "Please, test the product produced from our labor and arcane knowledge."

Derek shook the vial, pulled the stopper, and used it to liberally apply the cloudy-blue, viscous liquid to his little finger.

It did spread easily, and left a clear blue tint to the warrior's finger.

"Gnome, open your candle."

Glenn did, and Derek held his finger several inches above the pinkish flame, and slowly lowered it.

After twenty seconds of raising and lowering, Derek said, "It works." He held up an index finger to forestall the words on the salesman's lips. "I want three more vials of this."

The salesman responded with a negative hand gesture. "The deal was for one."

"No," Derek said. Brute anger tinged his voice. Still, he remained seated. "It was for enough to cover and fully protect one arm, possibly both, so I can grab the treasure from a flame trap in a mine overrun with goblins."

Derek glanced down at his little finger resting on the table next to the everlast candle. "Dainty painting will take half the blue stuff's effective time." He placed both hands on the table. "No way in hell there'll be time in a dungeon to daintily paint your lotion on my arms. It'll have to be done quick and dirty."

"One vial," the salesman said, "or no deal."

Derek showed a wicked grin. Glenn thought it would've been more effective with his tooth missing.

The big warrior leaned forward. "I know the value of manticore *venom*," Derek said, his voice going low. "Even poorly harvested venom. So if it ain't four vials, it's no deal."

He continued his intense gaze at the unflustered salesman. "And if your invisa-guard just out of sword's reach to my left tries to stop us from leaving with our manticore stuff, or you won't open the remotely locked front door, it's going to get messy."

The salesman steepled his fingers again. "Are you making threats, warrior?"

Glenn was pretty impressed. Derek looked pretty menacing, and the salesman was unarmed. Of course he might be a magic user with spells, and the invisible guard might be pretty high-level tough.

"No, I'm just telling you that if it ain't four vials of your protection lotion for our manticore parts, you're going to allow us to leave with our poorly harvested parts and go elsewhere."

"There are no other alchemists in Riven Rock."

"We're just passing through Riven Rock. There are plenty of other cities with plenty of other alchemists. That goblin treasure ain't going nowhere."

The salesman ran a thumb and forefinger along his thin, extended mustache. Leaning forward he said, "Two vials."

"Three," Derek countered. "And a fancy padded box to put them in, so they don't get busted during travel."

**Twenty minutes later** Glenn was at a table in a half-brick, half-wooden restaurant called the Good to the Last Scrape or, to its regulars, The Scrape. Turnip and onion soup, as opposed to stew, wasn't quite as tasty as Glenn imagined. But it was filling. And only made him sweat a little more, with the hot day. A breeze would help, but not likely to do much with such small windows.

Derek hunched over his wooden bowl of turnip and onion soup, laughing to himself as he ate.

The woman who worked the counter across the room was busy washing wooden bowls and copper spoons. Three men at a round table near her were drinking cheap beer and playing a card game that sounded a lot like Go Fish. Except they said, "Go dig."

Anxious about what lay ahead, Glenn whispered to Derek, "You think they'll send someone to follow us?"

Derek looked up. "Naw, they're figuring we're leaving town."

"What if…" Glenn paused and looked around conspiratorially. "They talk to Yonn?"

Derek shrugged and scooped a spoonful of soup into his mouth. "That sniveling asshole? He heard me tell a few tales about fighting goblins in the swamp, and about a shaman and that big saber-toothed cat. They'll figure that's where we're going—if they even dig that far."

"You don't think they—"

"No, gnome, now shut up and eat."

Since Derek wanted him to shut up and eat, Glenn said, "This city doesn't have guards always showing up, like Three Hills City. But there isn't more…crime."

Derek looked up from his bowl. "You mean like dudes being killed in the street and stuffed behind some building?"

Glenn scowled and shot a glance to see if anyone at the card table was listening.

Derek rolled his eyes. He leaned closer. "Riven Rock's divided up into wards, with like nine groups that are in charge of them, like thirty or so. Localized folks, or hired guards watch the areas. The thieves' guild watches some. Only one wardian with more territory than them is some earth wizard. The wardians answer to some sort of Council of Three."

Derek leaned back and shrugged. "Don't make sense why it works." Then a dark look crossed his face. "Other than the asshole GM who thought it up said it does."

"How'd you find out?" Glenn asked. "About the wardians?"

Derek gave Glenn an incredulous look. "I asked Krogman."

"Oh," Glenn said.

"Just finish eating, gnome." Derek started laughing to himself again.

"What's so funny?" Glenn took a quick bite of turnip. "What are you laughing about?"

"Same thing as a few minutes ago."

Glenn wiped a sleeve across his mustache, in case food was stuck in it.

Derek looked down at his bowl then up with a feral grin. "Imagining the look on Breasty Mariposa Barbie's face when you tell her she'll have to get naked for the mission."

The big warrior turned red stifling a roaring laugh. He held up a finger, signaling there was more. "And…*you*, gnome, get to tell her she's gonna have to let someone help slather that blue stuff over every tiny inch of her naked, fairy body."

Glenn scowled. "Well, there's no chance she'll pick you."

"You got that, gnome. Probably be you." He pushed

his empty bowl aside and leaned forward. “With her nineteen point five Appearance Score, and your stubby fingers spreading slippery blue lotion over every curvy inch, how’s that gonna work out?”

# CHAPTER 41

**Being hauled around** in a wicker basket totally sucked. Instinctively, Stephi knew Ron was right. Being seen by people in town would draw attention and mess up their chances of pulling off that manipulative pawnshop owner's job.

People might be curious—at first. But deep down, they'd mistrust and fear her, just like any fairy. Total stupid ignorance.

Still, being a fairy, Stephi held deep-rooted distain for mortals. Those weren't *her* feelings. They were the stupid game's feelings of every single fairy and elf. She fought the revolting racist feelings as an elf but, as a fairy, suppressing them was ten times harder. Keeping away from the gawking peasants helped. Well, it didn't help, just kept her from constantly confronting the sick thoughts.

Deep down, in her real life, she'd looked down her nose at some people. People who got into college through grants and scholarships, and then wasted the chance. Flunked out. Things like that cried hypocrite, and ate at Stephi's thoughts, when she allowed. Luckily there was always something new happening, or some danger to distract her. Or, she told herself she was making a mountain out of a mole hill.

The sooner she got back to being herself, well, her weird game-paper elf self, the better. Her real self? That hope was on some mountain a millions miles away.

If she ever got to meet the narrow-minded idiots that created the stupid game, she'd kick each of them in the balls—twice. The dice rolling and paper game to the actual game world connection didn't make sense. Maybe the misogynistic men that wrote the game got some vibe, or unconsciously connected with the parallel universe that held this screwed up world, and just wrote that? Maybe stupid dreams influenced them? Wet dreams were probably more like it.

At that moment, all reality versus parallel world stuff didn't matter one pretty pink-poodle bit. She'd rather be a tall, gorgeous elf with ginormous boobs that everyone gawked at, like she was some supermodel porn star, over a hide-in-a-basket Tinkerbell. Despite having the looks and a chest that'd make Peter Pan forget pretty girl Wendy in two seconds flat.

Stephi sighed, feeling the wicker basket's bounce. Like she hadn't thought what it'd be like to be home, with her mom and dad, back with her sorority sisters, a hundred million times.

Lying on her side, she ignored the basket's swing. Glenn did an okay job, but Ron carried her with the most care.

The elf-turned-fairy took a steadying breath and mentally contacted her blue jay familiar. *Petie, slow look.*

After a few seconds, the blue jay responded. <Me-us slow look.>

One of the first things Stephi trained her familiar to do was to slow down while she observed the world through his eyes. The bird flicked his head sharply from view to view, working to get a different perspective. He'd done it so fast that the rapid-fire snapshots left Stephi with a headache, and little to show for it, other than a vague recollection of images. Even with slower, more deliberate views, adjusting to the shifted hues her familiar's eyes drank in, and the unfamiliar optics formed by the bird's different shaped eye and lens combination, was challenging. It was like wearing tinted, malformed goggles. A weird thing was, Petie, a blue jay, didn't pick up on the color blue all that well.

Stephi closed her eyes and focused on the

connection with her familiar.

Petie was on a roof, about a hundred feet ahead of Ron and Glenn. The pair strode down the empty street. Petie's vision after sunset was worse than a human's, and Stephi—if she allowed herself—could feel her familiar's intense apprehension over flying at night. His fear of flying into something unseen, or misjudging a landing, or being surprised by a night hunter.

Cats and owls were high on the 'flying around at night' list, but it took a while for Stephi to figure that out. As a bird, Petie's thoughts relied on images and emotions revolving around survival. To his mind, cats were hooked claws and bites, created from an amalgamations of feline encounters. The imagined cat's eyes, teeth and claws were large, out of proportion. A curved avian beak and claws, and a sensation of shadowy silence formed the owl threat, with anticipated piercing pain, usually along the neck or spine.

Petie warned Stephi. <Me-us fly.>

The warning was a throwback from before Stephi'd become a fairy, which had subsequently brought an internal ease when it came to flight. The magic user didn't want to break the warning habit ingrained into her familiar. She didn't plan on being a fairy forever. Or an elf forever. That thought *did* pinch her heart—she'd miss Petie.

*Fly*, Stephi mentally replied.

When they first arrived in the stupid game world, Petie communicated exclusively through images combined with intense, instinctual emotions. Since then she'd taught him twenty-two words.

Petie referred to himself as Me-us, and Stephi as You-us. The blue jay familiar considered himself and Stephi pair bonded. Almost mates.

No way she'd ever share that with Derek. The jerk would use it to make mean jokes. Well, more of them.

The good thing was, Petie knew who was in charge of the pair bond—her—and did what she asked without question.

Her familiar spotted Derek standing in the shadows between two buildings, one of them abandoned. That one was boarded up. When planning the assault on the glass shop, Kirby insisted he could break into the boarded-up place so they could use it as a base of operations.

While the party formed the plan, after Derek and Glenn traded monster parts for a heat-protection lotion, Stephi demanded privacy for removing her leaf and bark dress and getting the magical lotion spread all over her body. She demanded Derek go back and get enough to fill a small washtub so she could bathe in the liquid, but goober-kid Kirby said, "That's pretty much impossible." Ron called it, "An inefficient use of monetary resources."

Like either of them would want to perform a mission naked. Well, Ron might, if it would benefit the party. He was weird like that.

Derek made sure to remind Stephi, "The reason for this dumbass mission is to get the leprechaun's coin, so you can be an elf again. So suck it up, Whiny Winged Barbie, and stop bitching."

Pathetic thing was, the big jerk was right. Everyone was risking their lives for her. Ron reminded her, "It was what party members do, both out of friendship and obligation."

The friendship part covered everyone but Derek. He wanted to be friends with her—*more* than friends.

Friends with the muscle-headed jerk, in any way, shape or form? No. She'd sooner make friends with that leering, old, part-goblin that everyone insisted on hiring.

That Blizz and his donkey, and the hired mercenaries were driving the wagons, getting a head start on leaving the butt crack-smelling town.

Stephi's scattered thoughts returned to Derek. No. Even if he killed monsters and bad guys better than anyone in the party, obligation was the best she could stir up for him.

The thought about bad guys sent a cold shiver through Stephi. She clenched her hands into tiny fists and prepared to fly out into the night and cast her Slumber Spells. And it got worse after that.

Any moment, Glenn would open the basket lid and tell her it was time.

So much of her time as an elf—or fairy—involved life and death situations. Like, every other day she was like a modern-day city girl sprinting across the Roman Coliseum during a gladiator chariot race mashup. Always a desperate, erratic run that might end in success. Or complete disaster.

Through the basket, Stephi heard Ron say, "We have reached the launch point."

Glenn stopped walking and flipped up the basket lid. "Marigold," he whispered, "nobody's on the street. Time to go."

"Thanks," she replied, stood, and allowed the fairy magic to flow across her wings. Within seconds they blended with the shadowy, moon-lit darkness. It wouldn't make her invisible, but a lot harder to see. Knowing that, she jumped and flapped her wings, keeping near a brick building as she rose into the night sky.

*Warn me of danger*, she thought telepathically to her familiar.

<Danger watch> Petie replied, accompanied by an image of a bipedal cat with a human head and claws that resembled curved swords. Ron called them scimitars. <Us-me warn danger, Us-you.>

*Thank you, Petie.* Stephi waved back to Glenn and Ron. She rolled her eyes, realizing the two party members wouldn't be able to see her, or her waving hand.

The fairy beat her wings faster, dipping toward the road before zipping across the street, and between the back of the boot maker's and bakery. She didn't see the guard who was supposed to be watching somewhere along the street. Not her worry—not yet. One guard at a time.

The fairy continued until she was between the rear of the pottery place and the glass blower's shop. Kirby assured her that was the safest route to rise up and cast her spell. Taking her time, Stephi fluttered upward, hands touching the brick wall until she was able to grip the top ledge. She stuck her bare feet against the wall, stopped flapping her wings, held her breath and counted on her Camouflage ability as she peeked over the top.

A clean-shaven man in leather armor, with a sword on his belt and a crossbow leaning against the front ledge, squatted, looking over the building's front, down onto the street.

Stephi prepared to loose one of her two memorized Slumber Spells on the man. Something, a quick motion off to the right caught her attention. A small, furry creature was perched on the brick ledge. It rose to all fours, then on its hind legs, head shifting from left to right, eyes searching her direction.

A memory raced to the forefront of Stephi's thoughts. A trip to the county fair with Grandpa when she was a little girl. She had a nickel, and cautiously walked forward to hand it to a small monkey wearing a red and white-striped vest and miniature cowboy hat. The monkey's jolly owner, wearing an identical outfit, sent a tiny tug on the organ grinder monkey's leash—that's what Grandpa called the cute little animal—and the funny little monkey took the coin and tipped his hat.

Concern raced through Stephi's head. That carnival

monkey had worked for somebody. And the one now moving along the ledge, toward her, worked for somebody. It had to be a familiar!

Doing her best to remain calm, Stephi slowly lowered herself below the ledge, then shot away and flew in a tight right-hand turn around the corner. As she made her way between the glass shop and the bakery, Stephi had to find Kirby. Her Slumber Spell should've worked on both man and monkey. But, if it was a familiar, she remembered Ron saying they saved against magic spells at the rank of their master. If the magic user was over 4th rank, the whole deal would be blown. Even if the master wasn't over 4th rank, if his familiar all of a sudden fell asleep, he might come running. If that happened to Petie, she'd know, and do whatever it took to save him.

Stephi flew down the street and in between buildings and through an unboarded window in the abandoned building. Kirby squatted next to Glenn, both looking between slats, out onto the street.

The half-goblin sense something behind him and spun with cutlass ready.

Stephi fluttered back, up toward the ceiling's dusty rafters. "It's me."

"You forgot to say the password." He sheathed his cutlass and prepared to leave so Glenn could help coat Stephi with the magical lotion.

"Wait," she said, doing her best to keep her fairy voice down. "There's a monkey up on the roof."

"Did you slumber it too?"

"No, Gurk. What if it's a familiar?"

Glenn didn't say anything, but looked up at his half-goblin friend.

"Yeah," Kirby said, dragging the word out in thought. "Could be trouble."

He grabbed the sack Glenn was holding and

carefully emptied it of the boxes holding the bottled lotion. "I'm gonna sneak my way between the buildings and use this rope to climb up." He pulled a coil of thin rope from another sack that had been sitting under the opened window. It had a metal hook attached. Stephi remembered the rope was part of a backup plan.

"You'll have to haul this hook up and stick it over the ledge so I can climb up. Slumber the guard and the monkey. If either of them don't fall asleep, use your Dazzle Spell. That should give me time."

Kirby rubbed his hands together, forming the rest of the plan as he spoke. "I'll gag the monkey. Tie its hands and stuff it in the sack." He grinned wickedly. "Then I'll climb down, wake the monkey and take off running. If it's a magic user's familiar, he'll figure out his monkey's on the move—not at the building."

Then he frowned. "That means time'll be shorter, Marigold. You'll have to do the whole mission, uhhh, naked—which means you'll have less time protected to sneak in."

The thief made his way to the window. "I'm gonna let Lysine and Kalgore know the change in plan."

He began climbing out the window, stopped and grinned playfully. "Change places with me, Jax?"

"You wish, you little perv," Stephi said, a wide grin on her face. She had to admit, sometimes the kid was funny.

"I'll be waiting between the cobbler's and bakery," the thief replied to the fairy. Then he said to the gnome healer, "Good thing you got a high Luck Score, dude," and ducked out.

# CHAPTER 42

**Stephi purposefully ignored** the bulge in the front of Glenn's pants. She couldn't blame him. With her game-created 19.5 Appearance Score, it could hardly be otherwise.

The gnome healer was her closest friend—besides Kim, but that was different. If it had to be someone, she preferred Glenn see her unclothed, and rubbing hands across her naked body. Besides, he'd already caught a ton of glimpses while in the Dark Heart Swamp, helping her remove leeches.

Ron had as much, if not more, honor, and courage. The party leader's hands would've been less shaky than the gnome healer's. But allowing the gnome to help spread the magical potion—lotion—pissed Derek off way more than if she'd picked Ron. And the goober, junior high kid, Kirby? He would've lost it in his pants before ten seconds passed. That embarrassment might mess up their friendship, for who could guess how long. Besides, Kirby needed to be out there sneaking in the dark more than he needed to be rubbing blue fluid on her wings, hair, shoulders, back—and fairy-sized bum.

"How you doing, Jax?"

Stephi stood on a rickety crate in the middle of the abandon building's creaky floor. Glenn knelt behind her. His everlast candle lit the backroom they'd selected for the operation.

"Uhhh, got your wings and…hh-hair."

"Relax, Jax," Stephi urged. "Don't miss a spot or I'll feel it, and *you'll* have to heal it."

"Right," Glenn said, his voice quiet and meek. He ran a lotion-slick hand along the right side of her back. After a pause, a quick wipe up and down across her right butt cheek almost made her giggle. She managed to suppress it.

"Trade bottles," she said, no longer able to reach her arm in the top and reach any of the blue liquid. She picked it up and turned around.

The gnome's eyes widened, lingered several seconds on her bare, wet chest, before he looked at the floor. He focused on lifting the bottle in front of him. "L-let me get the funnel to fill that one from mine—I mean—the one I'm using."

"We don't have time to waste. First thing that'll lose protection is the gem holding Kim. I—we don't what to lose her, but I'll need her with me." They'd dipped the magical Alexandrite gemstone and delicate silver chain first to make sure it was completely covered. Ron assured them it would work, after coating the entire thing with some sort of resin he created from various leaves he'd gotten from a shifty herbalist.

She and Glenn briefly discussed using strategically placed leaves to cover her "naughty" parts. But the plant matter soaked up the magical lotion like a sponge. When it came down to it, Stephi preferred extra lotion on her body than risk burning up due to modesty.

Stephi huffed, beginning to lose patience. "Look, Jax, you're gonna have to take a close look at me in a minute anyway. Make sure I'm completely covered, so I don't burn up. Part of the plan, so be a man and help me out."

Stephi was scared. But she'd felt that way so much since arriving in the stupid game world, that hiding it had become almost second nature. Scared trumped embarrassed every time, but she didn't want to guilt Glenn into action…unless she had to.

Glenn bit his lip and blushed. Stephi could see it, even in the flickering light, beneath his tea-colored skin. Her hands went to her hips. "You weren't this way in the swamp."

"You weren't like you are now," Glenn said, defensively.

"Just look at me and tell me what the problem is, so we can get this done and I can go out there and risk my life."

"Forget it," Glenn said, placing the tin funnel in the mouth of his tiny bottle.

"Jax, just spit it out so we can get on with this, and you can make sure it's right."

Glenn met her angry gaze, then concentrated on pouring. "When you were an elf, it was different. Now…" He paused while he finished pouring. He wiped the inside of the funnel with a finger to get at the viscus liquid remaining on its surface. "Getting, aahhmm, sexually aroused…"

Stephi leaned forward, still looking up. The movement caused her breasts to protrude even further. "Time's a wasting, mister."

Glenn threw up his hands in exasperation. "It's like you're a little kid and me near bursting with an erection—it's like I'm a sicko pedophile."

Stephi lifted her hands from her hips and clasped them in front of her chest. She'd never considered that. It didn't make sense to her—but it did to him. She saw it in his eyes.

"Jax," she said, reaching a hand out to her friend. "When I was a freakishly tall elf, like twice your size, even with that difference I always thought of you as a man. Not a boy."

The way Glenn leaned back from her before extending his hand and taking hers told Stephi that she'd caught her friend off guard. "You need to think of me the same way, now that you're twice as big as me. As a woman. Just a midgety one. "

Glenn took in a deep breath. "Okay."

"I picked you to help me with this stupid lotion

because you're my friend, and I trust you."

Glenn snorted a laugh. "I thought you chose me to tick off Kalgore."

"That too," Stephi said, showing an impish smile.

They both laughed.

Stephi dipped her hand into the newly filled bottle. "Now let's get this over with, so I can survive in that glass oven."

"Furnace," Glenn corrected, poorly mimicking Ron's voice. He wiped his wet finger across Stephi's neck, where she'd missed a spot, and smiled. "So we can get that coin back and you can be freakishly huge, again."

"Tall," Stephi said, pointing up at Glenn, waving a finger. "Huge makes it sound like I was fat."

# CHAPTER 43

**The higher she** made it up along the glass shop's rear wall, the heavier the hook and rope became. Good thing the little goober only needed a thin rope. And the good sense not to stare at her naked body. He'd muttered an apology, after his yellow goblin eyes caught a glimpse when he handed her the hook. She hardly heard his muttered words. Not because she didn't care, but because Glenn insisted on pouring a few extra potion drops into each of her ears.

They'd already wasted two minutes while five dirty workers noisily made their way down the street, toward the underground bars. Three in the morning was a little late to begin partying. She needed to party, at a real bar, with her sorority sisters.

Kirby'd wrapped a brown scrap of cloth around the hook so that the iron in its steel didn't burn her hands. No way she wanted any part of the metal to brush up against her. She'd accidentally stepped on a nail in one of the wagons, and it burned like stepping on a hot frying pan. Ron, while healing her up, admonished her, saying, "That errant step cost one hit point." He explained, in his lecture voice: "Falling face-first onto a sheet of metal will cause two four-sided dice of damage per round of contact."

Being a fairy sucked. This whole world sucked poodle paws. Stephi wanted another bitch session with Kim, but there wasn't time. She'd have to contact Kim right after Slumber Spelling the monkey and two guards. Again, Ron's advice refocused Stephi. "Focus on accomplishing one task at a time. Those that follow will await their turn."

He'd make a good dad, Stephi thought. Boring as

hell, but good.

Before she poked her head up, she reached out with her fairy mind, trying to connect with the animal she was able to summon. Less than a block away two pairs of pigeons roosted in their nest. She called to them. Obediently they awakened. She sent the image of the ledge opposite to the one beneath which she fluttered. She directed for them to fly there, land, warble and coo until they felt danger from anything atop the roof.

Within thirty seconds she heard the pigeons' wings flapping as they landed.

Stephi thought to Petie, *Look here,* and mentally shared an image of the glass shop's roof.

The blue jay responded. <Me-us slow look.>

Stephi got an image. The man was in the same spot, walking toward the pigeons. The magic user's monkey minion was moving her direction. How had that little furry thing heard her? So much for the distraction. Then she thought about Kirby below.

Moving quickly she lifted the hook and affixed it too the ledge. The weight gone she flew to the right.

The monkey squealed a warning. The pigeons panicked and fled.

Doing what she could to Camouflage herself, Stephi fluttered up and began her Slumber Spell. The monkey was trying to lift the hook but Kirby's weight on the rope was too much for the little primate. The leather-clad guard was already racing over to the squealing monkey.

Stephi remained unnoticed as her spell went off. The monkey slumped to the rooftop. The man slowed, slumped and dropped like someone had switched off his brain.

She shot back down and angled toward Kirby, who was nearly to the top. He climbed as well as any monkey.

"Both are asleep," she said and raced away. The second guard was next on her list.

She kept between the glass shop and the bakery, landing just before the street, and peeked out. The guard was across the street, looking up at the roof where the other guard should be. Had the pigeons drawn his attention? Or was it the monkey's squeal?

Didn't matter. She whispered the words to her second Slumber Spell. The man shook his head, like a bout of dizziness had struck him. He didn't go down.

Damn, she thought, and went to Plan B. She didn't have time to try and Charm him. It was the wing Dazzle Spell. As she flew across the street, she redirected the fairy magic buried in her core to flow to her wings.

She fluttering up in front of the man. He raised a hand, preparing to bat her away. The stupid man thought she was a big bat or something.

Stephi warned Ron and Derek nearby, saying, "Flash bulb."

Brilliant light erupted from her wings, catching the man by surprise. He staggered back, shook his head, then smiled up at her. He reached for a dagger on his belt.

Derek came running, metal armor scraping and clanking, but Petie's jeer call covered the noise. The big warrior plowed into the distracted guard with his shield, knocking him to the ground. A powerful hack from Derek's long sword followed. It should've killed the guard, but it didn't.

Since the guard wasn't dropped by her Slumber Spell, he was above 4$^{th}$ rank. That meant he had a bunch of hit points. Nothing she could do. She'd left her tiny bronze rapier behind. She looked down at the necklace holding the Alexandrite gemstone, equivalent size to a strawberry hanging above her ginormous fairy boobs. Even if she channeled Kim, to borrow her Monk Warrior skills, she'd be about as helpful as a Kung Fu toddler.

The guard, on his feet, wielded his dagger expertly as Derek tried to close. Ron arrived, tossed a tiny scroll case up to Stephi, and said, "Mystic Missile." He then raised his spear and entered the fray. Stephi looked around while opening the leather case. The street remained empty, except for a short figure moving toward them—it was Glenn.

The fight's sound consisted mostly of grunts and thuds. Forth rank or above, the ambushed guard was proving a match for Derek and Ron.

Stephi focused her fairy vision, which wasn't as acute as her elven sight. Still, there was enough to read the arcane words and release the spell. It was written down by Coleen Sammae and produced four amber balls of energy. They darted from Stephi, and slammed into the battling guard.

Ron's spear thrust to the guard's spine ended the struggle.

Derek shoved his sword back into its scabbard. "Come on, Striptease Barbie," he said, beginning to trot across the street. "Lysine'll take care of the body."

Stephi didn't have a comeback ready—other than "Jerk." Instead of saying anything, she stuffed the scroll back into the case and tossed it to Ron.

Flying over the big warrior's head, she heard him grumble, "That gnome better hurry up with the sledgehammer."

It took Derek a minute to swing wide, and then make his way between the rear of the boot maker's shop and the bakery. By the time Derek got to the heat pipe running from the glass shop to the pottery shop, Kirby was already gone. Through Petie's eyes Stephi saw him running north with the filled sack over his shoulder.

"Go up and get the hook," Derek ordered in a hushed voice, "while I bust apart this pipe."

She didn't argue. In the planning, Ron said to retrieve the hook and rope, if they were used. Before grabbing the wrapped hook, Stephi looked over the ledge, onto the roof. She spotted the guard, sprawled out exactly where her Slumber Spell dropped him. Liquid—blood—pooled around his head and shoulders. The kid had slit his throat.

She gulped down a bit of vomit that crept up her throat. Everyone said they were just NPCs, and the party's survival was paramount. Was Keri Lovelace, the owner of the Glade House, not a real person? Did that dorky doofus, Jurome's brave death mean nothing?

A cracking *thud* snapped Stephi back to the present. She carefully lifted the hook and descended. Ron was there, watching the street while Derek's powerful arms drove the sledgehammer against the heat-conveying pipe. The fourth blow separated it.

Stephi dropped the hook and rope and fluttered up to Ron.

"Are you prepared?" he asked. The man's eyes didn't even stray to her liquid-blue naked body. Even Derek had been more focused on the mission than trying to catch an eyeful. That impressed her.

She was tempted to shake her head in answer to Ron's question. Both in the negative and as a response to everything still sounding like she had shower water stuck in her ears. "Does it matter?"

He placed one hand on his chest where his wooden holy symbol to Gaia hung, and touched her shoulder with his other hand. A few arcane words later he nodded. "Your protection is now supplemented with a Minor Heat Resistance Spell."

"Thank you, Lysne," she said.

"Come on," Derek hissed. His eyes lingered on her a moment. With the scant light and his human eyes, not like he'd see much. He pulled a long crowbar from his belt and prepared to work on prying out the pipe's iron grate. "I ain't looking forward to fighting more guards."

Stephi doubted that. She held up a finger as she

concentrated. *Kim, I'm borrowing your Warrior Monk Dodging Skills.* Letting her friend know wasn't necessary, but it was polite.

Kim replied, <Don't use them unless you must.> As always, her voice in Stephi's mind sounded like it came from the bottom of a deep well. <You won't earn experience points, if you do.>

*I know, Byeol. Stupid experience points won't mean anything if I'm dead.*

<True.>

Stephi had shared the details of the plan the party came up with. She told Kim a lot of things. It was a weird relationship. Stephi had to initiate all contact, and Kim could only respond on topic to what Stephi brought up. But it was better than nothing, for her and for Kim.

Within seconds Stephi felt her body infused with an exceptional sense of calm, balance, and snap reflexes.

Around Derek, a crackling flash went off, filling the air with the smell of ozone.

"Come on, Mariposa Streaker Barbie," Derek growled, tossing aside the metal grate he'd pried out of the clay pipe. "Since I can't get a decent eyeful in the dark, hanging around, flapping your wings is wasting everyone's time."

Stephi flew over and landed near the open pipe leading into the glass furnace. "Jerk."

Derek shook a bone scroll case holding a mixture of lead and copper beads before handing it down to her. "Nice maracas."

Stephi sneered and spread her wings, preparing to release a Dazzle Spell. "Wanna see a little more?"

"Kalgore," Ron said, restrained anger in his voice, "move to Position C. Remain alert and prepared."

"Right," Derek said. He picked up the sledgehammer and crowbar, and trotted away.

Ron's eyes lingered a half second on Stephi's body

before meeting her eyes. "Remember, hold your breath. The Heat Resistance Lotion only protects that to which it is applied. Your trachea and lungs are not included."

She'd already been warned of that. The warrior druid's spell would protect her entire body, but it wasn't strong enough compared to what was supposed to be in the furnace.

Intense heat flowed out of the pipe, causing Stephi's damp fairy hair to wave, like it was caught up in a steady breeze. "Thanks for the reminder," she said, her voice a little shaky. She tucked back her wings before getting on her hands and knees in front of the pipe.

"I have the utmost faith in your ability to succeed," Ron said. "You should have the same."

Right, Stephi thought to herself. She took a deep breath and scuttled into the pipe.

# CHAPTER 44

**Adequate light wasn't** going to be a problem. Intense, yellowish-white immediately revealed a second steel grate Derek had managed to knock out. It lay several inches in front of the opening into the furnace area. Stephi didn't think the magical lotion would protect her from that.

Reminding herself that she had only as long as she could hold her breath to complete what she needed to do, Stephi maneuvered the bone scroll case to push the circular grate aside. The scroll case was two-thirds her height, and it took nearly fifteen seconds to accomplish the task while confined to the pipe. Thankfully the pipe wasn't made of iron, or they'd have dressed her in some sort of confining body suit. She imagined moving like an inchworm. Like that would've helped things along.

Grate out of the way, she peered inside.

The furnace was probably six feet across and wide, and eight feet high. The opposite side had a hole about eighteen inches in diameter a little over six feet up. Someone was apparently working glass, because a pole with a glowing glob stuck to the end was being withdrawn. She wouldn't have seen it if the porthole had been in the middle of her side of the furnace. Instead it was offset to the left. Because, in the middle was a squat pillar of flame, intense, like a giant welding torch.

A thin spread of liquid glass lined the floor, nearer the furnace's opening where drops or beads must have dripped off of the poles stuck in. She saw a circular raised area, an inch high. Resting on the elevated area burned the pillar of flame, an elemental spirit of fire, if Ron was correct. He was rarely wrong. Atop and along the edge of the one inch raised circular area were runes, magical symbols that held the elemental spirit captive within the circle. Above the fiery elemental hovered some sort of clear barrier, also with runes carved into it. It was slanted, like a roof, to keep glass from dripping down onto the magical runes that formed the containment circle.

Whoever created this setup, and captured that fire monster—spirit—was powerful. And was going to be super-duper pissed at whoever messed it up. In Stephi's mind, the pawnshop owner moved up three rungs, from greedy conceited bastard to greedy, super major conceited bastard-asshole!

And what the hell was she supposed to do?

She had to get the lead and copper to melt across the circle of magical runes. Since she was a fairy, a magical creature, she couldn't do it directly, like by tossing them on the runes. Glenn or Kirby or anyone else in the party could. But not her. So she had to *set up* a process by which it happened *naturally*.

Kirby had carved a hole along the bottom of the bone scroll case and the cap. He stuck a sheet of lead over the case's hole to plug it. When she turned the cap and aligned the holes, the lead near the fire would melt and release the beads, which would melt and break the circle.

But, with the circle's elevation, that wouldn't work.

She was about to go back out and ask Ron for advice, and get a fresh breath of air, when Petie shouted into her head, <Fighting!>

Stephi sent, *Okay*, then cut him off. Time was running out, and she needed to concentrate.

Once whoever made this oven circle prison for the fire monster showed up, the party was not only over. The party was dead. She'd witnessed what high-rank spell casters could do to low-rank characters. She hated it when Derek called the party a bunch of low-rank peons.

But that's what they were.

Time was also running out another way. Her lungs began insisting that breathing was something she should be doing. Only, she reminded herself, if she wanted to cook her lungs.

Stephi looked around, lamenting that she wasn't an engineer. She refused to take shop class, and never paid attention when setting up physics labs in high school. She always got the boys to do it for her.

Well, none of those people were there. If she didn't do something, Glenn, Kirby and everyone outside would die. She'd be stuck, alone, as a fairy. If she didn't die, too.

She was naked, with nothing but the stupid bone case. Maybe she could fly out and find something in the shop. But there were people, and the glass guardian things.

Then her eyes fell on the round grate. Lying on the floor, it was about an inch tall. It looked heavy, and just touching it would burn her. An image of playing shuffleboard with Grandpa came to mind.

She flew over and shoved the scroll case against the steel grate and pushed. Feet braced, shoulders and wings working, Stephi immediately remembered why she always made her brother shovel snow.

The metal disk scraped across the stone floor easier than Stephi anticipated, especially when it met the liquid glass. For a second, it slowed, but only for a second. Nevertheless, the physical exertion caused her lungs to burn with the need for air.

The case jolted in her arms when the grate ran up against the edge of the elevated circle. Rather than walk through the thin sheet of liquid glass, Stephi flapped her wings and lifted the scroll case. The melted glass wouldn't burn her feet, but it'd probably harden when it cooled. Then that jerk Derek would call her Maracas Mariposa Cinderella Barbie, or something else stupid.

The fairy put her strength and Kim's balance into the effort, struggling to keep from exhaling while balancing the cap-end of the scroll case on grate's rim and crossbars. She aligned the cap's hole with the circle, carefully placed her left foot on the rim of the cap. Then she held it in place, and slowly twisted the bone case. The intense heat had already caused the scroll case to become brittle.

She mentally thanked Ron for insisting a small portion of the magical lotion be used to, "Reduce the frictional coefficient, should the cap and bone case expand unevenly due to differential exposure to intense heat, or other unforeseen factors."

She spotted the lead plug, already glistening. Taking an additional second to ensure the case wouldn't topple once she let go, Stephi fluttered away and turned toward the pipe exit.

Before she flapped her wings twice, white fire engulfed her, then shoved her aside. The lead had already melted and broke the magical barrier. The unexpected force hurled the hapless fairy against the wall. She rebounded from the impact, having the air knocked out of her. Reflexively, Stephi breathed in.

Searing, agonizing pain filled her chest.

She collapsed to the stone floor, lacking the ability to scream.

# Chapter 45

**"Dying! Dying!" Petie** screeched, landing in front of Glenn, franticly bobbing and flapping his wings.

Ron or the others might sense the blue jay's distress, but the gnome healer could interpret it.

Glenn had been keeping in the shadows, watching Derek pound the crap out of a pair of nosy drunks. The gnome healer broke from his cover and sprinted across the street. Careless of who heard, he yelled toward Ron, "Marigold's dying!"

He pounded his way toward Sterjin's Glass, no clue what he'd do once he reached the magically sealed main door. Two thirds of the way there, he unslung his shield. He'd try ramming it open first. After that, his cudgel. If that didn't work, at least he might've triggered the doors magical defenses, leaving Derek free to break through and save Stephi. He knew Ron and Derek would come running.

Three strides away the steel-reinforced door flung open. Glenn lowered his head and plowed forward, colliding with a man desperate to leave.

Glenn's momentum and low center of gravity bowled the man back. Glassblower and gnome tumbled to the floor in a jumble of flailing arms and kicking legs. The gnome rolled away from the glassblower. Away from the scrapes of shuffling feet on the granite floor, along with shattering glass. The man near him frantically got to his feet. His leather apron blackened along with patches of his flesh.

Before the door swung closed, Ron slipped in. Anticipating violence, the warrior druid ended the burnt man's life with a spear thrust to the throat.

Ron kicked the dying man back into the room,

closed the door behind him and dodged right. He grabbed the gnome's arm and yanked him back behind a fallen display case.

A raging battle filled the center of the display area. Two swift, beautiful women of glass exchanged blows with a fiery whirlwind. They slashed with their crystal daggers while dodging tentacles of flame whipping out of the spinning tornado of flame. The glass golems' attacks appeared to weaken the enraged fire elemental spirit, like a cup of water being tossed into a raging campfire. Minor in individual effect, but enough would eventually snuff the flames.

As the room's temperature rose, smoke began filling it.

The glass women's swift movements avoided most of the flame attacks. When they failed, portions of their bodies melted like blue-tinted wax.

Ron gripped Glenn's hand and began a spell. Upon its completion he said, "Minor Heat Resistance."

Glenn nodded understanding as the effects of the room's heat diminished.

"I shall seek Marigold out here," Ron said. "You shall seek her within the furnace."

Without a word Glenn moved to his right, his heavy boots stomping on broken glass. In a rush he raced toward the counter that separated the display area from the fabrication area and furnace. At the last second, the gnome healer ducked and raised his shield, barely deflecting one of the melting women's daggers. Although she didn't cut him, the solid strike jarred his shoulder, causing at least a hit point or two of damage.

The distraction cost her greatly, as the fire elemental got in a flank strike. Realizing the greater enemy, the glass guardian turned and attacked the fiery elemental spirit.

Glenn climbed over the counter, stepped over a body

burned beyond recognition, and reached the circular opening to the furnace. Knowing it was going to be dangerously hot, beyond what Ron's spell could counter, he discarded his shield and cudgel, reached up and pulled himself into the opening. Because the magical lotion covered his palm and fingers, he felt none of the furnace porthole's residual heat. But, squeezing through it, his leather jerkin didn't fare as well. Still, Ron's spell dampened the effect on both the gnome and his attire.

Even though the gnome's body blocked most of the flaring light through the porthole, narrow shafts revealed Stephi on the furnace's far side. She lay sprawled on her back with wings unmoving.

She appeared unconscious but uninjured, yet dying.

"I see Marigold!" Glenn shouted, his voice nearly cracking. "She's in here!" He hoped Ron heard.

Glenn finished squirming through the hole and tumbled to the furnace floor. On hands and knees, he frantically crawled around the broken magical circle, toward her, beginning the words of his spell before he made it there.

A welling tear evaporated before reaching his cheek. He placed a hand on Stephi's beautiful face, completing his Minor Heal Draw Spell.

Searing pain filled the gnome healer's chest. He collapsed onto the stone floor, unable to scream.

# Chapter 46

**The minute it** took for Glenn's lungs to heal was the most terrifying he'd ever endured. It was like he'd inhaled molten lava, and then proceeded to suffocate, surrounded by fresh air. Laying on the furnace floor, gasping to no benefit, he wondered if his spell succeeded.

It came down to being able to heal enough hit points to enable his respiratory system to function. He was so terrified that he hadn't noticed Stephi sit up and grasp him in a joy-filled embrace.

Her emotional shift from elation to alarm coincided with Glenn's first successful, yet anemic breath. He sat up and returned the embrace, with each breath that followed renewing his strength and vigor.

Glenn's eyes snapped wide, remembering Ron was in the building, the same room as those battling magical creatures. Had the warrior druid heard his shout that he'd found Stephi? Or was he still seeking her? Or worse, injured or slain by the fiery beast or glass maidens?

Orange flickering light shone through the furnace's porthole.

He pushed Stephi away and held her at arm's length. His mouth and throat were parched-earth dry, but he still managed to say, "Go. Find Petie and Gurk." He pointed at the exhaust pipe for emphasis. He'd purposefully mentioned the two closest things to her heart. No way he wanted her flying through whipping fire tentacles and slashing crystal daggers.

"What about you?" she asked.

The gnome healer got to his feet. Still pointing and without much of a voice, he said, "That's faster. Petie and Gurk." He coughed and swallowed, trying to wet his tongue and throat. "I'll be out in a minute." He *didn't* add, "Maybe."

With amazing speed and agility, Stephi tucked her wings and darted into the pipe. Seeing her leave, Glenn trotted around the raised circle and hauled himself up and began squirming through the porthole. He hadn't thought about the monsters until he was halfway out—just in time to see the two glass maidens turn and face his direction.

Flames licked along the edges of several toppled cases, but the fire elemental was gone. The shop must've had some sort of ventilation system because less smoke filled the room than before.

The two maidens moved his direction, their movements no longer swift. They came on, slow and ungainly, looking like wax figures that some sadistic goon had gone to town on with a blowtorch.

Glenn felt like Winnie the Pooh after eating too much honey and trying to squeeze out of Rabbit's hole. He wasn't fat, but the furnace's porthole wasn't built to crawl through, not even by a gnome. There was probably some latch or other mechanism to access the furnace, but he hadn't taken time to discover it. He squirmed forward, knowing he'd plop down on the floor just in time to become a perforated gnome.

Ron stood and leapt over a toppled case. He took the glass guardians from behind with his spear. Glenn was sure Ron's first strike was true, but it merely glanced off the female guardian's molten-slashed back.

Glenn remembered, in the game, some creatures required silver, or magical weapons, to score damage. The warrior druid had some magical rings added to his ringmail armor. That improved his armor class, but he had nothing magical to attack with. Derek's sword was the party's sole magical weapon.

The warrior druid's maneuver, however, drew the glass guardians' attention, allowing Glenn to escape the furnace and drop to the floor. He picked up his shield and cudgel and prepared to aid his friend. His cudgel's business end had bands of silver worked into it. They *might* prove effective—if he managed to hit. Compared to a second rank warrior's 'to hit' table, his healer's one was crap.

"I shall occupy the glass golems' attention," Ron said, backpedaling around a fallen cabinet, "while you depart." He deflected an award dagger thrust with his spear shaft. The second glass guardian closed in on him. "Tell all to make haste to Rendezvous One."

Glenn nodded and remained still until the backs of both guardians were to him. He then clambered over the counter and made a dash for the door. It was closed, but not locked. He kicked a broken board onto the threshold so the door wouldn't close and looked back over his shoulder. Even a half second's delay to open the door might spell Ron's doom.

Glenn shouted, "I'm out!"

Ron dodged one attack, but caught a glancing dagger thrust in the shoulder. Grimacing, he ducked a third awkward slash and broke for the doorway.

Glenn raced toward the street, nearly crashing into Derek. Stephi fluttered above the big warrior's shoulder.

"Lysine's coming," Glenn said, clearing the doorway. "The glass warriors'll be chasing him."

Kirby shouted from around the corner. "Two guard dudes coming!"

All subtlety and subterfuge of their sabotage attack was gone.

"Run, Gnome," Derek ordered. "Fly Girl Barbie, the thief's gonna need help. You're with me."

Derek took off, sword and shield ready, followed by Stephi and Petie. The latter wasn't flying nearly as nimbly as he normally did, even at night.

Glenn ran the opposite direction, toward the

underground. It wasn't the direction of Rendezvous One, but he could turn right at the corner and get out of sight. He might be able to outrun the glass women, damaged as they were. Then again, maybe not. He bet they didn't get tired.

He circled back around, toward the right direction… he hoped.

**Glenn crouched in** the shadows of a half-collapsed brick wall, once part of a two-story building. He was five blocks south of Krogman's Wagon Repair Shop. The small well house across the street was Rendezvous One, and near the shantytown's stench.

Petie arrived first, landing on the round well house's slanted roof. Glenn sighed in relief. Stephi was okay, and on her way. Petie wouldn't be so calm if things were desperate. Glenn looked around before stepping out of the graying shadows. Sunrise was about an hour away. Glenn guessed the laborers and artisans were stirring in their beds, preparing to face the morning and long work day.

Glenn waved to get the bird's attention. The blue jay flew over and landed on the broken wall. He warbled and chirped, telling Glenn to wait.

A few minutes later Glenn spotted his friends. Ron was leaning heavily on Derek's shoulder. Kirby trotted ahead, carrying the big warrior's shield and the druid's spear. Stephi followed a short distance behind, flitting from building to building. If Glenn hadn't been looking for the fairy he wouldn't have seen her. Actually, she must have failed her Concealment roll, or he made some sort of detection roll. Either way, it didn't really matter.

Ron looked pretty bad, bruised and bleeding. Probably a single hit point remaining.

Glenn waved to get their attention, then ran toward them.

"Hey, Jax," Kirby said, grinning. "We all made it, dude."

Glenn grinned back and they gave each other a high five. The gnome lost track of Stephi. She was probably Camouflaged, because he failed some roll. He was pretty sure she'd put on her leaf and bark attire. A pang of guilt tugged at his disappointment.

"Gnome," Derek said, "stop playing patty cake and heal Lysine."

Derek lowered Ron against the wall of a cooper's shop. "Thief, come with me to get the horses." He looked over his shoulder. "Jumbo Tinkerbell Barbie, until Lysine's one hundred percent, make sure the gnome doesn't do anything stupid."

# CHAPTER 47

**Before sunrise, Glenn** had been only able to partially heal Ron, adding four to the warrior druid's hit point total. Ron had used his only memorized Cure Minor Wounds Spell on Petie, who'd slammed against one of the glass shop's narrow windows in a vain effort to reach Stephi.

Derek berated Ron for the foolish gesture while Stephi thanked him profusely. After sunrise, a quick Minor Heal Draw Spell brought Ron up to full strength. They were on the road out of town minutes after that.

Stephi'd been fortunate that she had Kim's hit points to draw from. Similarly, Ron's recent rank advancement saved his life. Probably Glenn's and Stephi's as well.

Only two rode horses, since only Derek and Ron had taken the Horse Riding and Handling Skill. Kirby rode with Ron and Glenn got stuck with Derek. Stephi flew alongside. Occasionally she flew up to search the road behind to see if they were being followed, and ahead, to spot their two wagons. It was easier than looking through Petie's eyes.

"Lysine's Minor Heat Resistance Spell saved everyone's ass, Gnome," Derek explained. "It ain't powerful enough to stop massive heat damage, like being stuck in the forge with a pissed-off fire spirit elemental. But you only take half damage, and if you make your saving roll, only a quarter damage. Stephi probably suffered a Critical Strike, being next to the elemental and breathing in that super-heated air. But made her save and only went to zero hits. Unconscious with her lungs fried, she lost another point per round. So good thing you hustled your gnomey waddle-butt to her rescue."

That he used "gnomey" told Glenn the big warrior

was in a good mood. They all were, having accomplished their mission. The elemental spirit had been released, the glass guardians were horribly damaged, and the shop itself was a wreck. Several guards and two glass blowers were dead. No one was alive that got a good look at any of them, except the monkey familiar. He only saw Stephi—a fairy. Once the party got the leprechaun's gold coin, that trail would dry up on anyone following it. Only way things could've gone better was if the fire elemental had destroyed the upper apartments and set the office building aflame.

Stephi fluttered down, a concerned look on her beautiful face. She said to Ron, "There's a couple soldiers in armor lying in the sand and patchy grass near the road." One eye squinted as she bit her lower lip. "I think it's where we were supposed to meet up with our hired people and wagons."

"Your observation is troubling," Ron said. "Return to the overwatch position."

Derek was about to kick his mount into a gallop but Ron signaled for him to wait.

"Let us not rush into a concerning situation."

Derek held his mount to a trot, matching Ron's pace, but not without cussing under his breath. The bouncing made Glenn even more uncomfortable. That fact probably soothed the big warrior's volatile mood.

**Glenn stood watch** on the road while Stephi remained fifty feet overhead.

Kirby rolled over one of the six bodies. "Recognize this dude?"

"Yonn," Derek snarled. "Don't recognize the others."

Ron stood, a finger to the side of his chin as he observed the placement of the bodies and the abandoned campsite. "Three wagons, drawn by horse teams, and the small hoof prints of what is likely a donkey."

Derek said, "Looks like they came in on horses and got their asses handed to them."

"They ain't got anything of value on them," Kirby said. "Except their armor."

"Yeah," Derek said. "No weapons, neither." He lightly kicked one corpse. "Mardin or Trumble yanked their crossbow bolt out of this guy's face."

"Our men-at-arms and hired drivers prevailed in the fight," Ron said.

"Yonn," Kirby said, seething anger in his voice. "Probably hired by the thieves' guild. This guy in leather armor was probably leading them."

Derek spat on the ground. "They wouldn't send only a thief and five men-at-arms against the wagons, if we were with them."

"That means somebody was watching us," Kirby said. "Or at least our wagons."

"Fortunately I opted for the Tracking Skill," Ron said. "Thus, that no enemy retreated and returned to Riven Rock is closer to established fact than mere speculation."

"We should catch up to our guys soon as we can," Kirby said. "They'll know if anyone got away."

"Lilac isn't a guy," Stephi shouted down in her fairy voice.

"They might need healing too," Glenn added.

"Agreed," Ron said returning to his mount.

"I'm gonna move the bodies over behind those rocks," Derek said, pointing to an outcropping about fifty yards away.

Kirby looked up at Derek in puzzlement. "Buzzards and gore crows'll tell anybody that comes looking for them where they're at."

"No sense making it easy by leaving them here," Derek said. "Plus, bodies right by the road'll raise questions for anyone coming by."

Kirby gestured by tipping his head. "Main road's five miles that way."

Derek turned and snarled at Kirby, "Think I don't know that, thief?"

Ron told Mardin and Blizz to take the side road out of town to be less conspicuous. It was an older, less maintained route that eventually merged back into the main road.

"No, dude," Kirby said to Derek. "I know you know." The thief scratched his head. "Just make sure we cut the straps to their mail armor and slice open the gambeson underneath."

Derek grinned ferally and nodded. "Good idea, thief. The vultures can get at them faster."

**Glenn rode in** the trailing wagon, on the bench next to Blizz.

They'd found the wagons camped five miles further down the road. Ron expended all of his Minor Cure Spells to bring the surviving men-at-arms up to full hit points. Glenn expended one Minor Heal Draw Spell to cure Lilac. The draw of the severe wounds transferred and draw on his hit points suggested Lilac was tougher than a typical man-at-arms. He wondered if Ron, who'd hired her, knew that.

Her unexpected ability to fight and absorb damage proved lucky for Blizz, Simmer, Mardin, Trumble and Kronk. Not so much for Harold. They'd buried him in a shallow grave. They covered it with rocks to protect him from scavengers.

Blizz and Mardin had apparently prepared Trumble and Kronk for traveling with a gorgeous fairy. Nevertheless, they only dared look upon her from afar. Seemed trust in fairies was lacking among humans pretty much across the board. Glenn suspected it was the Charm ability. He hadn't seen Stephi use it. Heck

Stephi's Appearance Score could pretty much get her anything she wanted.

Glenn said to Blizz, "Lilac's tougher than she looks." He thought about that statement. Her stocky build and crooked nose. "And she looks like she can take care of herself."

"I sure am glad Mr. Lysine hired her on," Blizz said while flicking the reins to his horse team. Crates of coal made for a heavy load. But not nearly as heavy as the overloaded wagons the horses previously hauled. "We'd all be dead, weren't for her."

The old half-goblin licked his lips and cocked his head. "Them hired swords that Yonn fella was with…I mean, Mardin, he knew trouble was brewing. Him and Trumble shot their crossbows before it came to close fighting. Mardin was leading them to fight hard, but they was losing, 'till me and Lilac took'm from behind."

Blizz laughed at himself. "Mostly her doing all the taking. They'd discounted her, 'cause she's a woman, and me? An old, worn-out half-goblin." He paused, glancing up into the morning sky, recalling the moment. "They turned to hacking their swords on her, but she kept giving it, and wouldn't go down. Mardin and Kronk rallied and that was it. Not one got away, and we got their swords and horses."

Six sturdy mounts, tied in strings of three, followed behind the trailing wagon.

"Cost Harold his life, though." The animal handler's head drooped. "I liked him, that Harold. Didn't know him long, but he was like you, Mr. Jax, and Mr. Lysine. Talked to me like I'm more than a worn-out old half-goblin."

Glenn suppressed a prideful grin. "You're okay in my book, Blizz."

"Hearing that from a gnome? Makes me wonder at how the world sometimes shows you a shiny copper coin edging out from under a pile of bear skat."

The gnome healer didn't know exactly how to take that. He decided it was more of a complement than anything else.

# CHAPTER 48

The ride back was akin to a race where the runner kept looking back over his shoulder, expecting at any moment to see a pack of wolves closing in for the kill. Or at least that's how Glenn felt.

Everyone else was on edge, too. Kirby fitfully muttered in his sleep, often snapping awake, covered in sweat. Ron remained silent about any concern. His vigilance, day and night, as they traveled through the dry, barren land said enough. Derek grumbled and yelled at the men-at-arms for any small misstep, until Ron intervened. Only Lilac appeared unfazed by the big warrior's bouts of anger.

Stephi, while watchful, was the most positive. So much so that a friendship between her and Lilac showed signs of budding. Their stations were different, animal handlers and drivers being lower than men-at-arms. Although Lilac addressed Stephi as Miss Marigold, as a sign of respect, Lilac wasn't an average hireling. Stephi's being a fairy didn't throw her off. Glenn figured both women longed for female companionship.

They met several caravans traveling south, toward Riven Rock. Glenn and Stephi kept out of sight during the passing meetings. A fairy and a gnome would be far more memorable than humans and half-goblins, should the southbound caravans be questioned by northbound pursuers.

No bands of bandits, manticores, or other Wandering Creatures Encounters impeded progress. They came across the damaged wagon they'd stripped of wheels and abandoned. Not much was left. Horse bones lay scattered and the wagon's wood and metal scavenged.

The party crossed the Snake Claw River and drove

through Three Hills City's main gate. This time Lieutenant Reginald Voss, always fancy with his oiled, curly hair, assessed a mere eight silver coins as tax. Apparently coal imports were something Duke Huelmer encouraged.

Glenn inhaled the city's smells. There was sweat and manure on the air. The odors were neither intense, nor rancid. Three Hills City had its problems, but it was ten times better than Riven Rock. No wonder the Villar's thieves' guild from Riven Rock was interested in expanding to Three Hills City.

Stephi was more than ready to immediately get the leprechaun's coin from the pawnshop owner. Ron counseled the wiser course would be to deal with him well-rested rather than weary.

When the party arrived at the Glade House, Ron hired a runner to inform Higslaff, through a note, of the wagons and cargo to be retrieved, and the desire for a meeting the following morning to complete their business.

Ron paid the men-at-arms and hirelings. Derek and Kirby took the horses to the stables, including the six extra. Glenn did the unpacking and helped the young maid, Elise, fill a wash tub so that she might work on the party's dirty clothes.

Once Stephi privately informed the Glade House's owner of the party's success, Keri offered to take Stephi to visit the duke's garden. Glenn wanted to go, too. It was a beautiful place and he sort of wanted to see the garden's fairy, Emma.

Instead of rudely inviting himself along, Glenn retrieved the creel basket and handed it to Keri. After the two women departed, he trundled up to the party's rented room, intent on enjoying a long nap.

# CHAPTER 49

**"Yes!" Kirby shouted**. "This day rules."

Glenn, tucked under Stephi's bottom bunk—which she didn't use—stuck his head out and looked up to the top bunk where Kirby slept. It was still dark outside, and the small open window didn't lend much light. Enough for Glenn's eyes, but certainly not enough for Derek's human ones.

"What the hell, thief?" Derek's annoyed grumble wasn't really a question.

Ron, in his bottom bunk, propped himself up on an elbow, a curious look on his face. "The walls of this boarding house will not sufficiently muffle excessively loud voices, Gurk. Moderate your volume and explain your predawn proclamation."

Stephi fluttered in the window from her rooftop perch. Fairies, like elves, didn't sleep. Not exactly. Maybe meditated or something, but they definitely didn't sleep.

Glenn opened his everlast candle, bringing the flame to life.

Derek groaned. "Is that necessary, gnome?"

"I had the dream," Kirby said, his croaking voice excited, but hushed. "I'm a third-rank thief. Rolled a four on my D6 for hits."

Glenn knew it was more metaphorical rolling, having experienced the dream once himself. The process mimicked exactly what would happen if Kirby had gained enough experience points to advance to third rank while playing the actual *Monsters, Maces and Magic Game.*

"I believe that brings your hit point total to a respectable fourteen," Ron said.

"Yup," Kirby said.

"That's so cool, my little man." Stephi flew over and hugged the half-goblin thief, well, his shoulder, and kissed him on the cheek.

Glenn was so happy to hear Stephi call his friend that. She hadn't in so long. It hadn't fit. Now, having finished the mission, and with the leprechaun's gold coin as payment, she'd soon be back to her tall elf self.

Derek punched his pillow and sat up in his top bunk. "Why'd it happen last night?" He stared accusingly. "What'd you do yesterday to earn the experience points to put you over, thief? Steal something? Cash in something that should've been party treasure?"

"No, dude," Kirby said, "I didn't steal anything—although I had tons of chances. And I didn't cheat the party."

"Why do you have to be so mean, Kalgore?" Stephi fluttered over, stopping a foot from the big warrior's bed. "Are you jealous because Gurk's higher rank than you?"

"Ha! Warriors are always tougher than thieves. They go up ranks faster in a pathetic attempt to compensate."

"Each character class has merit," Ron said. "We are fortunate to be a balanced party."

Derek ignored Ron and looked past Stephi, to Kirby. "What skill did you take?"

"Stone Masonry."

"You planning on building a castle, thief?"

"Come on, dude," Kirby said, hopping down from his bed. "Gives me a five percent bonus to Finding and Removing Traps in stone structures and underground complexes with stone construction."

A wide grin crossed the half-goblin thief's face. "Plus, I can build a castle, if I want to." He put his hands on his hips and puffed his chest out. "I'll even build you a room on the east side, so the sun won't wake you up early."

Stephi flew back next to Kirby and rested a hand on

his shoulder. "Maybe then Kalgore wouldn't be such a Mr. Grumpy Pants."

"Butterfly Barbie," Derek said slamming his head down on his pillow and facing the wall, "why don't you go do something useful, like go suck some flower nectar."

**Higslaff didn't appear** pleased about the entire party's arrival to retrieve the leprechaun's gold coin in payment for their service. Ron was insistent, and Higslaff couldn't come up with a reason to deny the full party's involvement.

It'd take a lot to dampen the party's high spirts. Certainly more than a sour, stingy businessman. They were getting the coin to return Stephi to her elf self. Plus, Kirby'd had the special dream.

Once up in Higslaff's office, Stephi seated on the corner of the pawnshop owner's desk, and the other four party members seated on stools arranged in front of it, the owner leaned back in his chair.

"So," he said, "tell me of your success."

Bonnar sat on a stool off to the right. He combed his fingers through his blond beard and leaned forward with interest. On the table next to him rested his war hammer. It was a less than subtle suggestion that the party members should mind their manners.

Ron reached into his satchel and pulled out a written voucher. "This states what was earned through sale of the goods we delivered to Riven Rock, minus the cost of the coal we returned with. That commodity, along with the wagons and horses, were delivered to the agreed upon stables."

"So I was informed," Higslaff said, his words drawn out slightly.

"During the journey toward our destination, one wagon and horse team was lost as a consequence of a manticore attack."

Higslaff's eyebrows rose. "A fierce foe. One that's fortunately rare to come across."

"Yeah," Derek said. "We dealt with it. Lost some of your cowardly men-at-arms in the fight. Half of them ran."

Ron put a hand on Derek's forearm. "More on that in a moment."

Derek relaxed and Ron continued his report. "As to the results with respect to our assigned task, four guards and two skilled glassblowers were slain. The elemental fire spirit held within a magical circle was released, doing substantial damage to the shop's interior and wrecking the majority of items for sale within the shop, prior to its departure.

"Two glass golem guardians were also severely damaged, yet not destroyed. A substantial amount of resources and magical effort will be required to bring them back into service as effective guardians."

After a half-moment of silence, Higslaff sat up straight in his chair. "In truth, I expected more."

Kirby hopped to his feet and leaned on the desk. "Dude!"

Ron reached forward and put a hand on the half-goblin's shoulder. "Gurk."

Kirby threw up his arms and sat back down. The party had agreed Ron would do the talking. The warrior druid was less likely to get thrown off or distracted by anything the pawnshop owner might say or do.

Ron folded his arms across his chest. "Before you express disappointment, your assignment of Guard Captain Nickson and the man-at-arms, Yonn, to accompany us, handicapped our effort."

Higslaff cocked his head and squinted an eye. "Handicapped?"

Ron went on to explain the guard captain's

attempted betrayal, and how their need to deal with the situation drew suspicion from the local thieves' guild, complicating the party's effort to complete the assigned task.

He then explained how Yonn was part of a group that attacked the wagons prior to the party joining up with them after the completed mission. And that it was likely he informed on them to the local guild. The party did not return to investigate that aspect.

Higslaff waved a hand in dismissal. "Krogman's failure. He should've warned you sooner."

"We disagree," Ron said. "Nickson and Yonn were your men, and should have been better vetted before assigning them to accompany us to Riven Rock. That oversight not only endangered the success of the mission, but our lives as well."

"A matter of opinion," the pawnshop owner said. "Such ventures are fraught with unknown dangers. I figured you were up to the task. That is why I sent you."

A moment of silence fell in the room. Glenn wasn't sure where things were going to go. They'd earned the coin, but thought additional payment was in order, due to the handicap of Nickson and Yonn's participation.

Ron cleared his throat. "Marigold utilized two of the three spells inscribed upon the scroll you provided. As Marigold will soon be returned to her full stature, we request that you provide her with a scroll containing an identical Fire Blast Spell."

Glenn remembered looking at the scroll. The scribed magical lettering and symbols were the equivalent size of a four point font.

Ron continued. "In addition, we request compensation for imperiling us with assigned traitorous individuals."

"Curious requests." Higlsaff leaned back in his chair. "I am not in the habit of paying extra for a job accomplished to the bare minimum."

Derek laughed. "But you're in the habit of sending backstabbers on missions?"

Glenn remembered Ron, Derek and Kirby agreeing that appealing to the pawnshop owner's honor would be pointless. But, suggesting how it might impair his reputation? That would better garner a favorable response. And Derek, an impulsive hothead, blurting that out brought the incompetency point home. Should it get out, nobody would believe anything was Krogman's fault.

Glenn put a disapproving frown on his face and glared at the pawnshop owner.

Higslaff rubbed his chin in thought. "I suspect Marigold has become used to a fairy's ability to blend into the background. Become invisible to an average observer." He tilted his head, making eye contact with Stephi. "My employee, Coleen Sammae, will instruct you in the casting of Render Unseen." He leaned back again. "That is, once you've gained sufficient knowledge and skill to master spells at a higher tier of complexity."

"Render Unseen?" Stephi asked.

"Invisibility," Derek said. "Better in some ways than what you can do as a fairy. But worse in others."

Higslaff's eyebrows rose at Derek's explanation. Most warriors weren't well-versed in spells magic users cast, especially illiterate warriors.

"No deal," Kirby said. The half-goblin's voice was both authoritative, and tinged with anger.

Everyone turned toward the thief.

Kirby made eye contact with Stephi, then locked gazes with the pawnshop owner. "In addition to handing over the leprechaun's coin, Marigold will retain the tiny scroll with the Fireblast Spell. You'll provide one with two Mystic Missile Spells equal to the one the small scroll held. And you'll hand over an additional fifty gold coins to the party."

Higslaff looked from Kirby to Ron. "With which of you should I be carrying on this conversation? You, Kalgore? Or Gurk?"

Ron nonchalantly shrugged. Glenn thought that was out of character, especially in the current situation.

The warrior druid said, "Did you not, a mere moment ago, address Marigold directly concerning compensation for your dispatching hirelings of dubious loyalty? An act which not only endangered the mission's success, but put our lives at additional risk." He spread his hands, gesturing to everyone in the party. "We are of one mind on this issue."

Ron's eyebrows pinched together. "We suspect that you have eyes and ears in Riven Rock, beyond those of Krogman and his associates, and have some knowledge of events. You do not strike me as an individual prone to believing an adventuring party's claim of success. Not without sufficient proof. Yet, those most easily accessible, who might confirm our claim, are no longer directly in your employ, or dead."

Derek shrugged again. "On the other hand, we have a reputation of successfully completing missions."

Without thinking, Glenn nodded. They'd recovered the magical necklace for the Church of Apollo, and they'd rescued the elven baronet's daughter, White Ash, from a tribe of goblins.

Higslaff grinned. It wasn't a friendly grin, as it didn't reach his eyes. "Fifty gold coins in trade for what my shop has to offer."

"Seventy-five gold," Derek said. "Everything on your shelves is a sucker's price."

"Sixty gold coins in trade," Higslaff countered. "That is in addition to the scroll escribed with the spells Gurk requested."

Ron looked to everyone in the party to determine if

all agreed with the terms.

Glenn, wanting to be a part of the negotiations, figured he wanted to close a potential loophole. "The leprechaun's coin turned over now. The scroll with spells should be delivered to the party at the Glade House within one week from today." Glenn scrunched his nose before adding, "And no time limit on when the sixty gold in trade can be used."

"The timeframe for returning the magical coin was never in question," Higslaff said.

He pulled a skeleton key from his pocket and unlocked one of the desk's lower drawers. After some sort of maneuvering, which the party wasn't able to view, he placed a gold coin on the table.

Ron reached into a pocket for the copper coin the leprechaun had provided. It appeared identical to the one on Higslaff's desk. "May I place this copper coin close to the gold coin upon your desk?"

"For what purpose, Lysine?"

"To identify the gold coin's authenticity, Higslaff."

The shop owner nodded.

Ron placed the copper coin on the desktop and slowly slid it toward the gold coin. When the two were within five inches, the gold coin began sliding toward the copper one.

Ron lifted the copper coin from the desk.

"Interesting," Higslaff said. "Works like a lodestone would with iron. You didn't do this before."

"Circumstances vary," Ron said, offering no further clarification.

The way the pawnshop owner licked his teeth told Glenn they'd managed to agitate the man.

Ron reached his right hand across the desk. "For completion of the assigned task, we get the leprechaun's coin immediately, two Mystic Missile Spells as described by Gurk, to be delivered to us at the Glade House within the week, and sixty gold in trade, redeemable by anyone in the party, with no assigned date of expiration."

"Mighty formal, saying the same thing twice," Higlsaff said, shaking Ron's hand while pushing the magical gold coin across the desk with his left. "I am more inclined to reasonable intent of the agreement rather than one needing a magistrate to untangle."

"Understood," Ron said. He picked up the gold coin. "With various voices involved in the discussion, I desired for the understanding to be clear and concise."

"My understanding of leprechauns," Higslaff said, "clear and concise, with no loopholes is most desirable."

**Once on the** street Derek asked Kirby, "What stuck the burr in your undershorts?"

It looked like the day was going to be clear with lots of sunshine. The party hurried back toward to the Glade House for lunch and then to summon the leprechaun.

"Something didn't seem right about what that dude was offering. I tried to figure out why, which triggered a Diplomacy Roll. I got the notion like, even though he was offering a Render Unseen Spell for Marigold, it felt like he was gonna get something out of it."

From inside the creel basket, Stephi asked. "What was he trying to get away with?"

Kirby shrugged his shoulders. "No clue. My skill in Diplomacy isn't high enough to figure that."

"I gotta admit, thief," Derek said, "that was pretty smart." He slapped Kirby on the back, knocking the half-goblin forward a step. The big warrior laughed. "That slimy salesman couldn't hide your digging under his skin pretty good."

# CHAPTER 50

**The party made** its way to the coppice of trees that were said to be Duke Huelmer's exclusive property. They'd learned there was a lot more to the restricted grove of trees and the delicate balance between Polayney, the immortal wood nymph, and the rulers of Three Hills City.

The late breakfast of corn cakes and honey sat like a brick in Glenn's stomach. It wasn't that the duke's guards might catch the party entering the restricted stand of trees. They entered from the river's side, careful that nobody might spot them. Glenn's gnomish instincts tickled his thoughts, suggesting they were being followed. Nobody else sensed it, not even Stephi and her fairy senses, supplemented by Petie. Derek's deriding laugh settled it. The gnome was being paranoid.

In any case, the goal wasn't to remain among the trees for long. And facing the leprechaun worried Glenn far more than the duke's men.

Sure, this time Ron and Derek were there. Ron had the silver dagger made by the silversmith while they were away, and Derek had his magical sword. They could hurt the leprechaun. But so much was on the line for Stephi. Heck, things could end up being even worse. How? Glenn couldn't imagine. And that's what had his stomach tied in a knot.

When they got to the spot near the center of the coppice where the leprechaun, Bataí Fidil na Maidine, and his pot of gold had originally appeared, Ron said, "Kalgore and I shall conceal ourselves behind those two trees." He pointed to a pair of large yew trees. "Summon the leprechaun using the name he provided. Kalgore and I shall monitor, and respond as might be required."

"More like 'shall be required,'" Kirby said with a gloomy certainty. His mood was in stark contrast to the sunny day that shown down into the sunlit area before them.

That Kirby was worried things wouldn't go well had to be upsetting to Stephi, Glenn thought. Heck, it made him feel worse.

Derek looked from the hole in the foliage above to the twelve-foot diameter patch of sunlit grass before them. The green area extended another fifteen feet before becoming lightly wooded. Logically there shouldn't be a hole in the canopy, but there was. To nobody in particular, the big warrior said, "The leprechaun wants his coin back as much as Flutter Wings Barbie wants to be an elf again." He drew his sword from its scabbard strapped across his back. "This time he won't be so cocky..." The warrior spun his sword in a series of fancy slashing attacks. "Not when he sees this."

"Whatever, dude," Kirby said. Then he glanced to his left at Stephi fluttering eye-level next to him. "It's gonna work out, Marigold. Just not as easy as Kalgore thinks."

Stephi said, "I hope so, my little man." She sighed. "I hope so."

Kirby looked to his right, making eye contact with Glenn. "Remember, Jax, you and Marigold have to do the talking. You're sort of fae, so he'll be more honest dealing with you."

"We already have a deal," Stephi said.

Derek slid his sword back into its scabbard. "Like Lysine said, it ain't a done deal until it's done."

Stephi's hands went to her hips. "Lysine didn't say that."

Glenn stepped forward. "Let's not argue and just get this done and over with." He wondered why Ron hadn't stepped in to stop things. "Okay?"

"Agreed," Ron said. He signaled to Derek and led him back behind the trees.

Once they were out of sight, Kirby said, "You get in between us, Marigold, and then say his name." He checked his bandoleer of darts. "Don't show you're scared. If you have to, pretend you're arguing with Kalgore."

Stephi gave a half smile, which blossomed into a full one. "I can do that."

"Cool."

Stephi took her position between the half-goblin thief and gnome healer. "You ready, Jax?"

Glenn put on a stern look. "I am."

"Okay," Stephi said, her voice ending in a nervous higher pitch. She turned her gaze up to the opening in the trees. "Bata Fidil!"

# CHAPTER 51

**Glenn didn't know** what to expect, but it wasn't a thirty minute wait. After the first ten, he and Kirby sat down with Stephi landing in between them. She didn't sit.

Maybe it was Glenn's gnome senses kicking in when he felt a tingle across his skin, like someone gently drawing a comb across it. The buzzing bugs and nearby birds fell silent.

Stephi looked around, wide-eyed. "Petie says he's coming."

Glenn and Kirby got to their feet. Stephi fluttered to a height equal to theirs.

A shimmering rainbow dropped down like falling streaks of paint. Where it touched, the meadow grass began roiling. Or maybe the soil beneath roiled and the green blades shivered. The effect lasted mere seconds before a huge iron kettle—or pot—of gold appeared. The rainbow remained, causing the gold within the pot to sparkle.

Bataí Fidil na Maidine strode around from behind the pot, chest puffed out and shillelagh in hand. He was attired exactly as before: Crayola green shirt with brown buttons that matched his brown trousers, and brown bowler hat. The hat sported a green feather stuck into its brick-red ribbon. His boots were also Crayola green and came to an upturned point at the toe.

The leprechaun's curly red hair held wisps of gray, but this time appeared damp, as if he'd just showered. His freckled cheeks framed a wide, insincere smile.

Glenn reminded himself that the diminutive man, at least a foot shorter than himself, was dangerous. Not because of his physical prowess. Magic was the leprechaun's strength.

But Bata Fidil came when called because the party had something he wanted. So he wasn't one hundred percent in control of the situation. They had leverage, too.

"Took you long enough," Stephi challenged, hands going to her hips.

Bata Fidil quirked an eyebrow. "And exactly how fast can *ye* go from one continent to the next?"

Glenn hadn't thought of the world having continents. He'd have to see if Keri had a map of the world among the books in her third-floor workroom above the Stickley Café.

The gnome scrutinized the leprechaun. The distance travelled *might* be a factor, but it wasn't the whole reason for taking so long to arrive. He looked around, and in the trees above, and listened. Maybe Bata Fidil had some sort of familiar too, one that he'd sent ahead, or had scurry out of sight during the rainbow's initial distraction. If so, Ron and Derek might've seen it. They would've seen how the leprechaun appeared, too. It's possible he didn't know Ron and Derek were hidden among the trees behind him.

Glenn recalled the feeling someone, or something, followed them to the grove of trees. Did leprechauns use crystal balls or some kind of magic pools to see elsewhere? He vaguely recalled that from his junior high stint playing *Dungeons & Dragons.*

He tried using his nose, but the sharp scent of yew trees overpowered anything subtle the gentle breeze might carry upon it. At least in the brief time he had to test the air. It was up to him to begin the negotiations.

He cleared his throat. "We brought the coin. Your gold coin—the one stolen from your treasure pot by that the dwarf, Benxcob."

The leprechaun's face squeezed together like he'd unexpectedly bit into a lemon. "What happened to the thieving dwarf?"

Glenn wasn't going to admit any connection to the dwarf's death. "We took it from him."

Bata Fidil shook his knobby stick. "So, ye killed 'em?"

"We got your coin, as agreed." Glenn gestured with his right hand to Stephi. "Change her back to the way she was, as you agreed to do."

She nodded and fluttered down to the ground, a half step ahead of Kirby and Glenn.

The leprechaun squinted an eye. "First, I want ta see me gold coin." Then he spun to face behind him. "Annnndd..." He drew the word out, before finishing. "I want whoever yer companions might be, in the open, and comin' around from skulking behind me back."

Glenn suppressed the urge to smile at the leprechaun's cheesy Irish accent. Obviously owed to the game's designers.

The pot and shimmering rainbow, while blocking and distorting Glenn's view, they apparently didn't affect Bata Fidil's. His senses were far more keen than a gnome's.

"They're not skulking," Stephi said. "They're here in case you try double-crossing me."

Ron and Derek stepped from behind a pair of thick-trunked trees. They split up, and made their way along the edge of the clearing. Ron walked with cautious purpose and stopped at the leprechaun's two o'clock position. Derek strode with a sneer on his face. He stopped at the ten o'clock position.

Bata Fidil grinned in triumph, until the two party members halted before reaching Glenn, Stephi and Kirby at his twelve o'clock. "I said, together."

"You can see them," Glenn said.

The leprechaun squinted, looking around. "That ain't everyone."

"Petie isn't coming anywhere near you," Stephi said.

"Petie?" Bata Fatil rubbed a finger under his nose. "Nobody hiding, or no deal."

"He's not a *somebody* hiding," Glenn said. "He's a bird."

"And he's not coming anywhere near you," Stephi repeated.

A momentary gust of wind rustled the branches above. Remnants of it brushed across the meadow grass below.

"The blue jay." Bata Fidil tapped his brown bowler hat. "Yes, now I remember. A familiar?"

Glenn ignored the question. "Return Marigold to her former stature, as agreed."

Bata Fidil tipped his hat up with a finger. "Me coin. I want to see me stolen gold coin, first."

"You can sense it's nearby," Glenn said, counting on what Ron and Kirby had told him and Stephi. Derek agreed, but the gnome didn't give the big warrior's advice as much weight. "So you know it's here."

"You tell him, gnome," Derek urged.

Bata Fidil cocked his head Derek's direction and mumbled something under his breath. A few seconds later, Derek's breast and backplate dropped from his shoulders and thudded onto the meadow grass.' The leprechaun's spell had rotted the armors leather straps.

Derek clenched his teeth and held his tongue. He still wore chainmail and had his shield. But who knew what else the leprechaun might pull.

Stephi had gone from nervous to the edge of fuming. She turned to Kirby. "Gurk, put my cloak on the ground and then show this annoying little man the stolen coin that *we* got back for him."

"Callin' someone little sounds funny, coming from you, miss fairy."

Stephi spun back and pointed at the leprechaun.

"You promised," she said. "You gave your word, remember?"

"That I do," Bata Fidil said, an eyebrow suddenly raised. He tilted his head and squinted.

Kirby laid Stephi's cloak out on the grass, and set her boots next to it. Then he reached into a fold in his boot and withdrew the golden coin.

"Why, you let that mongrel lay hands on me coin?"

The party gave the coin to Kirby because he, being third rank, had the best chance to make Saving Throws against any spells the leprechaun might cast.

Without a word, Kirby slid over and handed the coin to Glenn. The gnome held it up for the leprechaun to see, and then stuffed it deep into his pocket.

"Now," Glenn said, "please undo your magic and return Marigold to her former self and stature."

"Well, Jax, is it?" The leprechaun straightened his hat and then rubbed his hands together. "Doing that and regaining me coin is the point of being here. Right?"

Not wanting to say anything that might muck things up, Glenn nodded agreement.

Stephi fluttered down, and quickly lifted the hood and stepped underneath. She stretched her short arms along the shoulders, as far as they would go into the sleeves.

Bata Fidil frowned. "Awww, no glimpse of yer fair body for me green eyes as before?"

Stephi let out a long breath. "No, Mr. Fidil. Sorry." Somehow, she managed to keep her tone light and friendly.

Derek argued that she should stand buck naked. It'd distract the leprechaun from any mischief he might plan. Ron disagreed, indicating that, "Marigold's nudity would distract not only the adversarial leprechaun, but every individual involved in the encounter." And, "There is a considerable probability a leprechaun will be less susceptible to such a carnal distraction."

"Disappointing." With a flourish of his left hand and a mumbled series of arcane words, the leprechaun completed his Transmorph Spell. Or undid his previous Transmorph Spell. Stephi's wings shrank and disappeared. At the same time she grew, as if a camera's zoom lens was a real, physical effect. As she returned to her stature, her head lifting the cloak by its hood, she pulled the front closed, covering her more than amply endowed body.

Glenn watched, amazed to witness the spell's effects. The first time, she'd disappeared within her collapsing garments. Kirby had a ring that could similarly cause size changes, but on a far more limited basis with respect to both size, and duration.

During the middle of the Transmorph Spell's effects, Bata Fidil muttered something else. Glenn's attention shot to the leprechaun. The gnome internally berated himself for getting distracted.

Within fifteen seconds Stephi stood, filling her travelling cloak as she once had. She looked around, and down at her companions, her face moving from elation to relief.

"Now, you'll be returning me gold coin I've been missing."

"I'll give it to him," Stephi said. She extended her left hand down toward Glenn while clutching her cloak with her right, keeping it closed.

Glenn dug for the coin in his pocket, and took his eyes off the leprechaun for a second. "Just a sec," he said. "It's tucked beneath my coin pouch." He realized something was wrong the same instant Stephi did. Her boobs were up too high. Normally their bottoms rested at a height to lightly brush the top of his head, if he stood close enough. Now, they were more than a hand's spread higher. And she wasn't even wearing her heeled boots.

Either Bata Fidil had shrunk him, or he'd overdone Stephi.

Glenn shot a glance past Stephi, toward Kirby. And unless his half-goblin friend had been shrunk too…

Stephi's beautiful face twisted in anger. She took a step toward the leprechaun. "You little creep."

"This is coming apart, dude," Kirby said. "Give me back the coin."

Glenn complied and tossed it to his friend.

Ron, comprehending the deteriorating situation, shifted his spear to his left hand before pulling his silvered dagger from its sheath.

Derek drew his sword. "Fix her right."

Kirby drew his cutlass. "Yeah, dude."

Glenn unslung his shield and pulled his cudgel. He, Derek and Ron wielded weapons effective against the magical leprechaun.

Bata Fidil took a step back toward his pot, a playful grin on his face.

"Departing without properly rendering the promised service will not earn the return of your treasured gold coin." Ron spoke as if lecturing a freshman who'd failed an exam due to partying instead of engaging in adequate study. "This potential impasse can be resolved without resorting to violence."

Glenn sure hoped so. He'd seen what high-ranked magic users could do. What a magical creature like Bata Fidil could do frightened him. Killing the little man wouldn't solve Stephi's new problem. It would leave them with a pot full of gold. That selfish thought bit at Glenn's conscience, until he rationalized they could spend it on finding someone to cast a spell to shrink her back—if that could be done.

"Oh, my dark-skinned friend," Bata Fidil said, "impending violence isn't nearly the concern for me as it is for you." He tapped his shillelagh three times against the cast-iron pot. "Or, 'twill be the case, momentarily."

The rainbow shuddered like a flag waving in the wind. Then an undulation in the colors, originating from above the trees, descended. From behind the pot of gold stepped a hissing lizard man. Standing nearly seven feet tall and armed with a nasty-looking trident, the man-eating creature stared at the party assembled against the leprechaun who'd summoned him.

A second undulating wave descended, depositing a hulking ogre. The huge brute smelled of foul sweat and fetid blood, the latter emanating from the stains of recent victims coving his spiked club. Glenn had encountered a couple ogres in the *Monsters, Maces and Magic* world. This one looked like their big brother.

The third and final wave brought forth a monster three times worse than the previous two, combined. The big monster didn't even acknowledge Bata Fidil as the others had. Rather, it immediately turned its black-eyed gaze upon the party. The monstrous beast stood over twice the height of a man. It wore an assortment of crudely sewn furs over its broad shoulders and around its waist, covering only a portion of its mottled-green skin.

Glenn recognized it as a troll. His gnomish heritage—shared nightmares of his race—left no doubt. One of his few *D&D* characters back in junior high died fighting a troll. During that game encounter the troll monster regenerated from all wounds his party inflicted. Only fire and acid were effective. None of which they had.

Where the similar-sized ogre lumbered, the troll stepped away from the rainbow, showing tight muscles, ready to spring into action. Although the troll carried no weapons, it arrived spoiling for a fight.

It smiled menacingly, showing double rows of pointed teeth. Everything on the troll's face seemed pointed. Its ears, its long nose, its chin. The black nails on each hand were sharp too, resembling talons more than anything else.

"Might you be thinking on amending your notion of violence?" Bata Fidil asked. He leapt up and backwards, landing atop his pot's mound of gold. A nimble feat certain to impress any tree frog. He extended his hand. "Now, I'll be having me stolen coin, and be on me way."

"You'll be on your way like a fall leaf taken up by a winter's gale, Bataí Fidil na Maidine," a high-pitched, female voice from behind Bata Fidil and his three enforcers announced, "once you fulfill your promise to Marigold."

# CHAPTER 52

**"Emma Glade Flower,"** the leprechaun said, slowly turning atop his pot of gold. "Tip of the afternoon to ye."

The leprechaun's back was now to the party. But, of the other three, only the lizard man had turned to face the fairy fluttering a half-dozen feet above the ground, where the meadow grass began.

Someone else on their side would certainly help, Glenn thought. He was pretty sure things would come to blows. Sucking it up, giving the leprechaun his coin, and letting Marigold continue in the game world a foot taller than before seemed like a viable option. But Glenn knew how bullies were. Show weakness, and giving the coin despite the fact that Bata Fidil had broken his end of the deal would encourage him to greater boldness. Probably sick his three goon monsters on them anyway once he had the coin in his greedy little hands.

Yeah, a fight was coming. PCs in a game—no question, they'd fight for Stephi's honor, and because the creepy leprechaun was trying to cheat the party. But the stakes were higher. A player character in a game dies? Roll up a new one. If his party died, there wouldn't be any new PCs for them to run.

The gnome healer gripped his cudgel. A fight was coming. One based on RPG rules. Armor Class Tables and Character Stat Modifiers, unseen Dice Rolls and Saving Throws. Intellectually, Glenn knew that was going on all the time, every interaction with NPCs and action, including combat. But he ignored that reality whenever possible. Now, he couldn't. All the tables and charts and dice were weighted against him and his party, and in the leprechaun's favor. One small fairy added to their side wasn't going to change odds.

Glenn realized he hadn't been listening to the conversation between Emma and Bata Fidil. He'd been thinking, and keeping an eye on the ogre and troll, trying to be ready to get Initiative, if—when—they tried something.

"Yer mistaken," Bata Fidil said. "I *did* return her to her former size and self, as agreed. Then added a bit." He lifted a hand to show a small space between his forefinger and thumb. "No more than a firkin of a hogshead."

"They bargained in good faith, and upheld their end," Emma said. "A cradling bough of a hundred-year oak could've held up no better." The fairy remained at a distance while tipping forward to look down at Bata Fidil. "You spurned their effort to return to you your heisted coin."

"The elf maiden has the stain of greed on her hands." He stomped a booted foot on his gold coins, causing them to *tinkle*. "She plotted to take all of me gold."

"For which you turned her into a fairy," Emma said. "Then you used that to prod her and her friends like a spotted dog herding sheep to do your bidding."

"She, and they, need a reminder," Bata Fidil said, looking back over his shoulder at the party. "Sure as night follows day, me three friends'll take back me coin, if they refuse to hand it over."

At that, the troll flashed his pointed teeth and the ogre thumped his spiked club against the ground.

"You will risk every coin of your gold, for one?" Emma replied. "Based upon a slight already punished?"

"Risk?" The leprechaun tilted his head, focusing his senses to the left of the fairy. "The unseen one standing next to you has to be the forever-meddling Lovelace."

Glenn noticed some of the grass there appeared trampled.

The leprechaun laughed and spoke to the spot. "You

must realize, Lovelace, here your spells will have no effect upon me. And raising fire among the trees, should you wish to harm my companion?" He held his arms wide and slowly turned. "Certainly the wood nymph protecting this grove will frown upon that. Or worse."

Keri, the Glade House owner, was with Emma? Maybe she was using a Render Unseen Spell. That gave Glenn some hope—but not much. The leprechaun was right. He'd planned all the angles. It took a powerful magic user to reliably affect a leprechaun. Magic Resistance was how Ron and Kirby explained it. And Fire Blasts to battle the troll? Even if the party avoided the magical flames, the trees would certainly suffer.

The leaves in the canopy above began rattling, as if a breeze ran through them. The branches were moving, but not back and forth. They were stretching inward. The leprechaun looked up and realized this a fraction of a second after Glenn did.

The sun's rays blocked, the rainbow faded to nothingness, stranding Bata Fidil atop his pot of gold, along with his nearby enforcers.

The stakes just got higher. Bata Fidil couldn't use his summoned rainbow to escape. Without it, his pot of gold wasn't going anywhere—unless the ogre or troll carried it for him.

"Turn me back," Stephi interjected. "Like you promised."

Still atop his gold, the leprechaun spun back around. "No, me tall elven maiden. You'll be handing over me stolen coin."

Stephi held up a fist and shook it. "How about I hand you a fat lip!"

Bata Fidil's held his sides while emitting a scornful belly laugh. The ogre, troll and lizard man joined in.

"Come ahead, ya saucy tart," Bata Fidil said, gesturing her toward him. "I'd like to see ye tr—"

Before the leprechaun finished his taunt, Stephi bounded ahead, planted a foot and performed a lightning-fast, spinning wheel kick.

Her heel struck Bata Fidil in the head. The blow knocked the leprechaun from his perch atop his pot of gold and sent him tumbling.

Glenn knew what a solid hit looked like—one that did hit points of damage—compared to when a creature immune to normal weapons took a hit and sloughed it off. Bata Fidil *lost* hit points.

Stephi turned and pursued the leprechaun as the little man got to his feet and stumbled back, left hand cupping his thumped ear. Surprise and awe filled his face as he processed what just happened. So intent on dealing with the leprechaun, the towering elf maiden was oblivious of the ogre's backhand blow, until it sent *her* tumbling.

The leprechaun shouted, "Take the coin!" and the fight was on.

Derek hadn't waited for the leprechaun's order to his goons. He intercepted the ogre before the brute it could follow up on its successful attack.

Kirby shouted, "Lizard dude's mine," and loosed a spread of darts as he charged.

Glenn didn't shout or wait. He pounded toward the leprechaun, cudgel held high.

A stream of four emerald-green Mystic Missiles slammed into the ogre's back. That same instant, the source of the attack appeared. Keri Lovelace. On the far side of the meadow, she pulled her curved dagger and began striding forward while speaking the words of her next spell.

The fairy, Emma, shot ahead of her partner. Building up as much speed as her iridescent wings could manage, she zipped in front of the fierce troll's face and released her Dazzle Spell at pointblank range. Unaffected by the spell, the troll sprang after her and snaked out his long arm. He snatched the fleeing fairy from the air and slammed her to the ground like King Kong did to bi-planes that strayed too close.

Ron hurled his silver dagger at Bata Fidil, grazing the leprechaun across the shoulder. It wasn't much, but the single hit point of damage foiled the spell the leprechaun was casting.

"Jax, assail him with vigor!" Ron shouted the instructions while racing, spear raised high, to save the imperiled fairy. "Inhibit successful spellcasting."

Glenn intended to do that. He closed and swung his cudgel, but his nimble foe sidestepped. The gnome cocked back again, pressing his attack, but the leprechaun got initiative, and finished a brief spell. He followed it with a swing of his shillelagh. Glenn interposed his shield. The move saved his life. Upon impact, the gnome's shield, forearm and shoulder shattered in a clap of thunder.

Glenn staggered back, somehow managing to hang onto his cudgel. He knew the magically-enhanced blow had bludgeoned away all but a handful of his hit points. He shook his head; he wasn't done with the fight. Muttering the words to cast a Minor Heal Draw Spell upon himself, the gnome healer dropped the wrecked remains of his wooden shield and, with grim determination, stalked back toward his smirking foe.

Kirby was locked in combat with his own foe. They went at it toe to toe, like gladiators. Kirby's nimbleness and slashing cutlass against the lizard man's superior strength and the longer reach of his wicked trident. Although he was third rank, the thief's inferior 'to hit' chart and lesser damage inflicted by his weapon ultimately destined him to defeat—barring a Natural 20 Roll. Of course, the lizard man could just as easily roll a 20.

Derek and Stephi battled against the ogre. Despite his magical sword, and being two on one, the big warrior stood battered and bruised, while Stephi was down on one knee, struggling to get back to her feet. Giving up on that, she loosed one of her pink Mystic Missiles into the brute. Although the ogre had taken several powerful sword blows, the single bolt of energy wasn't nearly enough to take him down.

Ron and Keri battled the troll. Ron did his best, wounding the troll consistently with his spear but, as anticipated, the wounds quickly closed up. The powerful, regenerating monster ignored the warrior druid and went after Keri. She'd cast Flame Blade upon her dagger, and the flames that coated the curved blade ensured every successful strike didn't automatically heal. Because of this, the troll focused his fury on her. And his nasty-sharp teeth and two clawed hands backed by tremendous strength dealt out far more damage than a flaming dagger.

Emma had backed away from the battle, one wing broken. But the tiny fairy hadn't quit. She seemed to be concentrating, chanting the words to form some sort of enchantment.

After ducking under a clawed fist that hooked several strands of her straight brown hair, Keri loosed a sharp, trilling whistle.

Was she calling in reserves? Glenn sure hoped so.

# CHAPTER 53

**Two small canines**—Rocky and Chili—bounded from their concealment within the tree line. Bata Fidil was proving too nimble for Glenn to hit, probably due to some sort of Agility Spell. Now the leprechaun had to split his attention among three foes. The two dogs bit at his thighs and ankles, and tugged at his trousers and sleeves. Barking and snarling, the pair darted in and out like a pair of mongooses—mongooses armed with Silver Strike in their snapping jaws. Yes, they were small dogs, but to a three-foot tall foe, they were closer to pit bulls than terriers.

Kirby managed to dodge another trident attack, but wasn't quick enough to avoid the spinning lizard man's tail strike. The thief went down, stunned, probably at zero hit points. The green-scaled monster lifted his trident to finish the half-goblin thief, preparing to ensure Kirby never climbed to his feet again.

The three-tined death stab never fell. A buzzing swarm of thumb-sized hornets descended from the branches above. They attacked the lizard man. His scaled hide was hard and thick, largely proof against the hundreds of determined insects and their venom-filed stingers. But the riled swarm attacked eyes and mouth, and sought out gashes left by the thief's cutlass and piercing wounds inflicted by his darts.

The cold-blooded monster hissed, slapped and spun. He quickly determined neither his trident nor his slapping hands and swinging tail would suffice. Tossing aside his weapon, the lizard man fled, racing full tilt toward the distant sound of the river.

The hornet swarm followed, continuing its relentless stinger attacks.

With Emma's aid, Kirby's fight ended in a draw. Barring outside assistance, the same wasn't in the cards for the rest of the party. Still standing toe-to-toe, Derek got in another solid sword blow. It wasn't enough to drop the ogre, who knocked the big warrior back with his spiked club. The blow toppled the warrior onto the meadow grass.

Derek wasn't dead, nor was he getting back up to continue the fight.

Stephi loosed her second Mystic Missile into the ogre. The hulking brute, bloody and pissed, spun to face her.

Rather than resorting to her Running Skill to flee, she took a determined Martial Arts stance and prepared for the single combat onslaught. Actually taking note of her for the first time, the ogre's gaze dropped to her dangling-open cloak. His leering grin showed yellowed teeth between his upturned, warthog-like tusks.

Stephi rolled her eyes. "Is everyone in this stupid world a pervert?" Maintaining her stance, she giggled her bountiful chest. "That's it," she said, laughing under her breath. "Give me a bigger target to kick."

While Ron remained unscathed, Keri was anything but. She'd struck home with four attacks, but the damage totaled only a fraction of the troll's hit point total. Ron had wounded the troll faster than the monster could heal, but not nearly enough to approach dropping the ferocious brute. Once Keri was down, being only a second rank warrior druid, Ron had little hope of prevailing alone against such a foe.

Keri backpedaled, chanting the words to a spell. The troll pursued. Ron followed, once again driving his bloodied spear into the troll's back.

Keri extended her left hand, pointing at the ogre. A stream of four emerald-green Mystic Missiles impacted the hulking brute along his neck and spine. The ogre staggered forward, then grunted in surprised pain. Stephi stepped back, having completed a stepping punch to the brute's engorged genitals. The tall elf watched the ogre collapse onto the ground with a resounding *thud.*

Keri paid for her assist. A clawed fist slammed down on her shoulder, driving the woman to her knees. The dagger fell from her grip and its flame extinguished.

Barking in high-pitched alarm, Rocky and Chili abandoned their fight with the leprechaun and raced to save their imperiled owner. As much as he wanted to help Keri, Glenn couldn't leave the leprechaun and allow him an uncontested moment to wreak mayhem and death with his spells.

Bata Fidil, however, was distracted by the turn of events. The determined gnome ensured the leprechaun paid for his momentary lapse.

The leprechaun suffered a cudgel blow to his ribs. The successful strike's four or five hit points wasn't enough to drop the leprechaun, but the sneer said it got his attention. Rather than dodge and continue observing the intent of his remaining goon enforcer, the leprechaun's face went red before he wildly attacked Glenn with his shillelagh.

The gnome healer did his best to fend off the crazed leprechaun but, somehow, the little man managed three attacks per round of combat—thrice what Glenn could manage. The shillelagh connected two out of three blows. Not for many points of damage per hit, but enough to nickel-and-dime Glenn, while he whiffed every attack.

Keri tried to roll away. The troll's clawed hand latched onto the Glade House owner's leg. Before the monster could lift her from the ground, Rocky snarled and darted in, attacking the troll's ankle. Chili leapt up, her teeth clamping down on the troll's little finger.

Ron swung his spear like a staff, striking the troll

across the face. Stephi ducked in close to punch, failing to score a hit.

The troll swung his left arm, a fist connecting with Ron's shoulder. The blow sent the warrior druid tumbling back. Unable to shake the little black and white dog from his finger, the troll dropped Lovelace's leg and clenched his right hand into a fist. Emitting a guttural snarl, the troll drove his fist like a piston toward the ground. The brave little dog, caught between the troll's bugling knuckles and the unyielding ground, yelped when fist met earth. Her piercing cry was so sharp it drew everyone's attention.

Chili was dead. The impact left her shattered canine body lying broken within the fist-shaped impression.

# CHAPTER 54

**"Cease!"**

The command rumbled down from the branches above and resounded off the standing yews.

Glenn felt the compulsion to stop his attack, but sloughed it off. He couldn't give the leprechaun an inch, while hoping what remained of his party could somehow defeat the troll. Besides, the leprechaun kept coming at him, snaking beneath Glenn's shield and striking a solid blow against the gnome healer's shin.

Ron, Stephi, Keri, and even Rocky disengaged and backed away from the troll. The fierce beast ignored the command and pressed his attack, this time focusing on the spear-wielding warrior druid.

Ron stood ready, but the attack never came. Sinuous roots reached up from the ground, through the flattened meadow grass, and coiled around the troll's feet, holding them in place. The roots didn't stop there. They continued their twisting climb, even as the troll stopped and tore at them with fingers and claws. It continued until a stalemate in the struggle was reached just above the troll's knees.

The same happened to Glenn, but he didn't fight the roots. He simply twisted his hips and neck to see what was happening.

Bata Fidil rose above the ground, like a helium-filled balloon, halting beyond the reach of the entangling, snake-like roots.

No one else was threatened by the trees' animated subterranean appendages.

Trying to keep his shield between himself and the leprechaun floating above the meadow grass, Glenn saw the little man had lost interest in him. The gnome followed the leprechaun's gaze, peering to the far side of the small clearing.

A tall, lithe woman with flowing, moss-green hair and deep mahogany-colored skin strode into the clearing. A diaphanous veil and flowing gown partially hid her face and otherwise unclothed body. The garments shimmered like dew-covered spider webs reflecting a morning's sunrise.

The wood nymph, Polayney, raised an arm and pointed an accusing finger at Bata Fidil. "You brought conflict into my wildwood. Death into my home."

Bata Fidil remained where he was, arms crossed in arrogant defiance. He cocked his head, looking around until his eyes fell upon the broken body of Chili. He started to say something, then thought better of it. Instead he pointed his own accusing finger at Stephi and said to the wood nymph, "You know as well as I do, the blame falls upon her, the one that they call Marigold."

"What?" Stephi said, a look of disbelief on her face. Her eyes narrowed as she pointed *her* accusing finger. "Don't you *even* try to blame me, you—you mean little man."

The troll ceased his savage attempts to free himself, but clearly hadn't given up. Thigh muscles bulged as he continued to twist and attempt to pull his legs free.

Ron sidestepped until he stood to Stephi's left. He tipped his head upward, speaking quietly toward her ear. "Marigold, refrain from being further drawn into their dispute."

The towering elf maiden cocked her head and stared down at the warrior druid. Glenn kind of wondered, too. She was sort of at the center of the conflict…wasn't she?

Ron signaled to Stephi, and she bent so that he might whisper into her ear. It wasn't difficult to determine what he said because she immediately grasped the front of her cloak and pulled it closed over her exposed chest—and more.

That Glenn hadn't paid attention to her wardrobe malfunction said how distracted the conflict had left him. He wondered if Stephi's flashing had distracted Derek. Probably not. He'd been fighting not only for the party, but for his very life.

The big warrior lay motionless on the ground, as did the half-goblin thief. Without his breastplate, Glenn observed Derek's chest rise and fall. Kirby's chest did the same. Next to Chili's broken body was Rocky. He laid with head, ears and tail down on the edge of the impact impression. The brave dog quietly moaned, mourning the loss of his companion. Keri Lovelace reluctantly moved from her surviving canine to stand on Stephi's right. She, Stephi and Ron listened attentively to the intense exchange between the leprechaun and wood nymph.

"She is a sylvan creature," Polayney said to Bata Fidil. "Your words and deeds were suited to dealings with a mortal, not a distant cousin." Beneath her gossamer veil, the wood nymph's gaze wandered toward the prone bodies of Derek and Kirby.

Bata Fidil threw up his hands. "Her words and actions, they're not those of an elf maiden. Rather, those of a pesky girl with human blood."

"She is more than an elf maiden," Polayney countered. "Her flesh was able to harm your flesh."

The leprechaun's nose scrunched up. To that, he had no reply.

"You will effect a suitable resolution and depart," the wood nymph said. "Or it shall be I who draws the next and final blood."

The leprechaun shook his head. "Yer magic canna harm me. Nor can ye confine me here." He crossed his arms. "And plenty of mischief in return can you expect for centuries to come."

Polayney took a step closer to the leprechaun. "The blood would be that of your hirelings," she said. "As for centuries to come..." The wood nymph gestured with her right hand and roots anew emerged from the soil. They coiled around and covered the gold-filled kettle. "Endure those same centuries in the company of your fellows, bereft of your treasure of gold."

Fellows? Glenn thought. The gnome healer shuddered at the thought of a company of leprechauns.

He wondered, without his pot of gold, would Bata Fidil's magical prowess be weakened? Would the loss of ranks—if the *Monsters, Maces and Magic*'s game creatures such as leprechauns had ranks—accompany Bata Fidil's loss of prestige among his fellow leprechauns? If nothing else, Bata Fidil would be like a king whose scepter and crown jewels had been confiscated.

While leprechaun and wood nymph stared each other down, Emma dropped her Camouflage and made her way next to the gnome healer. In addition to the fairy's broken wing, she limped heavily.

Even though he was down ten or so hit points, he still had two Minor Heal Draw spells. Keeping an eye divided between the leprechaun and wood nymph, and the still straining troll, he whispered to the fairy, "Get closer so I can heal your wing."

Emma stepped right up next to the roots holding Glenn in place.

Curious as to how a broken wing would manifest itself, Glenn whispered the words to his spell and touched the small fairy's shoulder. Pain in his right scapula answered the question.

Emma's wing straightened. She grinned broadly as she fluttered up into the hair. She swooped back down and laid a light kiss on Glenn's nose. The fairy acted so quickly, the kiss was over before the gnome knew what was happening.

Bata Fidil ended the silent standoff. “Fine.” He threw up his arms and stomped around in a circle. “But I’ll be settling with the elf maiden, and her alone.”

Not waiting for a reply, the leprechaun waved a hand, gesturing for Stephi to follow him over to the far side of the glade.

“Be strong,” Keri urged.

“Contemplate what is proposed,” Ron said. “Rely on your high Intelligence Score.”

If what the warrior druid said seemed out of place, none of the NPCs took notice.

Still clutching her cloak closed, Stephi huffed and walked wide around the unconscious ogre and followed Bata Fidil to the meadow’s edge. With their backs to everyone, they began their negotiation. Glenn could hear discussion, but not what was said.

Emma flew around the roots gripping the gnome healer, momentarily resting a hand on the thicker tendrils holding him in place. Seconds after she did, each withdrew and disappeared beneath the soil.

“Thanks,” Glenn said.

Emma giggled and flew over to Keri and settled on the Glade House owner’s shoulder. The two began conferring. In the meantime, Polayney had moved next to the troll and silently convinced the monstrous creature to cease his struggles. Once he complied, the roots holding him in place withdrew.

The troll lifted each foot, ensuring he was free then stood straight and motionless, like a statue. In the depths of a wooded area, Glenn wasn’t sure he could see the troll. It wasn’t like the troll was using some sort of spell power like Emma. Instead he relied on coloration and stillness to blend in. In Glenn’s book that made him even more dangerous.

Glenn trotted over to stand next to Ron.

Keeping an eye on the troll, the warrior druid patted Glenn on the shoulder. "This day is progressing toward a most memorable one."

Glenn hoped "memorable" also meant worth a lot of experience points. He glanced up at Ron. "Think it would be okay if I healed Gurk?"

"Bide," Ron said. "It may unbalance the tranquil mood the wood nymph is working to maintain."

Stephi turned and shouted over her shoulder. "Lysine, what's a 'Firkin of a butt?'"

"In measure of wine cask units," he said, "eight gallons of one hundred and twenty-six."

Stephi's attention returned to her conversation with Bata Fidil. She shook her head, drawing Glenn's attention to her long wavy hair. The leprechaun stomped his booted foot. His face turned an even darker shade of red.

After a few more moments of discussion, Stephi asked, "Lysine, what's a pin of a tun?"

"In measure of wine cask units," Ron said, "four gallons of two-hundred and fifty-two gallons."

"What's that about?" Glenn asked Ron.

"Component measurements to establish a fraction. Firkin of a hogshead, eight out of sixty-three. Firkin of a butt, eight of one hundred twenty-six."

"And," Glenn said, "four of two fifty-two. Why's Marigold asking you all that?"

"Based upon the discussion between Bata Fidil and…" Ron gestured toward the wood nymph who'd moved to kneel next to Rocky. "I believe Bataí Fidil na Maidine is attempting to extract some measure of a concession from Marigold."

Keri and Emma joined the wood nymph. Keri knelt with tears welling in her eyes and petted her surviving canine companion.

Glenn felt the pang of loss. The little dog had

touched his heart during his stay at the Glade house. He sighed and took a long, steadying breath, and pushed the sadness into a corner. At the moment the fate of Stephi and his party concerned him more.

Stephi reached down and shook hands with Bata Fidil. Even as they shook, Glenn watched Stephi's stature decrease. Not a lot, but enough that her cloak hung a little long in the sleeves and hemline.

With that, the tree canopy retreated, allowing sunlight to reach the meadow. The roots holding the pot of gold withdrew and returned to their place beneath the meadow grass.

With the brightest smile Glenn had seen in months, Stephi actually skipped over to him and Ron.

She picked Glenn up and hugged him to her barely covered breasts and spun around. "I'm back!" As if to emphasize the fact, from the trees behind Petie belted out a joyous song. Glenn interpreted it as, "Happy, happy, content. Happy, happy, content."

Glenn turned his face to the side after returning the gesture with a quick hug. He tried to find appropriate purchase for his hands to push away. Now wasn't the time to get aroused. "Maybe I should heal Gurk now?"

Stephi nearly dropped the gnome. "Oh," she said, embarrassed, and placed Glenn on the ground. "And the little…leprechaun, he wants his gold coin."

"Jax," Ron said, maintaining a wary stance as he faced Bata Fidil, who was striding toward the party, "I shall expend one Minor Cure Spell upon Gurk after retrieving the gold coin from his person and delivering it to Bataí Fidil na Maidine.

"Marigold, remain vigilant," Ron continued. The warrior druid was already walking toward the fallen thief. "Jax, accompany me."

Glenn trotted to catch up. Ron intended to reach Kirby before the leprechaun.

Ron knelt down and withdrew the coveted coin from a hidden pocket in Kirby's left boot. He turned and handed it to Glenn.

The gnome's eyes widened. The round coin was cold in his grip, like it'd been lying in a pile of snow. Ron was only one quarter elf, not enough to be treated fairly—well sort of fairly—as a gnome by a leprechaun.

Bata Fidil stood in front of Glenn, right hand extended.

"When I give this to you," Glenn said, holding up the coin, "our agreement is complete and satisfactory to both sides?"

"That it will be, Jax, the oddest gnome I've ever had the displeasure of meeting."

Not waiting for a response, Bata Fidil snatched the coin. A mongoose hyped up on methamphetamine couldn't have been faster. The leprechaun turned and gestured toward the troll. "Pick up Loagull so we can be gone." He tossed his returned gold coin onto the pile within his pot before waving his hands. The rainbow returned.

The troll managed to lift the bulkier ogre over his shoulder. The lizard man trotted onto the scene, picked up his trident, and Loagull's spiked club and joined the troll and leprechaun next to the rainbow.

In an iridescent flash, the leprechaun and his henchmen were gone.

# CHAPTER 55

**Derek sat up** and asked, “What happened, gnome?” He looked around. “Where’s the ogre?”

Glenn hadn’t been able to heal Derek to full hit point strength without sacrificing and keeping some of the sustained damage. Derek could suck it up.

Kirby was on his feet as well. Ron had used two of his Minor Cures on the thief and was walking over to offer one to Keri when Rocky began barking and wagging his tail. A higher-pitched bark accompanied him, but somehow it sounded distant.

Glenn rubbed his eyes. Running around Keri were both Rocky and Chili. Keri clasped her hands and laughed while Emma flittered above the wood nymph and clapped her hands.

The gnome healer looked closer. The ground had leveled out where the little black and white dog’s body had lain. And the revived dog looked different as she chased Rocky around their owner’s feet. Less substantial? A ghost?

“I have bound Chili’s spirit to my tree,” the wood nymph explained. “Henceforth, she shall be a guardian of my grove.”

Keri wiped a tear from her eye, a tear of joy. “Thank you, Polayney.”

Ron led Stephi and Kirby over to Glenn and Derek. The warrior druid offered the big warrior a hand. Derek accepted and got to his feet.

“We should thank her too,” Kirby said. He whispered to Glenn, “Don’t look at her if she drops her veil. Her looks can kill.”

“Gnomes and elves get bonuses to their Saving Throw,” Derek said. “Half-goblins get a minus two.”

"Maybe Marigold should do the talking," Kirby said.

"I believe I may have appropriate words to accompany our thanks," Ron said, and led the party over to the wood nymph.

The beautiful wood nymph watched the party approach, Ron in the lead. Glenn couldn't determine if her visage was haughty or regal. Or if they were one and the same.

Ron bowed his head. "Polayney, most gracious of wood nymphs, might I offer a song to show our gratitude?"

Polayney, behind her gossamer veil and gown, nodded once.

Glenn decided it was regal.

Ron cleared his throat and began to sing.

*"Bonny Portmore, I am sorry to see*
*Such a woeful destruction of your ornament tree*
*For it stood on your shore for many's the long day*
*Till the long boats from Antrim came to float it away."*

Ron's voice was a combination of singing, representing who he was now, and lecture, carrying the tone of who he really was. But somehow, the duality proved both majestic and appropriate.

Standing straight, looking up, his arms stiffly at his side, the warrior druid continued.

*"O bonny Portmore, you shine where you stand*
*And the more I think on you the more I think long*
*If I had you now as I had once before*
*All the lords in Old England would not purchase Portmore.*

*All the birds in the forest they bitterly weep*

*Saying, 'Where shall we shelter or shall we sleep?'*
*For the Oak and the Ash, they are all cutten down*
*And the walls of bonny Portmore are all down to the ground."*

Glenn wasn't sure but, at the mention of the weeping birds, behind the veil he thought he saw tears begin running down the wood nymph's cheeks.

Kirby whispered into Glenn's ear, "I didn't know Lysine was a *Highlander* fan."

*O bonny Portmore, you shine where you stand*
*And the more I think on you the more I think long*
*If I had you now as I had once before*
*All the Lords of Old England would not purchase Portmore.*

When he finished, Ron bowed his head once again. "That is a song from our home. It expresses the loss of a forest there, as yours here has been decimated.

"May your grove one day return to its former majesty."

# EPILOGUE

**Glenn shook his** head as he looked at his fishing pole's bare hook.

"Stripped again, dude," Kirby said, sitting on the bank next to his gnome friend. "You suck at fishing even more than me."

Rather than show anger, Glenn dropped his stick pole on the ground next to the river bank and wandered the dozen steps up to the willow tree. There Stephi sat, barefoot with her long legs outstretched and her beautiful face half-hidden by her broad-brimmed straw hat.

Glenn said, "When I level up—"

"Rank, not level," Kirby corrected, attempting to mimic Ron's voice.

"Oh, shut up, my little man," Stephi said playfully. She wrapped an arm around her gnome friend after he plopped down next to her. She squeezed his shoulder. "What were you going to say, Jax?"

Since completing their deal with the leprechaun and she was no longer a fairy, Stephi had remained in high spirits.

Glenn stared at his boots. "When I go up a rank, I was thinking on picking up a Skill Level in Fishing."

"No way, dude." Kirby kept his eye on his wooden bobber floating in the little inlet along the Snake Claw River. "Kalgore'll give you hell for that."

Stephi huffed and squeezed Glenn's shoulder again. "Who cares what that big jerk thinks?"

"It isn't just for fishing here," Glenn added. He plucked a blade of grass, examined it, then flicked it away. "Out adventuring, being able to fish will get us food."

"Maybe." Kirby shrugged. "Kalgore's bow and Marigold's Slumber Spell can do better than fishing."

It was Glenn's turn to shrug. He listened to Petie warble in the branches above and sighed.

The trio sat in silence, each deep in their own thoughts.

Out of nowhere, Kirby said, "That was so cool, Marigold, when you kicked that leprechaun dude in the head. The look on his face!" The thief turned and did his best to show a wide-eyed expression of surprised disbelief.

All three laughed, although the gnome's laughter came a second delayed and sounded forced.

Kirby turned back to watching his bobber. "Marigold," he asked," how long did you know Byeol's Heirloom Item was Silver Strike?"

"After Jax killed that creepy husk mummy," Stephi replied. She pushed up her hat's brim and smiled down at Glenn, who, for some reason, remained in a glum mood. "Remember that, Jax?"

"Sort of," Glenn said. "I was too scared to really remember most of it."

Stephi sat back, resting against the willow tree's trunk. "What's wrong, Jax? Everything turned out fine."

Glenn gazed up into her green eyes. "Why'd you let the leprechaun get away with not turning you back exactly as you were before?"

Stephi's frown faded. "Did Lysine tell you?"

Kirby turned around, eyebrows raised. "What's not the same?"

"How do you know, Jax?" She didn't sound happy. "Did you listen in on our *private* conversation?"

Glenn didn't know Ron knew. Rather than deny her accusation, he asked, "You want to know how I knew?"

Kirby set down his pole and made his way up to the tree. "Was it that firkin, hogshead, wine barrel thing?"

Stephi ignored Kirby's question and addressed Glenn. "Well, *yeah*, or I wouldn't be asking you."

Glenn was caught between anger, embarrassment and frustration. Better to just say it and get it over with. "Because, Marigold, I do a lot of looking up. From my angle, looking up at your face, I have to look past your breasts. It's different than before. They're a little higher up."

"Well," she said, no anger or bitterness in her voice. "I don't blame you, Jax. It's hard not to notice my biggest assets." She put a hand under each and hefted them. "They're like the first thing *I* notice every time I look in a mirror."

"There ain't many mirrors I've seen big enough for that," Kirby teased.

From her seated position Stephi lightly kicked Kirby in the shin. "Too bad you were unconscious, Gurk." From beneath her hat's brim she winked at Glenn. "I totally lost my cloak for most of the fight after you were down. With your eyes closed."

"No way." The half-goblin thief looked to the gnome for confirmation.

Stephi giggled. "You're right, my little man. No way."

"I'm glad you're back to calling me that," Kirby said. "Even if I am now a little little bit littler compared to you…before you got a lot littler because you got fairyed."

"You little jerk." She threw a stick at him. The thief deftly caught it and grinned, showing his pointy teeth.

She threatened to throw another. "That's not what I mean and you know it."

He laughed and replied, "I know."

Stephi turned to Glenn. "I let that mean little leprechaun get away with a pin of a tun because it sounded like a tiny amount." She playfully elbowed Glenn in the shoulder. "I was right, too. Lysine did the math and it was only one and a half percent. We measured and it's only one and a quarter inch difference."

Petie flew down and landed on Stephi's shoulder.

She tipped her hat's brim back down. "It was silly to think that there'd be a big pot of gold sitting in the woods, just waiting for us to take." She rubbed a finger along Petie's throat. "Even though it's only a little, little bit, it's enough for me to notice. Enough to remind me not to go and do something stupid like *that* again."

"I tried to warn you," Kirby said.

"I know. And I'd still be mad at myself if it weren't for Lysine."

Before either gnome or half-goblin could ask, Stephi explained, "Lysine told me, 'Life perpetually strives to surround us in oppressive darkness, especially in this aberrant concurrent world. When it succeeds, we must strive to seek the tiniest bit of sparkling light that inevitably pierces such darkness. When things are bad we must look upon that shimmer of beauty, at that which is sustaining, to carry us through the worst days. Look forward, for there remains the possibility of better days.'"

Kirby asked, "Lysine said *that*?"

Stephi gave a look of exasperation. "Those weren't his *exact* words. A lot of them are mine. But he did say 'perpetually,' and 'inevitably' and 'sustaining.' And now that I think about it, 'persevere' instead of 'look forward.'"

Kirby nodded understanding. "My sixth grade English teacher said that memorizing important speeches and poems can be important. But it's more important to understand them." He kicked at the grass, thinking back to that memory. "Put them in your own words so that they have meaning to you."

Kirby sat down, facing his two friends. "That's what

gets him through here, every day?" His gaze fell to his lap. "Man, he's either one pessimistic dude, or his life before here must've sucked worse than mine."

"I think it's inspiring," Stephi said. "It tells me he'll never give up."

After a moment of silence, where all three contemplated their party leader's words, Glenn asked, "So, what light came through in this last adventure?"

"We made new friends," Stephi replied, as if it was obvious. "Emma and Polayney."

"I think with the wood nymph," Kirby said, "it was mostly Lysine's song."

"Better than that pawnshop owner," Glenn said.

Stephi patted Glenn on the leg. "I agree."

"Me, too." Kirby nodded. "But he's a contact who knows we get things done. Might lead us to more adventures."

"We'll need those to get more gold and experience points," Glenn said, staring out across the slow-moving river. "So we can get back home."

**The End**

# About the Author

Terry W. Ervin II is an English teacher who enjoys writing fantasy and science fiction.

Fairyed is the fourth book in Terry's Monsters, Maces and Magic series (LitRPG fantasy). He is the author of two other series: Crax War Chronicles (science fiction) and the First Civilization's Legacy Series (fantasy). Terry has also written a post-apocalyptic alien invasion novel titled Thunder Wells, and a short story collection, Genre Shotgun. Finally, Terry co-authored Cavern, a Dane Maddock Adventure, with author David Wood.

When Terry isn't writing or enjoying time with his wife and daughters, he can be found in his basement raising turtles.

To contact Terry, or to learn more about his writing endeavors, visit his website at www.ervin-author.com and his blog, Up Around the Corner, at uparoundthecorner.blogspot.com

Made in the
USA
Monee, IL